Samuel Peter Spreng

The Life and Labors of John Seybert

Samuel Peter Spreng

The Life and Labors of John Seybert

ISBN/EAN: 9783337400019

Printed in Europe, USA, Canada, Australia, Japan

Cover: Foto ©Raphael Reischuk / pixelio.de

More available books at **www.hansebooks.com**

THE LIFE AND LABORS

OF

JOHN SEYBERT,

FIRST BISHOP

OF THE

Evangelical Association.

———

BY

REV. S. P. SPRENG,

Author of "Rays of Light on the Highway to Success."

———

They that be wise shall shine as the brightness of the firmament; and they that turn many to righteousness as the stars forever and ever.—DAN. 12:3.

———

PUBLISHED FOR THE EVANGELICAL ASSOCIATION BY
LAUER & MATTILL, AGENTS,
CLEVELAND, O.
1888.

DEDICATION.

To the Evangelical Association, whose first Bishop he was;
To the Bishops now living, the senior of whom is a spiritual
son as well as a successor in this high office;
To the ministers and members, for whose emulation his
remarkable example is here portrayed, and
To the Church universal, of whose bright lights he was
one of the brightest, this record of the life of
Bishop John Seybert is affection-
ately dedicated, by
THE AUTHOR.

(2)

PREFACE.

THE story of Bishop John Seybert's life is herewith presented to the Church, in the fond hope that its perusal will serve to keep alive in every Evangelical heart the love of the Church and rekindle the spirit of self-sacrifice which characterized our fathers, by means of which the foundations of the Evangelical Association were laid, and without which our peculiar church-life can not be perpetuated. Bishop Seybert was of all our fathers the typical Evangelical preacher; in every element peculiar to our ministry, in simplicity of life, in singleness of purpose, in self-sacrificing devotion to the vital truths of the Gospel, he was the example and the pattern. His memory should be kept alive to the latest generations, and especially should the English and modern portion of our Church become well acquainted with the record of his life.

Nearly a generation has already passed away, since the grand old man was taken from the earth, and yet until now, no record of his remarkable life has ever been offered to the public in the English language. For years there has been a growing desire among our ministry and membership for such a work, but various obstacles delayed its publication until the present moment. Not only do the people desire it, but the exigencies of the times, and of the future demand it. The present modest volume is a slight attempt to meet this demand, as well as to pay a deserved though humble tribute to the extraordinary character and career of the first Bishop and first regular missionary of the Evangelical Association.

In the preparation of the book we have had access to the Bishop's journals, which cover the entire period of his public ministry, from 1820–1860, and give a complete record of his daily deeds and experiences. The perusal of that journal, written in his beautiful hand-writing, was a privilege of unspeakable preciousness. In that journal he gives a concise account of *every day for forty years; scarcely a day is omitted.* At the close of each day he could indeed say :

> " One more day's work for Jesus,
> How sweet the work has been,
> To tell the story,
> To show the glory,
> Where Christ's flock enter in ! "

Another thing should be stated, that in all his private journal entries there occurs not a single word of unkind criticism or a disparaging, uncharitable remark, concerning any person, nor a word which indicates the least vanity or self-esteem. There are not many of whom this can be said.

The *"Life and Labors of Bishop Seybert"* in the German language, by the late Rev. Solomon Neitz, the eloquent preacher of the East Pennsylvania conference, was also consulted, and the literature of the Church in general was drawn upon, besides consulting Bishop Seybert's still surviving contemporaries.

It is the prayer of the author that the book, despite its faults and imperfections, may prove a great spiritual blessing to thousands, and that it may aid in the advancement of the kingdom of Christ, and in the spread of the Evangelical Association.

S. P. SPRENG.

LIFE AND LABORS

OF

JOHN SEYBERT

(THE FIRST BISHOP OF THE EVANGELICAL ASSOCIATION.)

CHAPTER I.

PARENTAGE,—EARLY TRAINING,—CONVERSION.

DURING the War of American Independence, Henry Seybert, then a lad of fifteen years, was brought to this country among the German mercenaries employed by George III. of England, in his war with the American colonies. At the close of the war young Seybert refused to be "redeemed" by the British government, preferring to try his fortunes in the new Republic which had achieved so brilliant a victory over one of the foremost nations of the world, rather than to return to Europe. The result was that the lad was thrown into prison at Lancaster, Pennsylvania, from which a philanthrophic gentleman, named Schaffner, released him, by the payment of one hundred dollars as a ransom price. He served his benefactor three years for his liberty, working at his trade as a tailor. It was in this way that the father of a future American bishop earned his personal liberty, and attained to citizenship in the United States.

Soon after this he became acquainted with Miss Susan Kreuzer, a poor, industrious orphan and a native of the Kingdom of Wurtemberg, to whom he was married Sept. 5, 1790, the marriage ceremony being performed by the Rev. Henry Muehlenberg, a distinguished minister of the Lutheran Church. The young bride had, at the age of four years, lost her father in the deep Atlantic. The young couple were thus emphatically thrown upon their own resources, but German economy, industry and energy enabled them soon to acquire a reasonable competency, so that at the untimely death of Mr. Seybert, in 1806, the family was in possession of a respectable property.

John Seybert, the subject of this biography, was their first child, and was born July 7th, 1791, at Manheim, Pennsylvania. He was followed by three brothers, Henry, Christian and David. Daughters there were none.

When John was about thirteen years old, an important change occurred in the religious life of Henry and Susan Seybert. The mother was the first to realize the need of a change of heart. For though both she and her husband were accepted communicants in the German Lutheran Church, they became conscious that all was not right in their hearts. The Holy Spirit wrought powerfully upon their minds, and they were thoroughly awakened from their previous false security. They began to hunger and thirst after righteousness. But since their unconverted spiritual advisers of those times could give them no relief, they began to look about for other means of grace. They accordingly attended the meetings of a company of pious, converted people, in the vicinity, and were soon rejoicing in the saving power of Christ. They now had prayer-meetings in their own house, which, though it caused them sore persecution, served greatly to strengthen them in the faith of the Gospel. This also became the means of the first religious impressions upon the mind of their eldest son John. He heard the voice of the Spirit calling him, frequently and earnestly, but youthful pleasures held for a while complete control over him. He says of himself: "I was a bad boy; my life, from youth up was one of wickedness, though my parents tried every possible means to check and control me. Neither coaxing nor scolding, neither kindness nor sternness availed. They did not spare the rod, but I was incorrigible, I loved sin."

Henry Seybert was a man of impetuous spirit, whose temper sometimes overcame his judgment; he frequently became exceedingly angry, and at such times did what he afterwards regretted with great sorrow. He possessed the choleric . temperament, which sometimes led him to punish his children with such severity as to rouse their anger, make them vindictive, and increase their stubbornness. "My father," says the Bishop, "would have succeeded much better, had he understood the wholesome art of first moistening the rod with his own tears." Mrs. Seybert was the opposite of her husband. She was a gentle spirit, in whom the melancholic temperament predominated, and of a serious, quiet, sedate disposition. She had great self-possession, and sought to rule her children by the persuasive power of love, rather than with the iron sceptre of physical force. Says the Bishop, speaking of his mother: "She frequently prayed with and for her little ones, but she had to wait a long time before she was permitted to see any fruit of her labor in me. My parents often remarked afterwards, that I was worse than all other boys of the same age, and worse than any of my own brothers. They declared that wickedness manifested itself in me at an unusually early age and increased in virulence with added years. The weakening of the carnal nature, in fact, is not to be thought of so long as sin reigns within us, but it rather grows constantly by means of the very wickedness which it produces."

When young Seybert was about seven years old, he was sent to school where he soon learned to read and write in both German and English. At the same time he was sent to his parents' pastor for catechetical instruction, with a view to the rite of "confirmation," as it is called. "But," says he, "we candidates for confirmation were a set of godless sinners, practicing all manner of wickedness, in the intervals between our lessons." At length, however, a circumstance occurred which resulted in preventing him from being confirmed. Mr. Seybert's father, namely, meanwhile lost all confidence in the minister, because of his unchristian conduct, and therefore objected to the confirmation of his son. It was well. Perhaps, if John Seybert had been allowed to finish his catechetical education, and to be "confirmed," in his unregenerate state of heart, he might have lived and died a deluded man, having the form of godliness, but denying the power thereof. Nothing can be more baneful than to be declared a Christian by a mere ceremonial ordinance of a lifeless church, when the subject has not the consciousness of Divine pardon. This is a "strong delusion." Mr. Seybert, we are entitled to believe, escaped this delusion by Providential interference. Otherwise he might never have been converted, and as a result would, undoubtedly, have lived a commonplace life, if not a life of vastly pernicious influence. It is hardly to be supposed, however, that such a man could have lived without exerting a great influence, either for good or evil. At the same time there is no doubt that the quickening and renewing grace of God lifted him out of comparative social obscurity, extended the sphere of his life, enlarged his capacities, and widened immeasurably the horizon of his actual influence. John Seybert, like Saul of Tarsus, had naturally too much positive strength of character, and too great natural endowments, not to have become a leader among men. It was, therefore, specially fortunate that the grace of God rescued him. He himself expressed the following conviction: "Had I been confirmed by the Church in my unregenerate state, and admitted to the Holy Communion, perhaps I should not have been converted for a long time as yet. As it was, through the influence of my comrades I fell deeper and deeper into sin, and the evil passions grew in power in my soul, so that I felt a positive hunger and a burning desire for the delights of sin.

I practiced evil with alacrity, while I felt a strong aversion to that which is holy and virtuous. I was now thirteen years of age, and desperately wicked."

He began to recognize the awakening influence of the Holy Spirit in his fourteenth year, as the result of the conversion of his parents and the consequent change of life which this effected in them. Mr. Seybert gives the following account of this experience. "It frequently occurred to me that I also ought to lead a better life and to follow the pious example of my parents. But alas! this was all that came of it. The devil led me to believe that it was much too soon for me to be converted, and thus taught me the dangerous habit of procrastination. True, I promised myself to seek religion *sometime*, and so went on in the road that is truthfully said to be 'paved with good intentions.' Oh, procrastination is the weapon which the 'strong man armed' employs to guard the palace of the human heart against the 'Stronger' lest he be robbed of his armor and the spoil be taken from him.

"Nevertheless my poor heart was melted more than once, and that at times in public places. The influence of the Spirit of God became occasionally irrisistible. I remember especially a certain 'big meeting' where the preaching affected me so powerfully, that, on the way home, I lingered behind our company, so that I might weep over my miserable and sinful condition, unseen by mortals, and that I might have opportunity to meditate, undisturbed, on the patience and longsuffering of God, in bearing with me so long. On another occasion at a meeting of the United

Brethren, I was so mightily wrought upon, that I wept loudly enough to be heard, and friends came to me, urging me to enter into the conflict for my soul's salvation, immediately. And I did pray, and entreat God to give me peace. But my will would not yield fully. However, I became willing, upon this, to attend public services and prayer-meetings. I also felt at this time a strong inclination towards those things which are pure and of good report. Virtue and sin had begun a struggle upon the battle field of my soul. It was a desperate conflict. Whenever I attended the meetings of God's people, my good resolutions were greatly strengthened, my convictions deepened, and like Peter I wept bitterly on such occasions. At other times I was overcome by the power of evil, which still maintained dominion in me, for I was not yet born again. I was not made free by the Son of God. After these seasons of sinful abandonment I suffered terrible compunctions of conscience, for I knew better than I acted." Such was the religious experience and inner life of John Seybert, when a lad of but fourteen years.

Two of his brothers died in infancy. He says beautifully concerning this: "The Lord took these children out of the polluting companionship of sinful men, into the fellowship of the redeemed in heaven, because he loved them."

When he was not yet fifteen years of age, the Lord also called away his father, in March 1806, at the early age of forty-five. The death of Henry Seybert was the occasion of important events. Within one

2

year of her husband's demise, the widow, who was now the only support of the two remaining sons, John and David — the eldest and the youngest — fell into bad hands, which doubtless would not have been possible, had Mr. Seybert remained living. The representations of that religious enthusiast, George Rapp, would have made but little impression upon Henry Seybert's firm and settled character, whereas the gentle nature of his wife, softened still more by her recent severe bereavement, was very easily impressed by Rapp's deceptive Pietism. — But to be explicit.

A society had come from Germany to this country, who professed to be Divinely commissioned, and specially and specifically sent to this western Republic, to establish here the Millennium. Their founder and leader was George Rapp. He had selected a stretch of land about twenty-five miles north-west of Pittsburgh, Pa., for his home. Here he built a village and established his society. The village and the society were named "Harmony." One of the families of this society obtained a home in Mrs. Seybert's house, through her kind-heartedness and hospitality. This occasioned frequent visits from other members of the society. No sooner, however, had these chiliasts — for such they were — become acquainted with the Seyberts, than they began to display a strong disposition to secure them as new adherents to their scheme. They succeeded in misleading Mrs. Seybert, so that she became confused in her religious conceptions. The Harmonists represented that they alone in all the wide world of Christendom, were on the right way, and claimed to be the special favorites of God. They proclaimed that God would now speedily gather all His scattered sheep together into their particular society, and the village of Harmony was destined to become the new Jerusalem. They urged immediate and literal separation from all worldly' society and occupations, and union with themselves ; just as Lot left Sodom and as the disciples had fled to the mountains at the destruction of Jerusalem. In the society of the Harmonists alone, was there absolute security, etc.

By these, and similar representations, these people finally persuaded the mother to forsake her already fatherless children. About thirteen months after her husband's death, she left her two boys,—the youngest but eight years of age—left everything the family had, regardless of the dying instructions of her husband, in his last will and testament, according to which she was to have remained upon the family estate until the eldest son, John, should reach his majority,—and followed these people into their settlement west of Pittsburgh. Nothing could prevent her from taking this step. She disregarded all the entreaties of relatives, and the advice of friends, steeled her heart against the helpless orphanage of her boys, and went to Harmony. Such is the power of fanaticism, and such the unnatural influence and tendency of erroneous religious teaching. When men wrest the Scriptures, they do it to their own hurt ; when they supersede God's word, by the teachings of conceited human wisdom, they ruin themselves and all who follow them. False doctrine has always been inimical to the best interests of humanity; truth alone always works well, and is followed by humane and elevating tendencies.

Some account of the life of George Rapp and his colony may be in place here. George Rapp was a native of Wurtemberg, Germany, born in 1770, who, already in early life, believed himself to be favored with revelations from God. These pretences gradually developed into the conviction that he was called to restore the Christian religion to purity. In the course of time he withdrew himself from civil and also ecclesiastical obligations, and labored to construct a civil and ecclesiastical organization of his own with a community of possessions, pretendedly modeled after the apostolic church. Being prevented by the civil government from carrying out his scheme, he emigrated to the United States in 1803, with his followers, and at the close of 1804 founded a colony, called Harmony, as stated above. Its members were supposed to live in perfect harmony, and complete equality of possessions, rights and duties was to prevail. Later, Rapp sold this colony, and emigrated to Indiana. Among these Harmonists, about 1809, at a time of high religious excitement, the principle and practice of continence or marital abstinence was introduced. In Indiana they settled in the valley of the Wabash, in Posey Co., but suffered so terribly from the malarial fevers which were prevalent in that country, which was at that time the far west and uncultivated, that they turned their steps eastward again. At that time, it is believed, that the organization already possessed property worth half a million dollars. Rapp returned with the faithful to a point within eighteen miles of Pittsburgh, on the right side of the Ohio river, in Beaver county, where the colony of "Economy" was founded, which soon became the head-quarters for the Harmonists, and which exists to the present day, as a wealthy community. They cultivated the soil, constructed respectable buildings along an avenue of green trees, and caused the desert to blossom abundantly.

Mr. Rapp acted as leader, high-priest and preacher, and, demanding implicit faith in his teachings, he exacted unconditional obedience to his legislation. He controlled all the common property of the colony in the corporate name, and regulated and prescribed all their social customs as well as their religious rites, and even made marriage contracts dependent upon his consent. He exacted a novitiate of four weeks' duration, and the transfer of all property of all candidates for membership in the community.

The Harmonists suffered, however, a considerable loss in 1831, through an impostor named Bernhard Miller, alias Proli, who, under the pretence of being of princely ancestry, introduced himself as Count Maximilian of Leon. He settled in Pittsburgh, announced himself as the Lord's anointed, and claimed to be called to judge the world and to inaugurate the Millennium by the organization of the society of the New Jerusalem. The "Count" joined himself to

Rapp and his society, in the capacity of a prophet. Rapp guaranteed to him and his younger associates the privilege of matrimony, and true community of goods. The Count, however, soon withdrew from the colony with three hundred adherents, and compelled Rapp to pay over to him the respectable sum of $105,000.00 as his share of the common property. This sum he squandered like a prodigal, eventually cheated his followers, separated himself from them and settled in Arkansas. He at last perished miserably. Rapp, whose colony is practically a Protestant conventicle that has not increased in members, died in 1847. A Mr. Baker became his successor.

These were the people who so sadly interfered with the family life of the Seyberts, by deceiving the widowed mother. Notwithstanding the conduct of his mother towards himself and his brother, Mr. Seybert never in his life allowed himself to think of or treat her otherwise than kindly and respectfully. His journal shows that he never failed to visit her to the end of life, whenever possible, and always enjoyed it. He believed that she was sincere, though strangely misguided. She really believed that to be the way to save her soul, and she was specially deceived by the semblance of asceticism which was involved in the doctrine and organization of the Harmonists.

The Bishop's remaining brother David, however, was very differently affected. The affair created in him a life-long, bitter and inextinguishable hatred towards his mother. He never wanted to hear anything about her after that. His youthful heart received too severe a shock ever to recover from it. John, on the other hand, continued to the end of life to respect and love her, especially after his conversion in his twentieth year. He frequently visited her at the colony, during his ministerial career, and invariably spoke affectionately of her. She died, only about a year before he himself passed away, at the ripe age of ninety-two years, and after her death he frequently alluded to her in his sermons, stating that he expected to meet her in heaven.

John Seybert exhibited great firmness and an admirable adherence to his religious convictions. After his mother had forsaken him, he proceeded forthwith to take the place of a parent to his yet tender brother David, and labored hard with his hands to sustain himself and his brother on the paternal estate. He was industrious, and avoided extravagance and loaferism. Though not yet converted, he firmly believed in God and in the Bible, and though at times he was led into sinful indulgences by evil companions, yet he maintained his integrity of character. This trait also manifested itself quite positively in his subsequent bearing towards the Harmonists. His mother with her associates tried every possible means to induce him to join them. At the early age of sixteen and seventeen he firmly withstood all their efforts to entangle him in their delusion. Neither entreaties, threats, nor blandishments availed. His mother wrote letter after letter; her efforts were reinforced by the ablest apostles of the society, but all to no purpose. As long as she followed the directions of his father's testament, he treated her wishes like the edicts of a king, but after her abandonment, he did what he believed to be right, while listening patiently and respectfully to all she had to say.   And all her efforts were necessarily directed to him, since his brother's heart was closed against her forever.   When blandishments and flatteries failed, the Harmonists began to hurl anathemas.   They declared that all outside of their community would be the victims of unspeakable calamities and awful destruction.   But John replied with manly firmness, and emphatically refused to have anything whatever to do with them.   As a last resort, they sent special emissaries to him, who tried to picture the peculiar delights and beauties of their conventicle, in glowing colors, in the hope of enticing him.   They evidently judged, and rightly too, that John Seybert would make a valuable addition to their number.   But, though he was himself a decidedly eccentric personality, yet he never took any stock in the eccentricity of monkdom.   Its seclusion accorded ill with his practical view of life and of the Christian religion.

These occurrences, and sad changes in the family life, had the effect to dampen Mr. Seybert's religious zeal, and temporarily obliterated the pungent convictions he had previously experienced.   His advancement towards the kingdom of grace was severely checked, and for the space of three years his religious life was indeed "A barren waste, and howling wilderness."

He might have adopted the language of Carlyle

during this period: "A nameless unrest urged me forward. Whither should I go ? My loadstars were blotted out ; in that canopy of grim fire shone no star. Yet forward I must; the ground burnt under me ; there was no rest for the sole of my foot. I was alone, alone ! A feeling I had that, for my fever-thirst, there was and must be somewhere a healing fountain." He ceased to attend the meetings of the people of God, and came near yielding to the boisterous public voice that "these praying people"—meaning the Evangelicals, principally,—are the false prophets and deceivers, of whom the Scriptures gave warning. At length, however, in his nineteenth year, he agreed with an associate to go on a certain occasion, to hear one of these reputed "deceivers" preach. The service was to be held in a private house. When they arrived at the house, his companion hesitated, but Seybert led the way and the other followed. It so happened that young Seybert sat upon the end of a bench which extended to the table behind which the preacher sat. As people kept coming in he was crowded nearer and nearer to the preacher, until at last he could get no nearer. · The preacher was Rev. Matthias Betz, a mighty preacher, who was at that time serving Lancaster circuit with Rev. John Dreisbach, of precious memory. The Bishop frequently declared that Betz gave him "the finishing stroke" that night. While young Seybert sat there waiting for the service to begin, he keenly observed everything about him in the room. During Bro. Betz's opening prayer the Spirit of God got an overpowering hold upon his heart.   He afterwards related, that during this prayer he shuddered convulsively and that new and strange feelings possessed his soul.   This experience during prayer, well nigh cured him of the suspicion that the preachers of the Evangelical Association were false prophets.   Here is his own account of what followed: " After prayer the preacher rose, stood behind the table, read a text of Scripture, and began to preach. Before he was half-way through, I was thoroughly convinced that he was a true servant of Jesus Christ. I was also convinced that I was no Christian, but a sinner who richly deserved the wrath of God.   Then and there I received a wound from the sword of the Spirit, and a stroke from the hammer of the Word, from which I never recovered, and the effects of which will continue with me through all eternity. Praise the Lord for it !"

That sermon and that prayer broke the long slumber of his conscience, and John Seybert was no longer able to delay seeking Christ.   His associate was similarly affected, and both went home buried so deeply in thought, that scarcely any conversation passed between them.   It was the beginning of a new life for Seybert.   The next morning he rose early, in a contrite frame of mind, and about six o'clock formed the resolution to consecrate himself from that hour wholly to the Lord, soul and body, and with all that he had for time and for eternity.   He had coolly counted the cost, and deliberately determined upon this course, regardless of consequences.   With streaming eyes he prayed the prayer of the Publican, as he rose from his knees: "God be merciful to me a sinner"! Then he repeated stanzas of hymns which expressed the burning desire of his heart to be free from sin. He continued his struggle of soul all that day, by repeating some of the penitential Psalms, until his tear-stained eyes were too dim to read. His associate pursued for a while the same course, but grew weary and gave up the struggle. Seybert went on. He soon became more courageous, and willing to take up the cross; he attended public services, eager to hear the hated "preachers of repentance," sought the Lord publicly as well as privately, separated himself from the world, and devoted himself with energy to the salvation of his soul. Withal he had to suffer persecution. In those days, whoever espoused the cause of Christ had to expect that, and no one became a member of the Evangelical Association for the fashion of it. Such a step was anything but fashionable. John Seybert, however, was too sin-sick to care for persecution; besides, he had taken it into the reckoning beforehand, for he knew what the step he took involved. Accordingly he sought consolation and counsel among the "praying people." He sought to grasp the idea of faith in the sufficient merit of Jesus, and continued to wrestle day and night in prayer and entreaty, in strong crying and tears, with unabated earnestness, until, in his own favorite phrase, he was *"converted deep into eternal life" (tief ins ewige Leben hinein bekehrt).* He knew the *time* and place of his conversion very definitely. It was *June 21, 1810,* when the awful struggle finally ended in victory, and rest came to his tried and weary soul, after two .ong months of incessant striving to enter in at the strait gate.   In harmony with the man himself and everything connected with his person, this important occurrence was also somewhat singular.   He awoke early on the twenty-first of June, feeling unusually depressed and sad.   The burden of his sin became at length unbearable.   Everything about him had assumed a sombre aspect, himself the centre of sadness, and in his own estimation the most miserable being on earth. As he walked out of the house that morning, he again and again groaned his oft repeated prayer: "God be merciful to me, a sinner, for Jesus' sake!"   Meanwhile he had reached the well, the trough of which the members of the family were accustomed to use for the purpose of washing themselves.   He stooped to bathe his tear-stained face in the clear water, when instantly he became conscious that the load of guilt had been rolled from his soul, and that the blood of Jesus was applied to his heart.   He realized at that moment that he was washed with the washing of regeneration and the renewing of the Holy Ghost. The fashion of his countenance was altered, and prayer was changed to praise.   Old things had passed away, and behold, all things had become new.   He had received "beauty for ashes, the oil of joy for mourning, the garment of praise for the spirit of heaviness."   He was "a new creature in Christ Jesus." Thenceforth John Seybert was a Christian.   Thenceforward he served the Lord with almost unexampled ardour to the end of his days, a blessing to his day and generation. He was a burning and a shining light. He became a great winner of souls, and turned many to righteousness. To many a seeker of religion he afterwards gratefully related how the Lord had saved him while washing his natural face in a trough by the well. "There by that well," he exclaimed, "the Lord converted me deep into eternal life; there he blessed me for the first time, and I will not forget it to all eternity. My heavy load was suddenly gone, my sorrowful spirit was made instantly happy, and I was full of the Holy Ghost. Hallelujah!"

Such a conversion is the greatest possible event in a man's life, and such it proved to be in John Seybert's case. The whole course of his life was changed by it.

CHAPTER II.

HIS CALL TO THE MINISTRY, AND THE BEGINNING OF HIS WORK.

IMMEDIATELY upon his conversion, Mr. Seybert united with the Evangelical Association. For a while he continued at his trade as a cooper. The society to which he belonged, however, soon urged his appointment as exhorter, and in accordance with their wishes Rev. J. Dreisbach, the first Presiding Elder of the Evangelical Association, licensed him as such. This was his first office in the church, the functions of which he discharged with great zeal and exemplary faithfulness. Soon afterwards he was elected class-leader. He keenly felt his unworthiness and unfitness, as he expressed it, for such public service in the church; but, yielding to the importunity of the preachers, he accepted the position, serving in this capacity for a while in two classes, one in Manheim and the other in Mt. Joy, seven or eight miles distant. The Lord blessed him and his classes greatly; their prayer-meetings were seasons of great spiritual power and rejoicing, and sinners were convicted and converted in them.

With his accustomed modesty he speaks of his call to the ministry in his Journal: " For sometime I had felt a deep inward constraint to preach the Gospel, but on account of my sense of unfitness, I was very careful not to mention it to anyone, and went on quietly in the discharge of my duties as class-leader, when, without any solicitation on my part, the brethren received me into the ministry as a local probationer. This was in 1819, and I made my first attempt to preach with 1 John 3:8, 9, for a text."

Bishop Seybert's call to the ministry was never doubted by the people of God, nor by the devoted servants of Jesus Christ. He was himself the only one who ever was troubled with any misgivings on that subject. It soon became clear to all that he was indeed called of God, for his ministrations had a powerful effect upon his hearers, and produced profound impressions, often setting everything in commotion. It was no uncommon thing for sinners to break down in bitter tears of penitence, under the fervent appeals of the youthful class-leader, while the saints were greatly edified and quickened by his stirring exhortations. He was evidently endued with the Holy Ghost. Of course, his sermons at the first were not in themselves remarkably excellent ; indeed sometimes they were rather inferior productions. He was no intellectual prodigy. But it was clear that he was deeply in earnest, had the salvation of souls at heart, and was a chosen vessel of God's mercy. Besides, he was assiduous in the study of the Scriptures, instant in prayer, active in pastoral visitation, and constantly devising means and methods to rescue the perishing. His great self-denial, his modest bearing, his affable manners, his philanthropic disposition, and withal his eminently Christian walk and conversation, secured for him, without his seeking it, the universal confidence and respect of mankind.

In respect of his special equipment for the work of the Gospel ministry, it was from above. He had at the outset but limited literary attainments, owing to the general want of educational facilities within his reach at that time. Schools and colleges were as yet comparatively scarce, and those that did exist were little adapted to fit a man for the work of a preacher in the Evangelical Association. His spiritual equipment was, from the beginning, excellent. He had but one purpose in preaching, and that was to save sinners. In this purpose he was so earnest that he frequently forgot his text, while being led out to plead with sinners to be reconciled to God. His commission was Divine, and he cared more to please his Master than to achieve a finished literary style, in order to gain the applause of men. But he improved rapidly. From the beginning he took great pains to educate himself, and certainly attained a very high degree of literary knowledge. It must not be supposed that Bishop Seybert undervalued education. On the contrary, he was a widely read, versatile and a highly self-educated man.

The Spirit of wisdom and of grace was upon him. In a few years he attained eloquence of speech, and soon became renowned as a man mighty in the Scriptures. He could have adopted Isaiah's words : "The Lord God hath given me the tongue of the learned, that I should know how to speak a word in season to him that is weary." He has seldom been excelled in the facility with which he learned to explain and defend the great doctrines of salvation. In a short time he had acquired the reputation of being deeply learned in divinity. However, he sought more to speak in the demonstration of the Spirit and of power, than in the wisdom of men. As a result, opponents were never able to withstand him. Their classical learning availed them nothing. Already in his first years he vanquished hardened and embittered opposers, so that they fled tremblingly and confused, or fell smitten down by the power of God. God himself had equipped him by nature, as well as by graces and gifts of the Spirit. To this he added stores of knowledge and strength of intellect by close application to the study of all the sources of information to which he could obtain access, especially the Holy Bible.

At the age of twenty-nine years, ten years after his conversion, John Seybert started out as an Evangelical itinerant. From that day to the end of his life, he was prominently and actively identified with the conflicts and triumphs, the labors and successes, the sufferings and joys of the church in whose service he was engaged. He saw the Evangelical Association enjoy a period of wonderful growth in his lifetime, and himself performed no small part of the work which led to that success. When he first joined the Evangelical Association, it had about four hundred members, seven itinerant preachers, and ten local preachers ; when he entered the ministry, the church had not quite two thousand members, twenty itinerant and forty local preachers ; when he died, it had forty thousand members, and five hundred and eighty-eight itinerant and local preachers.

Concerning the important step of entering the ministry, he writes in his Journal as follows:

"I started out as an itinerant, September 12, 1820, and at first served in stead of Rev. John Klinefelter, who was sick at that time. The second day I felt greatly encouraged, and fully determined, if it be God's will, to labor in His vineyard with my Evangelical brethren. I should have gone sooner, had I been certain that the Lord wanted me to go. However, I had no rest at my cooperage, and concluded that the only way to get into the clear, concerning this matter, was to make an effort. If the Lord blesses my labor with the awakening and conversion of sinners, and the edification and encouragement of saints, I determined I would serve Him in this way with all my ability, wherever I might have to go, whatever crosses I might have to bear, and however long the task might last.

"With this sentiment I set out for my first appointment. I had laid aside my worldly affairs, was sound in mind and body, and had but one desire, and that was, to do whatever God required of me. The third night after leaving home, I had a remarkable dream. I thought I was in my brother's meadow at Lancaster, Pa., and saw springs of water flowing from the south, and turning their streams toward the east. I then went under an overhanging rock that is in this meadow, and saw other springs of water, one of which was much stronger than the rest, and had exceedingly sparkling water—indeed it seemed to be literally '*living* water'!—I felt greatly strengthened by this dream, but had a terrible conflict with the devil next day. A few evenings later I dreamed I was preaching, and that a sinner was converted under the sermon."

Though he gives no explanation of these dreams, he evidently regarded them as omens of good. He afterwards became quite an adept in interpreting his dreams, and certainly experienced some remarkable realizations of his premonitions.

About a week after this, Bro. Seybert had a remarkable time. At this time he felt with peculiar weight his unfitness for the work, and endured a severe temptation. That evening, notwithstanding his miserable state of mind, he was to preach. The congregation gathered, and he took Rom. 2: 4, 5, for his text, and began to speak. Then he realized the truth of the saying: "My strength is made perfect in weakness." God blessed him so that he was able to preach with great unction and much feeling. A sick woman in the house, during the closing prayer began to cry out in terror, "Lost! lost! lost!" and entreated the company to pray for her. Her very weakness lent pathos to her touching appeal, and every one in the congregation fell to weeping. She was soon converted, and after that lived for God.

From the time of his entrance upon the public service of the church, he kept a journal, in which his personal experiences are related in very simple language.

His style of composition was a copy of himself — simple, direct, inornate and quaint.   We only regret that extracts from the journal must necessarily lose much of their original flavor and idiom in the translation. In the original it fairly "holds the mirror up to nature." This journal is the principal source of information in many particulars, and we shall follow its guidance.

On the way to an appointment at Bro. Lehn's, he was obliged to stop in the city of Lancaster, to dispose of some temporal business matters which, he complains, caused him much distraction of mind. That evening his text was Eph. 5: 14.   He remarks: "I felt wonderfully weak and empty.   Still the meeting was not quite without blessing, for two brethren exhorted afterwards."

Next day he set out for Manheim, his native place, where he preached at sister Krahl's.   He says, many people ran together, some of whom "behaved very badly, yea worse than brutish — *devilish*.   Preaching was very difficult under such circumstances.   Everything was fearfully dark and locked up.   Fortunately there was present a talented young preacher, a stranger, who followed with a powerful exhortation, so that Israel got the victory anyway.".

From here he went to Bro. Breidenstein's, where he met the brethren Zimmerman and Peters.   The former preached, the latter exhorted, and Seybert closed the meeting.   The meeting was blessed.   Then he remarks : "Saturday, 30th, my meeting was at Bro. Eby's.   Here God had mercy on me once more and blessed me.   Praise the Lord!"

October 1st, he preached at J. Walter's, from St. John 1: 11, 12.   At this place there were many people, and preaching "went hard".   But the Lord refreshed the people from another source.

Monday he preached from Rev. 3: 20, to eight attentive auditors, one of whom fell into great distress of soul.   She was so wrought upon by the Holy Spirit, that she wept aloud, and began to pray.   This gave Seybert courage to go on in the work.

On Tuesday his appointment was at Bro. Stroh's. During the day he felt sad and depressed in spirit. With this feeling he went into a wood, as he himself tells us, fell down upon his knees, and made his complaint unto God, entreating His help in this time of need, and, he adds: "the Lord heard me.   In the evening preaching went well, beyond all expectation in fact.   It was a glorious time.   The Lord be praised forever !   Next evening, however, I felt empty and forsaken again, and it was hard to preach.   And then, to make the matter worse, two very large dogs came into the assembly, and began to fight most savagely right in the midst of the congregation of worshippers." It is easy to imagine what disturbance such an incident would occasion, under such circumstances.

Mr. Seybert then gives a characteristic account of a "big meeting", which was held Oct. 6th, near Washington, Pa., as follows :

"Bro. Zimmerman preached the word with life and power; Bro. Barber also spoke with great unction. The preaching of these brethren was not like that of the pharisaical hypocrites and of the college fledglings, who filled most of the pulpits of the day. It seemed as if the gates of hell must tremble. On Saturday night we had a glorious time ; some struggled for liberty, while others leaped for joy and shouted victory. Sunday morning at eight o'clock there was an experience meeting, during which the excellent experiences, related by the people of·God, so moved the unconverted that they wept freely and became penitent. Then followed a sermon by Bro. Erb, on "leprosy", which occasioned much sobbing and weeping even among the votaries of fashion, who had ornamented their necks with 'ruffles'. In the afternoon the power of God came upon the people in a still more wonderful manner. Many were moved to repentance, among others a little girl of ten years began to pray most piteously for mercy, and ceased not until she had entered in at the strait gate. There was great rejoicing in Israel over this affecting incident. The holy fire was still aglow on Monday morning, breaking out afresh during family prayers at Bro. Herr's. I know of at least six persons who were converted at that meeting, and several others continued earnestly to seek the Lord after the meeting closed. One family in particular experienced a wonderful change. First the mother was converted, then a son-in-law, at a camp-meeting which he ventured to attend ; soon afterwards his wife yielded ; upon this a son became concerned for his soul ; then the rest of the children, and last of all the father was also saved —all in about two months."

On the fifteenth of October Mr. Seybert, while on

a journey, was caught in a cold rain. It rained so long and so hard that he was completely drenched, even his shoes filled with water. It should be explained that he never wore boots, and always rode on horseback, until age compelled him to change to a more comfortable mode of travel.— But he declares this experience did not in the least discourage him. He went about his Master's business in all kinds of weather.

Here Mr. Seybert also makes note of the suicide of a wealthy cattle-dealer, which occurred about that time in Lancaster, Pa. Commenting on it he exclaims : "This man was a poor wretch, and ended his own life in terror, though he had two thousand dollars in his pocket!"

At a certain meeting, Nov. 15th, a great commotion was caused by a sister who, after the service had closed, made a wonderfully pathetic appeal to the unconverted. She wept so exceedingly in her agony for souls, that she might well be called a sister of the prophet Jeremiah of old, who once exclaimed:.. "Oh, that my head were waters, and mine eyes a fountain of tears, that I might weep day and night for the slain of the daughter of my people!"

During the early part of his ministerial career, Seybert had many tribulations to endure. Like all God's saints he had to be tried as by fire. Neither did he overcome the sinfulness of his nature without severe struggles. Scattered through his journal, such sentences as these afford some glimpses of his inner life:

"To-day Satan tried me sorely. I realized strong

feelings of envy and anger within me, which pained me deeply."

Again :

"This was for me a hard day. My temptations were of such weight and force, as to be well-nigh unendurable. It seemed as though all the pollution of the pit of hell was being poured over my poor soul."

Again he says :

"To-day my wanderings were again full of sadness. I was troubled all day with uprisings of anger and of impatience. This was miserable company."

During this year (1820) he experienced his last difficulty with the Harmonites, who had so unfortunately victimized his mother. Upon certain grounds which do not appear, Mrs. Seybert laid claim to part of the estate of her late husband, and sent several members of the society to negotiate with her sons. The younger son emphatically objected to giving her a single cent. The elder, however, desirous of peace, and anxious to have done with this disagreeable affair forever, was disposed to give their mother more even than he felt it really his duty to allow her. His wish finally prevailed, and a sum of money was accordingly given the Harmonites, who had all things in common, and the account finally closed.

Through December of that year, Mr. Seybert reports "good times." He enjoyed bodily health, was in good spirits, and had great delight in the Lord's service. Of a sermon which he preached on the 14th, he has this to say :

"At the beginning my heart was fearful and diffident. But, blessed be the Lord, the man-fearing spirit soon left me, and I began to realize a deep concern for my hearers. Eternity in all its vast sweep opened to my view, and it was as if I saw heaven opened, and caught glimpses of its ineffable blessedness and glory. The vision thrilled me with unspeakable rapture, so that I felt moved to praise the Lord with shouts of joy. The people of God, full of the Holy Ghost, shouted God's praises. The dark power of Satan was broken, and Israel had a glorious victory."

On one of these days he attended a specially powerful experience meeting. A class-leader complained at this meeting that something was yet lacking in him; in fact, he confessed that he did not have religion enough. Seybert encouraged him to seek that which was lacking in his spiritual condition, immediately. This the brother at once resolved to do, and that with fasting and prayer. Then the grace of God poured like a river into his soul until he was so filled that for a time he was unconscious, or, rather, entranced, while the rest of the company were so filled with the love of God, that they gave vent to their emotions with shouts and jubilations. There were also some 'dry bones' in the congregation, which were stirred by the mighty movings of the Holy Spirit, and began, as it were, to gasp for life. One sister was so inspired with zeal, that afterwards with fastings and prayer she struggled against Satan for days, and obtained so grand a victory that, under the powerful effusion of God's Spirit, she lay entranced for thirty-two hours, and awoke feeling unspeakably happy.

Such occurrences were frequent in those days among God's really spiritual people. The contrast between. God's true people, and the dead, cold, heartless, spiritless formalism which prevailed in the old churches, was on this account the more marked and convincing, especially when these demonstrations were followed by purity of life and rectitude of moral character. These peculiar demonstrations and manifestations were unmistakably the work of the Spirit of God, and were adapted to the social and religious condition of the times in which they occurred. They had a convincing effect upon the thoughtful as well as upon the thoughtless, proved the supernatural character of true religion, and were the means of many conversions. The general spiritual apathy was so great, especially in those circles among whom the Evangelical Association was called upon to labor; the belief in experimental religion and spiritual life had become so nearly crushed and obliterated by the semi-rationalism imported by the clergy from the universities of Germany; the standard of morality was so low among the masses of nominal Christians, that, unless the work of reformation, in which the Evangelical Association was engaged, and to which she was undoubtedly called, had been accompanied by such mighty demonstrations of the Spirit and of power, as would brush away the scales from the eyes of deluded thousands, and stir as with an earthquake of moral power the public religious consciousness, the effort must be futile and abortive. Such a work, a work namely of reformation for the *restoration of Spiritual life*, was and is the mission of the Evangelical Association, and in the providence of God, Jacob Albright was the Luther of German religious life in America. God makes no mistakes, and these, to our times peculiar manifestations, that developed in the earlier stages of that religious awakening which was the result of the preaching and labors of the Evangelical ministry, need no apology.

After Bro. Klinefelter had recovered from his sickness, and was again able to fill his own appointments, Seybert, at the beginning of 1821, was sent to York circuit with Bro. Barber. His first sermon was on the occasion of a watch-night, Jan. 12th. Such all-night meetings were often held, and not only on New Year's eve. He preached from Rev. 22: 17. This was a favorite text of his throughout his life. Bro. Seybert describes the service as follows:

"I was still in the first part of my discourse, and had just been speaking of how God calls sinners to repentance by his Spirit, and was explaining that the 'bride', spoken of in the text, meant God's true Church, and was showing how the Church says 'come', when a woman in the congregation suddenly began to cry out, LOST! LOST! LOST! and instantly fell to weeping and praying aloud. Now that another preacher, namely Jesus, had begun to preach, I stopped; and, since two more souls began to cry for mercy, we at once prayed with these penitents. Before the meeting closed, all three were saved."

This was the beginning of a work of grace in which forty souls were brought into the marvellous light and liberty of the people of God. This was a great encouragement to the young preacher, and from that time on, Seybert was satisfied that his call to the ministry was genuine.

Feb. 10th, he had a meeting at Mr. Reber's, where the people were fearfully wicked. They behaved in a most heathenish manner, talking aloud and laughing in the preacher's face, and carousing about the house. These people certainly served their father—the devil, with all their might; but Seybert says he also preached to them with all his might, concerning the awful damnation of the wicked, taking a German hymn for a text. However, they closed the service early, and all became quiet as though all were over. In this way they got rid of the mob about midnight. Thinking that the meeting was closed, the rabble left with horrible roarings and shameful bellowings. After the mob was gone, they engaged in further exercises, and the Lord blessed them so gloriously that the meeting ended with a shout. This was "stealing a march" on the devil. The stratagem succeeded, the servants of Satan were foiled, and God's people had a feast of fat things besides, even though they had to wait until after midnight for it. In those days, however, the people were not as anxious to have short services and an early close, as many are in more modern times. It was not unusual to keep up services all night, even until at the break of day the rising sun gave the flaming signal for part-

ing. Many instances of this are recorded in Bishop
Seybert's journal.

Bro. Seybert loved to have conversions during his
meetings, and took great delight in seeing them *"get
through"*.

At a meeting, Feb. 14th, a woman was so mightily
wrought upon by the Holy Spirit of God, during
preaching, that she came near fainting away. She
fled to an adjoining room, threw herself on a bed,
and would not permit the arrow of conviction to enter
her soul deeper. She resisted the grace of God.
Seybert remarks: "This fish, though already caught
in the Gospel net, and even already pulled ashore,
yet fell back, I fear, into destruction. Still, she is certainly severely wounded, and at least a few arrows
of conviction are fast in that soul, and for this reason
I am not without hope that on some future occasion,
if the Lord spares her life, she may yet be rescued.
I pray God to give this woman no rest until she turns
unto Him."

Bro. Seybert was at this time greatly encouraged,
because his labor was not in vain in the Lord. Sinners were being saved. This only increased his
earnestness. His soul was eager to wrest spoil from
Satan. This was the passion that nerved him for toil,
and moved his soul with deep agonies. Like Rachel
of old, his cry was, "Give me children, or I die." He
would quickly have resigned his office as a minister of
the Gospel, had not the Lord given him spiritual sons
and daughters. However, the success of the work
provoked great opposition from certain quarters.

Under date of Feb. 21st, 1821, he writes:

"While the work of conversion in this benighted community is progressing irresistibly, and a soul is being saved here and another there, Satan also has his emissaries abroad. These are Protestant clergy,—hirelings,—men whose god is their belly—whom he has stirred up to oppose the work of the Lord. They are wolves in sheep's-clothing, and in their rage the wolf nature very clearly appears. They set up a fearful howl, because we (whom they call false prophets) have invaded the land to deceive the people." Wonder why they have suddenly become so concerned for the souls of the people! But they care not for the sheep, only for their wool. These are the very scoundrels of whom Isaiah says: 'His watchmen are blind; they are all ignorant; they are all dumb dogs, they can not bark; sleeping, lying down, loving to slumber. Yea, they are greedy dogs which can never have enough, and they are shepherds that can not understand: they all look to their own way, every one for his gain, from his quarter. They say, 'Come ye, I will fetch wine, and we will fill ourselves with strong drink; and to-morrow shall be as this day, and more abundant.' (Isa. 56: 10, 12.)

"Accursed generation of Balaam! And these delectable gentlemen warn the public against *us*, when we are endeavoring to rescue souls from the Devil, and are trying to bring them to the Lord Jesus Christ, in order to save them from their horrible vices!

" But the vulgar mob, which interferes with our services, belongs to these accursed shepherds, and is led on by them. Though consisting nominally of Christians, they are adepts at profanity, and lying, habitual drunkards, bold sabbath-breakers, and in every respect perfect disciples of Satan, following closely in his footsteps, and sometimes even growing impatient because the fiend himself does not go fast and far enough. They fairly out-devil the Devil! With their preachers, who are ungodly belly-servants, they oppose those who want to serve the Lord. They set themselves, and these rulers take counsel together against the Lord and against his Anointed. But 'He that sitteth in the heavens shall laugh; the Lord shall have them in derision; He will mock at their calamity; He will laugh when their fear cometh.' Meanwhile His work goes gloriously on. Hallelujah!

"But this is not enough. After the people have been saved, this Christian (?) mob does all in its power to recapture the escaped birds, for which they employ all sorts of means. One tempts them with the brandy bottle; another comes with a deck of cards; another invites them to a dance, and so on, almost *ad infinitum*. If by any means they are successful in luring any one away again from Christ, this Philistine brood tear their mouths open and fairly scream with delight. 'O yes!' they exclaim vauntingly, 'didn't we tell you they are all hypocrites?' The outcry becomes general; young and old, poor and rich, great and small—in short all sorts of sin-cripples, pastors included, join in the chorus, 'Our prediction has come true: this movement will soon collapse; before long you can pen all the Albrights

together in a corn-crib.   Perhaps some lying old wise
acre among them will yet add his opinion, saying, 'I
for my part never could have any confidence in these
praying people!'

"They are very much opposed to our 'evening
meetings' and to all that they are pleased to call
religion enthusiasm.   But when *they* hold 'evening
meetings' at the beer saloon or in the ball room—
that is perfectly justifiable.

" According to *their* notion, it is only necessary to
say that John was a little tipsy on election day, to
prove that he is ' all right again '.   That is a demonstration that *he* has been ' restored ' and has left the
'*Albrights*',—Elizabeth was not at the meeting last
Sunday, because she had been at the ball all night
Saturday.   That, shows that she is no longer among
the 'deceivers'.   The leader cries out, ' That will do
for Elizabeth, but these *Albrights won't go to dances.*'
To this mob, the only proof necessary that persons
are 'all right', is that they swear and drink and dance
and fight.—But this is enough for us too.   *We* also
understand these signs.   *Such is the manner in this
land of moral midnight, when any are truly converted
to the Lord Jesus Christ.*

" After the mob has in this way done all it can, it
then begins to peddle out innumerable lies concerning
us.   One asks another, whether he has also heard
that the preacher is an adulterer,—when he himself
may be guilty of it.—But then such a thing does not
unfit him to be even an elder or a deacon in *his*
church.   If *he prayed*, he would soon be unfit, and

would be expelled. Another, who has already been
in jail for stealing, tells his associates that the Gospel
preacher has more than once been guilty of horse-
stealing, and is known at home only as '*the ignorant
horse thief.*' 'Humph!' says an old card-player, 'the
whole thing (meaning the Evangelical Association) is
going down—faster than it came up. Our parson
told us last Sunday we should be careful, may be
they give the people some kind of poison so as to
deceive them the easier!' Thus they belie and slander the true servants of God. They carry about with
them a perfect 'Pandora's box' of filthy epistles.—
And yet, in spite of all, the Lord's people are the
light of the world and a salt to the earth."

This is a severe arraignment, but it is no exagger-
ation. In fact, it was evidently impossible to exagger-
ate the condition of things among the nominal
German church-members of Pennsylvania in those
days, and Bro. Seybert felt perfectly justified in his
satirical, vigorous and severe attacks upon them.
Some of these localities were perfect hot-beds of
iniquity, and their parsons strained every nerve to
prevent the early success of the Evangelical Association, for if the Evangelical Association were
successful in its work, their occupation would soon be
gone, and they opposed Seybert and his compeers
much in the same spirit and with the same motives,
that actuated Demetrius the silversmith and his fellow-
craftsmen, in the Ephesian uproar against Paul. Had
it not been for the prevalence of religious liberty
protected by civil law, the Evangelical itinerants

4

would have been shot from their horses, or burnt at the stake, as late as 1840.   It is unpleasant to be obliged to make such statements, but we could not otherwise be true to the facts of history.   Whatever may be the moral status of those religious organizations to-day, we would fain throw a covering over their past in this country, if we could do so, and still write an intelligent life of Bishop Seybert.

Need enough, one should say, for the preaching of the pure Gospel to those people.   The degenerate condition of morality, and the deplorable religious life of the German people of America, made the work of JACOB ALBRIGHT, and the organization of the EVANGELICAL ASSOCIATION, an imperative necessity.   It was this that inspired the ministry of that great and good man, and resulted in the organization of this branch of the Christian church, which was not only the first to do anything, but which has done as much as, if not more than any other single organization or agency for the religious reformation of the German population of the United States, Canada, and even Europe.

About this time, Bro. Seybert lost his voice in consequence of over-exertion.   Under this affliction he felt "tempted to labor more moderately."   This "temptation", however, he soon overcame, and he began earnestly to pray for the restoration of his voice.   Upon this he made an attempt to preach, and behold, the Lord so blessed him that a sinner was convicted.

Some time in February (1821) Seybert purchased

Godfrey Arnold's "Portraits of the first Christians," and read it so diligently that he nearly committed the entire work to memory, for he was a great and careful reader.

Soon afterwards he records this in his journal:

"To-day I had a dispute with an unconverted man, who asserted that our people were as false as Satan himself. In vain did I challenge him to name or point out a single drunkard, swearer or Sabbath breaker among us. I furthermore told him that in his church no hypocrisy was necessary, since godliness itself was at a discount among them. This he admitted to be possibly at least correct. I succeeded so far in convincing him of the error of his ways, that he promised he would never again partake of the Holy Communion in his present state of heart. He further confessed that he was unsaved, and that his church was really in a state of decay."

March 4th he says he preached to three hearers, which was followed with excellent results, but upbraids himself, because at first the idea of preaching to so small a congregation was repugnant to him, until he thoughtfully *considered the worth of one immortal soul*, when he was enabled to address himself to the task with energy and courage.

On the same date he wrote of this place:

"Here the saying of Jesus is realized, when he said, 'I am not come to send peace, but a sword.' A Roman Catholic lived here, whose wife and two daughters were converted. He himself was a drunkard, and abused his wife barbarously after her conver-

sion.   One day when the husband was engaged in the
brutal act of beating his wife again, she began to praise
the Lord aloud, manifesting great joy in her sufferings.
The genuineness of this extrordinary manifestation
was so apparent that he became alarmed.   But, in an
enraged manner he turned to his eldest daughter, and
peremptorily ordered her out of house and home, if
she did not at once quit this 'foolishness', as he called
the true service of God.   However, she was ready
for him, and promptly told him she would go without
being driven away, which she immediately proceeded
to do.   Upon this he fell to beating the youngest
daughter most unmercifully with the ramrod of his
gun, until a splinter struck her near the eye, causing
the blood to flow in streams.   But the monster procured another stick and continued beating the child
still more, simply because she prayed!"

About the time when Bro. Seybert was to leave
York circuit, he says the devil set some of his faithful ones at work to besmirch his reputation, if possible
ruin his character, and so counteract, if not destroy, his
influence for good.   This they attempted to do by
circulating a series of scurrilous lies about him.   One
story ran to the effect that he had a wife near Baltimore, Md., who could not live with him on account
of his quarrelsome disposition.   Another story was,
that he had behaved himself indiscreetly towards
persons of the other sex, and that police detectives
were after him.   This, they said, was the reason why
he wanted to leave York circuit.   This class of stories
were circulated with special alacrity, because Bro.

Seybert was a celibate. He was never married. He says: "These very things only proved that my call to the ministry is divine, since I knew they were false, and I was conscious of living a life of chastity, sobriety and integrity. I rejoiced that I was permitted to suffer persecution for righteousness' sake."

Soon after this he deplored the fact that he did not realize the solemn importance of eternal things as he ought, in his ministerial office. He had to fight against lethargy, and the devil seemed determined to ruin him, he thought. "I am tried by lusts of the flesh", he says, "which, though they never get the victory over me, yet cause me much trouble, and I have a strong desire to be saved from these things — the sooner the better. God certainly must hear my ardent prayers, and He will surely deliver me from this buffeting of Satan's messenger, this thorn in the flesh. I do ask the Heavenly Father to do this speedily for the sake of the Redeemer's bitter sufferings. Amen! Amen."

May 31, 1821, Seybert preached his first sermon at a camp-meeting. The meeting was held at Philip Breidenstein's in Lebanon Co., Pa. God blessed the young preacher and gave him power and life, so that he was enabled to tell the people the truth with effect. Among other incidents a fashionably dressed young lady fell into distress of soul; she was so wrought upon that she became disgusted with her stylish articles of ornament, and tearing them off, she fell upon her knees and began to cry for mercy and salvation. This enraged the wicked, so they made an attempt to get the poor penitent away from the place of prayer, but the people succeeded in preventing this. The young lady was praying in a tent, and they prayed with her and for her until she was filled with light and life from above, and was translated into the kingdom of God's dear Son. The people of God, who had wept with her, now rejoiced with her.

At this meeting, Seybert remarks, Rev. H. Niebel preached in great power, and with wonderful unction, for two hours, and Bro. Erb preached a sermon of similar power, of two hours and three quarters in length.

In June, 1821, John Seybert attended his first conference session, and was regularly received into the itinerancy. Up to that time, since Sept. 1820, he had served "under the Presiding Elder". He says they had glorious times during that conference session, which convened in New Berlin, Pa. Bro. Seybert, however, demurred because he was given charge of a work so soon, as he felt himself entirely unfit for such a grave responsibility. He was given charge of Union circuit, with Rev. F. Hassler, a young probationer, as his colleague. But since "the brethren" had so ordered it, he meekly submitted, and the Lord blessed him.

Soon after conference, he happened into a meeting, where he did not like the preacher very well. He says: "The preacher belonged to that class who 'live in kings' houses' (to judge from the 'soft raiment' which he wore), rather than to the humble followers of Jesus. He was dressed like a worldling, and by no means looked as if he could 'endure hardness as a good soldier of Jesus Christ'. In explaining his text, he came near reasoning away the history of Creation, and jumbled together a wonderful conglomeration of astronomical guesswork and astrological dreamings, far beyond his own ability to comprehend, and much more that of his congregation. It was indeed a cold meeting. One could detect no life nor fire in the people, and alas! none flashed from the preacher either."

Sometime in July, he preached twice at a new place. In the morning he had good success, but in the after-noon "it went hard". There was a large congregation present, among whom were many proud, vain, puffed up people. Somehow he had not the gift of explaining the Scripture that particular afternoon, and the power of speech itself was almost gone. There sat before him such a mass of "children of darkness", that their spiritual coldness chilled him and he "had a hard time breaking the ice". Seeing at length, that all exegetical skill was gone from him, he abandoned his text altogether, and began to reason of righteousness and judgment to come. In this he persevered until at least some icy hearts began to melt, and tears flowed down some cheeks, then Seybert exclaimed, "Thank God for victory any way!"

CHAPTER III.

DIVERS EXPERIENCES.

The first Bishop of the Evangelical Association was now fairly launched upon his ministerial career. He already enjoyed the confidence and respect of his co-laborers, and had many seals to his ministry. He persevered in the same spirit in which he began. He grew in ability, increased in usefulness and power, and if possible in zeal and devotion. He was indeed a burning and a shining light. Here follows the record of his varied experiences as culled from his Journals.

Dec. 5th, 1821, he had a very remarkable dream: He thought he was told of a pit that was very deep, and had water in it. He was informed furthermore that several persons had fallen into it. With his companions he decided at once to visit the spot. On their arrival his companions were afraid to approach the pit, as they were made aware that the earth around it was undermined, so that only a frail, thin crust remained, which could not bear their weight. At this moment a strong feeling of sympathy possessed Seybert for the unfortunate people who had fallen into the pit. Hastily seizing a stick of wood, he began to knock off the loose earth around it, until he found solid ground. He then obtained a windlass, of the kind used in old-fashioned wells, with which he drew two men and one woman out of the pit by means of a rope. They were in a forlorn and pitiable plight indeed, for the pit was a place of great misery. After this he beheld the pit utterly destroyed, and to the astonishment of all, a bright stream of water gushing from it. This dream awakened in him confident expectations of conversions.

Bro. Seybert regards the following incident as authentic, which he relates in his journal. An extremely wicked man was converted to God. His name was Kashar. Upon his conversion his wife began to persecute him terribly. She swore at, scolded and blackguarded him shockingly. Suddenly, one morning, she appeared entirely composed and peaceable. All who knew of her conduct were amazed at the transformation. After repeated efforts to secure an explanation, she finally became more talkative and told them the cause. She related that in the previous night a form in gray appeared before her. She believed it was a spirit. The apparition offered her a bag full of gold and silver, if she would only continue to persecute and abuse her husband. This dream so shocked her, that she resolved to cease from her shameful conduct. She soon afterward requested religious services in their house, and sought the Lord without delay.

From the remarks of Bro. Seybert, recorded at some length in the previous chapter, concerning the parsons and members of certain churches, the reader might come to the conclusion that he was bigoted, and of the opinion that none were right except his own church. But this is far from the truth. He acknowledged merit wherever he chanced to find it, nor did he forbid any man to cast out devils because he followed not his company. He says: "Jan. 26th I visited a Reformed minister named Felix, who lived on Union circuit, where I was preaching that year. This man treated me with the greatest courtesy and consideration. When he saw me coming he hastened out to meet me, without either his hat or his coat on, and grasped my hand in a friendly manner. But not knowing at first who I was, he shook my hand with great heartiness a second time upon learning my name. I have never found another such friendly, benevolent, humble-looking Protestant preacher, possessing withal such a Christ-like spirit as this man. His dress, manners, conversation and disposition indicated a humble, sincere Christian and true embassador of Jesus Christ. We had a good time together, exchanging our views on the great, vital truths of our holy religion. He would under no consideration allow me to leave before dinner. His wife also was exceedingly hospitable and accommodating. Mr. Felix then saddled his horse, and rode a piece ways with me, that I might not lose my way."

One night he thought he went fishing, and also caught some fish, but neither with a hook nor with a net, but with his bare hands. Afterwards he thought he also captured a beautiful dove, and then a very cross young bear. His dream awakened his curiosity, and expectation.

The next day he called upon a newly awakened family, on the way to his appointment. After they had conversed a while on divine things, he asked the brother whether they would not unite with our church. At first the brother thought they were unworthy, but the woman said, "O yes, let us do it." After consideration the man consented. Seybert remarks confidently: "Here I had now caught my fish or my dove, in reality. I was now on the lookout for the bear." For this he had not long to wait. A few evenings later he was preaching in a private house, when some malicious person threw a brickbat through the window at the preacher with such violence and such well-directed aim, that the pieces of glass flew into his face. "This was the cross bear," he says.

Bro. Seybert, as the reader is aware, was a German by birth, by training and by practice. True, he could speak in English, and even read and write, but it was in an exceedingly broken manner. No one who knew his acquirements in this respect, would for a moment suppose that he would ever undertake to preach in the English language. But with him, souls were everything and reputation nothing. He would attempt anything to save a soul.

It was March 23d (1821), that he undertook to preach in English for the first time in his life. He had a congregation almost exclusively English. How could he serve them in their own language, much as he desired to do so, was the question. After talking a while in German, he ventured to say a few words in English. No sooner had he begun this, than the power of God came upon the people, and the effort was as blessed as it was stammering and imperfect.

And really, it "went" better than he imagined it
would. An English brother afterwards came up and
gave him some money for salary. He seemed very
well pleased, and encouraged him. He thanked God
and took courage.

May 12th, in Marietta, he had a North American
Indian in his congregation, which pleased him, for he
had often been told of the Indian's reverence for God
and His house, and was delighted to find it true in
this case. He bluntly remarks, "A great many, who
have all their religion in their mouth, could learn
from this Indian how to behave in the house of
God, in a manner becoming a civilized and enlightened race."

May 20th he came home to his brother and preached
to his neighbors and acquaintances in his old cooper-
shop. When he first saw the people he felt somewhat diffident. But he began to pity their souls, and
upon this he " broke through" and everthing "broke
through wonderfully", and tears flowed freely. He
however, hastened to praise the Lord for the successful issue of the meeting, and ascribed all to his
Divine Master.

In June, 1822, the Annual conference met again in
New Berlin, to hold its fifteenth session. At this
time there was as yet but one conference. At this
session Joseph Long, the second Bishop of the Evangelical Association, was received into the itinerancy
on trial, and John Seybert, the first Bishop, received
his ordination as Deacon. Bro. Seybert makes the
following observations on this event:

"It caused me great depression of spirit and a severe mental struggle, when it was reported that I had been elected to the office of a Deacon. Could I have chosen, I would have greatly preferred to be retained a while longer as a probationer, for I felt that I was not fit for anything else. Nevertheless I submitted as cheerfully as I could to the decision of my brethren, and will seek to do the best I can by the help of God."

He was appointed to Canton circuit, Ohio.

On his trip to his new charge in the West, Bro. Seybert attended a camp-meeting in Fayette Co., Pa., where a very sad event occurred. Sunday afternoon, under deep and solemn emotions the Lord's Supper was celebrated. On this occasion a brother named Bernd had been specially happy in seeing his own children participating in this great ordinance of God's house. At about five o'clock, while he was sitting by his tent in quiet and sweet contemplation, he suddenly fainted, and falling into the arms of his wife who was near him, he immediately expired, without being able to utter a word. Eleven of his children were on the encampment at the time. The sorrow into which the family were plunged was indescribable, while the alarm on the camp-ground was something awful. Bernd was a man greatly beloved by his family, and highly respected in the community. The corpse was left on the camp-ground, and prepared in a tent for burial. The funeral services, held in the auditorium, were exceedingly solemn, and made a most profound impression.

On Canton circuit, that year, Bro. Seybert labored with great success. Many were converted. He also got rid, more and more fully, of his harassing doubts concerning his call to the ministry, though even yet he was occasionally troubled with them.

July 19th he heard a sermon on Col. 3:3. The first part of the sermon was good enough, but the latter part greatly disgusted Seybert, "because he discussed matters not germain to the subject at all. When he spoke of infant baptism, he asserted that not all who die in infancy are saved, and that mother Eve would instruct the innocents in heaven." "Such trash was not edifying."

Two days later he heard another preacher, who preached "a very dry, cold and powerless" funeral sermon. Indeed, it was more of a tirade against heretics than anything else, utterly devoid of anything that could comfort the afflicted friends, or encourage the congregation in Christian living. The hearers had a very tedious time. "He is one of those of whom the Lord complained of old that they 'temper with untempered mortar.'"

Under date of Aug. 12th (1822) Bro. Seybert refers to the barbarous conduct of the people about Lancaster (Fairfield Co.), O., relating an instance where, at a meeting of United Brethren, a brother was so cruelly beaten that he died a few days afterwards.

August 15th he was overtaken by the darkness of night in one of the great primitive forests of Ohio. It was impossible to find his way out again. At length, he found a log hut in an opening, where, for money, he was shown the way. It was his purpose to reach his destination, if it took all night, which it came very near doing, for he arrived very late indeed.

Meanwhile his colleague, Bro. Wagner, had already been attacked with malarial fever, so prevalent in Ohio in those days, so that he could not keep up with his appointments, and on the 25th Seybert himself was attacked. But he stoutly refused to succumb, lest the circuit be "neglected". Still it often became simply impossible for him to reach his appointments. In this to him unwonted experience he was sorely tried in spirit, so that at times it seemed as though his little craft (*Glaubensschifflein*) should sink beneath the troublous waves. He however wept and prayed much; often stopping on his journey in the shadowy depths of those great forests to plead with God, wrestling until he was blessed.

Near Lisbon, about this time, a wicked man died a terrible death. In his last hours he blasphemed so terribly, that it became impossible for anyone to remain in the room. In his despair and rage the miserable man tore pieces of plaster from the wall and hurled them at his poor children, acting like a demoniac. In this condition he went into eternity. At his funeral the most barbarous scenes were transacted. The father of the dead man was so drunken, that he was hauled in the funeral procession like a dead swine, and one of the brothers was so intoxicated that he was left at the house, unable to go to the burial. Though it must be confessed that there was a certain savage fitness in all this, yet, who can fail to shudder while contemplating it. *"My God,"* he exclaims, *"what scenes in Babel!"*

Nov. 15th, when he preached at Bro. Rausch's, a drunkard came into the service to create disturbance. He had first exchanged clothes with an 'Amish' man. With this singular outfit he came in, causing great merriment, for his attire was really comical. But the merriment did not last long. "The almighty word of God got hold of him," so to speak, "by the nape of the neck" so that he began to weep violently. It was the end of his foolish conduct. From that hour he was a different man. "O that God would thus graciously save every disturber," Seybert fervently prays.

January 18th (1823) Bro. Seybert preached a sermon with which he was, it seems, very well pleased. He says of it :

"Last evening my preaching was blessed." Song of Solomon 6:9 was his text. He felt that great grace was given him, and when he came to the words, *'terrible as an army with banners'*, he finally applied them to the coming of Jesus Christ to judgment, when He shall come with a shout, and a great noise as of a trumpet, with ten thousand of his saints, and all the holy angels with him, on the day that shall burn as an oven, when consuming fire shall go out before him, which shall destroy all the wicked, root and branch,

> " When the sun is cold,
> And the stars are old,
> And the leaves of the Judgment book unfold."

During this application the audience broke out in sobbing, weeping, shouting and praising. A young lady became penitent, with whom they afterwards prayed until she found pardon and peace. She afterwards united with our church.

Under date of Feb. 9th he finds fault, both with himself and with the people. He mourns over his infirmities and imperfections and shortcomings. He felt a great lack of ability to perform the duties of his office ; while he was to preach to others he felt himself so far below the mark. With the people he found fault, because they praised him and told him he could preach grand sermons, and so forth. He wished they knew how poverty-stricken and miserable he really was, then they would no longer flatter him, and so occasion temptation in his depressed and feeble state of soul.

One day in March he had a meeting, where his effort seemed specially to please a certain pedagogue in the community. After the service had closed he sat down beside Seybert and began to "sing his siren song" to him. This, Seybert did not want to hear. Then the stranger began to abuse the other Christian denominations of the neighborhood in a very indiscreet fashion, which so angered an old gentleman who was present and overheard the conversation, that he uttered some hard words, seized his hat and hastened to leave the house. Seybert, however, hurried after him, spoke kindly to him, and tried to subdue his passion. Next morning he returned quite early, to see Seybert; they had a long, earnest con-

5

versation, and finally parted in peace. "This trouble", says Seybert, "was occasioned by the indiscreet school-master."

About the middle of May (1823), Bro. Seybert closed his labors on Canton circuit, Ohio, and after a year of faithful toil, prepared to return to annual conference. During this conference-year he endured all the hardships of a pioneer circuit rider on the frontier. His horse frequently became saddle-galled, owing to the long journeys over the unbroken, muddy roads of Ohio at that time. In fact, his route often lay through trackless forests, where the paths (not roads) were hard to find. Besides, the intrepid itinerant was often sick. But still he says, "The Lord gave us good times. Blessed be His name!"

On his way home, when he reached the eastern boundary line of Ohio, he alighted from his horse, fell upon his knees, and devoutly thanked God for Divine assistance, guidance and protection on his circuit during the past year. The soil of Ohio had become sacred to him, and on that consecrated ground he would once more praise the Lord, and there he would raise his Ebenezer.

That year in Ohio was a memorable one. To follow him in all his journeys, and relate all his experiences, would make a volume itself. His colleague was sick with fever nearly the entire year, and Seybert had to work alone over a territory nearly as large as that occupied by the Ohio conference now. Once we find him at a camp-meeting near Lancaster, then lodging with a family at Painesville, and then looking for new appointments in the valley of Sugar Creek. During the Summer he had the ague until he was prostrated; the Winter was unusually severe, and in the Spring the roads were unspeakably hard to travel. His trouble was increased by the fact that his horse became severely saddle-galled. There was not a single church of our denomination in the State at that time. They preached mostly in private houses, and they were miserable huts, without stoves. But the foundations were being laid for a great future. The membership of the circuit increased forty-five during the year.

O for the spirit of the fathers, to come upon us, their sons! Let us be thankful that things have changed for the better; that the work is less exposed and less laborious; that salaries are better. But under God we owe it to the men who braved the perils of a new country, and by their toil have caused the desert to blossom abundantly with joy and singing. We are reaping where they sowed. Let us honor their courage and emulate their zeal.

Sitting in his brother's house at home, May 27th, Bro. Seybert was talking earnestly, as usual, concerning the affairs of the kingdom of God, making special allusion to the sufferings of God's people from of old, and to the self-denial involved in following Jesus, when a neighbor's wife, who was listening with rapt attention to his conversation, suddenly became penitent, and interrupted the preacher's conversation with loud cries for mercy. Seybert said, " I guess we ought to pray." This they at once proceeded to do, and continued till late in the night, and the woman was converted.

At the conference session in 1823, held June 2d in Shrewsberry, York Co., Pa., Bro. Seybert was stationed on Schuylkill circuit, in Pennsylvania. The conference session lasted but three days. Ten preachers of the already small conference located, and consequently the remaining preachers were compelled to take large fields of labor without help. Seybert was obliged to serve his extensive circuit without a colleague. It had been served formerly with two preachers. Notwithstanding the extent of his charge, the indefatigable Seybert sought for new appointments, and with this purpose, soon after conference visited for the first time the city of Philadelphia. Here he was entertained by a gentleman named John Mann, at whose house he held a prayer-meeting, the first evening of his stay in the city of Brotherly Love. The second evening he preached to them. The third day he spent in visiting from house to house, meanwhile getting into a dispute with a couple of young theological students, concerning the sad decay of the Protestant churches of the land. They also differed in reference to the nature of the preparation necessary for the ministry of the Gospel. Seybert, of course, insisted on the necessity of a change of heart and the gift of the Holy Ghost, while these young students contemplated only literary and scientific education and intellectual training. That night he preached again. Next day he left the city to follow his regular appointments. This was the first effort of the Evangelical Association in the Quaker City, where we now have a large and influential membership, and a number of beautiful and commodious church edifices.

In June he had an appointment at a place bearing the rather startling cognomen of "Devil's Hole". On the way to this appointment he was obliged to stop at a tavern along the road, to feed his horse, where he says he "encountered the *Devil's people* before he got to *Devil's Hole.*" The tavern people were just at dinner, when he rode up. They behaved in a most frivolous manner at the dinner table. Seybert sat down quietly on the piazza, where these "sons of Belial" afterwards began a flippant conversation with him. Upon this he reproved them for their wickedness in very plain terms. But they confidently asserted that no one could be good, and that there are no longer any upright people in the world. Seybert relates: "However, I soon drew my spiritual sword (the Bible) out of its sheath in my saddle-bags, and began to assault the rabble vigorously with it. I explained to them what true religion is. But there was one particularly devilish individual among them, who became so angry under my assault, that he could not conceal his irritation, but his rage was evident to all. I, however, gave them solid blows in quick succession, so that one by one they slunk away like beasts of prey who had lost their spoil; and after I had conquered the whole swarm I yet administered an earnest exhortation to the landlord and his family, representing to them the temporal and eternal consequences of such a life.   Before I left, the worst one of the crowd came back and apologized for his rudeness."

On July 13th he tells of a remarkable prayer-meeting at the house of Bro. Cook, near McKeansburg.   As it was in harvest, Bro. Cook had a large number of laborers in his employ, mostly converted people, who also attended the prayer-meeting.   Bro. Seybert read a part of the 18th chapter of St. Luke, and gave an encouraging exhortation on prayer.   He showed the true characteristics of prayer both as to its spirit and its form.   During his remarks the power of God already became manifested in the meeting.   When they began to sing, after the exhortation the manifestation of the Divine presence became still more glorious, and soon they experienced such a mighty outpouring of the Holy Spirit, that there was not room enough to receive it.   It was as if the flood gates of heaven had been lifted.   The South wind breathed into the garden until the spices thereof flowed out.   There began an unusual demonstration of shouting, leaping and rejoicing, and many of the friends seemed quite overwhelmed in the sea of eternal love.   One could no longer distinguish the voices, for the outpouring of the Spirit had been in accordance with Joel's prophecy.   Sons and daughters, old men and maidens, and *all flesh* seemed to be filled. So great was Seybert's enjoyment of this mid-harvest prayer-meeting, that he records this desire:

"O, I wish that, during the remainder of my earthly life, I could have a vivid realization of this wonderful prayer-meeting at least three times daily!   I know it would nerve me for the battle, and would be an incentive to faithfulness in the midst of tribulation. Blessed art Thou, eternal King and Saviour of the world, that through Thy holy blood Thou hast triumphed over the might of hell, and hast delivered us from Satan's power, and hast pardoned our transgressions, and hast overcome principalities and powers, and divided unto us the spoil! We praise Thee both now and forever! Hallelujah!"

During a sermon of great plainness and power about this time on Rev. 3:20 at a new appointment, a young lady suddenly began to cry out, "I am lost! I am lost!" Her outcries were so terrible that it was impossible for Bro. Seybert to continue his sermon. They prayed with the penitent lady until she was saved.

At a certain place Bro. Seybert asked for permission to preach in the school-house. At first there was little objection; but when the authorities came together, they began to look upon him with suspicion, and promptly declared that they would much rather have it to do with a rabid dog than with a 'shouting preacher.' Seybert could endure this very well; still it grieved him that these people thus despised God's word and God's servants to their own damnation.

However, to repeat all similar occurrences recorded in Bishop Seybert's journals, would make this work monotonous, for such things frequently took place. It is certainly remarkable that the efforts of this plain, simple, unassuming man were crowned with such signal success and powerful effects.   From a worldly stand-point his preaching was by no means extraordinary, except for simplicity and disingenuousness. There was no display of classical lore, nor parade of high sounding phrases.   There was no appearance of formal theological erudition, for in that he had not been systematically trained.   Nevertheless, in God's hands he was mighty to the pulling down of strongholds.   Not many preachers of any age can point to more signal demonstrations of power under their preaching than occurred under the preaching of John Seybert.   Few sermons are interrupted by the cries of penitents.—Has the salt lost its savor, or the sword of the Spirit its edge? Nay, verily, but those who wield the sword are too often better used to carnal weapons.   The feats of modern eloquence and polished speech, are feeble, compared with the spiritual power of this great and good man.   John Seybert belongs to the age of spiritual giants, and, "take him for all in all, we shall not look upon his like again." The Lord made but one Seybert, and then broke the mold.

On a certain occasion Bro. Seybert had to hasten very much in order to reach his appointment in the evening, but arrived late.   He rode directly to the church, and immediately rushed into the crowded and expectant congregation, taking with him, as was his custom, his Bible and hymn-book, hastily snatched out of the saddle-bag.   The sermon proved effective. Sinners began to weep and pray, and several were happily converted before the meeting closed that night. In his journal of that day there appears the following devout acknowledgment: "O God, how good Thou art unto Thy servants! For even when they are obliged to drive 'like the driving of Jehu,' in order not to reach their appointments too late, and therefore have no time to prepare themselves to preach, Thou givest them on such occasions *that* message which is best for the people, and also pourest out Thy rich blessing. Amen."

Malarial fever, which had given him so much trouble the previous year in Ohio, again attacked him this Fall. Oct. 10th he was subject to a very severe attack of it, while riding through a long stretch of woods. Compelled to stop and lie down, he unsaddled his horse, turned him loose, and, using his horse-blanket for a bed, and his saddle for a pillow, the weary itinerant lay down in excessive feebleness. Before doing so, he tried to pray, but fainted in the attempt, and sank down on his improvised couch utterly exhausted, mentally committing himself to God's faithful care. There lay the zealous, sincere, faithful, ever-restless servant of God, far from human help or sympathy, in the autumnal shadow of an ancient wood, under the canopy of the sky, in pathetic and helpless solitude, burning with fever. He reminds one of Elijah, faint and ready to die, lying under the Juniper tree, save that he was more resigned than the prophet. After lying there for some time, the fever subsided ; he suddenly felt new strength and life thrilling his whole frame, as if an angel—one of those ministering spirits who are sent to minister unto the heirs of salvation—had come on silent wing to bring him a Divine strengthening. He immediately arose, saddled his horse, and went on his way.

During this conference year, the historical revival at Orwigsburg broke out under the labors of Bro. Seybert. This was one of the most remarkable revivals in the history of the Evangelical Association, not so much for the number, but for the character and subsequent usefulness of the converts. Seybert was closely identified with it, and some of the most extraordinary effects that ever followed his preaching occurred there.

The revival began in the Fall of 1823, when Seybert served Schuylkill circuit, but it proved to be more than a merely transient excitement; it lasted without serious interruption for several years. The way for it was paved by Rev. Adam Kleinfelter, who, as early as 1818, preached at the residence of Daniel Focht, Esq., the proprietor of extensive iron works and a gentleman of great prominence and respectability. Mr. Focht was soundly converted, besides several of his neighbors. No sooner had these few begun earnestly to serve the Lord, than persecution broke out. Parents persecuted their children, and children persecuted their parents. But the work could not be hindered in this way, for it was a genuine work of grace. God blessed His people wonderfully both in secret and in public, with the joy of the Lord which was their strength. Besides, they were pious, and led a chaste, quiet, holy life. Mr. Focht was elected class-leader, and in later years became useful in the church as a local preacher.

Seybert preached his first sermon there July 15th, soon after his appointment to Schuylkill circuit. His text was Ezekiel 33:11, and the service was held in the Court-house, Orwigsburg being at that time the County seat of Schuylkill Co., Penna. The preacher was somewhat embarrassed by the novelty of his surroundings. August 17th he preached in a grove near the city from Rom. 2:4-6. His experience was peculiar. For some reason, he felt tempted to stand during the opening prayer. But, "breaking through" as he called it, he fell upon his knees to pray, and instantly a wonderful baptism of power came upon him. The Divine effusion was so powerful, that Seybert afterward asserted his belief that this was the real beginning of the Orwigsburg revival. The multitude melted down, and the Word of the Lord had free course and was glorified. Seybert hereupon erected a stone on the spot, called it *Ebenezer*, and with his own hand engraved the date upon it for a memorial, a spiritual landmark.

The conversion of Bro. Focht was the first breach in the wall. He frequently preached to the people, and in 1822 obtained permission to preach in the Court-house. Many were awakened in that Court-house. Rev. J. Breidenstein also preached there. On one occasion the Court-house was closed against him, but nothing daunted, he went to the School-house, where many heard him gladly. "But as usual", says our Church historian, Rev. W. W. Orwig, "the pastors of the German churches were his principal opposers. By slanders upon his personal character, and by assailing his doctrine, they endeavored to alienate the people from the preacher, and to shake the public confidence in him; but they failed." Breidenstein preached Jesus as a perfect Saviour; God blessed His own Word, and, like the Bereans, many began to search the Scriptures daily whether these things were so. This was in 1822. Then came Seybert in 1823, who set the ball rolling. September 14th, after again preaching in the Court-house, he was to have spoken in the evening at a School-house, some three miles from the city. But it was closed against him at the instigation of the parson. A much despised citizen now offered Seybert his house, where he preached from St. John 1:11, 12. God wrought so mightily that there also the walls of Satan's kingdom began to quake. "This", says Seybert, "was on the east side, whereas that powerful meeting in the grove was on the west side, and now there was trembling in Satan's ranks all around."

October 30th, after preaching in the morning at the court-house, he visited a condemned murderer in prison in the afternoon, whom he earnestly sought to lead to repentance. In the evening of that day he had an appointment in a large tavern some distance east of the city. He was greatly concerned for his evening service. Accordingly, some time before service he went out into the woods on a mountain, and spent the time until service in meditation and prayer. Thus he went directly from the lonely mountain sum-

mit·into the crowded congregation. His text was
Acts 3:22, 23. He began to speak with feelings of
hope and faith mingled with fear and trembling, yet
believing that God would help. During the sermon
the power of God was manifested in His word. Sinners began to tremble and quake, and there was a
general inquiry, what to do to be saved. Now, as
Seybert used to say, "the ice was broken". The
work of conversion soon spread, and the slain of the
Lord were so many that Seybert sent for Bro. Focht
to assist him. Focht continued the meeting successfully in Seybert's enforced absence on his extensive
circuit. December 7th seven souls were saved in
one of Bro. Focht's meetings. In January (1824)
Seybert was again on the ground. Three future
ministers of the Gospel were soon after converted, as
young men. They were Samuel Rickert, and Joseph
M. and Jacob Saylor. A class was now organized.
The work progressed gloriously.—Some wonderful
meetings were held. All classes of persons were
converted, — "drunkards, swearers, card-players,
fiddlers and drummers".

May 21st Seybert held his first communion service
at.Orwigsburg. He says:·

"I had glorious times seeing sinners coming home
to God in crowds from all directions. Within six
months forty souls were happily saved, and I was
enabled to·report to conference seventy-five newly
converted, while at Orwigsburg especially a good
foundation has been laid for the future work of the
Evangelical Association."

The revival continued without abatement for several years. Some of the most influential families of the denomination, such as the Orwigs and the Hammers were converted here. In 1826 a church was built, and the society has continued strong and flourishing ever since.

In connection with this revival Bro. Seybert was the hero of a hazardous undertaking, in which he came near losing his life. He had to cross the Schuylkill river near Orwigsburg at a time when the river was much swollen. He was warned not to attempt the ford. But he said, " I have an appointment across the river, and in the name of the Lord I am going to ride in. The Lord can help me through." He was on horseback. Getting upon the saddle with his knees, the intrepid circuit rider ventured boldly into the mad torrent. The horse soon got beyond his depth, and was compelled to swim with his rider on his back. The noble beast, to the astonishment of the spectators, bore him safely to the opposite bank, and Seybert filled his appointment that evening in spite of storm and flood.

Seybert was not easily scared. " I have an appointment,"—that was the irresistible argument of his conscience. He would not miss an appointment if he risked his life to reach it.

Jan. 25th he had a meeting at the "Church of the Blue Mountains", where the people behaved in a brutal manner, throwing clubs through the windows with such force that many of the audience were seriously injured by the flying splinters of glass. In fact, the floor was stained with blood. This occurred in a community where there was a church, and among citizens who boast of their freedom of conscience.

Feb. 14th, just before preaching, some one brought Seybert a book which he had bought a long time previous, but which he no longer expected to get. So it happened that he had not just then the neces-. sary amount of money to pay for it, which was one dollar. This awkward circumstance, however, did not embarrass him. He thought, "Well, I must preach now, and afterwards I will find some way to arrange this matter." After the service, a man who had been greatly moved by the sermon and had become deeply interested in the preacher, crowded his way through the throng, grasped Seybert's hand warmly, and upon withdrawing it, left a round dollar in the preacher's palm. This was promptly used to pay for the book. The generous friend, however, knew nothing of Seybert's special need.

One day in March he was called upon to baptize the infant child of unconverted parents. The child was sick unto death. He therefore first addressed an earnest word to the parents, endeavoring to impress them with the importance of saving their souls, upon which they promised, by the help of God to prepare for eternity. The child was then baptized, and the remarkable fact is noted in the journal that immediately upon its baptism the child suddenly became well.

Under date of April 18th, 1824, he writes: "The

people here in Berks County are awfully benighted. They call themselves church-members, but they are unspeakably wicked. In one of these churches they had the communion of the Lord's Supper last Friday, being Good Friday, and then on the following Easter Monday they had a big dance, in a tavern near the self same church. Here they employed ten musicians, and served the Devil with all their power, by swearing, drinking and fighting. This Christian (?) rabble howled so loudly that they were actually heard two miles away. These are the people who can not bear the least noise, not even a stifled sob in Divine service. But I have not heard that they thought their shameful frolic too noisy! O consistency!"

Conference time again approached, and Seybert started on his way thither. When crossing the Susquehanna bridge, he encountered a young man who was in great trouble, just returning from the Lancaster Fair, where, he said, his money had been stolen. But the toll-keeper would not let him pass over the bridge without paying his toll. During their parley Seybert came up, and, learning the difficulty, said to the youth: "I will pay your toll for you, if you will promise me never to go to another Fair." The young man replied, "But I might have business that would compel me to go." "You can go where your calling takes you," Seybert explained. "Well, then," said the youth, "I will promise never to go to Lancaster Fair again." "You shall not go to *any*," Seybert insisted; "if you do, you may look out for yourself how to get over the river." Driven so closely, the youth sincerely promised never to go to another Fair. Seybert thereupon paid the toll, and the two rode together over the bridge. During the ride Seybert took occasion to point out more explicitly the perils to which the young expose themselves in attending these County and State Fairs. He used to call them "*The Devil's camp-meetings*". And if he were living now, he would have no reason to change his opinion.

Soon afterwards, as he was riding along one day, a group of ungodly young men accosted him with: "I believe you are a '*strabler*' parson!" "No sir!" Seybert replied, as he stopped his horse a moment and faced the rabble, "I *was* a 'strabler' once; the people on the dancing floor are the 'strablers.'" With that sally he turned his horse and rode away, leaving the rabble to bear as best they could their chagrin. —This word 'strabler' is a word belonging to the Pennsylvania German dialect. It is untranslatable, and was applied in derision to the early Evangelicals, because of their lively demonstrations in religious service.

Speaking of the spirit of persecution which manifested itself at that time in that part of Pennsylvania, Bro. Seybert relates many incidents, and states among other things that the members of a certain church had proposed to join the militia, if that organization were summoned to murder the "praying people", and then remarks: "These are some of the so-called "good Christians" of the modern University educated preachers!" This shows, furthermore, how

6

the beast of Rev. 13:11, which arises out of the earth, represents certain denominations of nominal Christians who, like the dragon, have the spirit of murder, and utter voices of Satanic malice. It also shows what this dragon would do if it had the power, and if our excellent civil government did not put a bit into its blasphemous mouth."

At Orwigsburg he had trouble with a sister who had set a bad example. She had fallen from grace through the practice of backbiting. Seybert threatened and pleaded with her, but apparently in vain. "O", he exclaimed, "when will the earth be delivered wholly from this terrible evil."

During that year in Schuylkill circuit, Seybert had seventy accessions, and the membership of the charge increased fifty-nine, numbering nearly two hundred at the end of the year. Among those whom he reports as newly received, occurs the name of Francis Hoffman, who afterwards became a useful preacher in the Evangelical Association.

CHAPTER IV.

ORDINATION AGAIN.—ELECTED PRESIDING ELDER.—

Bishop Seybert was ordained as an Elder in the church, at the seventeenth session of the conference, being the fourth which he attended. At the same session of conference, Bishop Joseph Long was elected to the office of a Deacon. His second ordination caused Seybert a severe conflict of soul. He feared conference was making a mistake, to commit this solemn trust to him so soon. True, he had served the full length of time according to Discipline, but, he said, "It is plain enough that I am not worthy of this high office." He earnestly desired to make further proof of his ministry, and would have served joyfully as a deacon for a third year. It was even proposed at the same conference session to elect him to the office of a Presiding Elder, which, however, was not done.

He was stationed on York circuit that year, with J. Bixler as his colleague. This was the charge upon which he had labored so successfully during the first year of his ministry. They had one day's respite after conference, and then immediately began their appointments.

One day in June, 1824, as he was riding through a strange country, he happened to meet a farmer, of whom he enquired the way to his destination. The farmer was just bringing in his horses from the field, but directed Seybert in a very civil manner. However, immediately he began to question the latter, whom he surmised from his dress to be an Evangelical preacher, concerning the manner of our public worship,—the earnest exercises—the camp-meetings, etc., expressing promptly his doubts as to the Scriptural warrant for such proceedings, and then added, with some vehemence, 'And you also anathematize all others.' This brought Seybert from his horse in a hurry. Taking his Bible out of the saddle-bag, he began to substantiate our position and methods, both from the Old and the New Testament. As to loud praying he read Psalm 50:15, and the fourth verse of the sixty-eighth Psalm. To this the farmer objected, that it applied to the ancients only and had no reference to modern times, but Seybert told him the same God still lives, that the nature of His work has not changed, human nature is the same in all generations, — sinful and corrupt and in danger of eternal death. If it was proper for the ancients to cry aloud whether in distress or in joy, then it is proper for us too. He reminded him that the Lord Jesus himself prayed "with strong crying and tears". Our camp-meetings he justified on the ground of the Feasts of Tabernacles celebrated among God's people of old, and showed from St. John 7, that our Saviour himself preached at one of these Tabernacle meetings. As to cursing other people, he said it simply was not true, which he invited the farmer to test to his own satisfaction, if he would attend our services and hear for himself. The farmer was unable to reply, and seemed quite overcome. Before riding on, the faithful Seybert sought to convince him of the necessity of his own conversion, and they parted as friends. Seybert thought, as he rode away, the man was not far from the Kingdom of God, for which he was glad.

A few days later he heard a preacher deliver a funeral discourse from John 3: 3. It was an instructive and edifying sermon. The preacher, he says, was orthodox, taught both the necessity and the possibility of perfect cleansing from all sin in the blood of Christ, and demonstrated that all who desire to enter Heaven, must seek after holiness with all their hearts. Then he adds, significantly, "He may have been a messenger of God, *but he lacked one thing: an unction from the Holy One.*"

In July of that year he wrote of his experience, as follows:—"I am enjoying a most delightful and blessed experience after the inner man. I am fully translated into the marvellous light and liberty of the people of God. The enemies of my soul seem overcome and driven from the field, and the everlasting arm of Jesus Christ is around me, as He presses me to his comforting bosom. I am therefore enabled to enjoy my travels, possessing as I do a healthy body, a contented mind and a quiet conscience, especially in this halcyon period of the year, when bright sunshine and gentle winds mingle the perfume of the flowers with the golden glory of the harvest fields. My heart is filled with peace."

During the month of August of that year, a "big

meeting" was held near the village of Marietta on the Susquehanna river, at which Bro. Seybert was instrumental in the awakening, among others, of John Sensel, a blacksmith, who, after a profound penitential experience was gloriously saved. Sensel afterwards became a successful minister of the Gospel. He was one of the most effective preachers of repentance of his time. His rich, sonorous voice woke many a sinner from the slumber of sin, and won many to the feet of the Crucified One. One of his favorite sentiments was, "*Without grace, no sermon.*" And indeed, Sensel was exceptionally helpless when he did not realize the unction of the Holy One, but when filled with the Spirit, he was a power. Sometimes the place seemed literally shaken when he preached. But he was a man of unceasing prayer. He would rather miss three meals than neglect secret devotions once.

At a glorious camp-meeting in August (1824) near Orwigsburg, among others, Chas. Hammer and Richard Rickert were converted, who afterwards became eminently useful in the service of God and the church.

One day in December Bro. Seybert entered a store to purchase some stationary. But he was refused. The proprietor would not sell any paper to a "*strabler*" *preacher.*

He frequently makes mention in his journal of specially blessed seasons experienced during family worship with various families. For instance:

In January, 1825, at Bro. Alspaugh's, they were so

blessed while engaged in family prayers, that they were constrained to praise the Lord aloud before they could eat breakfast or before they could even prepare the meal."

On another occasion about that time, the people were so filled with "the joy of the Lord which is our strength" at family prayers, that they did not care to eat at all. In that community he says, "the Devil and wicked people try in every way to hinder the Lord's work: *but it is useless, as long as the fire of God's Spirit burns like that on the family altars.*"

On the 9th of January, 1825, Bro Seybert visited an uncle and his family for the purpose of seeking ·an opening to preach. The privilege was given him, and he preached to them and their neighbors. His relatives were deeply impressed, and when he left them next morning they were greatly moved. One of the sons had been converted, but acknowledged that he had back-slidden to a certain extent, and did not live as consistently as he should, and consequently was rather a hindrance than a blessing to the family in their efforts to seek religion. Bro. Seybert very pertinently remarks: " How necessary it is that professors of religion demonstrate that which they orally profess, by living and acting in conformity with the word of God, lest the name of God be blasphemed both among the baptized and unbaptized heathen of the land. The unchristian conduct of those who have been enlightened, always was a greater obstacle to the progress of Christ's cause than all the bloody persecutions that have ever raged, and more detrimental to the religion of Jesus, than all the malicious literary attacks of skeptics and atheists."

Barbara Eckert, one of the most devoted and pious members of the church, was bitterly hated and persecuted by her father and relatives, because of her earnestness and zeal in the service of God. At the time of her conversion she was a domestic in the service of an intelligent Christian family. After she had found the pearl of great price, she went home to visit her parents. However, her father was enraged over the matter, so that he refused to allow her to finish her term of service, and kept her at home to keep her from the "pernicious" influence of her Christian employers, in the hope of diverting her from her religious purposes. But she was firm in her purpose, and had the moral courage to erect a family altar at home. While she prayed, her father raved and swore like a mad man. Nothing daunted, Barbara persisted until her mother herself was brought under conviction through her godly life. Upon this, her father, seeing he could not induce her to give up her religion, and enraged because even his wife was following the same way, drove his daughter from home.

After being driven from home she was more devoted than ever, and seemed to be wholly charmed by the love of God. She enjoyed in a remarkable degree the life and power of God. Soon after her banishment from home a "big meeting" was held at the house of Bro. Young. The persecuted saint was there. She was said to have spent the whole week previously in fasting. She left Young's to go to a neighbor's house, and never returned. She was never seen again after leaving Young's. Many of course conjectured that a secret murder had been committed. But, Seybert concludes, those who knew her most intimately whispered with significant mien, "God can do to-day what He did in Enoch's day."

Bro. Seybert's young colleague could not endure the fatigue of preaching and the exposure of travel, consequently rendered him but feeble assistance, notwithstanding his willingness and devotion. To make matters still worse, Seybert himself got sick and had to take to his bed, where he remained for four weeks. This was a sore trial, because, as he felt, the circuit was suffering from neglect. But a certain young brother (Joseph M. Saylor), whom he had been instrumental in saving the previous Winter, was able to supply the work, to Seybert's great relief. He remarks that this spell of sickness, which he considered a loving visitation of Providence, taught him two things: First, the value of good health, and, second, to be joyful in affliction; and he regarded it a great blessing.

At Steintown Bro. Seybert baptized several children March 16th, one of which was remarkable, the daughter of a Justice of the Peace named McCrary. This child displayed unusually strong religious inclinations for one so young. Soon after her baptism, which rite she had earnestly requested, she realized the saving grace of God, though she was only a little more than four years of age. She became sick, and did not desire any medicine, but wished to be baptized, die and then go to heaven. At her death, which occurred soon after, she admonished her parents very earnestly to prepare for eternity, and died in great peace.

May 29th, 1825, a tent-meeting was begun at Bro. Ernst's, which deserves a place in our Church annals, chiefly because it was the occasion of the severest and most serious persecution ever experienced at any camp-meeting of the Evangelical Association, so far as known. On Wednesday and Thursday a wonderful awakening took place among the multitude. Among others a poor cripple was converted, who confessed publicly, that before the meeting he had been hired by the mob to stone those engaged in the services. He had come into the congregation with his pockets full of stones for this diabolical purpose. The Word of God, however, got such a hold upon him immediately, that he sank to the ground with his stony weight. He was made spiritually whole. The preaching was marvelously powerful. Several sinners literally fell to the earth unconscious, under the hammer-strokes of the truth of God. This power, so strange and mysterious to the blind masses of people, occasioned such a terrible rage among the rabble, that they fell upon these profoundly awakened and quaking penitents like bloodthirsty tigers fall upon their prey, and dragged them violently away to a neighboring house, where they had an ungodly doctor, who undertook to restore these *sin-sick and spiritually wounded souls* by bleeding (phlebotomizing) and by dashing cold water upon them. Unlike Shakespeare's physician in "Macbeth," this fellow *could* or *thought* he could,

> "Minister to a mind diseased,
> Pluck from the memory a rooted sorrow,
> Raze out the written troubles of the soul."

They also had a preacher, there named Boyer, one of the many blind guides of the day, who sought to console these awakened and smitten souls in their sinful condition, and to quiet their fears by applying his untempered mortar. An insolent rabble gathered around this ungodly spiritual adviser, with clubs, pitch-forks and such other murderous weapons as were at hand. They prowled about the woods like hyenas. This pack of howling wolves Parson Boyer called "his *sheep*", for whose spiritual, or rather ecclesiastical safety he attended the meeting. At the same time he kept continually threatening to 'whistle for his hounds', to chase the 'foxes' into their holes!

Seybert sarcastically remarks: "By his own mouth these church-members were both his '*sheep*' and his '*hounds*'."

On Thursday afternoon and evening the devilish brood was greatly augmented in number. That was a sad and fearful night. The Satanic rabble was well equipped with clubs and pitch-forks, for their hellish work, and well drilled by their commander-in-chief, who kept himself in the back-ground, having great confidence in the obedience and desperate character of his hosts. They lay in ambush about the encampment, under cover of the darkness, waiting for a signal from their wily leader.

Rev. D. Manwiller was preaching, when the club-armed rabble came in and began to tear off the boards from the preacher's stand, and to fling clubs and stones among the worshippers in a very reckless manner. No one's life was any longer safe. Their brutal actions were made more terrible by awful profanity and cursing. The service was broken up, and the devil took possession of the place, in the person of Rev. Boyer and his mob. To restore order was out of the question. The rabble had torn down the fire-places with which the encampment was lighted, and raged frightfully. Remonstrance only made them worse. The hellish performance was kept up all through that hideous night. Their howling and screaming was more terrible than that of wild beasts. At times they would bawl like calves or cattle, then crow like cocks, swearing meanwhile and cursing one another and the worshippers promiscuously. These people were mostly so called church-members.

Oh, how that persecuted company wished for the day! they cried more than once during that night, "Watchman, what of the night? Watchman what of the night?—Still there were also some decent people on the grounds, who, though they were not converted, yet stood by the people of God. On Friday some of the rowdies left the ground and the confusion was somewhat diminished.

As to casualities, Bro. Ernst, on whose premises the meeting was held, was beaten unmercifully with a club, during the night. Bro. D. Loos was dangerously wounded with a pitchfork, while many were bruised and stunned by flying stones and other missiles. No one was killed, however, which, under the circumstances, was a veritable miracle, and must be attributed to the merciful intervention of our Heavenly Father.

Many of the friends were now in favor of closing the meeting at once, but others wanted to have at least one more service held. The latter was accordingly done. Amid the ghastly ruins of their temporary sanctuary, and amid the continued howling of the rabble, Bro. Seybert preached from Psalm 43:3, and God's Spirit wrought mightily through the word. They broke up the meeting on Friday noon, however, one day sooner than they had originally contemplated.

Such occurrences are a dark blot upon the history of this land of religious liberty, sad mementoes of the unhappy past, and an eternal disgrace to the old German churches in America. It would be impossible to-day to believe such things, but for the indubitable evidence of the most trustworthy witnesses. Should any member of those churches scan these pages, let him be thankful to Almighty God that he lives in a brighter day. Neither let him ever again think or say that the Church of Jacob Albright had no mission in this country, no occasion for its existence.

The annual conference which met June 6th, 1825, elected Bro. Seybert to the office of Presiding Elder for the first time. This was a surprise to him and by no means an agreeable one. He thought the brethren greatly over-estimated him and knew nothing of his great deficiencies, or they would not have entrusted to him this important position. However, he determined to seek more grace, and live nearer to God, in the hope that perhaps he could get along at any rate. He was assigned to Canaan District, embracing Schuylkill, Lancaster, York and Franklin circuits. One of these circuits was alone greater than an entire District is at the present time, in most of our conferences. Bro. Seybert was no less successful in his new position, than he had been in his former one. Awakenings and conversions continued to occur under his labors. He was a Presiding Elder who saved souls.

He relates that in October he preached in a hotel to an attentive audience. He also lodged there. When he awoke in the morning he was somewhat perplexed concerning family worship in this public house, and felt inclined to shrink from suggesting it to the landlord. After coming down stairs, and breakfast being ready, he was quite agreeably surprised to find the landlord coming into the room he occupied, and, after the usual morning salutation, accosting Seybert with "I suppose the minister will pray with us this morning before breakfast?" "O, yes," he replied, "I consider it my duty, where I lodge at night to hold family worship with the family, when it is permitted."—But that morning he had almost determined not to venture to suggest it himself. He now conducted service with much delight, but afterwards felt heartily ashamed of his "lack of moral courage".

Nov. 14th Seybert visited a penitent man who was extremely timid, fearing persecution if he should espouse the cause of Christ openly. He specially feared a brother of his, who had in some way learned his state of mind and threatened to shoot him if he went with these *"knee-crawlers" (knie-rutscher)*.

This menace scared the timid soul, but the Lord opened his way by a terrible visitation of Providence. On his way home from his errand of intimidation the wicked brother was suddenly taken violently ill. In a few hours he became speechless, and was never able to utter another word. He finally died in great agony. In this way the Lord opened the way for the brother, and took away an unprofitable servant. "Be not deceived; God is not mocked. For whatsoever a man soweth that shall he also reap."

In his old home, during this year, Bro. Seybert was also called upon one day by a police officer. However, his offense was nothing grave. When he was yet in business there, he had become security on a note for one of his neighbors, who had proved unfaithful, leaving Seybert to pay the note, and for this the officer of the law came to see Seybert. But he immediately paid the note and so escaped arrest. Seybert lost a great sum of money in just this way, during his life.

Following is a letter which Bro. Seybert wrote to a life-long intimate friend, in Reading, Pa., who was however a member of another denomination. This letter gives further glimpses into the life and work of Seybert at this time:

York County, Pa., March 2d, 1826.

Dear Friend and Brother in Jesus!

"Your letter to your friends in Manheim I delivered in person. The man seems, however, unconcerned as regards things of eternity; still, in a general way there is an improvement in spiritual matters in the town, for during the last five weeks there have gradually been some conversions. I am well in soul and body, and earnestly desire the same blessing for you and yours.

"Since I left you I have had many a severe conflict and trial to endure, and have been assailed from within and without, by Satan and by the world. But the Almighty is my faithful and ever present Helper, and He helps me through. *Blessed be his dear name!* In order to look up new preaching-places I have ventured north, even into the land of midnight (Jer. 3: 12) and preached the Word there, where I had blessed and melting seasons. There is hope for that region, especially in the Mahanoy valley. In the vicinity of Orwigsburg it still goes well. Usually in our services there great weeping occurs among the unconverted, while the people of God engage in shouting and praising the Lord, and weeping. · Conversions are still going on, for the Lord is at work in spite of all the opposition and persecution on the part of the ungodly parsons. Not long ago one was converted whom Babylon the Great regarded as a strong pillar. He also united with the people of God, which caused no little crashing and cracking in the old Babylonian edifice. The foundation, which is built on the sand, and the roof which rests upon dangerously rotten reasoning—in short, the whole hellish building trembles. Several strong posts have been shaken loose by the fall of the great pillar aforesaid, besides many beams and joists have been lifted out of their places, and the whole structure is crazy and out of shape. Unless Babel's builders quickly fasten the broken parts and loose pillars and beams, they will soon fall out also.

"But to return to Manheim, my birth-place. Only recently I had a meeting there, in which the power of God became marvellously manifest while I was preaching from Rev. 22:17. A general power of repentance came upon the people, and the slain of the Lord were of all ages, from the child of twelve to the man of fifty. There are still seeking souls there even now, while many have obtained pardon in the blood of Christ. Since the Lord works so mightily in Manheim, there is great uneasiness in the kingdom of darkness. The fact that the sons of Belial are doing their utmost to hinder the work is proof enough of this. In several cases, parents have beaten their children unmercifully, because they wished to lead a godly life and desired to abandon the prayerless ways of their parents. But this has been of old the characterestic of the Babylonians to persecute and oppress God's people. However, the work of the Lord is not hindered.

"You also know something of the Reformed minister, John Winebrenner, do you not? The same is earnestly engaged in the Lord's work, labors with great success and God is with him. This can not be denied, by the ungodly and even all the Egyptian sorcerers can not gain say it.   Winebrenner preaches in a certain locality, in Cumberland county, where the people are boundlessly wicked.   But since he is preaching there, a work of grace has broken out, and it is asserted that the people of Lisbon and vicinity are nearly all awakened and converted.   This man manifests great zeal, and is no respecter of persons or station.   He preaches to the wicked and the good, among the high and the low, the rich and the poor, Methodists, white or black.   He is loved by the good, and by the false teachers he is hated and persecuted.

On last Tuesday evening I had a meeting in York county, during which such distress of soul seized the unconverted, that I could not continue my remarks. The people wept and began to cry for mercy so loudly, that I could not be understood.

Now, dear Bro. Rein, I wish you God's blessing a thousand-fold, so that you may be enabled to continue faithful to a happy end in the well begun work. Your wife also shall pray earnestly, live a holy life, and continue to seek that which is good through suffering and in patience, as her purpose also is.   Tell your daughter to consecrate her youthful years to the service of God; above all let her follow Jesus in humility, avoid pride, and God will bless her.   Greet G's. for me.   They are to remember me in prayer, for they are my friends beloved in the Lord.   It would greatly delight me, if you would write to me as to how the work of the Lord prospers in your city.

Your Brother in Christ,   John Seybert."

At the conference session of 1820 Seybert was chosen President. There was as yet no Bishop in the Evangelical Association. Though the Discipline provided for the office, it had not been filled. Until a Bishop was elected, the Presiding Elders were the highest functionaries in the church.

In June of this year Seybert visited John Winebrenner, the founder of the society calling itself " Church of God," also commonly known as " Winebrennarians". Bro. Seybert says they had a very edifying interview, and mutually obligated themselves to pray for one another, and also agreed that Seybert should be welcome to preach at Winebrenner's appointments, and Winebrenner should be equally welcome at Seybert's appointments. At the close of the interview they knelt together in prayer, and the above covenant was practically observed by both of these brethren, until Winebrenner assumed an independent attitude, began to promulgate some singular notions and prepared the way for the organization of the "Church of God", as a separate branch of the Christian Church, when further fraternization became impracticable.

In 1826 Bro. Seybert broke the fallow ground for the work of the Evangelical Association in the valleys of Likens, Mahantango, Mahanoy, Pauls, Armstrong and Deep Creek. In this enterprise, however, the Presiding Elder of Canaan district subjected himself to great persecution. Already on his first tour over the lofty Mount Mahantango, his preaching resulted in awakening sinners, and many inquired what must

be done to be saved.   This aroused the spirit of persecution at once, which was at first directed against
the preacher himself.   One man distinguished himself above all others for his insolence and anger.   He
sought to ascertain the time when Seybert would
again cross the mountain, loaded his gun, and announced that he was going out to shoot "this Seybert".   No one doubted the desperation of this mountain terror, for all knew he was vicious enough to
execute his threat.   He went out to the mountain
early in the morning of the day designated for Seybert's return, and waited and watched the entire day
for his harmless, unsuspecting victim.   But no Seybert appeared; he had crossed the mountain early in
the morning, and while the would-be-assassin was
lurking there, his intended victim was innocently engaged in visiting one family after another of awakened
souls, in the valley below, who were hungering and
thirsting after righteousness.   The ruffian with others
like himself would no doubt have been at the services
in the valley that evening, but so certain were they
that Seybert had not passed over the Mahantango,
that they made no effort to go to the services.   After
discovering that his game had eluded him, the ruffian
swore that he would shoot Seybert from his horse before he should ever again reach his appointments.   He
was no doubt in earnest, and would have accomplished
his diabolical purpose had not Providence interfered.
Before the faithful itinerant returned, the would-be-
assassin was dead and buried.   Surely, as Luther has
written in his great hymn of the Reformation.

"A mighty fortress in our God."

Though no one informed the "Governor" of the plot, as in the case of Paul, yet God knew it and defeated the purpose of Hell by sending the death angel to palsy the murderous heart and hand.

Bro. Seybert was a good prophet in regard to the progress of the work of the Evangelical Association. There are instances in which his predictions were minutely realized. In 1827 he made the following prediction, concerning the above named valleys:

"'There is at present much excitement about salvation, and many inquiries after the way of life. The people are uneasy in their sins, and eager throngs assemble at our services. This uneasiness of the public mind is destined to become general, for the morning twilight of the day of grace is breaking upon the midnight of these valleys and mountains:

The clouds are lifting,
The shadows shifting.

It will soon be daylight, for the day-star has arisen, and the Sun of Righteousness will speedily burst upon the scene with his glory, and darkness will flee away. All the efforts of Satan to prevent it will be in vain. A great change is imminent here, and a mighty spiritual revolution will be enacted on this romantic arena. These valleys will be redeemed. This desert will yet rejoice and blossom as the rose; it will blossom abundantly, and rejoice with joy and singing. All flesh shall see the salvation of our God."

This glorious prediction, like many other similar ones, was strikingly fulfilled. He was endowed with a remarkable prophetic ken. He stood upon the mountain summits, and his acute intellect saw with precision what the outcome would be, for he had a just appreciation of the power of the Gospel, which is the power of God unto salvation unto everyone that believeth.

The conference session of 1827 was held in Orwigsburg. During the conference session the people streamed to the services in great and eager crowds, among them many newly converted, The work here was now well established. A society of one hundred and forty zealous and active members was already organized.

Seybert started on a Saturday in September from a camp-meeting in Virginia, to visit his mother, and rode fifty miles that day. Sunday he crossed the Alleghany mountains, for he had an appointment to preach that evening. He reached his mother's home at Economy on the following Friday. The visit of her son caused her much joy. The next day he spent in visiting from house to house among the Harmonites.—They had meanwhile changed the name of their society and town, however, calling it 'Economy' latterly. On Sunday he went to church with them in the morning, when Rapp preached. The evening they spent in playing on musical instruments. Wednesday evening Rapp held a church trial with a member who was found guilty of stealing apples from a neighboring orchard. Rapp asked the society what should be done with the offender. No one spoke. After waiting in silence for a while he exclaimed impatiently, "Is there no one here who has a familiar spirit?" At last a young man arose, and suggested that the thief should be prohibited from attending public meetings for two weeks. This was accordingly done, Rapp adding to the punishment that during the two weeks he should live on bread and water, and no one should give him a welcome.

On Friday Seybert left to go to Ohio. After preaching a number of times and visiting Bro. Erb, he returned to Economy before the second Sunday. The Lord's day was spent similar to the one described. He remained another week, taking a much needed rest, meanwhile applying remedies to cure a trouble-some cough which had settled upon his lungs. Among these Economists he says no one is in want, a consequence of the community of goods. Their domestic habits are simple, cleanly and economical. The same is true of their dress. They seem to love each other sincerely. Those who are married practice continence, hoping in this way to present themselves to Christ as a Bride without spot or wrinkle, or any such thing. They seldom, if ever, have prayer-meetings, never saying grace at table, nor holding family worship, contending that one must "pray inwardly". They consider baptism unnecessary, and disregard feet-washing, but they esteem the Sacrament of the Lord's Supper very highly. They profess that Christ will soon come and establish his kingdom among them and by them. It may be remarked here, that Seybert always spoke favorably of this institution.

January 30th, 1828, he went to Harrisburgh on his way east. Here he visited Rev. J. Dreisbach, who was at the time a member of the House of Representatives of Pennsylvania. Dreisbach showed Seybert the hall of the Representatives and the imposing Capitol buildings, the arrangements of which the latter thought very excellent. He was glad to see his ministerial brother there, and hoped he would also do his duty in his present position to the glory of his Lord and the welfare of his country. "But", he exclaimed, "how much greater is the dignity and honor of a minister of the Gospel which I am permitted to hold! O thou eternal Jehovah! Who am I poor worm, that Thou hast counted me worthy of a place among Thy children? Though I were a thousand times better than I am, I would by no means be worthy of this dignity. I could not even claim merit enough to be a door-keeper in Thy house. How can I be worthy of such an office as the Gospel ministry! Nevertheless I praise Thee with all my soul, that Thou hast counted me worthy, putting me into the ministry, through Jesus Christ. Amen."

Seybert not only engaged in pioneer work in rural districts and villages, but also opened the way for the Evangelical Association in large cities. He visited the cities of Reading and Philadelphia for years, occasionally, and was greatly esteemed by the honest Germans of those places, for his simplicity of manners, his disingenuousness of mind, his self-denial, his condescending interest in the common people, and his industry. During the current year (1828) he made some progress in laying the foundation for our work in those cities, which has now assumed large proportions.

In April he visited one of the German clergy in Womelsdorf. Seybert, during their conversation, asked him as to the state of religious matters there, and the parson replied that everything is "all right". But Seybert did not agree. "This preacher," he says, "calls everything all right, while at the same time the masses of the people there live like veritable heathen. For instance: Just about that time two church-members had a heated quarrel at a dance. The quarrel ended in a fight, but in a few minutes they professed to make peace. One of the belligerents, who was the fiddler, began to play again, and the dance went on. Meanwhile the other went out, procured a knife, came back and stabbed the fiddler, killing him instantly. At the funeral of the murdered fiddler the parson aforesaid declared, the brother had fallen asleep in Jesus; that he is in heaven, and has no sin to account for. The murderer was alone the sinner. This preacher calls this getting along well in religion! Surely, this is the prosperity of the wicked, the security of the sons of Belial. And no wonder that such a state of affairs exists when the spiritual leaders cry *'peace, peace,' when there is no peace.*"

The conference of 1828 met in June, at New Berlin. On account of increasing interests and more business complications its session lasted an entire day longer than heretofore. Up to the previous year there was but one conference in the Evangelical Association, and that conference had to transact the business and govern the affairs of the entire Church.

In 1827 the Western conference was formed, — which afterwards became the Ohio conference, but for several years the most important business was still transacted in the Eastern conference. This made the session of 1828 unusually lengthy. At this session Joseph Long, (afterwards Bishop) was for the first time chosen as Presiding Elder and placed in charge of the one district composing the new Western conference. Long was thus the first Presiding Elder, regularly serving in the Western or Ohio conference. Seybert remained on Canaan district.

During this year a sort of union camp-meeting was held in Cumberland Co., Penna., originated by Rev. John Winebrenner, at that time as yet a minister in the Reformed Church. It was to be purely non-sectarian, and ministers of four different denominations were present and participated, besides even some who belonged to no branch of the Christian Church. Bro. Seybert, who, as we have seen, was very favorably impressed with the character of Winebrenner's work, was also present and preached. The meeting was very largely attended, and no less than sixty-two tents were erected. The meeting produced an extraordinary spiritual commotion, and the close is said to have been very affecting.

The only serious objection Seybert had at that time

to Winebrenner's work as a spiritual reformer, was that in his opinion he did not lay stress enough upon the virtue of self-denial and non-conformity to worldly pleasures and ·fashions. — Of course, later on, when Winebrenner began to drift away from the beaten track of orthodoxy, and announced his extreme views on baptism and insisted upon feet washing as an ordinance, Seybert could no longer endorse the course of his former friend.—Accordingly he took the opportunity at this camp-meeting to preach on this subject of self-denial, for he thought the people were dressed in a very vain and worldly fashion, entirely unbecoming for Christians. Seybert was thoroughly at home on this theme, and his preaching was often startling in its immediate effects.

On this occasion he made a profound impression. Some of the "haughty ones in Zion", as he called them, threw into the straw useless articles of ornamentation, or rushed excitedly into their tents to divest themselves of articles of dress which their aroused consciences condemned. This was preaching with effect upon a subject which is undoubtedly neglected too much in our day, by Evangelical preachers. Seybert, however, never prescribed any particular mode of dress; he only insisted upon propriety, simplicity, plainness and economy. He opposed fashionable apparel chiefly on the ground of the boundless extravagance to which it leads, and because, to his mind, it was indicative of conformity at heart to the world.' To him personal apparel was an important index of the state of the heart. He thought a Christian ought to dress like a Christian, and not with the vanity and display of a peacock. Was he wrong?

In September he was taken very sick, so that he was confined to bed for twelve days. He stayed with a family named Wise, whose kind hospitality he gratefully acknowledged, and whose sterling piety he greatly admired. His sickness was so severe that it was feared his career would end. He experienced no fear of death or eternity, and expressed himself prepared for the mortal change. Contrary to all expectations however, he recovered, and before he had sufficiently recuperated, he was again in the saddle. Occasionally he was compelled to stop and lie abed for several days. Frequently he lay down by the road-side in the woods. In the evening, if he was too feeble to preach, he exhorted or held class and prayer-meetings. Thus the intrepid pioneer kept on, and actually recovered in the midst of his labors. It was almost impossible for Seybert to adjust himself to the idleness which sickness imposed. However, on a certain occasion in a conversation, he asserted that he had learned through sickness to serve the Lord in a new way. Upon being asked for an explanation, he said: "Not long ago, when I had to succumb to severe sickness, I had a very hard conflict with myself, because I could not be contented with doing nothing. Suddenly it flashed upon my mind that we must not only *labor* according to the will of God, but also *suffer* according to the will of God."

Near the city limits of Lebanon, Pa., there stood an old one-story brick church, built upon a great, solid limestone-bedrock for a foundation, and therefore a very firm and substantial building. It was owned by a defunct society of Mennonites, the few remaining members of which, however, generously opened their house for the use of other preachers. Seybert was always welcome to use it and frequently preached there. In April, 1829, he with several other ministers held a special meeting there. This meeting was evidently characterized by considerable lively demonstration, upon which several of those who had control of the property, sent word to Seybert that he could not be permitted to hold any more of *that kind* of meetings in the old brick, for, they said, "*it would not stand the jumping and shouting!*" But Seybert gave it as his opinion, that the building was perfectly safe, standing as it did upon the great limestone rock; he thought there was much more likelihood that "certain cold and formal Christians could not endure such lively meetings."

About this time, while on a prospecting tour through Lehigh county, he visited a venerable gentleman, eighty-five years of age, belonging to the "Schwenkfelders", otherwise known as *Tunkers*, who had long cherished an ardent desire to see another preacher of the Evangelical Association before he died. His delight, therefore, at seeing Bro. Seybert, was very great, and he treated him very effectionately.

Seybert says:

"I also attended a meeting of the Schwenkfelders, where a man named Schultz preached. These people seemed to be a very sociable, virtuous society, outwardly humble, and simple in their dress. But it seemed to me that in respect of the inner spiritual life they were far below the mark. I gave my host several tracts on the subject of conversion and salvation from sin. I found four classes of people in this vicinity:

First, the rough and extremely wicked.

Second, the respectable and moral, who have never been awakened.

Third, those who were struggling with conviction.

Fourth, some who may have had some knowledge of a genuine Evangelical experience."

Our sainted Bishop never failed to chronicle in his journals an appreciative reference to the beauties and delights of Spring. In his strictly itinerant mode of life, too, he had abundant opportunities to witness and enjoy the annual resurrection of nature. He was blessed in this respect above modern pastors, who find themselves mostly shut up within the brown, dull walls of the library, or tramping with weary feet the sombre pavements of the city — that sacrilege in God's beautiful temple of nature. Scarcely a blade of grass helps to soften their footsepts; scarcely a flower greets their languid eyes, as they pace the tread-mill beat of their daily round of duties. Some of them would, we think, gladly bear the hardships of the glorious old-time itinerants, for the exuberant joys and exquisite pleasures which blessed them.

Give us green fields, shadowy wildwood, meandering brook, fleecy clouds flecking a soft blue sky visible from horizon line to horizon line, pure air perfumed from the tinted chalices of God's flowers, and sunshine that comes clear and straight from heaven, not filtered into shadow through clouds of smoke and dust and soot from a thousand impudent fire throats!—But we started to copy an entry from Seybert's journal, written in the Spring of '29:

"At this season of the year traveling is pleasant. Everything is beautiful; the weather is delightful; the earth is carpeted with green; a glorious wealth of flowers is displayed in meadow and on hillside, and the very air is full of the most pleasant odors. In the soft evening the trill of the frog is heard, and in the morning the feathery tribes sing their choruses of praise, while the cooing of the turtle-dove lends its subduing enchantment to the song. One can now drink in the delights of nature and the glory and goodness of the Creator, with all the five senses."

During this Spring he went to Dauphin county, to look up a new field of operation, and was invited to the house of a man named Henn. But when he began to arrrange for family prayers, the housewife became angry, and began to curse, scold and swear, though Mr. Henn himself was pleased to have his guest pray. Seybert prayed in spite of the angry woman, and continued praying until she became quiet. But seeing that the prayer had touched her husband's heart, set her to raving anew, and she finally threatened to scald Seybert with boiling water.

Upon this he spoke gently and kindly to the woman, and was permitted to remain all night; but he left early next morning without breakfast, though he was obliged to make a long journey fasting.

On the last day of May, 1829, he concluded his labors on Canaan district, where he had now labored for four years with great zeal, faithfulness and acceptability. He had many spiritual sons and daughters there, for whose welfare and spiritual advancement he was greatly concerned. He writes:

"To-day I must leave my dear Canaan district. My heart is filled with sadness at having to give the parting hand to so many warm friends, to whom I have become so closely attached. And yet, my soul is moved to grateful praise unto God, for his unspeakable goodness to me during these four years. With such feelings and thoughts in my heart, I could not do otherwise to-day than stay behind my traveling companions, on the way to conference, to commune with my heavenly Father about these things."

CHAPTER V.

FURTHER EXPERIENCES AND DEEDS AS A PRESIDING ELDER.

The session of his conference, for 1829, met on the first of June in New Berlin, elected Bro. Seybert a second time to the office of Presiding Elder, and assigned him to duty on Salem district, embracing Union, Centre and Somerset charges in the State of Pennsylvania, and Lake circuit, in the State of New York. He was also elected Trustee of the fund created by legacies bequeathed to the Evangelical Association, whereupon he prayed for a special wisdom to perform the duties of this new trust to the best interests of the Church.

During this conference session a somewhat amusing incident occurred. Seybert with several other ministers was sitting one evening on the piazza of Mr. Maize's house, where they were being entertained, quietly conversing on religious topics among themselves and with the family, when a vicious neighbor, named Maurer, came up Penn's creek, on the banks of which Michael Maize's house was situated, for the purpose of annoying the brethren. He was a fiddler, and stationing himself near where they were sitting, began to play some giddy dancing airs. This he knew would annoy these plain gentlemen, but they were not long in divining his purpose. Accordingly,

8

while he was vigorously engaged in playing his dancing airs, they began to sing in a hearty manner, "Our dying day is coming on". They sang so lustily that the violin could no longer be heard, and the disconcerted musician, with a chop-fallen scowl, thrust his fiddle under his arm and trudged angrily away, muttering some harmless imprecations upon the men who had so signally defeated him. They fairly sang him down. He must have been a miserable creature. He committed suicide soon afterwards.

After conference, on account of some business, Bro. Seybert returned once more to Liken's Valley. Arriving there he found that in his absence, the devil, through his willing creatures, had scattered a whole pack of lies about him. One story ran that Seybert had a wife and children somewhere, whom he did not support, and that he was in communication with bad characters. Another was to the effect that he had stolen a horse and saddle from his father. Seybert remarks:

"These lies would never have been circulated about me, had not a genuine work of grace broken out in that section, wherein many sinners were snatched as brands from the burnings and happily converted deep into eternal life. This is what made the old father of lies scatter these stories concerning the poor itinerant."

During this trip Bro. Seybert fell into an earnest dispute with a Lutheran woman, who was rather bold, and unceremoniously attacked the Presiding Elder on various points, expressing her dissent in very positive terms. She seemed specially intent on establishing the assertion that there were no saints living in that day, and that none ever lived who were "not afraid of thunder". Bro. Seybert tried to show her from Scripture, that the true Christian has no occasion to fear, or to live in constant trepidation and anxiety. Pefect love casteth out all fear that hath torment. The loud thunders may momentarily frighten timid souls, or startle nervous people, but they still have no actual fear, if they are true children of God, who trust in their Heavenly Father as they should. He was however, apparently making no impression upon her. At last he happened to espy an old Lutheran hymn-book, lying near him, which he quickly seized and began to read to her from its pages: —

> "Roll, ye dread thunders, in majesty rumble,
> Shake, in your wrath, the dark clouds over head :
> Smite with your might,
> 'Till quaketh the earth, neath the shock —
> Still standeth my faith on the Rock."

The woman thought, her "faith" would stand firm too: she agreed with the poet. Then Seybert read on:—

> "Darken the heavens, ye storm-clouds, with blackness ;
> Terrify earth with the hurricane's roar :
> Rush, ye mad floods ;
> Break o'er thy bounds, O wild sea,
> Your power alarmeth not me !"

The woman said, what *she* dreaded about a storm wasn't the thunder so much as the frightful lightning. He read again:—

> " Flash, ye quick lightnings, like a sword from its scabbard!
> Pour your hot fires from the vials of wrath
> On the doomed world ;
> Shoot from the bow the swift dart :
> Yet shall peace dwell in my heart ! "

"Oh yes," she interrupted again, "if a person hadn't any sins anymore,—but who that is not free from sin, can witness such a scene without fear?"

"Why, listen!" says Seybert, and reads on:—

> " Jesus the mighty, hath pardoned my sinnings !
> I am saved from all sin by the blood of the Lamb !
>   He is my Friend,
> Holds o'er me his banner, beneath me his arm,
> So nought can my spirit alarm ! "

The woman admitted that probably such a defiance of a thunder-storm might be possible, if one is in such a state of grace as the poet here describes and professes to enjoy, but such people are scarce now-a-days. Bro. Seybert, however, confidently assured her that there were already quite a number right there in Liken's valley, who were gloriously and consciously saved in Jesus, and that their number was rapidly increasing. He was right. Gradually that valley became a truly Christian community. The old lady could not resist the double argument of her own hymn-book and of the logic of facts around her, and was silent.

July 7th. 1829, was his thirty-eighth birth-day, on which he visited an aged saint, seventy-five years old. The brother was so feeble as to be almost helpless. While relating his Christian experience, he was so powerfully blessed that he sank from his chair under the weight of glory that filled his soul.

In September, during a blessed camp-meeting, Bro. Seybert was one day engaged in baptizing a number of persons, immediately before celebrating the Lord's Supper. While engaged in this solemn ceremony, a woman came into the meeting terribly enraged, because the evening before her husband had been converted. Just as Seybert was about to offer the prayer in the ordinance of baptism, she came in, picked up a stone and attempted to pound her kneeling spouse, who was one of the candidates for baptism, upon the head. Several brethren interfered and prevented her from executing her brutal purpose, when she began to pound the altar, and screamed like a demoniac, cursing and swearing in a most blasphemous manner, in the midst of solemn worship. Finally, finding that she failed to break up the service in this way, this feminine demon drew from the folds of her clothes, where she had concealed it, a large, murderous butcher-knife, wrapped in rags. While she was unwrapping it, some one dexterously snatched it out of her hands. This made her fairly wild. She charged that her husband had been seduced from his "faith" by these people, and now the whole family would go to hell! She was going to kill herself. At length the friends succeeded in removing her from the grounds.

Bro. Seybert later reports the following happy sequel:

Several years afterwards this woman came to

another camp-meeting on the same grounds. She came in just as he was preaching. She took a seat, and stared hard at the preacher, while he in turn looked upon her with pity. The Lord blessed His word. The woman fell into great distress of soul, began to plead for pardon, and was saved. The change in life and manner was remarkable. "The Lord hath done this. *Hallelujah!*" he exclaimed.

The following incident throws a curious side-light upon the morals of the German ecclesiastics of that time:

On a certain occasion our Evangelical people at a certain place had a meeting where the schoolmaster and organist of the church partook of the communion of the Lord's Supper with them, and otherwise participated actively in the services. This created a great furore among his brethren. They accordingly met with their minister at a tavern or liquor house to hold a church trial. It was, by the way, a most suitable and congenial place, since the church was made up of swearers and beer-guzzlers. After drinking deep draughts of the distilled nectar of death, they summoned the aforesaid organist before them, to call him to account for his conduct. When the culprit appeared, they charged him with the crime of having prayed on his knees at one of these Evangelical prayer-meetings, and partaking of the Lord's Supper with them. As he manifested no sorrow, and would not promise to "do better", the parson solemnly declared him to be a fanatic, a heretic and a reprobate. The church expelled him, and, declaring him unworthy to serve it any longer, he was then and there deposed from his positions as schoolmaster and organist!—And this in Christian America in the nineteenth century!

Some days after the conference session of 1830, which returned Bro. Seybert to Salem district, he was troubled with a remarkable feeling of spiritual poverty. Under this feeling he withdrew from all society and sought solitude in a forest, where he wrestled all day until the sun set. Even then, only the fact that he had to preach, drove the weary wrestler back to the dwellings of men. Trembling with fear he appeared before his congregation, and began in great weakness to speak. Soon, however, "the Lord sent the light from the glory world into his soul", and he spoke with such demonstration of the Spirit and of power, that a young man in the congregation fell upon his knees in deep conviction, and began to cry for mercy. In a few minutes more an old sinner in his ninetieth year also broke down, and pleaded for mercy. These were the trophies he had wrung from the enemy, during the long, single-handed struggle in the woods that afternoon.

The fourth General Conference was held in November of 1830, in Centre Co., Penna. There were but eight members composing that body. Joseph Long acted as Chairman, and John Seybert as Secretary. Very important business was transacted, especially in regard to the Discipline and the articles of faith of our Church.

He closed the year 1830 with this retrospective remark:

"Dec. 31, 1830. This day closed the year A. D. 1830, which has been full of labors and experiences. I have traveled three thousand nine hundred and twenty-four miles during the past year (on horseback), and the Lord has been very good to me. I feel moved to prayer and adoration in deep humility before God, because He has been so kind, good and merciful unto me, and has frequently permitted me to preach the Word with great liberty. I have had good health, and all things necessary thereto. Blessed, adored and praised be His glorious Name in time and in eternity!"

On March 8th, 1831 he accidentally came into a meeting of English speaking people. Unexpectedly their preacher failed to come, and they wanted Bro. Seybert to preach. But to preach in German was out of the question. Seeing there was here a case of necessity, he concluded that under such circumstances a stammering and imperfect English would answer. Accordingly he undertook it, and preached his second English sermon. During this broken effort he presently began to feel the blessing of God mightily upon his soul, and God's children were blessed. Before he closed a youth fell into distress of soul, which did much to encourage him to try the English again under similar circumstances: for this was his chief concern, that sinners be converted.

In April one day, he visited a sister eighty-four years of age, who had served the Lord for many years. He prayed with her, and was delighted to find that, though she was very feeble physically, yet she was very strong in faith, in love and in the power of God. She became truly happy during the interview, and he found her familiar with the Word of God, and deeply experienced in divine things. "When the Lord blessed her, she expressed herself with holy laughter, such as is mentioned in the one hundred and twenty-sixth Psalm. She is a pious widow, waiting for her release, as Hannah and Simeon of old waited for the consolation of Israel."

Here is a characteristic incident :

Some time in September, Bro. Seybert came to Brush Valley, where he learned that the officers of the law were about to sell the home of a certain poor widow, in payment of a debt her late husband had left. Seybert, who was of a very benevolent disposition, thought the matter all over carefully, secured all the information concerning the case possible, and determined within himself to relieve the unfortunate woman.

On the day of sale he promptly appeared in the crowd, and bid for the house, until he was declared the buyer. Upon this he said to the Sheriff, "Please deed the property back to the widow", which the astonished officer proceeded to do, and Seybert paid the debt in cash, so that the house belonged henceforth to the widow without encumbrance. The surprised and overjoyed woman was anxious to know how she should repay her clerical benefactor, who had indeed proved himself a friend in need, though a stranger. His reply was, "I want you to lead a pious, godly life now, avoid luxury, extravagance and every evil forbidden in the Word of God, and if you think you can pay me back in small annual instalments, all right." She stated how much she thought she could pay every year. He replied, "If you can do that, it's all right, and if you can't, it's all right anyhow." She paid him back in small annual instalments, without interest, and he was satisfied. He had lent it to the Lord.

In October of this year (1831) his official duties brought him for the first time to Niagara. He stopped to view this great natural wonder, was deeply impressed with it, and was led to contemplate the majesty and power of the great God.

In the same month he had a remarkably powerful Quarterly meeting on the Mohawk river in the State of New York, during which he received twenty-five persons into the church. Seventeen members from the class near Niagara Falls, had come sixty miles to attend this meeting, and one sister had come ninety-two miles. The sister, he says, was specially blessed of God during the meeting. No wonder they had glorious Quarterly meetings in the days of yore, when the people went such distances, underwent such sacrifices, and came together in such numbers and in such zeal. Is it not worthy of modern imitation?

During this year Seybert traveled four thousand three hundred and fifty-six miles, preached two hundred and seventy-one times, and baptized thirty-eight persons.

Saturday, April 21st, 1832, was begun the first 'big meeting' in Log House, Lycoming Co., Pa. On

Saturday the services were held in Bro. Sindlinger's house, but on Sunday they met in a church. Many people were present, and James Barber preached from 1. Cor. 5:7, 8. There was much weeping. They then celebrated the 'Lord's Supper after baptizing three children and one adult. This was the first Evangelical communion service in those parts. On Sunday night Seybert preached and gave an invitation, when sixteen persons joined the church. He organized them into a class, and they elected Bro. J. M. Sindlinger as their class leader.* He remained five days, baptized a number of children, preached nine times, held two prayer-meetings, married one couple, and received in all twenty-one members into church fellowship, besides leaving many in the community who were serious and thoughtful.

About this time Seybert began to urge the need of parsonages, and was successful in having them erected upon the various charges of his district. He was a pioneer also in this matter, though he never expected to be under the necessity of using a parsonage himself, for it was his firm resolve to remain a celibate at least so long as he should continue in the itinerancy. He was unalterably opposed, as is well known, to all extravagance, but he advocated substantial and comfortable living for the ministry, and was anxious that everything, the temporalities of the church not excepted, be conducted decently and in order. He believed the ministry of the Evangelical

---

* Bro. Sindlinger afterwards became a prominent and successful minister of the Gospel, who died in October, 1883.

Association would be the more efficient if their temporal wants were adequately provided for.

Nov. 27th he preached in the northern part of New York, on the Mohawk, in a school-house, to a congregation of Methodists and enlightened Lutherans. He was kindly entertained, during his stay, by Mr. J. Dunkel, a member of the M. E. church. Mr. Dunkel was a very wealthy man, who, before his conversion, had been the possessor of slaves. However, when the Lord delivered him and his family from the slavery of sin, and translated them into the marvellous light and liberty of the people of God, he forthwith also liberated his slaves.

They had an extraordinary 'big meeting' in this vicinity about this time. The friends had come a distance of eighty-five miles from the north, fifty miles from the east, and similar distances from other directions.

Bro. Seybert was a born missionary. Whenever he found intervals of respite between his regular appointments, he spent them in explorations. Accordingly, in the Spring of 1833, he made a prospecting tour to Luzerne Co., Pa., in which he nearly froze. But of his experience among the people he makes the following observation: "The people were to some degree attracted by my labors, but they are an atrociously wicked set, being a new demonstration of the well known proverb: 'Like preacher like people'. For some of them complained to me concerning their preacher, that he is dissolute and unspeakably wicked. They said, he was so passionate that on the least provocation he would stamp his feet and swear horribly to vent his rage. Besides he often became beastly · drunk! Surely a worthless preacher."

Here is another letter, which details many interesting experiences, which we give therefore in full:

" Lewisburg, Union Co., Pa., March 9th, 1833.

Dear Bro. Rein:—Beloved in the Lord!—I write to let you know that since I left you in Reading last, I have been well, and am firmly resolved to serve the Lord while I live.

. "We are having good times generally in our meetings on my district, especially in Centre county, where a great revival of religion has begun among the Lutherans and Reformed. It has been spiritually dark beyond description in these parts. On Sundays before their divine service — rather idol worship—it has been their custom to visit the saloons, drink a goodly draught of brandy, and then, after the trifling pastime, they call the worship of God, was over, they would return to the saloon. The rest of the Lord's day was then spent in barbarous carousals, sometimes deliberately breaking in the head of a whiskey barrel, so that they might drink more freely. Often the bacchanal ended in some brutal fight until some were half dead. Many of their pastors were no better; they called these abominable wretches *good Christians*, comforting them in their sins, and vehemently warning them to beware of the influence of the ' Methodists' and 'Albrights'. But the Lord has blessed His Word proclaimed by us, and our services have been a great blessing to this benighted people. We have also introduced camp-meetings, greatly to the benefit of this region. First we obtained access to a school-house in Brush Valley. Soon a number of neighbors opened their houses, and a great work began there. In Sugar Valley we have had two camp-meetings, at which many have been saved. From there the fire got unto Nittany Valley, and set the Philistines' corn-fields on fire, and in Penn's Valley the fire is likewise burning gloriously. The 'dumb dogs', of whom Isaiah speaks, barked furiously and growled savagely too, at our preachers and our praying people. But they have already changed their tune. Since the senseless black-guarding did not help their cause, *they began to preach repentance too!* They publicly admitted that their churches were in a state of disintegration and decline, because of internal, moral and spiritual corruption, and they avowed their purpose to begin a reformation themselves at once. To make the matter still more plausible, they sent for some of their preachers from a distance, who played the role of evangelists, begging the people passionately not to leave 'the church', for it will now be cleansed. This was a trick of the devil, by which it was hoped to rock the awakened ones to sleep again. Still one by one they are leaving Babylon, and the redeemed are coming to Zion. They throw away their fashionable regalia of the devil's uniform, 'laying aside every weight and the sin which doth so easily beset them'. They walk by the faith of Jesus Christ, shouting Hosanna's and Hallelujah's as they go with Israel through the wilderness. It will not do to yoke believers with unbelievers, and therefore they are coming out from among them.

"Near Buffalo, New York, I also had abundant success. Fifteen sinners were converted in one of our meetings, and many others are seeking the Lord. O what a time of weeping and wailing and woe-begone crying for mercy! We have two preachers at work there now, and the work of the Lord is prospering in their hands.

"Last Fall I made a tour through that State as far as Albany, where a great work of conversion is going on among the Lutherans and Reformed. Of course, the devil got mad there too, just as he always does where people are being converted. I was greatly blessed in preaching among these people, and realized the power of God to such a degree, that I felt lifted up above all earthly things, and my soul was basking in the glory of the New Jerusalem. While I was preaching, many became spiritually drunken; some began to prophesy, praising God aloud, while penitents wept freely. I also found here a class of humble Methodists. I had never before found their equal for simplicity of manner and plainness of attire. I preached for them and we had a blessed time. I inquired of them, how they had managed so effectually to keep the fashions of the world out of their society, and was told, they were under a mutual agreement not to permit fashion to obtain a foot-hold among them.

"With greeting for yourself and family,. I am
    Your friend and brother,   John Seybert."

April 6th, he came to Womelsdorf, where, a very few years ago, pious people were extremely scarce. But, by the help of the Lord, our preachers have gained an entrance, and a revival of religion has resulted. The persecutors tried clubs and stones on God's children, but the more the sons of Belial raved, the firmer the converted people became, and the more the little flock increased. —

In May, 1833, Bro. Seybert took his departure from Salem district, preaching a farewell sermon on his last round, in which he exhorted the people to be faithful, to abhor all evil, to have the fear of God before their eyes continually, and above all, to avoid pride and vanity of life — particularly in dress, and to *serve the Lord in humility of heart and appearance.* During the delivery of this sermon on various occasions, the power of God was so mightily manifested, that, as he himself bluntly expressed it, *"pride got sick"!* and many were the useless ornaments of gayety that were thrown off. Whereupon he shouts, *"Hallelujah"!*

CHAPTER VI.

THE FIRST MISSIONARY OF THE EVANGELICAL ASSOCIATION.

At the session of the Eastern conference, in 1833, after having served two consecutive terms as Presiding Elder, Bro. Seybert offered himself to the conference as a missionary, provided the conference thought it proper to send him in that capacity. It was accordingly ordered that he should spend the ensuing conference year in explorations and pioneer work in the north-western portion of Pennsylvania, and open up new fields of operation. It was thus, that Bishop Seybert became the first regularly appointed missionary of the Evangelical Association. It was indeed true, that he had never been anything but a missionary, from the time he entered the ministry. That was the character of the man and of his work, whether in charge of a circuit, administering the affairs of a district, or laboring as a formally appointed and regularly sent missionary. That was, indeed, and is yet the character of the work of the Evangelical Association. It is a missionary church; its work is missionary work. It cannot be anything else and fulfill its calling. Its constitution forbids a merely conservative attitude; its circumstances preclude dependence upon wealth and popularity. It must be aggressive, or die spiritually and ecclesiastically. It is made to push "into the regions beyond". Otherwise there is clearly no room and no occasion for the Evangelical

9

Association among the ecclesiastical "Establish-ments". Should we ever lose the spirit of Paul and of our own church-fathers — the spirit of the Master's "last and great command" the Evangelical Association is doomed to become effete and corrupt.

John Seybert was the typical Evangelical preacher, *alias* missionary. Not a year of his public life passed that he did not seek new fields for Evangelical culti-vation. He was not, he could not be content to merely serve the regular appointments which he had received from his predecessors. Nor were his efforts unsuccessful. Each year he brougth the light of the truth to some benighted regions, and added them to his circuit or district. — A "station" was unknown in those days, in the Evangelical Association, and Bro. Seybert never had the privilege of serving one in his life. — He cared nothing for hardships nor exposure; the threatenings of the opposition did not alarm him; he was not deterred by the great moral darkness in any city or rural community; obstacles did not dis-courage him. In his peculiarly quiet way, with a composed manner that came from an all-conquering faith in God, he went forward with dauntless courage, preaching Christ and Him crucified, from house to house, and to the gathered throngs, and it proved a savor of life unto life to many.

But this year his work was formally and officially a missionary enterprise. Since, however, our church at that time had no organized missionary society, and had not as yet established any nominal missions, his charge was called "Erie circuit".

On leaving conference on this occasion, he wrote under date of June 12th:

"To-day I set out for my appointed mission-field in the north-western part of my native State. I go in the name of the Lord, and shall preach a pure Gospel to the baptized German heathen there, by the help of God."

On account of a necessary business trip to the State of New York, he did not reach the territory assigned him until July 12th. He was kindly received by a gentleman named Gingrich, near the city of Erie, Pa., and entertained with generous hospitality. This encouraged him. He began his work immediately after arriving. He spent Saturday visiting from house to house, and thus effectually prepared the way for his efforts on Sunday. Sunday he preached in the morning in a private house, and twice in the afternoon in two different school-houses, —at 1 o'clock and at 4. By this time he had open doors in abundance. His visitations on Saturday, from early morning till late at night, conversing on religion and praying with the people wherever suitable, paved the way, and gave him such ready access to the people. Three days more were now spent in this community in a similar manner. He inquired personally and closely into the spiritual condition of the people, and specially won their good-will by speaking kindly to every child in the household. After preaching on Wednesday night, and securing permanently a place to hold their services, he departed into Mercer county, but soon returned to the work near Erie, where he preached four times on one Sunday, and then could not meet all the demands that were made upon him.

He had to suffer a little persecution one day in October, from a wicked man, who abused Seybert, without the latter knowing, or being able to discover why. It had the effect, however, to draw him closer to God, and he was enabled to pray for his unreasonable enemy. In the evening there was still another enemy to trouble him. At first he blackguarded him, and when he knew of nothing more to say, he reproached him with being a '*bachelor*'. Seybert says: "I presume, he meant to insinuate that I was single because I could not get a wife, in which he was, however, greatly mistaken. I quietly replied, 'St. Paul was the foremost among the Apostles,' and one of the holiest of men, and he was not married either, being thus enabled to do the more in the vineyard of the Lord. My tormentor now referred to Solomon, who was reputed the wisest man that ever lived, and he had even more than one wife! I interposed that while Solomon was supposed to have been a very wise man, it was not his polygamy that gave him this reputation. Solomon became a backslider and a fool — for all backsliders are fools; but Paul remained faithful unto death without a wife, and certainly behaved more wisely than Solomon. This ended the discussion."

He had, in the course of time, obtained a foot-hold near Lake Conneaut, Crawford Co.. Pa., where he preached in a certain school-house that belonged to

two different parties. The edifice was well arranged
for preaching services, being provided with a pulpit
and convenient seats. The first time he preached
there a leading man of one of the parties concerned,
was deeply affected, and began to talk to his neighbors about living a better life. This caused uneasiness in the community, but the opposition became
more pronounced when this man with several others
undertook to hold prayer-meetings, and it was forthwith declared that Seybert should not have the use
of the school-house any longer.

When the missionary arrived there again Sunday
morning, he found a great crowd of people gathered
in front of the building, quarreling excitedly about
his preaching there. A majority of the one party
claiming ownership were in favor of letting him in,
but of the other party a majority were opposed to it.
However, in this opposition party the most influential
men belonged to the minority, who were in favor of
admitting Seybert. Fearing he should be admitted,
one man had run in and closed the pulpit door, when
another as quickly tore it open again, determined to
get him into the pulpit. Upon this the opposition
declared with fearful imprecations they would cut the
house in two, and roll their half away, and the others
might do with their half what they chose. At this
juncture Bro. Seybert interposed, and, turning to
those who had been awakened, counselled peace,
urged them to yield, and suggested to hold the meeting elsewhere, which was accordingly done and the
meeting was held in a private house.

The night following this occurrence, he dreamed he had lent his horse to a boy to harrow a ploughed field with, and thought the beast became truant and ran off with the harrow. Upon awakening he said to himself, "Look out! these enlightened people will not be faithful; they will serve me as my horse served the boy in my dream, they will run away." This fear was partially realized. About one-half of them became the hangers-on of another preacher, who interfered with Bro. Seybert's work and robbed him of part of the results. Still, he had the satisfaction of organizing a respectable class before the year closed.

On one of his trips to Mercer county he dreamed of being in a very splendid palace, in which, however, a few window lights in the upper story were broken. Through these openings some evil-disposed persons attempted to throw stones and water upon him, failing, however, to hit him. He went out and reproved them sharply, upon which they looked at him in a mocking, scornful manner, without, however, saying anything. Then he saw himself suddenly transplanted into a lovely flower-garden, full of the most beautiful flower-buds, just ready to open. But he soon perceived another person in the garden, who was breaking off some of those delightful buds, for which he promptly reproved him, saying, "Do let these buds alone until they open of themselves, and do not pluck them prematurely." From this dream he expected that he would find opposition in his work, and that it would suffer in its most promising condition, from hasty inter-meddlers. He also learned by it, that "we should never comfort seekers of religion too soon, but let them experience the grace of God for themselves. Comforting seekers prematurely is like plucking rose-buds before they are open. Let them open!"

During this eventful year, the tireless missionary did a deed one night, which is probably without a parallel in the annals of Christian work.

Weary with a long and laborious journey on horseback, Seybert arrived one evening at a house where he expected to lodge and rest. He soon discovered, however, that the family were going to a prayer-meeting on foot, four miles distant, that evening. Nothing daunted, the weary itinerant declared himself determined to accompany them. They went; Seybert was induced to lead the meeting, which became so interesting that it did not close until eleven o'clock. The meeting over, they trudged the four miles back again, along the tortuous windings of a primitive forest path-way. Undoubtedly the walk was lightened by songs of praise that rang out on the stillness of the night and re-echoed amid the solemn arches of the wild wood temple, and was enlivened by the recital of experience by the vivacious missionary. On arriving, Seybert sat down by the stove, manifesting great weariness. It was after midnight. He soon laid away his heavy, broad-rimmed felt hat on a bench beside him, took off his coat, which he hung upon a wooden pin in the wall of the rude mountain cabin, and began slowly to untie his shoes, preparatory to retiring. Suddenly, with a half-startled look upon his face, he sprang up, exclaiming: "*Just think!*"   In a moment his shoe was retied and the other as quickly pulled on again, and before the family who were sitting by and watching him could recover sufficiently from their amazement to enquire what was the matter, he seized his hat, explaining, "Why, I had promised to visit this penitent man up on the hill, last evening, and now I had forgotten it!"   The man he spoke of lived a mile away in a miserable hut on the summit of a steep mountain that was covered with briers and underbrush.   The family sought to detain him, saying, "it is now too late, you are tired, and the man is in bed asleep," etc., but the restless shepherd of souls would not be deterred from his purpose by any such considerations.

Though it was one o'clock in the night, and though he was almost intolerably weary, this man must be visited for his soul's sake.   Reaching for the doorlatch, Seybert hastened out into the dreary darkness of the lonesome night, to seek one of the lost sheep of the house of Israel,—

> "Away on the mountains wild and bare,
> Away from the tender Shepherd's care."

With hurried steps the intrepid missionary climbed the steep and rugged mountain side, through underbrush and thorns.   Arriving at the low, one story log-hut, he knocked at the humble door, waked the man up and remarked upon greeting him, "I could hardly keep my promise, but I thought, better late, than break it".   It must have been a startling summons to the sleeping sinner.   Entering the house

Seybert began immediately to talk with the man about the salvation of his soul. Presently he began to weep under the strong appeal of the humble missionary. Then the two knelt together in prayer, praying earnestly until day-break. A little before sunrise, the penitent found peace in believing, and began to praise the Lord. Seybert — after rejoicing in the new trophy of redeeming grace — now left and started down the hill. Light-footed as a deer, he fairly ran down, his face beaming with joy, and everything in his manner full of animation, for he had saved a soul. As soon as he got near enough to his intended lodging-place to be understood, he shouted at the top of his voice, "*What do you think! That man has been born into eternal life this morning!*" They now all hastened in their glad surprise to see for themselves what the Lord had done. There was the new convert, walking about the door-yard, praising the Lord with a loud voice, while the sun poured the virgin light of the morning over the landscape, and the birds sang their morning anthem to the God who made them. "Why!" exclaimed the happy convert, "the whole earth has become new!"

> "And all through the mountain, thunder-riven,
>   And up from the rocky steep,
>   There rose a cry to the gate of Heaven :
>   'Rejoice ! I have found my sheep !'
>   And the angels echoed around the throne,
>   Rejoice ! for the Lord brings back His own !"

At the close of this eventful conference-year, Seybert prepared the following report of Erie mission, from which it appears that like his great prototype, St. Paul, he belonged to that choice realm of high moral heroes who "turn the world upside down". He created a stir wherever he went, and Satan's kingdom always got a troublesome shaking up, when this simple, intrepid herald of the Cross began to preach. A mere selection from his report is here added:

"The families who first received me in Erie county, were Hershey's, Long's, Miller's, Gimber's, Metzler's, Brown's, Ripply's, Kurtz's and others. The Germans in those parts were divided among Catholics, Lutherans, Reformed, Dunkards and Mennonites, among whom, at the most, a very few were living a Christian life, while the masses were unconverted. In Warren county the German people were sunken in vice, but according to their profession, either Catholics or Lutherans. The former pastor of the church was said to have been a *regular* (!) drunkard, and their organist, a German who had served in the army of Napoleon Bonaparte, led them in dancing oftener than in worship.

"On my second visit to Warren, during preaching, one day, a respectable man by the name of Gross, fell to the ground as if struck by lightning, but it was the lightning of the Word. He began to pray and struggle, and ceased not till he had found peace and pardon in Jesus, and received the life of God. I made it my duty to visit rich and poor, and all classes and conditions alike, and consequently had plenty of visitors at my preaching services. At these services many were convicted. It seems to me that my personal visitation contributed more to that glorious revival than all my preaching."

"When I visited Warren the fourth time, I remained six days, preached nine times, and held four prayer-meetings. Upon this a glorious work of the Lord took place. Scoffers, persecutors, and despisers of God, broke down together under the Word of God, like trees in a cyclone. But there were also respectable moral characters among the penitents, ranging from men and women sixty years old down to children of ten years. The drunken parson could not accomplish anything against us, and so the German fiddler got his chums together to dance and carouse and drink, whenever the penitent souls met for prayer. This was done to prevent others from becoming concerned for their souls, and to disturb religious worship. The fiddler, who was the leader of the opposition, at length ventured into my meeting one day, and listened to the preaching of the Word for a while. He was arrested on the spot by the Spirit of God, and the great deep of his soul was broken up. He awoke suddenly from the long sleep of sin, and in agony cried out in the midst of the congregation, 'O Seybert, pray for me!'

"This naturally made a profound impression upon those present. It occurred to all that piping and dancing would soon be at an end now, for the ringleader himself lay on his knees, pleading for mercy. In consternation his whilom comrades whispered one to another, 'Behold, he prayeth.' He soon obtained pardon. Hallelujah!

"On another occasion, one of the most highly re-spected men in the community came to my services to make disturbance. I preached with much liberty of the eternal love and compassion of God in Christ Jesus, and our moral persecutor was struck by the Word of the Lord, and began to melt like wax. At the next service he came as a penitent, and in the presence of a large congregation, fell upon his knees in great distress of soul. He cried mightily unto God for salvation, and obtained it, being followed soon thereafter by his whole family. Two of his sons afterwards became ministers of the Gospel in the Evangelical Association. [This was Jacob Esher. One of the sons of whom Bishop Seybert here speaks, is Bishop J. J. Esher, who was then and there con-verted at the early age of eight years.] For all this we give everlasting praise to the King of kings.

"During this blessed year, the wicked world and the devil did not treat me very civilly either. The boldest falsehoods were circulated about me again, to awaken suspicions and prejudices among the peo-ple against me, and to destroy my influence upon my field of labor. They brought up the most shameful slanders, charging me with being not even virtuous and chaste. Several times things came to such a pass, that I thought it necessary to confront them with living witnesses in my favor, thus putting the adversary to shame. After this, certain sons of Belial started the tale that I had cheated my brother out of a sum of money. But I was not slow in writing to my brother three hundred miles distant, and soon received in reply a perfect vindication in writing. Then these Philistine busy-bodies said I had left a wife and children somewhere between Philadelphia and Lancaster, Pa., whereas I represented myself as a single man here in Warren and Erie counties. Upon this I wrote home again without delay, in answer to which a document was prepared, stamped with the county seal, and sent to me signed by twelve of my former neighbors and by a Justice of the Peace. This paper declared me to be an honorable citizen, and so the mouths of my persecutors were also stopped on that matter. The people were now ready themselves to defend me from these attacks. A so-called Reformed preacher had circulated the above falsehood with great industry, and it was necessary for the cause and the church which I represented, to vindicate the integrity of my character in this strange land. Thank God, that I was enabled to do it! At another place my enemies said I was a drunkard. This I thought may prove itself. They also asserted that I professed to be entirely pure and holy, and had not committed a single sin in eight years! In short, the pack of lies was too great to repeat them all, and too ridiculous to deserve attention. In spite of all, the Lord's work prospered most gloriously under the hand of his poor servant. For I wanted only to please and honor God and help my fellowmen.

"I have now served one year as a missionary on Erie mission, and have succeeded, by the help of God and in spite of the devil and all opposers, in opening twenty new preaching places, and have received one hundred and twenty-one members into the church, of whom at least one hundred were soundly converted during the year. I traveled on horseback a distance of three thousand and eleven miles, preached two hundred and eighteen times, and founded seven societies in which the Lord is worshipped in Spirit and in truth. To God alone be all the honor!

"I am happy on my way to conference. It is the last of May, and nature has donned her brightest robes. The fields are carpeted with green and decked with flowers of lovliest hue; the air is laden with odors sweet and trembles with the melodies of feathered choirs. It being locust year, locusts by the million join in repeating with trembling voices their 'Pharao'! O how unspeakably great is our God. How brightly His wisdom shines, His beauty and His power in all His works. Therefore praise Him, ye heavens, and, thou earth, bend in worship at Jehovah's feet! Amen."

Such is in brief the history of the first regular missionary enterprise of the Evangelical Association. It epitomizes our experience everywhere—the opposition of dead and formal churches leagued with that of the ungodly sons of Belial. It also augured the general success and prosperity that we now see attending our missionary efforts both at home and abroad. And what an inspiring as well as instructive example Bro. Seybert left his successors, the hundreds of missionaries who have gone out since and will yet go out under the auspices of the Evangelical Association!

In connection with this revival at Warren, Bro. Seybert in his subsequent travels frequently related the following alleged incident, when engaged in animated conversation in some domestic circle. We give it as he related it, leaving the gentle reader to form his own opinion of the matter. The date of the occurrence is Warren, Pa., April 1834.

One evening while the families Arnet and Gross were absent at prayer-meeting, their children, six in number, engaged in a childish prayer-meeting at home. The eldest of the group was 13 years of age, one was 12 and the youngest was 7. After their exercises had continued for some time, the youngest of the group, in some unaccountable way, became offended, and instead of praying, it mocked the others, finally going under the table in a sulking manner. What was the astonishment of the others, when, looking under the table, they saw an immense black dog, with unusually large, yellow, glaring eyes, sitting by the sulking child. They were certain that no dog was anywhere in the house. Presently one of the children said, "This is the devil!" The beast now walked around the little group, about the room, and pulled their clothes, and leaped upon the table. It also went into the cupboard and rattled the dishes. With all this the children experienced no terror nor alarm. One of them was unable to see the apparition. They continued their devotions. The father of the family, named Conrad Gross, soon returned, but noticed nothing unusual upon entering the room, except the vehemence and positive manner with which the children asserted that the devil was in the house. "Oh, pshaw!" he exclaimed, "away with such nonsense! what would the devil want in our house? — How does he look?" "Yes, yes," they cried, "he is certainly in the house — and it is a dog with great yellow eyes." But Mr. Gross could see nothing, though the children described the dog, and his movements, and pointed to where they saw him. Unable to silence the children, Mr. Gross finally said, "Let us pray," fell upon his knees and undertook to pray. Suddenly a thick, dark mist,— an impenetrable film, gathered before his eyes. Upon this he arose, opened the door, and in an imperative tone exclaimed: "Satan, I adjure thee in the name of Jesus Christ, depart from my house!" The children declared that they now saw the dog walk out at the door, and then slowly leave the house. Mr. Gross himself, however, saw nothing extraordinary, save the mysterious darkness that seemed to hold his eyes.

On Bro. Seybert's return from this missionary exploit, the conference, which met in New Berlin, June 2d, 1834, elected him Presiding Elder for the third time, and assigned him to duty on Canaan district. His circuits were Schuylkill, Lebanon and Lancaster. At this session he served as Secretary and also preached the ordination sermon. He began his work this time with great delight. He had pleasing anticipations of again meeting many of his spiritual children whom he found it so hard to leave on the expiration of his first term of service on that district five years before. He was also anxious to learn how faithful they had been in the cause of Christ. Though he never had much occasion for grief on account of apostasies among his converts, yet isolated cases of this kind also occurred in his experience. And every minister of the Gospel knows what a deep, poignant grief it causes the heart, to see the souls whom we have wrested from Satan's grasp, falling away again to the weak and beggarly elements of the world. At all events, Seybert was glad for the privilege of taking care for a while of his own gathered sheaves.

On Sunday, June 15th, he preached at the house of Mr. Henry Mertz, a man prominent among his fellow citizens, both in State and Church. Mr. Merz and his family had been soundly converted and had joined the Evangelical Association, together with some other families. The little flock had to suffer persecution, however.

Monday Seybert came to Upper Milford, Lehigh county, where he preached at Andrew Yeakel's,* who had formerly been a Schwenkfelder preacher, but had joined our Church, after his conversion. The power of God came down upon the people at this service, already during the opening prayer, in such a measure as to cause a tremendous commotion. A vigorous revival had been in progress for some time there, but also vigorous persecution. Wives forsook their husbands, solely because the latter began to pray, and parents drove their children from

---

* Uncle of Ex-Bishop R. Yeakel.

10

home, for serving the Lord and becoming religious. Public worship was frequently disturbed and violently interrupted, utterly regardless of the religious liberty which the laws of the land vouchsafed to us. Evangelical preachers were often shamefully treated on the street. Their life was openly threatened, if they would not leave the country. The rabble threatened to stone them, to club them, and even to shoot them. But the early preachers of the Evangelical Association, had the material in them that makes martyrs. They cared but little for the threatenings of Satan's vassals, and went bravely on, in the name of the Lord. And no one was killed. There was much more bravado in the enemies of the cause, than courage.

His forty-third birthday Bro. Seybert noted in the journal as follows:

"July 7th, 1834. To-day I am forty-three years old. Through the mercy and grace of God alone I have reached this age, and I am therefore resolved to serve my dear Lord with soul and body as long as I am permitted to live. But one thought occurs to me to-day which saddens me, and that is, that I lived in an impenitent state until I was nineteen years of age.

"This evening I had services near Lebanon, Pa., and we were blessed with a marvellous manifestation of the eternal life of God. The friends from town are still shouting on their way home — I hear their voices now praising God on the highway, while I am writing this journal entry. The air is so clear and still this evening too. I guess the Lord has bidden the wind to be still, so that his praise may be heard afar!"

July 20th, Bro. Seybert arrived at a Pennsylvanian village called Nazareth — a name, forever linked with the name and fame of Jesus, in the provincial *sobriquet* which derision gave him. The village had been founded by the Moravians, and had formerly been in good repute for the industry of its citizens, their good behavior, and an educational institution which they maintained in their midst. But at the time Presiding Elder Seybert visited the place, it had degenerated both socially and industrially, as a result of moral decay and a decline in religious interest. He was served there much as his Divine Master was served at Bethlehem: "there was no room for him in the inn". However, a gentleman named Werner, residing near, received him, and through his mediation Seybert gained access to the people and was enabled to lay the foundation of a good work.

In the Summer of 1834, a remarkable camp-meeting was held in Schuylkill Co., Pennsylvania, of which Bro. Seybert writes:

"During this meeting Bro. Henry Fisher (at one time editor of the Evangelical Messenger, the English organ of the Evangelical Association, in which position he died), preached one afternoon in such power that a general commotion took place over the entire encampment, and the convicting energy of the Spirit and of the Word was manifested to an extraordinary degree, especially when the invitation to come to the altar of prayer was given. The people cried out in loud lamentations, fairly staggering toward the altar, pleading for mercy in their helpless distress. Even in the outskirts of the audience, the spiritually wounded began to tremble. and quake, and cry out. They wrung their hands in agony, or smote upon their breast, wailing, 'God, be merciful to me a sinner'. In the multitude sat a woman with a child in her arm, who trembled and wept so sorely in her appalling spiritual grief, that by-standers relieved her of the child while she tottered toward the altar. The sisters encouraged her all they could, until she found peace in the Redeemer. She was wondrously changed. The very fashion of her countenance was altered. So signally was the power of God displayed, that many sensible persons who were cool enough to observe, declared that *the earth trembled*, especially on Friday night." And why not? Do we not read in the sacred records, that on a certain day the disciples of the Lord were assembled together in prayer, and "the place was shaken where they were assembled"? If then, why not now? Is the Lord's hand shortened? It is certain that human spirits are often made to tremble under the influence of the Holy Spirit of God.—Is it harder, or more miraculous for God, to shake the earth?

During this year Bro. Seybert held seven "big meetings", and five camp-meetings; traveled four thousand four hundred and six miles; visited very many families and prayed with them; christened many children and baptized many adults, besides preaching nearly three hundred times, and administering the Holy Supper of the Lord to many saints.

It was his privilege also, again to visit the Mahantango and adjacent valleys, where he had such memorable experiences on his first visits during his former term on this district, and witnessed with his own eyes the fulfillment of the prediction he made to the old German lady five years ago. There was such a change in the moral and social state of affairs, that the very angels of God must needs have rejoiced over it. He now had so many seals to his ministry, that the last lingering shadow of doubt upon that subject vanished from his soul.

On this trip he made the acquaintance of three European Catholics, of whom one was already converted. He speaks of him as "a talented man, not only learned, but converted", (*gelehrt und bekehrt.*) who also united with the Evangelical Association. The second of the three was in distress of soul and was seeking the Saviour. The third was also touched by the grace of God, and is convinced of the need of conversion.

Beyond the Blue Mountains in Pennsylvania, there was a place called "Paradise", which Bro. Seybert visited during one of his bold exploring expeditions in March, 1835. Like all earthly Edens, since the first one was destroyed, this was a Paradise but in name. The spiritual darkness was something awful, when Seybert first came there. There was no need to wish for the night to perpetrate deeds of darkness; the day was as the night, and both alike inky black.

Seybert planted the banner of the Cross there, and before its light the idols fell, the darkness fled, and vice crawled into caves to hide for shame. To his efforts under the blessing of God, it is due that "Paradise" was "regained".

The General Conference assembled May 25th, 1835, in Orwigsburg, Pa. All the Elders of the Evangelical Association were members. The delegate system was not introduced until the General Conference of 1843. The present session transacted very important business. It arranged for the publication of the "*Christliche Botschafter*", the first periodical of our church, and now the oldest, largest and most widely circulated German religious weekly newspaper in the world, having a circulation of nearly twenty-five thousand subscribers, at this writing. The influence of this paper in the development of our denominational interests is second to that of no other agency in the church. This General Conference also ordered the establishment of Sunday-schools. This order was executed forthwith in very many places. Before the close of that year, Sunday-schools were organized in the cities of Lebanon, New Berlin, Orwigsburg and Philadelphia. It has been a disputed point, as to where the first Sunday-school of the Evangelical Association was really organized. The school at Philadelphia was the first to publish a report, but the evidence seems to give priority to the school at Lebanon, where a Sunday-school had already been organized in 1832.

The chief matter to be chronicled here, however, is

the discussion in this General Conference, as to whether these Sunday-schools should be exclusively German, or whether the English language should be allowed to be introduced in them. In the debate Bro. Seybert strongly favored exclusively German Sunday-schools, principally on the ground that "the English speaking people were already amply provided for in this particular, by other churches. The Germans are in special need. Our church should work among them, and for their benefit. If the Evangelical Association does not help the Germans in the United States, nobody else will. God has commissioned the ministry of the Evangelical Association for the very purpose of bringing the Gospel with its light and life to the neglected German population of this country."

The Eastern annual conference met June 1st, 1835, in Lebanon. There were forty-five itinerants present. Seybert says it was the most blessed session he had ever attended.

One evening soon after, Bro. Seybert had an appointment at the house of a brother whose wife was opposed to having religious services there, having once even forsaken her family on that account. But seeing her husband would not yield to her wishes, she presently returned. On this particular occasion, Seybert arrived there sometime before dark, his horse was stabled and fed and he invited to the house. He shook hands with his customary cheerfulness with all the family, but the woman of the house acted very coolly toward him, and by no means welcomed him. One of the daughters was sick in bed, and the father and Seybert sat in the sick room conversing on the things of God. In the midst of conversation the wife and mother abruptly entered the room and began to abuse her husband in a most shameful manner, in the presence of her sick and feeble daughter. She precipitated a perfect torrent of abusive slander on "these converted people", and employed unrepeatable expressions regarding the preachers, asserting that she was determined not to tolerate their visits to her house any longer. Seybert said nothing. Her husband began to weep bitterly under her disgraceful attack, when she retired from the onslaught, but in a few minutes returned, scolding because these meetings caused her so much trouble. Upon this, Seybert arose and went to the house of a neighbor, who was also converted, where he got supper. Evening came at last, and in the gloaming he walked alone into a retired nook in a near field, asking God to stand by him in the performance of duty. The woman had appointed her neighbors, who were like-minded with herself, for the purpose of helping her to create disturbance in the service. But God's people met in a prayerful spirit, and the Lord blessed His Word mightily. Bro. Seybert preached from the words: "The Lord hath done great things for us, whereof we are glad". It seemed as though Satan were bound with chains, he says, and the ungodly were quiet; the Lord had thrown a spell upon them, and the "little flock", to whom is promised the inheritance of the Kingdom, had a most precious waiting before the Lord. Next morning the woman was in a better frame of mind.

During this Summer, Bro. Seybert attended a number of successful camp-meetings.

August 10th, 1835, he began a camp-meeting at Jacob Eby's, three miles south of Lebanon, Pa. Bro. Seybert preached the first sermon on Monday evening, and the Lord so blessed his people during the preaching of the Word, that to the right and left, there arose a great demonstration of shouting and weeping for joy. This became so general and so loud, that he finally ceased preaching and sat down himself, quite oppressed with the weight of glory. His heart was too full for utterance, and his voice could not be heard. He thought, "Let the children of God, who suffer so much persecution for righteousness' sake, rejoice; then let those who have been led to Gethsemane and Calvary, march down Olivet with shouts, and songs and hosannas to their King". —There was a just recompense accorded these people in these extraordinary out-pourings of joy, which they experienced in the midst of their fiery trials.

On Tuesday, Bro. Charles Hesser preached, and God's Spirit wrought wonders in the deep conviction of sinners. The saints were overcome with holy joy, and sinners cried for mercy with loud lamentations.

Wednesday it rained, but the work went on. Prayer-meetings were held in various tents all day, in which sinners were converted, and ever and anon shouts of victory went up.

Friday morning Bro. Seybert was to preach a sacramental sermon, but he says it was hard work. He seemed to lack the "inflowings of the power of the eternal world of light", and felt, oh, so poor in spiritual power. Still, with all the misery, the Lord so blessed His Word, that among the throng, several persons began during the sermon to weep over their sins. Afterwards nearly two hundred joined in the communion of the Lord's Supper. During the afternoon and evening of that day, there were such touching demonstrations of godly sorrow as are seldom witnessed. There were many conversions during this camp-meeting. Sixteen preachers were in attendance, and thirty-eight tents were occupied.

August 17th, he began another camp-meeting near Orwigsburg. It again fell to his lot to begin the meeting, and the altar was crowded with seekers of salvation, already at the first service, many of whom received pardon the same night. Upon this he exclaims: "What do you think of that?"

On Tuesday also the slain of the Lord were many.

Wednesday morning they were obliged to abandon preaching altogether, and labor with seekers. But in the afternoon Bro. Hesser preached a most convincing sermon on repentance, in consequence of which the number of the convicted was greatly increased.

Friday they had such a wonderful time, and the throng of seekers was so great, that Bro. Seybert says, "one might almost be led to think the strait gate might be over-crowded". For this reason this meeting was continued over Sunday.

Sunday morning he preached from Jer. 8, 21:22 —
one of his favorite texts. The gracious Spirit continued to work all day mightily. The spiritual tide
did not ebb and flow, but remained high. The meeting that evening had to continue all night, until the
morning dawned. It was so impressive and powerful,
that Seybert never forgot it.

Monday, August 31st, he held the third camp-
meeting for this season at Bro. H. Heppler's in
Mahantango Valley. Twenty-four tents were in the
circle, one of which was occupied by a Lutheran
minister and his family, whose wife was a member
of our church. Things have greatly changed since
the time Seybert was to have been shot dead for the
preaching of the Gospel there!

Wednesday afternoon of this meeting, the number
of penitents was so great, that the service continued
uninterruptedly until next morning. Many professed
to have been saved, and the shout of victory was
great.

In the Fall Seybert was taken sick with a fever.
His physician was successful in restoring him speedily, under the blessing of God, but peremptorily for-
bade his patient to exert himself for some time, which
he felt unable to observe. Seybert says of this:

"I am not to preach as yet. The doctor scolds me
for it. But God in heaven has blessed my sermon,
in spite of the doctor's grumbling. I havn't suffered
any harm, either. The fact is, I must work while it
is day, for the night cometh when I can no longer
work. When I once get within the gates of the New

Jerusalem, then I will rest. But so long as I sojourn in Mesech and dwell in the tents of Kedar, I have no rest, for it is written, 'work out your own salvation, with fear and trembling ever.'"

CHAPTER VII.

SELF-DENIAL AND INTREPIDITY.

In November, 1835, being in Philadelphia, Bro. Seybert heard of a number of German families living near the glass works at Waterford, New Jersey, who were without a preacher, and resolved to visit them. He was warmly received among them, preached several times, and baptized their children. His preaching affected these people profoundly, and he had reason to believe that his visit was not in vain. Then, leaving his horse in Waterford on account of the expense of its maintenance in Philadelphia, he returned on foot to the latter city. The distance was twent-eight miles, the roads were muddy and the weather rainy and stormy, but nothing of this kind deterred him from meeting his announced appointments. He arrived in the evening very tired. The next day he visited a large number of families, preached, and walked back to Waterford.

January 14th, 1836, he had an appointment in Mahantango Valley. To reach it, he was obliged to cross Mahantango mountain, which is hard to cross at any season of the year, and in any direction you may take. This time, when a deep snow covered it, the undertaking was really a formidable one. But he was determined not to miss his appointment, if there was any way to reach it. Finding his horse unable to carry him through, he alighted and walked ahead of him, slowly pushing his way through the white masses of the snow. Over and over again he was obliged to gather up all his strength, and then only slowly could he go on, step by step. When he finally reached the summit of the mountain, however, he saw at once the impossibility of getting through by the road. He had come up from the south, and the snow was much deeper on the north side of the mountain, besides being much more drifted. He called a halt. What was to be done now? He looked about, but there was none to help. Finally he hit upon a plan. Turning his face straight in the direction of his destination in the valley below, he started down through the woods, walking ahead of his horse. By that sheltered route the snow was not so deep and less drifted, but it led over rocks, logs and ravines, all concealed by the snow. Seybert and his horse toiled through underbrush and thorns, and stumbled over obstructions in great weariness. The remembrance of that trip made him shudder whenever he recalled it. But he finally reached the valley in safety, where he turned into the road again. Exhausted beyond measure, and tired enough to die, he reached the appointment, and a soul became penitent in the meeting that night.

The same month he again preached in Manheim, his native town. While there, he spent an evening with his life-long friends, Bro. F. Danner and family. There was also another friend and his wife there visiting. While talking with these friends, a neighbor came in, who was once converted, but had since backslidden, and had become very worldly. As soon as Bro. Seybert saw him, he felt a peculiar interest in him, and took pains in trying to bring him back again, into the Kingdom of God. He pointed out the dangerous situation in which he was, and asserted that the Lord would have mercy even upon apostates, if they repent and return to Him in sincerity and truth. After a few moments of silence, Seybert began to sing a hymn, and the friends joined him. They knelt in prayer, and he was enabled to pray with much fervor for the poor backslider. Rising, they sang another hymn, and, glancing at the man, Seybert saw he was deeply moved. Upon this he suggested prayer once more, and prayed for him still more fervently. This broke the man down, and he began to weep bitterly, and also began to pray for himself again. This brought the visitors upon their knees in great distress of soul, so that Bro. Seybert now had three penitents on their knees, with whom Bro. Danner and he labored until two of them found peace and pardon. This gave him great relief. All day he had been severely tried, while sojourning in his native place, because he thought it impossible for him to do any good there. For had not the Master himself said, a prophet is not without honor, except in his own home, and among his kindred?

Feb. 20th, Bro. Seybert began a two days' meeting in a newly erected meeting house in Lancaster Co , Pa. There were still some shavings and other loose pieces of lumber lying under the floor. Two vicious persons set this on fire during divine service, and while the house was filled with people. They had evidently hoped to accomplish a double purpose; namely, to disturb the service, and also to destroy the building. Whether accidentally or providentially, two brethren went out during service and thus discovered the fire. Without giving any alarm, these brethren with great prudence quietly put out the dangerous fire, without in the least disturbing the devout congregation of worshippers, who remained unconscious of the peril through which they passed. Bro. Seybert remarked: "Thus the devil's fire *under* the building was put out by the brethren, but the fire of the Lord burned mightily inside. *Hallelujah!*"

The Eastern conference had, up to this time, held its sessions about the first of June each year, but the last session of the General Conference changed the time to the last of March. This change made that conference year only ten months long. Seybert says:

"Through the mercy of God I have completed another conference year, which, though it was only of ten months duration, has resulted in more fruit than many longer years. Our Church, despised by men and hated by the devil, has taken a long step forward. On my district, the Lord has blessed us marvellously, bringing many sinners to repentance, under the preaching of His Word, which is a light to shine, and the power of God unto salvation, unto every one that believeth. It has pleased the Lord also to bless greatly my own feeble service, to the good of the Church and of the world."

In July, he visited Doylestown, the county seat of

Bucks Co., Pa., for purposes of exploration. He
called on a Reformed minister, who received him
kindly, but no door seemed to open for him, to
preach in the place. He therefore started out
through the country, in a north-westerly direction,
and found entertainment at the home of a man
named Albright, about eight miles from Doylestown. Next day being Sunday, Albright and his
guest attended a meeting of the Mennonites. It was
soon conjectured that the latter was a preacher, and
accordingly the minister of the congregation asked
him to preach for him "Certainly," he replied, "if it
is agreeable to you." "O yes," said the preacher,
"but will you also feel free to preach in our meeting?" "Under such circumstances I shall feel easy,"
was the response. The minister opened the service
with some introductory remarks and prayer, and
Seybert afterwards preached. It was a very solemn
hour. He was enabled to speak with great freedom,
and the people were deeply moved, so that they
declared that they had never witnessed such a scene
as that which followed. The Mennonite preacher
then kindly announced Bro. Seybert's appointment in
a neighboring school-house for that afternoon, took
him along home with him for dinner, and accompanied
him to the afternoon service. They afterwards visited
a member of the Mennonite society, who was sick,
where he was permitted to do the work of a pastor.
He was now obliged to stay all night with his newly
found friend and next morning they parted in great
peace."

11

September 18th, he baptized seven persons, "three of whom were baptized *under* water, and the other four *with* water. The baptism of the Holy Ghost came down upon *all* the subjects of baptism on this occasion, both upon those who were baptized *with* water and upon those who were put *under* the water. The Lord made no difference between them, nor showed any special favor to those who were immersed. The saints who were present were also greatly blessed."

Among the subjects baptized was a woman who, before her conversion, was noted for her fondness for display. But already during her penitential struggle she broke away from this vice and threw off her articles of useless adornment, burning them in the fire. One of the brethren whom he baptized that day, had been for fifteen years a very wicked man; an auctioneer by trade. He was very proud and vain, but since his conversion he had been remarkably humble, bore a modest demeanor and led a sober life.

About this time the work of the Evangelical Association in the Quaker City began to obtain a solid foot-hold and to enjoy remarkable prosperity. The difficulties with which it had to contend, however, were very great indeed. The attacks of its enemies were not vulgar and barbarous, like those in rural communities, but insidious and polite and for that very reason the more dangerous. The enemy appeared in the garb of refinement, civilization and culture, charming the public mind into carnal security.

And yet the Lord prospered Zion. Within two months above twenty-five persons joined the church, and the Spirit of the Lord continued to awaken the people.

The chapel became too small now, and it was found necessary to erect a more commodious house. The newly organized Sunday-school, which met twice each Sunday, numbered a hundred pupils. Not long before this, Bro. Seybert held a five days' meeting there, during which from twelve to twenty penitents were at the altar of prayer at every evening service, and every evening five or six found peace in Jesus. At one of these services it was very rainy and dark, and but few were present. But among the number was a lady ninety-four years old, who had to gather up all her feeble strength to get to the house of God. She listened very attentively to the preaching of the Word, which smote her with deep conviction, so that she tottered forward to the altar of prayer. The friends prayed with and for her, and pointed her to the promises of God, encouraging her to believe. Presently her faith laid hold of Jesus, and she obtained peace. This was indeed coming at the eleventh hour. This woman had spent almost a century in the service of sin, without God and without hope in the world, and now that the portals of another century or of another world were almost ready to swing open, she sought and found mercy at the foot of the Cross. Life's setting sun, after a long and weary day, is already gilding with twilight glories the horizon's western rim, but now the Sun of Righteous-

-ness suddenly rises in splendor on her soul. Thank God. Eternal day begins before eternal night could settle upon the spirit.

Incidents like this were by no means unfrequent in Seybert's ministry, and gave him much delight.

In 1836 he held a most successful camp-meeting near the city of Lebanon, Pa.

The friends prepared themselves for this camp-meeting by fasting and prayer, and came together in the fear of the Lord. There was accordingly no foolish jesting nor trifling conversation. Even while the tents were being pitched, an impressive solemnity pervaded the encampment.

There was no unseemly disputing for the best locations, as is sometimes the case on these occasions. Every one felt that they were on holy ground; that this was the house of God and the gate of heaven. Already at the first service in the evening a number of "backsliders and other sinners" came to the altar, and many were troubled. Bro. Seybert preached from Rev. 2:7, and the cries of penitents became so tumultuous that the sermon was interrupted, and they began to labor with seekers. Finally there was a general "breaking through into eternal life", which occasioned such rejoicing among God's children, that their shouts and songs were heard afar; the hills caught the echoes, and "Lebanon shook with praise". Many were so "utterly filled with the eternal love of God", that they fell overwhelmed with an exceeding weight of glory, as though they had been dead men.

Sunday a great throng was present, and the evening service, which lasted until midnight, was blessed with many conversions.

Monday he baptized a number of persons in the Quitapahilla creek, at which time the blessing of God came in showers upon the various candidates, but most especially upon the witnessing multitude who lined the banks of the stream.

Tuesday the interest of the meeting reached its climax. The solemnity of the occasion was such that the thousands who had come into the congregation simultaneously fell upon their knees, and devoutly joined in worshipping God. It was an impressive and overpowering scene. It was as when Israel on Mt. Carmel, at the sight of Elijah's fire signal, fell upon their faces and cried, 'The Lord is God! the Lord is God!' In the evening of that day the number of penitents was so great, says Seybert, that they could not find benches enough to accommodate them, and were under the necessity of turning the whole auditorium into an altar of prayer. The outcries and groans of poor sinners, mingled with the shouts of God's people over their deliverance rose to an extraordinary height, and continued until the dawn of the next morning. Wednesday forenoon this glorious meeting closed, but to many it will be memorable forever.

Up to this time the Eastern conference had determined the sessions of the General conference whenever the circumstances in their judgment made it advisable or necessary, and it did not meet therefore at regular quadrennial intervals, as is now the case.

The establishment of a publishing house and other important business made a session necessary at this time. Thus it was that only eighteen months elapsed between the last General conference and this. The General conference met in the house of Bro. J. Ferner in Somerset Co., Pa., Nov. 14. Bro. Seybert was present, and preached an ordination sermon on 1 Tim. 4:16.

About this time the custom of holding protracted meetings came in vogue in the Evangelical Association. Previously, the only special meetings that were held were camp-meetings, all-night services, and the so-called "big" meetings, which usually lasted two days. In 1835 Bro. Seybert held a meeting of five days duration in Philadelphia, which proved very successful. This induced him to hold other similar meetings, and he also advised his subordinates to introduce the practice on their charges. Almost simultaneously other ministers of our church began to hold protracted meetings. This method soon found universal favor, and was greatly blessed of God. Protracted meetings have ever since been one of the chief means of revival work.

At the close of 1836 Bro. Seybert penned the following grateful retrospect:

"I am profoundly moved when I consider how God has helped me during the past year in preaching and in all the duties of official administration. The Lord has also greatly blessed me while attending prayer-meetings, in laboring with seekers, in house-visiting when I prayed with families, and often in the secret closet. I am determined to be more faithful than ever. It is my intention to labor on until at evening the Master shall say, 'Call him home and give him his hire.'"

This resolution, frequently repeated, Bro. Seybert faithfully kept. With the last lingering doubt concerning his call to the office of a minister, which had troubled his conscientious soul, behind him, he was now fully launched upon the high seas of his stormy but useful life, steering boldly into the future. Like his great prototype St. Paul, he could look with consecrated scorn upon all the perils and troubles that awaited him, and say, *"None of these things move me."*

Early in 1837 Bro. Seybert held a meeting near Easton, Northampton Co., Pa., at a place he had visited occasionally since 1835. At first progress was very slow, but about eighteen months after he first visited the community and established the first appointment, a "glorious little class" was formed of some twenty genuine Christians. Among others a tavern-keeper who belonged to the Church, was soundly converted. Immediately after he had obtained eternal life, however, he dug out his sign post and took down his liquor sign. His conscience prevailed, and he would no longer consent to sell his neighbors liquid fire, and stopped the iniquitous business at once and forever.

Everywhere Bro. Seybert was among the foremost to penetrate into "the regions beyond", and to open new fields of operation for his church. Like Henry of Navarre his plume was always found tossing in the battle smoke at the front of the line. About this time the thrill of a general missionary enthusiasm was felt in the Evangelical Association; the missionary society of which Seybert was the first President, was formed in 1839; and with this organization a new impetus was given to the work. The work was accordingly vigorously pushed forward in every direction.

The ministry of that day was a hardy race of men. They were men of a high order, men for the times. And even among those grand men Seybert stood far up in the ranks. Though his district extended over ten large counties, yet he was constantly finding new paths, besides meeting all his regular appointments with scrupulous punctuality. He observed with delight the growing aggressiveness of the ministry. With his accustomed imperturbability he said:

"But, according to all appearances, I must bestir myself now, lest I should fall behind. Take notice, however, that I am not to be looked for in the rear ranks in this race. If any one wishes to see me, *let him look for me pretty well in the front, where they are still breaking ice.*"

These are the words of a hero. Here again we find the striking resemblance of our bishop to the apostle, elsewhere referred to. Like Paul, Seybert did not want to build on other men's foundations, or enter into their labors. He preferred to "break the ice" himself, to use a favorite and charmingly characteristic phrase of his. He would rather "plant", and leave some Apollos to "water".

About the time the work in Northampton county, mentioned above, began, Bro. Seybert had a somewhat singular dream, one night, while lodging in the vicinity of Springtown. He dreamed of coming to a place which appeared so dark and forbidding, that he came to the conclusion it must be a "place where Satan's seat is". Presently the dreamer espied a dilapidated saw mill. Under the broken wheel was a very dark pit. The thought occurred to him that this must certainly be the "nest" of the evil spirits. Happening to find a leather strap, he grasped it with both hands and struck into the supposed demoniacal rendezvous. The effort to exorcise the demons was in vain. In his dream he however thought, " I will try it again, for the devil certainly is there". He therefore smote into the dark hole with all his force, stroke upon stroke, until at last the "old demon" came rushing out and left the saw mill. The place upon this became somewhat brighter. Seybert then watched this dragon's pit until it became quite bright, and a stream of clear water flowed out of it, in which there were many fishes, of which he began to catch some; when he suddenly awoke.

Next day he rode farther with his traveling companion, a circuit-preacher. After they had ridden several miles, Seybert suddenly exclaimed with startled surprise, "See! there is the old saw mill!" By way of explanation he proceeded to relate his dream, and what surprised him was, that he had never seen that identical saw mill until he first saw it in his dream the previous night, closing his narrative with the remark that a work of grace may be expected in that vicinity, but not without severe conflicts.

Now note the following facts. The circuit preachers, after preaching in that vicinity for a while, became discouraged, because the people's hearts were so hard, resisted the Word, and persecuted the servants of God. When Bro. Seybert, at that time Presiding Elder on that district, heard of this, he promptly and vehemently urged the preachers there, to continue, and insisted they must by no means stop preaching in the vicinity of Springtown. He declared, the Lord certainly had a work for them to do there, which would certainly be fruitful, though they would meet with opposition in its performance. In compliance with his wish they accordingly continued, and as a result many precious souls were saved, a number of respectable people were brought to Christ, and a glorious reformation took place. The event proved that Seybert's dream was a prophecy, and was fulfilled. This is another illustration of the remarkable prescience with which he was endowed. His faith in his dreams of this character amounted to conviction, and he was seldom, if ever, disappointed in his sanguinary expectations aroused by these dreams.

This Spring the Ohio conference met March 6th in Stark county, and the Eastern conference met on the 27th in New Berlin, Pa. Three preachers located, and five were received into the itinerancy. The salary of an unmarried preacher was $56.40. At this

conference Bro. Seybert preached the ordination sermon. This he considered a very great task, "for on
such an occasion one must preach to the preachers",
he said.

In the Eastern conference there were four districts,
and the Presiding Elders were John Seybert, J. P.
Leib, Philip Wagner and Charles Hammer. The
Presiding Elders of the Ohio conference were Henry
Niebel, Samuel Baumgardner and John G. Zinser.
Of the traveling preachers of the Ohio conference,
Daniel Swartz, Louis Einsel, John J. Kopp and Henry
Bucks remain among us to this day, but all the rest
have "fallen asleep".

The next incident of note we find is the following:
The wife of a certain drunkard attended divine service on the camp-ground near Upper Milford, Pa.
On her return home her brutal husband maltreated
her most outrageously on account of it. About midnight the poor woman came to a neighbor's 'house in
such a condition, that it was feared she would die immediately.

Such cases, where wives were maltreated by their
husbands for attending the meetings of the Evangelical Association, were not rare. The strength of
character which the women of this region displayed,
however, was something remarkable. Some of them
were extraordinarily vicious, and unconquerable.
They rose up like Amazons, as furious and despotic
persecutors of their husbands, if the latter dared to
serve the Lord: On the other hand it is to be remarked, that in this same region, after these wives

saw their folly, they were equally firm on the side of righteousness. They were stubborn on the side of the devil, and immovable when once on the side of the Lord.

Under date of July 7th, 1837, he relates an incident which occurred in Old Berks county, Pa.

Finding his horse was lame, he took him to a blacksmith to have him examined. While he was engaged with the smith, a crowd of ruffians came up, who were profane and in every way all that Satan could wish. One of them was far worse than the rest, and distinguished himself by quite out-doing the rest of the crowd in extraordinary profanity and vulgarity. Seybert addressed him specially, and kindly requested him not to swear so, saying that it was a most abominable vice, and expressed the hope that he would learn to see his sin in all its hideousness. But this well-meant admonition only served to enrage him, and the fellow blasphemed still more. Finally Seybert remarked, "You will get over your swearing when you come to die". Upon this he asked eagerly:

"What's your name?"

"Seybert", was the laconic answer.

"I just thought you were this Seybert," shouted the bully.

Seybert said, "Yes, and I suspect you have been swearing so horribly for my special benefit; but such conduct only reflects on you, not on me."

But now he was enraged! He vauntingly challenged Seybert to a fight, but for this the latter had no relish. Then he began to curse our members, using every vile epithet he could think of, adding with vicious, over-boiling vexation, "and you are the worst wretch of all. You ought to be flayed alive like an eel, and torn to pieces." Seeing it was useless to take any pains with such a fellow, and as it would be casting pearls before a swine to say anything more, Seybert was silent. But he raved on for quite a while, and finally left with his disgraceful rabble.

Bro. Seybert was now "curious to know whether such a desperado was a member of any church." The by-standers informed him that he was a *"Reformed".—*

"Reformed", exclaimed Seybert, "surely he has been through the *devil's* 'reforms chool', else he would be a better man. For God does not reform people like that!"

Near New Holland, Lancaster Co., Pa., a two day's meeting was held May 6th and 7th, where there was a great throng, and good attention to the Word. Deep impressions were made. It was a gracious time. But a rabble of the sons of Belial disturbed the meeting by screaming, yelling, threatening imprecations and throwing stones and other missiles. However, the Lord sent his angel to encamp round about his people, and no harm befell the little flock. Bro. Seybert exclaims:

"Oh, that the teachers of these people cared more for their real welfare! We could then better enjoy the religious liberty which the laws of the land guarantee to us. Nevertheless, there are good prospects of better days. One infallible proof of this is that the whisky distilleries (poison machines) and beer breweries are growing less, and liquor drinking is on the decline. This I call one of *'the signs of the times'.*"

May 13th, being Pentecost, he had a meeting in Washington, Pa., and had a pentecostal time. The people here were almost Gospel-hardened. They had heard the Gospel so often and resisted the truth so long and so stubbornly, that nothing seemed to move them.

But there were also other hindrances to the work. The love of many waxed cold. There were also those who were slaves to fashion, and conformed to this world. Others strove about "non-essential doctrines, things to no profit, such as water-baptism and other forms and figures." "To what profit", asks Seybert, "is such disputing? Formalists and hypocrites should consider that the essential thing about religion is the *kernel* and not the *shell.*"

At Upper Milford an early camp-meeting was held, which continued over Sunday. Some of the friends were concerned lest the meeting should be disturbed by persecutors. But in Lehigh county matters seemed to have progressed to such an extent that they were enabled to hold divine services without being subjected to unlawful molestations. They had fought the battle through.

June 5th he began a camp-meeting in Stone Valley, Northumberland Co. Already the first evening there were conversions. The meeting grew better every day, and on the last two days there was a "sound as of a rushing mighty wind", and there was a great commotion among the *"dry bones"*. Many were filled with life from God, and could shout: *"Life! Life! Eternal life! Hallelujah!"*

During this Summer Seybert also held a camp-meeting near Orwigsburg. At first he "could not *break through* fully." Finally, however, people began to throw off their "silken vanities", and other unbecoming articles of apparel which belong to a life of haughty worldliness, but which have no consistency with a spirit of Christian self-denial. Then the spiritual atmosphere became purer, victory resulted, and a goodly number of sinners were converted.

Of the six camp-meetings which he held, the last one was held in Mahantango Valley. The quick and powerful Word of God "cut deep wounds into many hearts, which only Jesus Christ could heal with the Blood of His atonement". And indeed the Great Physician healed many. The behavior of the people was so excellent as to excite some surprise. No one had a loaded weapon to "shoot this Seybert", as was the case ten years ago.

From these extracts it appears that civilization and the elevation of public morals and the increase of intelligence always follow the preaching of the Gospel. Thank God! The Evangelical Association has never done any community any harm, but the results of her efforts have always been beneficient. If only all her enemies and opposers in ecclesiastical garb could say as much for themselves. Diluted or perverted Christianity is next to Paganism itself, the greatest curse that can befall a nation.

In the Winter of 1836 he had a blessed meeting of five days duration in Lebanon, Pa. A number of penitents were soundly converted. Among others a somewhat notorious character was converted, known as the "great drunkard of Lebanon". For about twenty years this man had led a most dissolute life, so that his family was thrown into extreme distress and poverty, in fact became dependent upon the benevolence of their neighbors. Meanwhile the wife had been genuinely converted, and began to pray most earnestly for the salvation of the wretched man, continuing night and day in unwearying importunity. Besides this she deported herself with great gentleness and exhibited much patience in the sad, distressful lot into which her husband's debauchery had plunged her. The Rum-devil had dragged him to the very portals of hell. But the Holy Spirit reached and awakened him, and granted him repentance unto life. He saw his condition, resolved to cease from his bestial habit, to forsake his besotted companions, and become a Christian. His companions made every effort to tempt the poor wretch back to his cups again, but in vain. He stood firm by the grace of God. Some who professed to be his friends urged him to "break off gradually, for fear it might kill him to quit too abruptly!" But he acted the man, boldly declaring he would rather die than take another drop of the sorcerous poison of hell. He would no longer walk in the counsel of the ungodly, nor stand in the way of sinners, nor sit in the seat of the scornful. He began to associate with God's people, attended their meetings and prayed publicly and privately for deliverance. His penitential struggle was protracted and severe, but God's children wept tears of deep sympathy with the unfortunate man, and ceased not day nor night to pray for his salvation. At last he was gloriously saved and filled with peace and heavenly joy. From this time on he lived a godly, pious life, treated his wife with becoming respect and sincere affection, and provided for his own household like a true believer. He became a remarkable example of what God's grace can do for the deeply fallen.

At last he approached death as a Christian. On his death-bed he was so full of spiritual life and power, that visitors were profoundly moved by his earnest and godly admonitions. Many were led to repentance by this means. When at last his hour came to die, he called his wife and children around his bedside, gave them his parting admonition and benediction, never letting go the hand until each had solemnly promised to meet him in heaven, and then passed peacefully away. Bro. Seybert concludes: "Now, ye drunkards, read, hear and consider this! Remember that though you are on the way to damnation, yet you can to-day be saved as well as this man, if you will quit your drinking, and turn to the Lord. The Lord help you to this end. Amen."

12

CHAPTER VIII.

LAST YEARS AS PRESIDING ELDER.

The work of the Evangelical Association in the city of Allentown began in 1837. The brethren Seybert and Altimos were the first to effect an entrance there. At that time it was a notoriously wicked city. The two missionaries could only secure the cold and inconvenient market house in which to preach the Gospel, while the authorities granted the use of the court house to an infidel for a lecture against Christianity the same day.

Such was the state of affairs in Allentown in 1837. The heralds of the Cross were left out in the cold, but the county hall was opened to a blasphemer of the name of the World's Redeemer. But they submitted patiently, and went to the market place at about ten o'clock, where Bro. Altimos preached from Heb. 13: 12–14. At about two o'clock they went again, and Bro. Seybert preached from St. John 1:11–12. It happened to be election day. Consequently the city was unusually full of people, and there was much disorder. Several of the crowd who gathered in the services attempted to disturb them by loud talking, others by boisterous laughter and all sorts of confusion. However, no attention was paid to this, it was patiently endured, and the preachers were exceedingly glad that some decent people were present, who gave close and respectful attention to the Word, and upon whom it seemed to have had a great effect.

In January 1838 Seybert preached at the funeral of a young lady, who had lived, up to the time of her sickness, without God and without hope in the world. She was the only daughter of a pious mother. There was much weeping on her funeral occasion, as the young lady had a large circle of acquaintances, and her spiritual condition was well known. On her death-ded she lamented her folly, in having neglected to seek the salvation of her soul In the days of health, and bitterly bemoaned her sad condition. Oh, had she heeded her good mother's fervent admonitions, she might have died in peace!

When at length her disease reached a very danger-ous stage, and eternity seemed to be casting its shadows over her, she got out of bed, despite her great weakness, fell upon her knees, and in a strong agony of fear cried unto God for mercy and grace. Hell seemed moved to meet her at her coming, and the pains of death got hold upon her. The effort exhausted her; she sank to the floor, and was lifted into bed for the last time. In this excited condition she went into eternity. Whether she obtained mercy in those last hours, God alone knows.

At Manheim, the following sad incident occurred about that time:

Here lived a man, who in his youth had been addicted to strong drink, and through excessive dissi-pations had contracted a disease in one of his legs which was pronounced incurable. Thinking he would have to die, he stopped his habits of intoxication, began to pray, and after a time professed conversion, upon which he led a pious and upright life.

The young man loved a devoted, virtuous maiden of the neighborhood, who was also well-to-do temporally. As every one entertained confidence that he was saved from his vices, and thought he gave promise of faithfulness and prosperity, they were married. On account of his blameless life the class elected him as their leader, and finally, as he evinced talents of no mean order, he became a preacher, was received into the itinerancy, and in due time was ordained as Deacon.

But he began to decline, soon after, both in temporal and spiritual things. His love waxed cold, and his zeal for the cause of Christ visibly declined. Now and then he was also known to taste of the sorcerous cup again. The conference was obliged to depose him from the ministry and expel him from the church. All efforts to save him were futile. If he did occasionally promise amendment and appear penitent, it was only the mood of the hour and passed away like a shadow. Soon he sank back into the terrible coils of the serpent of the still. In short, he became the chief of drunkards, and one of the most desperate and malicious men in the world. Once he tried to kill a man, but fortunately failed. At another time he attempted to set a house and barn on fire, but was prevented by being discovered. Thus he continued.

He had formerly been a successful school-teacher.

Some one asked him during the Summer of 1837, whether he would teach school the coming Winter, to which he replied, "By next Christmas I shall teach school in hell, conquer the devil, and refute the Almighty with my concordance". Shortly before Christmas he began once more to teach school. What a shame, by the way, to entrust the education of tender youth to such an outcast! But this used to be the custom in those parts, to employ drunkards and all sorts of street loafers for school-teachers. — Soon afterwards one of his neighbors· found him lying helplessly intoxicated on the street, loaded the drunken schoolmaster on his wagon, and dragged him to his door, like a dead brute. In the attempt to walk the few steps to his house, he fell, injuring one of his limbs, but as soon as it seemed sufficiently healed, he returned to the school room. On the way he became very sick, with a disease which in a few days sent him into eternity. *On Christmas he lay in his winding sheet.* Be not deceived; God is not mocked.

During the last night of his life, his chamber was a scene of horror. It was almost impossible to keep him in his room. He declared it full of demons. But he was compelled to take the fearful journey, which without doubt ended in a place of eternal torment where there is no peace nor rest.

At the close of his term of service on Canaan district, Seybert wrote a report, of which we give a brief extract:

"As the time of my departure from Canaan district

has now come for the second time, I feel inwardly constrained to write something of what God has done for us, during these last four years.

"When I came to this district four years ago, I found but three circuits, namely, Schuylkill, Lebanon and Lancaster. In the city of Philadelphia, a feeble beginning had been made in converting the Germans. Schuykill and Lebanon circuits I found in a prosperous condition, but on Lancaster circuit a sad state of affairs prevailed. As my district was small (extending only over seven counties), I spent part of my time, during the first two years of my term, in looking up new appointments, and that in dark regions eastward. The Lord blessed my efforts, and the boundaries of my district were extended about sixty miles farther in that direction.

"We now all united upon the whole district, to extend its bounds in all directions. By Divine assistance we were successful, so that we now have six charges instead of three; in Philadelphia there is a flourishing society and Sunday-school; fourteen preachers now man the field, instead of seven. Thus hath the Lord helped us."

March 28th, 1838, the Eastern conference elected Seybert for the fourth and last time to the office of Presiding Elder. For the second time he was placed in charge of Salem district, comprising Union, Centre, Columbia and Lycoming circuits. As always, this re-election was only an occasion for renewed humiliation. He sought grace anew for his duties. There was no pride of official station in him, neither was he ambitious for promotion.   When work was to be done he knew not himself, as Presiding Elder, but only as the servant of the Lord Jesus Christ.   Ecclesiastical power had no attractions for him.   All his life time he studied the task of the Greek philosopher, "Know Thyself".   And his modest manner showed that he had made progress in that fundamental branch of knowledge.   The real greatness of distinguished men is that they do not feel their greatness.   The strength of spiritual giants is explained by their consciousness of weakness.   Humility is a mark of worth.

Hardly had he arrived on his new district, before he was already exploring new territories.   On one of his exploring trips in the valley of the Catawissa, Seybert was overtaken in the month of April by a fearful storm.   He did not observe its approach long before it overtook him.   Riding listlessly along through the mountain-passes, buried in a deep reverie, he was suddenly awakened from his musings by the low muttering of distant thunder.   Looking upward with his calm blue eyes, he saw the massive clouds gathering overhead, black as night and angry, amid the wildest commotion.   Fierce lightnings leaping from its sombre folds, lit up the ancient mountain heights, as with the gleam of Jehovah's "glittering sword".   The mad howl of the approaching tempest was distinctly heard, and a dismal, hollow roar, as of heaven's artillery, crept along the valleys and rushed through the ravines.   The sky looked inky black, as the lightnings leaped from their ebony sheaths, and crossed swords above the smoking altar-summits of the everlasting hills. The heaped-up folds of the storm cloud threatened every moment to let go its torrents. Seybert rode calmly on in the fearless simplicity which a clear conscience imparts. He reached a human dwelling just as the rain began. Riding under a shed, he fastened his horse, took down his saddle bags and hurried to the house, where he was permitted to enter. By this time the storm was raging in full fury, and he was at first pleased with this timely shelter. He supposed he had found a Christian family, for he had noticed that one of the daughters was reading aloud from a prayer book as he entered. Presently, however, the man of the house became suspicious that his uninvited guest might be one of those hated preachers of repentance, of whom so much was said in those times. And thereupon his face wore a forbidding scowl. Seybert sat at a window, quietly watching the war of the elements without. His contemplative mind saw in the storm the evidence of the majesty and power of his God. To every thunderbolt that came crashing down through the agitated scene, and that sent its echoes rolling along the mountain sides, he inwardly responded "Amen". It was to him a delight to hear how

> "Loud and long
> The thunder shouts
> His battle song".

After the storm had somewhat subsided, the host, who seemed to have been driven like a wild beast into his lair, by the storm, ventured to question

Seybert. (It is notorious that the greatest sinners are the greatest cowards.) He began: "Well, where do you come from?"

"I come from the lower counties and am on my way farther northward to Catawissa", replied Seybert calmly.

"What are you after, anyhow?" was further asked gruffly.

"Why," was the answer, "I am an itinerant preacher, and my business is to proclaim the Word of God, to all who will hear it."

Upon receiving this interesting piece of information, the host, whose horrible suspicions were thereby more than justified, became enraged at once, and began to scold terribly:

"You don't need to come to *our* neighborhood; we have preachers and churches. too. You needn't think we are heathens here. Such cursed tramps as you are, may just keep out of our houses. You are a Methodist, and nothing else."

Seybert here interposed: "I would not be ashamed of being a Methodist, if I were one; but I am not a Methodist"—By this time the man was so angry that Seybert thought it best to leave at once, as he did not consider himself safe in that house. Politely thanking the family for their friendly shelter, which he had temporarily received, he mounted and rode away before the storm was over. He concluded he would rather endure the wrath of the elements, than the storm of anger that was brewing in this man. As he rode away, the monster watched him from the window, grinning savagely, because he was so successful in driving the preacher out into the storm.

At a certain camp-meeting in 1838, a *female drunkard*, in the most loathsome depths of degradation, was converted. She could gulp down incredible quantities of brandy, and was sunken far below the brutes in excessive dissipation. Her husband was already buried in a drunkard's grave, and her two daughters were accomplished worshippers at the shrine of Bacchus. During the meeting this female sot happened to arrive on the encampment in a comparatively sober condition. In all her repulsiveness of person, she took a seat among the assembled worshippers. This brought her under the sound of the Gospel, and she almost immediately fell under conviction. The truth flashed into her benighted soul, and she cried out, *"O Lord, save me!"* God had mercy upon her. He took her feet out of the horrible pit, placed them upon a Rock and established her goings. She is indeed a miracle of grace.

> "Jesus the prisoner's fetters breaks,
> And bruises Satan's head ;
> Power into strengthless souls he speaks,
> And life into the dead.
>
> Hear Him, ye deaf, His praise, ye dumb,
> Your loosened tongues employ,
> Ye blind, behold your Saviour come,
> And leap, ye lame, for joy."

From a report which Bro. Seybert wrote, after his second round on his district was completed, the following incident is of interest:

July 2d he held a camp-meeting in Tioga county, Pa., which was richly blessed of God.

Wednesday was Independence Day, and a volunteer company of militia came upon the grounds in uniform, with martial music and in all the glory of war, to hear a sermon. Bro. Seybert preached a sermon appropriate to the occasion, in which he showed in what civil as well as religious liberty consists, and sought to describe the prerogatives of both. In the evening one of the soldiers fell into distress of soul, cried mightily unto God for the pardon of his sins, until he was translated into the marvellous light and liberty of the people of God, and was fully enlisted in the army of the Lord. Quite a number united with the Association as a result of this meeting. Speaking of the condition of the people in a certain community in Tioga county, he wrote the following sometime during the Summer of 1838:

" When we began our work a few years ago in this region, the religious aspect of society was sad indeed. False teachers and the devil had confused and desolated everything, so that profanity, gluttony, intoxication, Sabbath-breaking and all sorts of vices were terribly prevalent. The passion for drink was so great, that brandy was lugged on their shoulders a distance of twenty miles, over the Alleghany mountains, rather than be deprived of it.

" Soon, however, some of the worst swearers began to pray, and some of the worst drunkards became sober, while some of the most quarrelsome received peace from God and became decent, peaceable citizens.

And the Scripture was fulfilled, saying: 'The wilderness and the solitary place shall be glad for them, and the desert shall blossom as the rose; it shall blossom abundantly, and rejoice with joy and singing.'

"Behold, what the **Lord by His Word and Spirit** hath wrought here! O, ye anointed men and youths, who have been called of God to preach, will ·ye not go out with us into the field against the Philistines which are towards evening and towards midnight! And ye, who have been blessed of the Lord with worldly goods, will ye not open your hands with benevolent deeds and gifts to support the Gospel and for the spread of pure doctrine, when ye see how much good the Lord does through this means! And ye poor, who would be glad to contribute, if you had the means, you can contribute by your *prayers.*—But let *all* pray the Lord of the harvest, that He may send laborers into His vineyard. For truly the harvest is great, but the laborers are few. On the contrary, there are many hirelings and horrible wolves who do not spare the flock."

August 11th and 12th he dedicated a new sanctuary in Union county, Pa., to the service of Almighty God. A large concourse of people was in attendance, and a considerable number of the friends on the district. The Word was preached in power, and made an irresistible impression upon the hearers. Believers were edified, instructed and encouraged, while many became convinced of the need of living a holy life, and were led to repentance. Sunday evening, a wonderful commotion occurred; many wept, not a few praised the Lord, and Bro. Seybert rejoiced that not only had the house been dedicated, but also the hearts of many of those present.

August 20th Seybert began a camp-meeting, during which they were favored with good weather and a large attendance. "Already on the first evening," he says, "we had a good time, but not until Tuesday did we have a perfect victory (*vollkommenen Durchbruch*), when many tears were shed by penitents who wrestled for salvation." The spiritual interest increased to the end of the meeting. On the last night there was much feeling, but on account of the throng, it was impossible to labor with satisfaction with the penitents. In this night several wicked persons undertook to drag from the altar and from the encampment a woman, who, in profound penitential grief, was pleading for mercy. When Bro. Seybert became aware that they were determined to execute their diabolical purpose, he remonstrated, and asked them at least to take the poor soul away in a decent manner. But in vain. They laid ruthless hands upon her, and literally tore her away in a most brutal manner and dragged her off. He remarks:

Here was an opportunity of observing the malice and bitter enmity of Satan and his serpent brood against the Kingdom of God. And this serpent brood are the rulers in Babel and in the kingdom of Anti-Christ. Had they the power, they would tear pilgrims away from the very gates of Heaven and drag them down into hell itself.

This incident occurred in September, 1838, at a camp-meeting in George's Valley, Centre Co., Pa.:

On Friday afternoon, Brother Berger preached on Heb. 2:3. His sermon produced a powerful effect; many people were awakened, and among others a certain woman was so wrought upon by the Spirit of the Lord, that for her there was no alternative but to seek the Lord. She began to tremble and weep. Her husband, who sat opposite her, soon observed this, and, fearing she would go to the altar of prayer, to which he was bitterly opposed, he promptly arose, went over to where his wife was, and took hold of her to detain her. She was just in the act of going forward, when he prevented her. He was not at all violent, but firm. There they both stood, the wife wanting to go to the altar of prayer, the husband keeping her back. In her distress, the poor, sin-sick woman now attempted to get upon her knees, right among the people where they were. But he also prevented this. Upon this, she began in her desperation, to pray standing, leaning upon her husband's arm. Most affectingly did she plead for mercy and for salvation, weeping so bitterly that it became a matter of astonishment how her husband could endure it, especially since he did not seem to be excited nor angry. But there the determined man stood, in the presence of a multitude, holding his penitent wife in his arms, unwilling to let her kneel down even. At last the light of salvation burst in upon the distressed and agonizing soul, and she found the Pearl of Great Price. By this time, however, the stubborn captor himself began to quake; he trembled like an aspen leaf, and tears involuntarily rolled down his hardened face, and it seemed certain that he would have to surrender himself. The probability was that he would sink down with his burden. But he held out. It was observed, however, that as they went home together, he was of sadder countenance than his wife, who was full of joy.

The camp-meetings this year were all blessed with revivals and many conversions. He who walketh in the midst of the seven golden candlesticks, and holdeth the seven stars in his right hand, had not yet forsaken his people.

At the above meeting above fifty were converted, nearly all of whom joined the Evangelical Association, notwithstanding that Bro. Seybert, as related by an eye-witness, urged very strongly and solemnly, that those who did so were called upon *forever* to deny themselves of worldliness and everything sinful, and must solemnly obligate themselves, to live godly lives according to the Word of God. This same witness relates how one day during this meeting, after the sons of Belial had vainly tried to break up the meeting by setting fire to the dry forests, and their fire always went out again, Seybert came upon the preacher's stand in that peculiar, animated hustling way of his exclaiming: "Now the devil's brush-fire is already out again, but God's holy, heavenly converting fire shoots its fervid flames higher and higher with every hour."

For some time he had been urging the various

charges to procure parsonages for their preachers, and he was pleased to see that his good advice was being followed.

During the year Bro. Seybert traveled three thousand one hundred and seventy-one miles, preached two hundred and fifty times, and held six successful camp-meetings.

New Year's day, 1839, he had the joy of seeing a "*Cripple* converted", referring namely to a man by that name. That day he also held a temperance meeting, in company with a Presbyterian and a Reformed preacher. It was somewhere in the Muncy mountains, where, he says, "there was a terrible state of drunkenness. The state of affairs was in fact almost unparalleled. But I am glad that right here five drunkards have been converted, and now live temperate, upright lives. But the number of drunkards is so vast, that I know of no similar locality. Among the many, however, there is one extraordinary drinker, who one Winter was so badly frozen while intoxicated, that both his feet had to be amputated. But it made no difference. Though he is without feet, he continues to drink. This demonstrates the awful power Satan exercises over those who yield to the slavery of drink."

About this time Bro. Seybert was permitted to see some of the glorious fruits of his pioneer labors among the crags of the Loyalsock mountains. It was indeed a wretched region, being almost inaccessible on account of the rocks and mountains. And the people were as rough as the country. But these were no obstacles to him. It seemed as if he delighted in taking the hardest routes and attacking the hardest places, where no one else would go. These places, too, were most in need of Gospel work. Their very wickedness seemed to be an inducement to him. He had great faith in the elevating influence of the pure Gospel, and afterwards it was a great pleasure to him to visit these places and notice the beneficient effects of his labors and of those who followed him.

On a certain tour over the mountains in 1840, in company with the late Rev. Solomon Neitz, his German biographer, and Rev. J. Sensel of blessed memory, Bro. Seybert led them over a long tedious mountain road, through snow three or four feet deep. His companions protested, for they could have taken a much more convenient and comfortable route. "No", he said firmly, "we will go by way of Loyal-sock, for there the people are glad when they see traveling preachers". He had many seals to his ministry there, and took a parental delight in visiting his spiritual children. He had "broken down some of the walls of Babylon" there, and he was going to see the ruins. The work was truly a success. One of the landlords, for instance, complained that he "could not sell one keg of whiskey now, where he used to sell five".

13

CHAPTER IX.

THE EPISCOPACY, ETC.

The General Conference began its seventh session, March 25th, 1839, at a place three miles south-west of Muehlheim, Centre Co., Pa., in Mosser's church. The work of the church was divided into three Annual Conference territories, called, respectively, the "East Pennsylvania," "West Pennsylvania" and "Ohio". These conferences represented work in the States of Pennsylvania, New York, Maryland, Virginia, Ohio, Indiana, Illinois and Upper Canada. Such was the extent of the field of operations. The Evangelical Association had at that time in all eighty itinerant preachers, thirty-six circuits, two stations and four missions. The total membership was about eight thousand.

Thirty-nine Elders, composing this body, were present. Rev. Thomas Buck was President of the Conference, and Rev. Geo. Brickley was its Secretary.

Following are the names of the delegates:

Thomas Buck, George Brickley, John Seybert, Joseph Long, Francis Hoffman, Charles Hammer, Michael F. Mees, Daniel Berger, James Barber, Daniel Kehr, John M. Sindlinger, Charles Hesser, Solomon G. Miller, Samuel von Gundy, John Lutz, Peter Wist, Henry Niebel, John G. Zinser, John

Sensel, Philip Wagner, Joseph Harlacher, John Young, John P. Leib, William W. Orwig, Henry Bucks, Elias Stover, Jacob Boas, John J. Kopp, Absalom B. Shafer, Peter Getz, Aaron Yambert.

On the third day of the session, being March 27th, 1839, the General Conference decided to elect a General Superintendent, or Bishop, and their choice unanimously fell upon John Seybert. This election was a great surprise to him, and of course came to him entirely unsought. It caused him great distress of mind. During the first few months after his elevation to the highest office in the gift of the church, he was known to weep almost constantly. He prayed much in secret, and several times burst out into a flood of tears in public. The more he contemplated the matter, the more crushing his new responsibility became to him. At first he could not endure the thought that he should be charged with the ecclesiastical superintendency over eighty preachers, three conferences, and eight thousand members. Frequently he exclaimed: "Why in the world did they not choose a man who is more suitable?" True, he was perfectly willing to devote all his talents to the work, but he considered them far too insignificant for this great office. The agitation of his mind, during the first few weeks, caused loss of sleep and appetite. Often he lay weeping for hours through the solemn vigils of the night.

It is needless to say that John Seybert did not seek the office. He had "greatness thrust upon him".

Following is the simple journal entry, on the evening of the day when he was so unexpectedly elevated to the episcopal dignity:

"Wednesday being the third day of the session, a Bishop was elected at about five o'clock in the afternoon. This important office unexpectedly fell to my lot, which oppressed me, and on account of the importance of the office, caused me to shed tears. My appetite failed, and sleep left me for a season. Gradually I felt relieved again, and felt disposed to submit myself to God and to my brethren, and formed the determination to serve the church in the faithful performance of the important duties of the office, and to labor for the glory of God and the welfare of my fellow pilgrims to eternity."

It has been a mooted question, whether the distinction of being the first Bishop of the Evangelical Association belonged to John Seybert, or to Jacob Albright. We present below the principal views which have been formally expressed by various authorities in the church.

The late Rev. Solomon Neitz, Bishop Seybert's German biographer, has the following to say:

"According to trustworthy accounts, the honored founder of the Evangelical Association was likewise elected Bishop of the little flock, shortly before his death. Neither is it to be gainsaid that the sainted Albright exercised all the powers of the Episcopal office in the Evangelical Association, from the time of its organization until his untimely death. He changed the appointments of the preachers as he pleased, and arranged everything in the Association according to his own best judgment. However, in important affairs he took counsel of his ministerial brethren. In the proper sense he was really Bishop of the Evangelical Association, from its organization to the end of his natural life, because he used all the powers and exercised all the authority of the office during that time, and did this to a degree of absoluteness, which none of our regular Bishops have had the right to do. But Albright's formal election took place only shortly before his death, and that too before the introduction of a Discipline, and therefore he can hardly be numbered as one of the Bishops within the meaning of the Discipline of our Church, which instrument alone defines the powers of the office. On the contrary, however, Bro. Seybert was the first to be elected under the laws and provisions of our ecclesiastical government, and therefore is *rightfully* called the first Bishop of the Evangelical Association."

Rev. W. W. Orwig, a member of the General conference of 1839, and author of Volume I. of the "History of the Evangelical Association", says:

"Bro. Seybert became the *first regular Bishop* of the Association, according to the rules of the Discipline. As to Mr. Albright, he was elected to this office before the Doctrines and the Discipline had been adopted, for which reason he can hardly be considered one of our Bishops. His case was in every respect an extraordinary one; for even before his elevation to the Superintendency of the Church, which happened but a short time before his death, he exercised, from the very organization of the Association till his death, all episcopal power, transferring preachers at will, and arranging everything in the Association as it seemed best to him, yet not always without consulting his brethren. He was, therefore, in the full sense of the word, *the Bishop* of the Association, exerting a power and influence upon it, such as no Bishop has done after him, and probably never will."

Rev. R. Yeakel, author of the "Life of Albright and his co-laborers", has this to say:

"The first conference, which met in 1807, elected Jacob Albright Bishop. The record of that conference is literally as follows: '4th. Jacob Albright was elected Bishop by a majority of votes, and George Miller was elected Elder.' The 'council' of 1803 already declared Albright to be an Elder, and he was ordained as such at that time. The conference of 1807 elected him *Bishop*. It is clear, from the fact that in doctrine and usage the conference was Methodistical, that they had a Methodistical conception of the word 'Bishop'. Side by side with her the M. E. Church was laboring zealously, with the godly and highly esteemed Bishop Asbury at its head. Yea, on the preacher's License which this conference issued, it named itself 'The Newly Formed Methodist Conference'. Who can doubt that this conference elected Albright Bishop in the Methodist sense? It was not looked upon as a mere title of honor or distinction. Jacob Albright was elected Bishop, and, according to the action of the conference and the terms of the record, is the first Bishop of the Evangelical Association, even though she did not at that time bear the present name."

It seems plain from the statements of facts in which all three authorities agree (and they are the only authorities at this time, who have expressed themselves on the subject), that, while Jacob Albright, the sainted founder of the Evangelical Association, was the first Bishop *de facto*, John Seybert was the first Bishop *de jure*. If it is without dispute that our disciplinary episcopacy is intended to be essentially Methodistic in its nature and functions, then Albright was in the full sense of the word the first Bishop of our Church. — But if there are any fundamental differences between the episcopacy of the Evangelical Association and that of the M. E. Church, then undoubtedly that distinction belongs to Bishop Seybert. And that important differences exist between the office as Albright and the Methodist bishops administered and the latter still administer it on the one hand, and as administered by the bishops of the Evangelical Association under the Discipline, seems conceded by all the authorities quoted. It seems evident furthermore, upon the testimony of trustworthy historical accounts, that Mr. Albright's administration of the episcopal office was practically much nearer akin to the episcopate of the M. E. Church, than to our own regular episcopacy as defined and limited by the Discipline. We repeat then, that Jacob Albright was the first Bishop of our Church *according to the facts*, and John Seybert was the first Bishop *according to the law*.

April 10th, two weeks after his election, the new bishop presided over the sessions of his mother conference. In this conference he had been converted, and by it received into the itinerancy. In its employ he had preached for a period of nineteen years. Now he was its presiding officer and belonged to all the conferences in the whole Church.

After this conference had been successfully held, Bro. Seybert began to feel more reconciled to his new position. It is, however, not to be wondered at, that he was at first oppressed by the responsibilities of his high and untried office. He had no precedent for his guidance, but had himself to make precedents for all time to come, and upon his conception and practical application of an untried law depended in all probability the permanence of the law, and the interpretations of his successors. Besides, he had to travel over an enormous stretch of territory, from Canada to Virginia, from Staten Island (New York City) to the Mississippi River, and this in an age when steam had not been generally introduced as the power of locomotion. It was an herculean undertaking.

Bro. Seybert mentions this first conference session as specially peaceable, and gratefully acknowledges the love and sympathy of the brethren. But when Sunday came, the Bishop shrank from the task of preaching the ordination sermon, and pressed another brother into service to perform that duty.

On the first day of this conference session, the first annual meeting of the missionary society of the East Pennsylvania conference was held. This society was organized in 1838, and was the first of its kind in the Evangelical Association. The General Conference which elected Seybert Bishop, in 1839, organized the Parent Missionary Society, and Bishop Seybert was chosen as its first president. He was in fact the chief mover in the introduction of organized missionary enterprises among us. He exerted a powerful influence in this matter in various ways. First, by his example in zealous missionary activity every year of his ministerial life. Second, by importing and introducing missionary literature. He imported the celebrated *"Basle Missionary Magazine"*, and presented the Publishing House with a very large number of these magazines. In this way the editor of the *" Christliche Botschafter"* had access to the best information to be obtained on the subject at that time, and consequently that organ of the Church presented the great subject in an intelligent and earnest manner. The Bishop also urged the preachers to inform themselves diligently on the subject. These exertions were chiefly influential in leading to the organization of the Missionary Society. This movement, in which Bishop Seybert was the master-spirit, resulted already in the first year in the organization of local auxiliary societies in many places. A considerable sum of money was raised by this means, and the missionary spirit was awakened in many of the young men of the Church.

At the same time, the first regular missions were started. They were four in number: New York City mission, Mohawk mission, Waterloo mission and

Black Creek mission. The two former were in the State of New York, and the two latter in Upper Canada. The East Pennsylvania conference, at its session in 1839, supplied these missions. It is thus seen in what a striking manner Bishop John Seybert was identified with the early missionary plans and enterprises of our Church. It is not too much to say that *he was the father of our missionary societies*, as well as the first missionary of the Church. Soon after his election to the episcopacy, he issued the following circular letter:

"An Appeal to the Ministry of the Evangelical Association.

"Dearly beloved! Inasmuch as the cause of the Lord rests heavily on my heart, and as I feel inwardly stirred and constrained, to devote myself to His work by day and night without ceasing, with soul and body, therefore I desire, through the *Christliche Botschafter*, to encourage our Evangelical friends, and in general all who love God, in this important cause, which also has been done by other brethren, and not without good effect upon sincere souls.

"But, as hitherto appeals have been made principally to the lay-members, I would at this time speak a word to their leaders, and communicate my thoughts and convictions to them in a simple and upright manner, especially since at the present time there seems to be a greater *lack of active ministers* in our Association, than ever before.

"The question first arises: Where lies the fault?

Certainly not on the side of God, who would that all men should be saved and come to the knowledge of the truth. The fault, then, must be with us. Evidently there is a lack of love to God and to our fellow-men in the hearts of many, as also a lack of the Spirit of Jesus Christ, the Great Head of the Church, our adorable Lord, who gave His life for us when we were yet enemies.

"There is an especial want among us of the following qualities, which the Master possessed:

"First: We lack the spirit of humility, which He displayed in the voluntary acceptance of the poverty and obscurity that marked the circumstances of His birth and early career.

"Second: That voluntary submission to the shame of the cross; we are not willing to bear the derision of every fool and devil's imp.

"Third: That willingness to suffer afflictions and tribulations without number, even unto death. Behold the love of Him, who was constrained by his very agonies to pray for His merciless tormentors.

"If there were more of the Spirit and qualities of Jesus among us in general, there would be less of the cares of the world to absorb our time, engage our attention and exhaust our energies; we would deny ourselves of all earthly things, and, without fear of want, without making provision for the flesh, in confidence in Him who upholds the sparrow and hears the young ravens when they cry, and clothes the lilies of the field with inimitable glory, we would surmount all difficulties, in order to execute the command of Christ, to bring to the world the glad message of her crucified Redeemer. There would not be so many unanswered Macedonian calls from Upper Canada and other localities, where they are in need of true shepherds and true preachers of the Gospel. The thousands of poor Germans in the States of Michigan, Ohio, Indiana, Illinois, etc., who wander amid perils in the moral desert in great throngs, like sheep without a shepherd, would in that case soon be fed with the bread of life.

"If the Spirit of Christ were dominant in us, there would not be so many who, in their best years, excuse themselves from active work, and locate, for the purpose of pursuing worldly objects. And many others would forthwith extricate themselves from their temporal complications to enter the Gospel ministry. Oh, it is to be feared, that many bury the pound which has been entrusted to them, and will eventually be adjudged slothful and wicked servants.

"As for myself, I am deeply grieved, because I hesitated until my thirtieth year, before I ventured out into the Gospel field, and because I did not begin earlier to blow the Gospel trumpet. However, with me it was not worldly greed, nor domestic affairs, that kept me back, but natural diffidence and a keen sense of my inability caused me to doubt my call and shrink from the magnitude of the undertaking. But I cautiously avoided temporal entanglements, which might at any time prevent me from going, and waited for a more positive Divine call and better fitness for the office, just as a sea-captain, with sails spread, watches for a favorable wind. Finally, however, my unrest became intolerable; I could no longer contain myself at home, and therefore, with Christ ventured out upon the stormy and tempestuous voyage which my career has proved to be.

"But now, many have located before they reach their thirtieth year. Just when by reason of practice and experience they are properly fitted for this important office, and when, by reason of physical strength and intellectual maturity, they could be eminently useful to the Church in defending and proclaiming her doctrines with ability and manly courage, they take the hand from the plough and look back. — Is not this a marvellous thing? Were these men really sent of the Lord, and have they turned back and become unfaithful? Or did they run without being commissioned from above? Let each examine himself — and the innocent shall be free!

"What then? Who will go into the battle-field where the fight is fiercest, and maintain his position under the banner of Jesus unto death? Who is willing and ready to *die in the field?* Reader, what think you? Do you know of one such? *I* know of *one!* Up, ye laggards! The harvest truly is great, but the laborers are few. Pray ye, therefore, the Lord of the harvest, that He may send laborers into His vineyard."

Bishop Seybert was a most diligent pastor. He improved every moment he could spare for the purpose of pastoral visitation. Nor did it take him long

to visit a family and pray with them. He was known
to make three or four such calls in a neighborhood
before breakfast, and a number of instances are known
where he visited twelve or fifteen families and then
walked twenty-five or thirty miles to an appointment
the same day. In connection with this subject we
subjoin an incident, taken from his journal, which
illustrates his sagacity and also his success in this
kind of work:

When he was Presiding Elder on Salem district,
he made a trip to the State of New York on a certain
occasion to hold a quarterly meeting in Alleghany
Co., N. Y. There was quite a society there, the
majority of the members hailing from Pennsylvania.
The remaining German population of the vicinity
were Europeans, who were strangers to experimental
religion.

Bro. Seybert arrived a few days before the beginning of the quarterly meeting, and, disliking to be
idle, determined to improve these days in visiting the
members and their German neighbors, in the interests
of the cause of Christ. Being a stranger in the vicinity, he enquired of the class-leader concerning the condition of Christianity among the people, and found
latter had little hope of seeing his neighbors converted; stating that they were extremely self righteous
and to make the matter worse, a foreigner living
among them well versed in Scripture, who was their
leader, and to whom they looked for guidance and
example. "This man's influence," the class-leader
said, "is powerful among them, for they believe

his words." Seybert inquired the man's name, and also his residence, and visited him without delay. He found him engaged in cobbling. Seybert greeted him cheerfully upon meeting him, and entered into conversation, which of course he very soon turned into the direction of religion. As the cobbler behaved very affably and seemed quite approachable, Seybert suggested: "You have here a very commodious room, which would be admirably suitable for religious meetings." To this he assented in a friendly manner, and consented that Seybert should begin.

Accordingly Seybert promptly fixed an appointment at his house, and at the appointed time many devout, attentive auditors gathered, upon whom the Word of the Lord had an emphatic effect. His text was Ezekiel 37:14, *"And I shall put my Spirit in you, and ye shall live."* After the sermon the man of the house arose and said to all present: " My house is open for such meetings. You may make appointments to preach here if you want to, and even if I should not be present always."

Meanwhile, the time appointed for the "big meeting" had come, and this gentleman attended the services. He was powerfully moved, fell upon his knees there, and plead fervently with the Lord for the pardon of his sins. The people of God prayed long with him, but he did not on this occasion as yet " break through fully " into the glorious liberty of the children of God. But he continued day and night in prayer and pleadings, in faith in the sacrificial death of Jesus, and presently obtained the pardon of his sins, and was blessed with an overwhelming measure of "Divine power from heaven". Afterwards he wrote Seybert a very agreeable letter, recounting what God had done for him, and averring the certain assurance which God's Spirit gave him that he was a child of God. This gave Seybert great joy, being permitted to see that his well-meant visit had resulted in a glorious fruitage. He fondly hoped 'a sheaf had been garnered for eternal life. This brother was subsequently received into our ministry and labored blessedly.

The conversion of this prominent and influential man, and his testimony to the truth, caused a great sensation among his German neighbors, so that in a short time nearly all were convinced of the necessity of conversion and true Evangelical repentance. Soon there were penitents and new converts in almost every family in the entire community. The aged mother of the aforesaid leading man became deeply penitent and was soundly converted. His wife was converted; his brother and wife were also saved. So that hurried pastoral visit became the cause of a genuine work of grace in which a whole community was brought to Christ.

Bro. Seybert related this under the constraint of love for his brethren in the Gospel, knowing from extended experience that "preachers can do much good for eternity by pastoral visitation". However, it was his conviction that on such calls "they must not forbear to speak to the people of the Lord and

His work, praise the ways of the Lord, and admonish the people to be converted and to live godly lives. They must also pray with them, else no fruit will follow. By these means persons are attracted, confidence in the preacher is awakened and strengthened, so that they will be inclined to attend the preaching services, and the attentive hearing of the Word results in enlightenment. And what impressions the words of the servant of God produce sometimes, when, full of the Holy Ghost and of love for souls, he converses in the privacy of the family circle on the great truths of the Gospel, and then seals the conversation by fervent prayer with outspread hands! Often where this is done in the right manner, there occurs a convulsive sobbing and violent weeping, and the newly sown truth takes root in the mellow, tender hearts, which will bring forth fruit unto eternal life. It may well be said of preachers who perform this duty aright: "How beautiful upon the mountains are the feet of him that bringeth good tidings; that publishes peace; that saith unto Zion: Thy God reigneth."

"But," the Bishop remarks, "it is greatly to be feared that we have done far too little in this particular. There is no doubt that we could be much more useful in our generation, were we at all times fully devoted to this sacred duty. The Lord bless us with zeal and love to prosecute His work as it should be! This is the earnest prayer of your co-laborer in the vineyard of the Lord."

The Bishop assiduously admonished his brethren

14

at every opportunity, to be faithful in this duty.   In his ordination sermons he strongly urged the pastoral obligation upon the young ministers.   He once remarked: *"The old preachers are hard to convert from laziness"*.

Leter-writing was but one of a hundred different methods he employed to enforce his views on this subject in the church.   The following letter he wrote to a young minister.

"Beloved Brother in Christ!—When I was with you last, I greatly rejoiced at what I saw and heard; and for what my heart felt I rejoice even yet.

" See well to it, both in your public preaching and in private conversation among the people, that the newly converted, and all professors of religion, are encouraged to growth in grace, to be separate from the world and its enjoyments, to deny themselves, and that they learn to avoid everything sinful. Strive to induce them by precept and example, to seek holiness and to obtain complete victory over indwelling sin, and that they be zealous in the exercise of godliness.

" See well to it also, that you keep everything in good order in your society, so that your successor on the charge may find delight in the excellent condition of things in the church, which you commit to him, and he will thus be enabled to begin and continue his labor with pleasure.   It is always hard, if a preacher, immediately upon the beginning of a pastorate on a new charge, is obliged to institute investigations, hold church-trials, adjust difficulties and differences, and reconcile quarreling parties, that should have been attended to by his predecessor.

"Take heed, however, unto yourself, that you lose none of your diligence in house-visiting. Do not become a lazy preacher, who is satisfied if he has only preached and afterwards had a good dinner. Experience has taught me that we can at times do more good among converted and unconverted by visiting, than by all our preaching. A preacher with but two talents, who is an industrious pastor, accomplishes more in the vineyard of the Lord, than he who has five talents and is indolent, slothful and frivolous in pastoral work — provided always that the former does not visit for the sake of gratifying a gluttonous propensity, rather than with a desire to pray and labor for the salvation of souls. I tell you, a very feeble instrument faithful and devoted, will accomplish threefold more than a man who on the pulpit makes a great noise, but otherwise is too lazy to feed his flock.

"Another thing, dear Brother in Christ! See to it also, that you do not become a careless, indifferent servant in the service of the Gospel, who neglects his appointments. Oh what a vicious habit that is! I have never known one yet, who ever overcame this sin, after having become addicted to it. Still I believe it to be possible, though difficult to be delivered from this evil. Yes, it is possible, but it will require a *deep* and *thorough conversion*. What think you? I tell you the truth, mark it well. I also have this confidence in you, that you will take pains to be an industrious, sincere and unblamable workman in the vineyard; a workman that needeth not to be ashamed, rightly dividing the Word of truth. Therefore have I written thus to you.

"I heartily greet you and all who may inquire after me, also especially the beloved and affectionate Bro. J. D., who is now afflicted, but who, by his powerful preaching, often richly encouraged me a poor, diffident and weak brother that I was, at the beginning of my Christian experience.

Remember me in your prayers before God.

John Seybert."

Is not this high ideal of an efficient ministry, as outlined by the first Bishop of our Church, worth pondering by the present generation?   Is not his example worth imitating?

Soon after the Spring conferences the Bishop visited the great metropolis, on his first episcopal tour of the East Pennsylvania conference, to inspect the newly established mission there.

May 6th, 1839, Bishop Seybert reached the populous and wicked city of New York, by means of railroads and steamboats from Philadelphia.   Our Church had established a mission there that Spring, in the interests of the neglected German population. He found the missionary well and in good spirits. He had rented a capacious hall in the northern part of the city, for one hundred dollars per annum, well located amidst a large German population.   "These Germans," he remarked, "are partly Roman Catholic, partly Lutheran and Reformed, and partly unbelievers. Indeed a large number were infidels.   Rationalism and skepticism were very prevalent, and the votaries of these isms were immeasurably sunken and depraved. Rationalism was entrenched there. These God-haters and Christ-despisers deride the faith of patriarch and prophet, and pretend to regard the prophets, Jesus Christ and his apostles as deceivers and seducers. For the most part these unbelievers are accordingly profane, slaves to drunkenness and in other respects vicious and depraved. O how the devil has despoiled the vineyard by letting loose the wild boars of false doctrine! What fruit these damnable inventions of so-called culture bring forth!" It is easily seen that the presence and influence of holy and zealous missionaries of the Cross was necessary in such a place. The establishment of our mission there was therefore indeed timely and important. In spite of the depraved and hardened condition of these people, quite a number had already been awakened and enlightened through the efforts of the missionary. Among them some extremely "hard cases", who, the Bishop thinks, might well join in Martin Luther's doggerel:

> "Ich bin ein wahres Sündenaas,
> Ein rechter Sündenknüppel,
> Der seine Sünden in sich frass,
> Gleich wie das Ross die Zippel.
> O Jesu! pack mich Hund bei'm Ohr,
> Wirf mir die Gnadenbrocken vor,
> Und schmeiss mich Sündenlümmel
> In deinen Gnadenhimmel!" *

---

* This I believe to be untranslatable, and therefore simply give it in the original romanized.—S. P. S.

From New York Bishop Seybert returned to Philadelphia, where, he says, one hundred and fifty-two brethren and sisters participated in the celebration of the Holy Communion.

Quite recently there had been another extensive revival there, and it gave him much joy to observe the good work the Lord has already enabled us to do. The influence of the meetings extended from the centre of the city, in all directions, out to the flourishing suburb of Kensington.

In New York and Philadelphia he had purchased some thirty volumes of books, which, besides some other baggage, he was obliged to carry, per *pedes*, a distance of twenty miles, to Lexington, where his horse was. He reached Lexington in an exhausted condition; but through the night he enjoyed a most refreshing slumber.

From here he went to Bucks county, where three years before he had spent such a pleasant Sunday in company with a certain Mennonite preacher. Since that time the work of conversion had spread there, which resulted in persecutions.

One day in May he went to a certain school-house in the afternoon to preach. But the building was locked, and the authorities refused to surrender the keys. In a grove near by, however, stood a large hickory tree, under which he took his stand, gathered his audience around it, and preached to them from the words: *"And the door was shut."* It was an affecting season. Many wept greatly. Three years before he had been treated very hospitably here, and was even permitted to preach in the Mennonite church; now even the school-house was locked against him. But the cause of this change lay in the fact that a revival of religion had since taken place, which reached some of the members of that church. One of their most prominent men had been converted, whose father, and grandfather on both sides, had been Mennonite preachers. This circumstance roused the ire of those who have the form of godliness, but deny the power thereof. They began to bestir themselves, and there was some lively running, riding and fighting, from house to house, to counteract Seybert's influence. It was in vain, however. The man whose conversion had occasioned all this commotion, was a diligent Bible student, remained firm, and became an efficient class-leader.

At Emmaus, Lehigh Co., Pa., which he called a modern Sodom, he was "egged" while preaching.

On the last Sunday in May they had a great day in Allentown. The synod was assembled, and "the devil sent one of his servants up in a balloon." There was much drinking, dancing and carousing. However, a spacious house of worship had already been erected by the Evangelical Association and a revival was in progress, and Seybert preached to a large and attentive congregation.

Many people were convinced of the necessity of conversion, through the earnest and persistent preaching of repentance by our preachers. But they were not willing to " bear the reproach of Christ, and though they became aware of the decay of their churches, and though practical Christianity was unknown among them, they were not willing to come out from among the world for Jesus' sake.   But when a rationalistic freethinker invaded the town, they left their churches to follow after him.   This is the natural result, when persons stifle their best convictions, and refuse to obey the truth, they are easily led into the folly of atheism."

Rejectors of vital godliness become practical infidels.   Those who are called and will not hear, who have the light, but will not see, are given over to the strong delusions, that they should believe a lie, that they all might be damned, who obey not the truth. Ultimately God abandons those who hold the truth in unrighteousness, and woe to that one who is forsaken of God.   The wrath of unrequited love is awful wrath.

In June, 1839, the Bishop stayed all night with some of his spiritual *children.*   Nineteen years ago these people were converted and declare that, as the instrument of their conversion, he was their spiritual father.   He was indeed glad to meet them again, and greatly rejoiced that during these nineteen years they had kept themselves from the "idol of fashion". Upon this he exclaims:

"Oh, how indescribably great is the goodness of my God, who has chosen me, unworthy as I am, as an instrument in his service to lead sinners to repentance.   Forever and ever will I adore Him for this unspeakable mercy."

July 4th he preached in Womelsdorf, on Col.
1:12–14. The ungodly, however, celebrated the day
"quite in their fashion, just as their father, the devil,
would have them keep Independence Day. They
fired guns, they swore, they drank to excess, and
amid hilarity offered unto devils the sacrifice of
pagans."

During the Summer of 1839, Bishop Seybert visited
the work in Upper Canada. Leaving his horse in
Seneca Co., N. Y., he made· the trip to Victoria's
dominions on foot and per canal-boat; though the
Bishop rode one day with a man named Rothschild,
whom he describes as a truly converted, pious, useful
man. The visit necessitated a journey of three
hundred miles, and he completed it with a total
expense of two dollars and eighty-three and a half
cents ($2.83½). This bill is itemized as follows:

Board going,	15 cts.
" returning,	12 "
Fare per canal,	$2.56¼ "
Total,	$2.83½

(Rothschild charged nothing.)

This small board-bill was not caused by "sponging",
but Seybert actually lived three days on a diet of
biscuits and water that cost fifteen cents, and on the
return trip twelve cents. Of course it is to be pre-
sumed, he did not pay for his victuals at the rates
which are charged at a modern railroad restaurant.
If he did, his feat would be one of starvation rather
than economy. This is the way the first Bishop of
the Evangelical Association traveled in 1839.

His traveling company on the canal-boats was anything but agreeable. Joking, fiddling, laughing, gambling, profanity and drinking, were the order of the day. Oh, how heavily the time dragged for this child of God in such surroundings. But when he left the canal-route again and traveled alone on foot, he soon forgot his misery, and became absorbed in contemplating the goodness and love of God, while his eye rested on verdant fields, and zephyrs caressingly cooled his cheeks and wafted to him the perfume of flowers, so that he was made to praise God in joyful songs.

At Galen, New York, he found a glorious revival in progress, chiefly among the Europeans. Recently four Catholics had been converted there. Seybert preached for these people from the words: "When the Lord turned again the captivity of Zion, then were we like them that dream; then was our mouth filled with laughter and our tongue with singing. Then said they among the heathen, The Lord hath done great things for them. The Lord hath done great things for us, whereof we are glad!" During the sermon there was a great commotion. Weeping, praising, shouting were the order. There was a live society of glorious Christians there! *"Hallelujah!"*

August 19th in company with six brethren from the State of New York, he crossed the line, and notes the fact that exactly eight minutes before noon his "American feet stood for the first time on British soil," and he was in the dominions of the Queen of England. Standing there, he fervently and devoutly prayed God to accompany him in his journeys in Canada, and to make him an instrument for the awakening and conversion of sinners also here. That evening he preached his first sermon in Canada, at the house of Moses Bayers, from Rev. 3:17, 18.

CHAPTER X.

VARIED EXPERIENCES.

The year 1840 was spent in traveling over the extensive and sparsely settled territory occupied by the Evangelical Association. The new Bishop held the annual conferences, of which there were for the first time three, and visited quite generally the various charges.

At Warren, Pa., where he had many spiritual children, whom God gave him as the result of his labors among them six years before when, as missionary he first brought them the bread of life, his arrival among them was the occasion of mutual rejoicing.

From here he went to Columbiana district, Ohio conference, and traversed the district, preaching as he went.

Then he went to Wayne Co., and preached at Christopher Felger's, six miles west of Wooster. Then he preached in an unfinished church near Lattasburg or Jefferson. They had a "melting time". Many wept, and others praised the Lord.

Friday, October 25th, he reached Ohio district, the last on his round. Though he did not reach every appointment on the various districts visited, yet he made quite a thorough canvass of the work.

On Sandusky district he attended a three day's meeting, which was specially blessed, for sinners were converted and God's people strengthened in the faith. On Ohio district he found the members engaged with alacrity in the service of the Lord. The newly opened Miami circuit, where the brethren had such great difficulties and were nearly discouraged, was now in a flourishing condition, and extended into the State of Indiana.

The Ohio conference, at its last (and first) session, organized a Conference Missionary Society, and at once sent a missionary to the State of Illinois. Tabor district suffered considerably during the year on account of sickness and through the death of several preachers, creating great gaps in the working force, making it necessary to abandon several new and promising appointments, and resulting in a contraction of the field of operation. However, these gaps were at least partially supplied by the entrance into the conference of a number of young men. Bro. Seybert prayed the Lord would give these young brethren grace, wisdom and unction, so that they may be steadfast messengers of His Word, and not soon quit the field in a demoralized condition, or perhaps with Demas, love this present world and locate from worldly considerations, as had so often been the case heretofore.

This first session of the Ohio conference was held at Emanuel church, in Walnut Township, Pickaway county, six miles north-east of Circleville, on what is now Cedar Hill circuit, beginning May 13th, 1840.

November 29th he crossed for the first time the State line into Indiana, and on the 30th preached in a school-house near Germantown. This was an un-satisfactory service. The crying of children, the howling and barking of dogs, together with the loud talking of scoffers and "sons of Belial", were very embarrassing to the Bishop in attempting to preach, nor could anyone listen with devotion.

Next morning he preached at the same school-house again, with better results. "The devil's imps and the dogs" were absent. He had an attentive and devout congregation, and was enabled to preach with liberty.

Bishop Seybert always repudiated the use of tobacco in any form, and frequently in his sermons at camp-meetings and ordination sermons expressed his disapproval of its use with characteristic severity. Especially at camp-meetings, where professors often were seen standing in the woods smoking cigars and pipes, when they ought to have been in the altar or elsewhere engaged in prayer, the Bishop spoke with vehemence and force on this subject. And when receiving preachers, he frequently asked, additional to the Disciplinary questions, the question: *"Are you also free from the use of tobacco?"* This he did, long before any conference adopted the rule and made it obligatory upon the presiding Bishop to ask this question.

From his journal we further learn that at the West Pennsylvania conference there was a notable lack of preachers in 1840, because some went to the East Pa. conference, some to the Ohio, and some located. A pastoral letter was therefore issued at the conference session, summoning the membership of that conference to more earnest prayer and sacrifice, so that the want might be supplied.

During the year 1840, the society at Philadelphia passed through a severe ordeal. The pastor, the Rev. J. Vogelbach, saw fit to forsake the little flock and join another denomination. This was an occasion of much distress to the good Bishop. Nothing gave him so much anxiety, as when irregularities and defections occurred in the ministerial ranks, through which the cause of God or the church should suffer harm. He was obliged, accordingly, as general superintendent, to hasten to Philadelphia in the interests of the work. Leaving his horse in the country, the Bishop walked into the city, where he arrived very weary, the roads being dusty and the heat intense. In the evening he preached to the distracted society from Matt. 8:22–27, on the presence of Jesus with his disciples in the storm. He mentions it as something remarkable, that his great weariness all left him by the time the sermon was over. He had enjoyed great liberty in preaching, and undoubtedly proved a son of consolation to the people. He aimed to effect peace, but Vogelbach withdrew, and with him his parents and a few others, giving as his reasons for this step the insufficiency of his salary, and the dissatisfaction that prevailed in the society because he protested against fanaticism in public worship. About this time the following incident occurred:

In one of the South-eastern counties of Pennsylvania lived a family of seventeen children, only two of whom could even read, while the rest were as illiterate as if they had been raised in the interior of the dark continent. One of the sons-in-law was occasionally seen at our services, at which his wife became enraged, and did everything in her power to prevent his attendance. Several times this untamed fury tore the clothes off his back after he was dressed and about to go. Sometimes she hid his clothes; at other times she set about demolishing their household furniture to keep him at home. At length it occurred that this furious woman herself came to a service at a camp-meeting. At first she stared like a wild beast that had suddenly and for the first time come among the habitations of civilized men, ready at any moment to run like a hunted deer. A hearty song was being sung, however, which seemed to have a subduing influence upon her. Nature's greatest poetic interpreter has said:

"Music hath charms to soothe the savage breast,"

and so it proved in this case, for finally she took a seat, but far on the outskirts of the auditorium, though near enough to be severely wounded by the arrows of truth from the Gospel bow. The bow seems to have been drawn taut that day, and it soon became evident that the woman was touched. As she listened with close attention to the preacher, her eyes became moist, tears coursed down her hardened face, and it was not long until, with a broken heart and a contrite spirit, she fell upon her knees, pleading for salvation. She was saved. Ever afterwards she proved herself a decent, meek, civilized and pious woman, a light to the world and a salt to the earth.

Throughout his life-time, Bishop Seybert had occasion to complain of the bad behavior of the people of his native county at camp-meetings. Among other incidents the following occurred in 1840, at a camp-meeting in that county:

The meeting was richly blessed in the conversion of sinners. But outside the tent circle, there was a perpetual, beastly howling among the ungodly clans. There was a rabble present, who must have been possessed by a legion of devils. These creatures did not conduct themselves like human beings, and in reality "they were only *human brutes (Thiermenschen)*, who either never had any reason, or if they ever had any, bequeathed it to their cattle, before they came to the meeting. They ran about in the woods with apparently brainless pates. They knocked one another about like oxen in a pen, screamed, swore and cursed each the other into the lowest hell". Such were the terms in which the indignant and outraged Bishop characterized the unchivalrous conduct of the people near his native heath in that day.

. On Mohawk mission, New York, in the town of Rome, a sister died in great peace, having been brought to Jesus by the efforts of our missionary. On her funeral occasion Bro. Seybert exclaimed: "The new Mohawk mission now has its first sheaf in God's heavenly garner. *Hallelujah!*"

In the vicinity of New Hamburg, in Upper Canada,

15

lived a great drunkard, whose wife was obliged to leave him on account of his brutality. Upon this he announced his intention of drinking himself to death; but this process of suicide proved too slow, so in desperation the wretch lanced an artery in order to bleed to death, and so released (?) the crazed spirit. Accidently some neighbors came upon the. scene, who stopped the bleeding artery and prevented his death. This seemed to bring him to his senses, causing him to reflect soberly. He quit his excesses, was converted to God, and truly led a sober, moral, godly life, free from drink. His wife returned to his home, and they conducted a happy Christian family life. "Is not this," asks Seybert, "a brand plucked from the burning?"

Friday, February 5th, 1841, he came to the city of Baltimore, Md., where he found the brethren engaged in holding a love-feast, in the midst of protracted meetings which had already continued ten days.

The Bishop remained until the 11th, during which time they had glorious meetings, for many souls were converted. Some sixty persons, of all classes, were converted during this revival, among them were several Catholics, of whom one lady, after she found pardon, immediately tore off her needless fineries of dress and trampled them under her feet. The society now numbered one hundred and fifty members, divided into seven classes. The meeting-house recently purchased, had already become too small to contain the multitudes who attended the services, and the erection of a new church edifice at a more suitable

location, near the center of the city, was already
under contemplation. During his stay he was specially delighted that the friends there have such lively
public services, and that there are "no long, frowning
faces visible when any are so filled with the joy of
the Lord, that they break out into shouting". He
also observed with pleasure, that the new converts
divest themselves of their "fashionable flippery".
"Oh," he exclaims "ye friends of Zion, deny yourselves of the world's vain display, and put on the
beauty of holiness!"

This year the East Pennsylvania conference met
March 17th, in Seneca Co., N. Y., the West Pennsylvania, April 7th, in New Berlin, Pa., and the Ohio,
May 12th, in Lafayette, Wayne Co. (now Ashland
Co.), Ohio. Seybert presided at each. He enjoyed
at this time the best physical health, and was enabled
to do his work with alacrity.

His journey from New Berlin, Pa., where the Publishing House was situated, to Ohio, was on this occasion a very severe one, on account of the immense
number of books which he took with him. Before
leaving for the Ohio conference, the Bishop ordered
one of the largest consignments of books ever issued
from the Publishing House at one time. And this in
1841, in a Church that has been accused time and
again of being indifferent, if not opposed, to matters
of culture and education. Seybert's order called for
twenty-three thousand seven hundred and twenty-
five volumes, which he intended to take with him on
his trip to the Ohio conference. Their weight was

twenty-five hundred pounds, and their cost, including a small quantity for Illinois, amounted to $4,306.25. Of course, many of these were small Sabbath-school books. In closing his order, he remarked: "You will probably think I have entirely overshot the mark, in ordering so many books; but if you were as well acquainted with the scarcity of books in the West as I am, you would judge differently." Rev. Charles Hammer, at that time General Book Agent, said: "Should such a large order be sent us again, we ought to have it a year before the books are wanted, in order to get them ready." The scarcity of books in the Western States was at that time so great, that some Sabbath-schools used the *Christliche Botschafter* and the Hymn-book as text books.

So great was Bishop Seybert's anxiety to have the families, schools and churches supplied with proper literature, that he undertook to forward these books and distribute them himself, mostly in Ohio, and also in Indiana and Illinois. He shipped them to the West per canal, and then distributed and sold them to the ministers and laity, taking all the financial risks himself. Though he lost no money in the operation, neither did he gain any. It was done solely in the interests of the Church. He was a far-seeing man, who fully appreciated the value and importance of education and intelligence. He not only wanted the preachers to be studious, but also the laity, and he provided for the children a liberal assortment of juvenile literature. All impressions to the contrary notwithstanding, Seybert thoroughly believed that intelligence should be fostered by the Church. He was a man of advanced thought and broad ideas. His plans were comprehensive. He thought of the future, and plainly foresaw that under the American system of free schools an era of general education was sure to come, and he wanted the Church to be abreast of the times. If any sentiment adverse to educational interests did prevail in the Church, the first Bishop did all in his power to counteract and dispel that sentiment. The great abuse of learning in higher literary institutions in Europe and America, had filled many of our members not only with indifference towards it, but with prejudice against it. But Seybert saw that the results of the abuse of anything were no argument against its proper utility, and he accordingly manifested a particular zeal in creating a healthy public sentiment on this question, believing that it was not too late to rescue learning from the vandal hands of the Philistines, and to create and spread a literature whose motto should be, "Holiness unto the Lord".

The Bishop's journey from New Berlin, Pa., the place of the West Pennsylvania conference session, to Lafayette, Ohio, the place where the Ohio conference met, was accordingly a most laborious one. Instead of riding on horseback, as he had always done, he employed a new conveyance, which he took to Ohio for a brother. Despite bad roads he reached Lafayette in due time.

After conference the Bishop visited a number of appointments in Southern Ohio, attended a successful camp-meeting at John Bright's in Fairfield Co., Ohio, and then started to visit the Fort Wayne mission, Indiana, going through Portland and Alexandria. After traveling a very long distance without finding a single house where he might feed his horse, not even a tavern, and the people along the road being very poor, he finally encamped in a wood, and while his horse was grazing, he engaged in reading the Bible, prayer and quiet contemplation. Meanwhile his horse played truant and ran away in the direction it had come. He started after it in great haste, and did not overtake it until it had gone a number of miles from the place of rendezvous. The race greatly exhausted the Bishop. It was night before he reached Alexandria. To make the matter worse, he got into a large, primitive forest, through the labyrinths of which he wandered for many miles in the dark, before finding his way out again. Next morning he passed through another forest, eighteen miles in length, and almost pathless, but had the good fortune to ride with the post man. The latter was a noisy fellow, however, blowing his horn so vehemently, that its shrill sound echoed and rolled almost continuously through the great woods. Only a few people lived along the road in this forest, in miserable huts.

Bro. Seybert reached Fort Wayne July 3d, and preached at Bro. Keim's in the evening. Next day, being Independence day, he traveled further west, while the people celebrated the day as usual with shooting, swearing, carousing, dancing and drinking. He remarks: "This is the way our western nominal

Christians give thanks to Almighty God for national independence and personal liberty of conscience.— Still, fortunately, it is not the God of Heaven, whom these people serve and at whose altars they offer their sacrifice of fools, but Bacchus, the god of debauchery, gluttony and dissipation. Yea, the devil gets thanks for these blessings, and surely they are not his due."

July 7th, 1841, Bro. Seybert celebrated his fiftieth birthday with this journal entry:

"To-day I am fifty years old. Oh, I would dissolve in tears of gratitude and praise to God, and appear in deepest humility before His throne of grace for the love with which He has crowned my days. I have now lived through half a century, in which millions not so old as I, have passed into eternity. O God! O God! O God! what shall I render unto Thee, because Thou hast borne me with so much patience until this day? I will present unto Thee my soul and body as a sacrifice, and devote all my future days to Thy service. Oh, do Thou qualify me, to be of some service to the praise of Thy excellent strength, and the benefit of mankind, through Jesus Christ!"

The Bishop, as one would suppose, believed in the special providence of God, and took refuge in prayer, even in small matters, with Him who counts the hairs of our head, clothes the lilies of the field, and sees the sparrow's helpless fall.

August 13th, 1841, he reached South Bend, Ind., where his horse became sick. He led it out of the

city into a grove near by, and tried every means
known to him to relieve it, but in vain. The baffled
Bishop saw his faithful beast lying on the ground in a
condition which gave no hope of recovery. He now
turned from the creature to the creature's God in
prayer. On his knees, with upturned face and tear-
ful eyes, he pleaded with God to have mercy on him
and restore his horse, so that he might not lose him,
because he needed him to fill his appointments. He
said, "*Thou hast often helped me in marvellous ways,
and Thou canst help me also in this time of need.*"
Upon this he arose, turned his eyes in the direction
of his horse, — and to his great joy the beast was on
its feet and stood demurely behind its master, quietly
grazing as if nothing had occurred. He led it back
to the city, fed it, and was soon ready again for
travel.

On his way to the West, he mentions among other
things that one Sunday he heard two preachers, one
in German and another in English, whose preaching
was "so superficial that the services were perfectly
quiet."* He does not mention who they were, but
he was evidently displeased with their preaching.

Thursday, July 15th, the first camp-meeting of
the Evangelical Association, in the State of Illinois,
began. This meeting took place on the farm of Bro.
J. Esher (father of Bishop J. J. Esher). Already
on the first evening the friends were happy and the
service full of life. There were also penitents at the
altar. On Sunday the people thronged to the

---

* "Wo es so leicht darüber herging, dass alles ruhig blieb."

encampment from near and far, and there were many attentive listeners, upon whom the Word made deep impressions. On Monday and Tuesday many came out from Chicago, of whom some had hardly arrived on the ground before they were convicted and became penitent. They came to the altar, and cried to God until He had mercy upon them. On Monday they had a most glorious communion season. In the last two nights the demonstrations of Divine power were indeed extraordinary.

There were eighteen tents, in some of which two or three families sojourned together. Several of the friends had come a distance of thirty miles with ox-teams, and that through bridgeless rivers and creeks, so deep that in fording them the water filled their wagons and spoiled their provisions. It may be well to mention this for the benefit of those in our time, who with good conveyances and generally good roads, often can scarcely be persuaded to go ten or fifteen miles to tent at a camp-meeting.

The order was so excellent that no police was needed, which was something unusual in those days. At this meeting they also received the first brother as a preacher on probation into our ministry.

At this camp-meeting there were miracles of nature as well as of grace. Many declared that the power and presence of Jehovah could be both, felt and seen, especially during a notable storm one evening. A thunderstorm is always dreaded at a camp-meeting. On this particular evening a lowering storm sent black battalions of clouds over the sky, charged with angry, muttering thunders on every side of the encampment. In all its terror the storm approached, apparently driving in full force directly upon the white semi-circle of tents. The enemies of the cause were already exulting in the belief that Divine service would be effectually disturbed and that the meeting would be broken up. But lo! just as the storm reached the encampment, its hurrying ranks parted and rushed past, close on either side, with fearful fury and destructive power, leaving the spot chosen for Divine worship *absolutely untouched and unharmed.* The phenomenon was so striking and so unaccountable, that even persons who made no profession of religion saw the finger of God. Bishop Seybert made no hesitation in declaring that the Lord had wrought a miracle there.

Accordingly, then, the first Bishop of our Church, on the occassion of his first episcopal visit to the State of Illinois, himself conducted the first camp-meeting of the Evangelical Association in that State, and received Rev. Christian Ebinger as the first preacher on probation there. Seybert was assisted in the meeting by Revs. J. Hoffert, A. Stroh and C. H. Lindner.

It is noticeable that from this time forward, Bishop Seybert's interest in the great West was enthusiastic and permanent. He took in at a glance its vast natural resources, and its consequent importance as a field of labor for his Church. So impressed was he with this, that his praise of the West was in the East deemed extravagant, and it subjected him to censure for partiality. But he had in view only the interests of the Church and of the cause of Christ.

After the camp-meeting near Chicago he continued his trip westward, preaching in Naperville, now the seat of North-Western College, and finally reached Illinois mission, in Stephenson Co. On the way he had a sad experience.

July 25th namely, he stayed all night at Bro. George Esher's. In this vicinity a sad condition of things prevailed among the friends. A bitter quarrel had raged among them for years, until the society became a total wreck and was hopelessly divided. This pained him the more deeply, because these people were mostly his own spiritual children, whom the Lord gave him years ago on Erie mission.

He preached on Illinois mission, and held a blessed two days meeting at Bro. John Falget's. Bro. Hoffer, the missionary, was pushing farther westward, and extending the field of operations across the Mississippi river into Iowa. The prospects were very favorable, but on account of Bro. Hoffer's rather feeble health, not much could as yet be accomplished. He was also obliged to leave his charge to attend a camp-meeting, a distance of one hundred and twenty five miles away, as preachers were scarce out there as yet.

At Milwaukee, Wis., a glorious revival had begun. A goodly number had already been converted and added to our church. The Germans were emigrating from New York and Buffalo and settling in this new commercial centre of the North-West in large numbers.

There was, therefore, a large and fruitful field of labor there for our Church.

In Chicago a fine society already existed, who worshiped God in Spirit and truth. Many Germans lived there also, among whom, the Bishop predicted, our efforts will yet bring glorious fruit.

In August his malarial troubles finally left him, and though sometimes he felt feeble, and traveling seemed laborious, yet he grew better and was in a cheerful state of mind.

At that time the Church was reaching out with gigantic strides, displaying wonderful enterprise in following on the very heels of immigration, and with commendable sagacity planting her banner so timely in the young giant cities of the upper lakes. In both of these cities, accordingly, the Evangelical Association has enjoyed a degree of prosperity, commensurate with the development of the population.

After this visit to the extensive frontier line of the Church, Bishop Seybert retraced his steps and started towards his native East, preaching through Indiana and Ohio as he went, and attending camp-meetings.

From August 31st to September 4th, he attended a blessed camp-meeting on the farm of Rev. Adam Haney (Hennig), near West Salem, Ohio, a few miles north of the site of the present permanent camp-ground of Cleveland district. There were 38 tents, occupied in many instances by several families, and there were sometimes 25 seekers at the altar at one time. From there he went to another camp-meeting in Stark county, which was very largely attended. One hundred and forty-six participated in the communion service.

Then he attended another camp-meeting farther east, where, while God's people rejoiced greatly, there was terrible carousing on the part of the ungodly rabble in the grove.

He also preached in Summit Co., Ohio, at the house of a brother who was once a hard drinker. He had been a "kind of Mennonite", but his wickedness knew no bounds. He was a powerful man, the terror of his community, and addicted to every form of vice. For eighteen years he was a toper, drinking rum as an ox drinks water, until he could devour three quarts of brandy daily. This wretch was however awakened through the preaching of the Gospel by our preachers, and being soundly converted, was delivered from his loathsome vices, and ever afterwards zealous in the Lord's service, for which, Bro. Seybert says, "let every one give glory, not unto us, but unto God."

In 1842, the East Pennsylvania conference was held March 2d, in Allentown, the West Pennsylvania conference April 6th, in New Berlin, and the Ohio conference May 11th, in Pickaway Co., Ohio. Though there were in all seventeen accessions to the ranks of the itinerancy at these conference sessions, yet the good Bishop was grieved over the fact that nine others located. While welcoming the new men, he wished to retain all the old ones, for only in this way could he realize his desire for the constant extension of the boundaries of the Association, for which he labored day and night.   Still the current year was a prosperous one in this regard.

After the conference, Bro. Seybert delivered a temperance lecture in the public hall, Allentown, to a large audience.   His address was applauded, and some twenty signed the pledge.

Bishop Seybert took another large quantity of books with him from New Berlin to the West, this year.   This time he sold his horse before starting, and traveled with his books per canal-boats, steam-boats and railroads.   This was with him a labor of love.   He paid the expenses of transportation, sold them to preachers and people for cash where he could, on credit where it was necessary, and gave them to the poor gratuitously.   So desirous was he to awaken a taste for study and reading among the people, that he cheerfully. suffered the loss of a hundred dollars or more, annually, in this way.   He believed that Christians ought to be reading people, and did all in his power to foster intelligence among them.   In fact, Bishop Seybert voluntarily assumed the laborious duties of a practical colporteur, in addi-tion to his legitimate official duties.   This fact is the more striking in a period when especially the German population of this country was uneducated, and was without taste for learning or appreciation of its value. Besides, it is a very practical refutation of the hack-neyed charge that the early preachers of our Church were opposed to education.   This was undoubtedly true respecting some of them, whose sentiments seemed especially, however, to militate against an "educated *ministry*". But this sentiment was not universally entertained, though, even had it been the case, it would not have been strange. The clergy of the German churches were, as has been seen, anything but pious. They were a godless set of men, and at the same time undeniably "educated" according to the standards of those times. In this way education and ungodliness became associated together, and the public mind attributed the wickedness of the clergy to their education. And the inference was correct, too, so far as these clergymen were educated in the skeptical and rationalistic universities of Europe. But sagacious men, like Bishop Seybert, saw well enough that education *per se* was not at fault, but the insidious scientific rationalism of the German schools, both in Europe and America, and rightly insisted that a Christian education is a great blessing. Bishop Seybert himself specially emphasized the idea that all educational systems must be thoroughly imbued with the Christian Spirit. That is a truth that will bear practical application to the end of time.

But we have unequivocal proof that Bishop John Seybert was a true and sincere friend of scientific culture. The story having gained currency that he was opposed to it, one of the financial agents of Union Seminary encountered great difficulty in securing financial support for that institution among the sturdy Pennsylvanians. The good Bishop upon this wrote the following remarkable document, the autograph of which Bishop R. Dubs discovered some years ago and has translated literally as follows:

"At the request of Daniel Kreamer, the collector of Union Seminary in New Berlin, the undersigned certifies that he is not against good schools, and that he also purposes to do something for the support of scientific culture, in case his circumstances will better warrant it.   John Seybert."

" March 15, 18—."

His trip to the West with his books was laborious and eventful.

April 20th he helped Bro. Hammer, the Book Agent, pack the books to take along to the West. He had "made up his mind to take a good lot along this time, so as to relieve for once the great want of books in the West."

Next day he set out early, as he had a long journey to make *per pedes*, from New Berlin to the canal, having hired a teamster to haul the books to that thoroughfare. In the evening of the first day he preached, and God's blessing came upon the people in such a manner, that there was a great commotion. One sister was so overwhelmed by the power of God, that she sank down in a rapturous entrancement, from which she did not awaken until at family worship next morning.

Next evening his literary cargo was transferred to a canal-boat, in which he traveled on that whole night. The weather was fine. Garden and field and meadow were already covered with grass and flowers, and the forests were putting on their resurrection robes again. The good man was enabled to praise the Lord with all his heart, on this account.

At Holidaysburgh he transferred his books to the railroad, and crossed the Alleghany Mountains per railway, and then resumed the canal for Pittsburgh. The captain and crew of this boat were awfully wicked, and the trip was therefore by no means an agreeable one.

At Pittsburgh he took the steamer Gloucester and sailed down the Ohio River to Portsmouth, landing at the latter port Sunday evening at five o'clock. On the steamer he fell in with a most ungodly rabble. Soon after sailing from Pittsburgh they searched for a liquor bar, which they found on board. They "drank down a heavy dose of liquid fire, and then began the revel". Amid frightful profanity they entered into "the Devil's service at the card table". Seeing this, he commended the boat, its crew and himself into the hand of God, and laid down to rest. He slept softly and awoke next morning happy in God. From Portsmouth he started northward along the Scioto River, and finally reached Circleville, May 6th, near which place the Ohio conference met. How glad he was to be among friends again and converse with them about the things of God, after being so long a time among "the sons of Belial".

After the session of the Ohio conference had been held, and the books had been disposed of, the Bishop purchased another horse, and started westward in company with Rev. J. G. Zinser. They went by way of Elkhart and Fort Wayne, Ind., and reached Chicago July 6th.

July 7th, 1842. "O God! what shall I render unto
16

Thee, or what offering shall I bring, for all the goodness which Thou hast shown me! Thou hast caused me to experience Thy great love, all the years, months, weeks, days, hours, minutes and seconds of my life. O God! I am pained at the thought of having done so little for Thy glory and for Thy kingdom. Oh, give grace and strength that I may dedicate my future life wholly to Thee, and that I may spend all my future days joyfully in Thy service, through Jesus Christ. Amen."

That day he began the second camp-meeting in Illinois, on the same ground where a year ago he had held the first German camp-meeting which was ever held in that State. They could have no preaching, however, the first evening, on account of a heavy rain and thunderstorm. But there was weeping and praying among penitents here and there in various tents.*

Next morning, Seybert was to have preached, but as there were so many penitents at the altar of prayer crying for mercy, the idea of preaching had to be abandoned again, and they went on laboring with the seekers. Before noon nearly all were gloriously saved. This caused such rejoicing among the saints,

---

* Readers may wonder how it was brought about, that there were penitents in distress of soul already on the first evening, and that before even a public service had been held. This is accounted for by the fact that in those days the people of God had the commendable custom of persuading as many of their unconverted friends as possible, to go with them to camp-meeting. These unconverted friends had been made the subjects of special prayers, and had been pleaded with, perhaps, for months. Some of them were serious or even penitent before they started to camp-meeting, and went with the purpose of seeking religion. Their Christian friends kept them in tow, and the result was, they were converted.

that shouting became the order of the day. Some of the new converts were overwhelmed with holy joy.

Thus they had a mighty victory at the very onset of the meeting, almost before they were fully aware of the fact, and had attained results before a single sermon had been preached. The meeting was equally good to the close.

A hundred and thirty-seven guests participated in the holy communion. It was a blessed time. At this camp-meeting the forests as a rule were vocal with prayer and praise before day-break. It reminded Bro. Seybert of those delectable times when Albright, Miller and Walter were yet among us and blew the Gospel trumpet. On the last two days of this meeting, which were the best of the feast, there were sudden and powerful conversions. Aged sinners sixty and seventy years old were moved to repentance and soundly converted. Men and women came sixty miles on foot to this 'meeting, with the purpose of seeking the Lord, and went home rejoicing.

Twenty-three tents graced the circle, and the conduct of the people was respectable, "for in this region the wicked parsons had not yet incited them against the children of God". This saved our people from molestation at these meetings. "It will furthermore be very difficult", the Bishop thought, "for an uncircumcised teacher to gain a foothold here now, because the light of truth is too great, and the prospect for a great religious revival is too apparent. On this account let us praise the name of the Lord."

. In September (1842), while traveling in the State

of New York, the Bishop came up one evening, a while before dark, to a temperance hotel. He could have gone farther, but seeing the "temperance sign" he concluded to patronize the place and stay there for the night. After the Bishop's horse had been put away and he had been shown to a quiet room, he soon sought an opportunity to express his delight at finding such public houses where no intoxicants are sold, and where "no drunkards are made". The landlord, however, was not long in informing his guest, that it had already cost him much persecution to conduct his business on temperance principles. He said the whiskey rabble had often treated him very rudely. On one occasion a crowd of these disciples of Bacchus overcame him, and so maltreated him that he barely escaped with his life. He declared, however, that notwithstanding these persecutions he was determined to carry his temperance enterprise through, let it cost what it will.

This aroused the Bishop. Shrugging his shoulders and nodding his head in that nervous manner so peculiar to him, he told the landlord that this was a good resolution, exhorted him to carry it out, and even if "the living devil's of hell" should attack him. "The cause," said he, "is a good one, and God will support you and give you victory and success. The devil and wicked people always will oppose a good undertaking, but with the help of the Lord it will nevertheless succeed."

On his return from the West, the Bishop often related the following story:

In Wisconsin a fiddler was converted. After his conversion he did not wish any longer to use an instrument that had so often been the means of leading him into dissipation and vice, and therefore traded the fiddle off for a pig. "This brother did wisely", the Bishop thought; "the fiddle could be of no possible use to him, because a converted man does not play at dances, whereas the swine could be of some use to his family."

The closing days of the year he spent in New York. In this greatest and most flourishing city of the United States the German citizens lived in frightful wickedness; they were sunken in vice and ungodliness, error and ignorance were their masters. In their so-called religious exercises barbarous scenes occurred. It was not unfrequently the case that the worshippers fell to quarreling and fighting in the house ostensibly dedicated to the worship of God. Rationalism, blasphemous deism and flippant universalism combined to work the temporal and eternal ruin of these people. Intoxication at every opportunity was their foremost vice. They were addicted to this sin in a frightful measure. For instance, at the festivities connected with the christening of a child, they indulged in singing Satan's songs, and ate and drank to such excess that twenty flasks of wine were emptied, and this at the house of a poor man. This is a sample of a German christening in New York City at that time. He found an earnest society of some fifty members there, however, and hoped it would yet prove a great blessing to the Germans of this wicked city.

During this year Bishop Seybert traveled five thousand six hundred and eleven miles, — more than in any previous year.

Bishop Seybert's life-long watchword was, " Not unto us, O Lord, not unto us, but unto Thy Name be the glory". Following is a remarkable occurrence, which he frequently related to warn preachers and others against seeking the honors of the world and the applause of men:

"A minister, weary with his Sunday forenoon service, retired to a quiet chamber to rest. Hardly had he lain down on the sofa, before he fell asleep and dreamed. He thought he was walking in a garden, amid flowers and shrubbery, and sat down under a shady arbor to read and meditate. It now seemed to him as if he heard the sound of footsteps, as of some one coming into the garden, and he at once arose to go in the direction whence the sound proceeded. Directly he was met by a particular friend of his, also a minister, a man of great gifts and splendid talents, and who was highly honored on account of his zeal in the public service. He noticed a singular expression of distress, anxiety and fear in his friend's countenance, but the two ministers greeted one another with the usual cordiality. The new comer inquired the time of day. *Twenty-five minutes past four o'clock,'* was the laconic reply. Said the other, *'It is now exactly one hour since I am in the spirit world, and I am damned!'* 'What! damned? Why?' exclaimed the shocked dreamer. Solemnly, sadly, but deliberately the answer came: 'Not,' said the unfortunate man, 'because I have **not** preached the Word of God, not that I have not been useful; for I have many seals to my ministry; there are many in glory to-day who can testify that I was the instrument of their salvation. But it is *because I sought the praise of men and the honor and fame of the world, rather than the glory of God. I have my just reward!'* The minister awoke. The dream made a singular impression upon his mind. He started towards his church for the evening service, musingly and in a strangely solemn mood. On the way he met a friend, who asked him at once whether he had been apprised of the great loss the church had that day sustained, and that the celebrated and talented Rev. —— *was dead?* 'No,' said he with surprise and amazement. Tremblingly he ventured to inquire at what time he had died, and the startling, laconic reply was, *'At twenty-five minutes past three o'clock this afternoon!'"*

CHAPTER XI.

VARIED EXPERIENCES—CONTINUED.

In February, 1843, one day Bro. Seybert preached at the house of a converted tavern-keeper in the valley of the Mahanoy. This man, before his conversion, manufactured brandy and kept a bar, but since his conversion he had learned to see his wrong. He broke his brandy flasks and poured their liquid poison into the streets. At the same time he ordered one of his employes to cut down the sign, and looked on with great delight until the Satanic banner came down with a crash. "Now the liquor traffic is at an end there", Seybert says, "and the place has been consecrated to the Lord's service. The tavern has become a house of prayer and a genial home for the preachers of the Gospel. Hallelujah to the Lamb that was slain! Praise the Lord!"

The same month the Bishop dedicated the first church in our Association which was furnished with a tower and bell. The church was built at Millheim, Pa., in 1842.

About this time a revival took place at Manhein, where wonders of grace occurred. Some of the worst men in the place were converted. One of them was a drunkard, who, while he yet held to his ancient faith, was often full of wine to overflowing. On one occasion he fell on the street in a drunken stupor during a severe hail storm, and lay there until he was stiff with cold, and his neighbors had to take him home, and only restored him to life and consciousness with much labor. They will have no trouble of that kind with him now, the Bishop thought, for he can go home alone, though he is "not always *exactly sober*, but *full of the ancient wine of Pentecost.*" "Another was saved at this meeting, who was so depraved and so deeply fallen, that no person could live with him, but after his conversion he was a real pleasure to his neighbors. Another man was converted who had often signed the total abstinence pledge, but always broke it again, being utterly unable to overcome his terrible appetite. It is very different now that the love of God is shed abroad in his heart. He is very devoted, and being a good singer, a very useful member of the society. His wife and children have also started on the narrow way, and are working out their salvation. Still another, who was known as a brutal prize-fighter, has also been brought to Jesus. Since his conversion, which, however, occurred already two years before, he has been fighting against sin and the devil. This man died in peace, having overcome by the Blood of the Lamb and by the word of his testimony, and already enjoys the fruitions of grace in the world of spirits." "O my brethren," the Bishop cries, "give God the glory for such triumphs of grace!" During this revival the Bishop delivered a powerful temperance lecture there, which resulted in much good.

This year the East Pennsylvania conference was held in Lebanon, March 22d, and the West Pennsylvania conference near Carlisle, April 5th. After these conference sessions were over, the Bishop, in company with Rev. J. Heis, went to New Berlin, where he had business at the Publishing House which occupied several days. During his stay he also attended the annual meeting of the Parent Missionary Society, and at its request preached a missionary sermon.

After transacting necessary business and visiting a considerable number of friends, besides preaching several times and delivering a temperance lecture, he set out for the session of the Ohio conference. Under Divine protection he crossed the Alleghanies in safety, and arrived at Pittsburgh April 28th, where he was kindly received and hospitably entertained by Bro. Herr. While stopping here he also visited a number of German Methodist families together with their preacher, who greatly desired that the Bishop should tarry and preach for him.

April 30th he rode through bad roads and inclement weather to Economy, to visit his mother, and found her in a good state of health for a woman seventy-five years of age. The visit gave her much pleasure. Two days later he reached the State of Ohio, and visited a few friends at Freedom. "I could hardly get away from them; they urged me so hard to remain and preach to them. There is a good prospect for conversions there."

Thursday he reached Greensburg, where he delivered a missionary address to a large congreation. This holy cause was handsomely supported there.

On Saturday he reached a "big meeting" in progress at Henry Meyer's in Wayne Co., Ohio. On Sunday afternoon, for the encouragement of the local auxiliary missionary society, a missionary sermon was preached and a collection taken, amounting to seventy-five dollars.

The Bishop arrived at Flat Rock, Seneca county, the seat of the Ohio conference, in good time.

There was a great deal of business, but it was transacted with dispatch, in a brotherly and harmonious manner. The boundaries of the work were greatly extended in the West during the last few years. So remarkably had the work increased that the conference was under the necessity of forming two new districts. A great field was open for faithful laborers.

During the Summer of 1843 Bishop Seybert was physically quite indisposed. He had contracted a violent cough, besides exhausting his strength by over-work.

We have now reached the end of Bishop Seybert's first term of office in the episcopacy—the General conference of 1843. His last regular meeting was held in August, in Illinois. He then traveled southward, spending several days among the Germans of Peoria, Ill., and from there he went to St. Louis, Mo. At the very urgent invitation of the pastor of the German Methodist society, he assisted in holding communion service and administered the rite of baptism among them. He observed that at that time fully one-third of the 30,000 population of

St. Louis were Germans. From here he retraced his steps and started for Dayton, Ohio. On the way he was troubled with attacks of chills and fever. To his delight he found the work prospering, especially at Mt. Carmel, Ill., Germantown, Ind., and Dayton, Ohio. Thence he made a flying trip through Sandusky district, Ohio conference, and Mohawk district in the State of New York, and finally, after a long and toilsome journey, he returned to Greensburg, Summit Co., O., which had been his objective point during all this circuitous tour. At this place the General conference met in October. The Bishop arrived October 20th, a few days before that body convened.

The chief business transacted by this General conference, with which we are properly concerned in this narrative, was the re-election of Bro. John Seybert to the episcopal office. Episcopacy in the Evangelical Association is not an order, but an office. Consistently with this conception, bishops are not elected for life, nor ordained as such by the laying on of hands, but are elected simply and lincensed for a term of four years. They are however eligible to re-election during life or "good behaviour" and satisfactory administration.

Bishop Seybert, it appears, considered himself in office, until on the ninth day of the session, the episcopal question was brought up. It was then declared that the Evangelical Association was without a bishop at that moment. Upon this the feasibility of electing two bishops, was taken into consideration. It was finally determined to elect two, on account of the rapid extension of the work. After discussing the merits of a number of candidates, who were sent out of the room during the discussion, the conference proceeded to an election. The result was that John Seybert was re-elected, and Joseph Long newly elected, to the episcopal office. Seybert made the following entry in his journal that evening:

"To-day I was *for two hours and fourteen minutes* relieved of the office of bishop, that being the exact time from the moment when my term of service was declared to have expired, to the moment when I was declared re-elected. I now feel more than ever the high importance of the position, and realize an inward constraint to devote myself with renewed energy and consecrated zeal to the work committed to my hands, to journey to all points of the compass, to execute my commission. The Lord give unto me and unto my colleague grace to do our duty, so that we may edify the Church and bless the world! Amen."

The religious services during this General conference were blessed from day to day with conversions.

At this General conference it was also resolved to labor more in the English language. An English conference was to be formed, if sufficient English preachers were together to warrant it; and if 800 subscribers could be secured, an English periodical should be published.

In April, after the East Pennsylvania conference had been held, he started, in company with Rev. Levi

Eberhard, for La Fayette, the seat of the Ohio conference. At John Herr's, near Harmony, Butler Co., Pa., they found a society of devoted Christians, who had been tried, however, as by fire. Seven families had been driven out of their houses by their landlord, for the Gospel's sake. But the Lord also drove out the wicked landlord, calling him into eternity.

In the Spring of 1844, Seybert was again present at each of the conferences. At the session of the Ohio conference, in La Fayette, Ashland Co., O., the Illinois conference was formed in accordance with the order of the General conference. The new conference, however, did not hold its first regular session until the Spring of 1845. Bishop Seybert was greatly pleased with the fact that the General conference had given him a colleague in the work, because it would enable him to take counsel in important matters, and would enable them to guard the flock and superintend the work more thoroughly.

On account of the poor state of Seybert's health, Bishop Long kindly relieved him of the chairmanship of the Ohio conference.

He was pleased that there was an addition of nineteen young men to the itinerant ranks, but he also censured severely the spirit which prevailed upon eight others to locate. One conference, however, was free from this evil; none of its members located.

After the conferences were over, the two bishops, Seybert and Long, divided the work into two Episcopal districts, Bishop Long taking the two eastern, and Bishop Seybert the two western conferences.

They separated May 16th, 1844, with mutual wishes of success and many expressions of affection.

There was a great contrast between these two men. One supplied indeed, what the other lacked. Both were perhaps equally pious, but Long, though less is known of him, was the greater preacher. Seybert was practical and spiritual in his preaching; Long was profound, and overwhelmingly powerful. When once Bishop Long was fully launched in his discourse, he swept his congregations along like a veritable cyclone. There was the element of majesty in his preaching, and few equalled him in the force and eloquence of his delivery. Seybert was a son of consolation; Long a son of thunder. Seybert had the advantage in the geniality of his disposition; Long being often morose and sometimes even acrid in his demeanor. The two bishops were mutual friends, entertaining sentiments of affection and profound respect for each other. The thought of jealousy never found any room in them. Each believed thoroughly in the other's sincerity, and they mutually confided in each other's judgment in matters of administration. The Church was safe in the hands of two such men.

Immediately after General conference, Bishop Seybert started on an extensive preaching tour. In Stark county, Ohio, he attended a "big meeting" in a new, unfinished meeting-house, which to his knowledge was the first of our churches in Ohio to be ornamented with a tower. On one occasion during this meeting he preached in such power and with

such eloquence, that he was unable to finish his sermon, for the tumultuous out-bursts of holy enthusiasm
and joy in the audience quite drowned the preacher's
voice, and he was obliged to "sit down in a storm".

After traveling extensively through Ohio, he went
back to Pennsylvania, through New York, preaching,
of course, as he went.   In February, one day, he and
Bishop Long together visited the grave of Jacob
Albright, the venerated founder of the Evangelical
Association, which filled these great spirits with profound emotions.   It would be worth something to
prosterity, to have a picture of that scene and know
what were their thoughts and conversation.

Samuel Baumgardner accompanied Seybert westward, and in eight days they rode a distance of three
hundred and eighty miles, which brought him to
Des Plaines circuit, Illinois.   This was a difficult trip.
It rained a great part of the time, and high winds
prevailed.   On account of freshets, broken bridges,
driftwood, the debris of demolished houses and barns,
and the trunks of fallen trees in some places filling
the roads so as to make them almost impassable,
traveling was both perilous and wearying.   At the
same time he was also weakened by rheumatic and
neuralgic pains, so that he greatly felt the need of
rest; nevertheless, he averaged 47 miles per day, and
preached during the next two days, being Pentecost,
in Chicago, Des Plaines and Dutchman's Point, and
"had glorious times".

Afterwards he attended a camp-meeting near
Wheeling, Cook Co., Ill., where fifty-two families

tented. At this meeting at one time, the slain of the Lord, who were on their knees and on their faces crying for mercy, were no less than thirty, most of whom obtained pardon before they ceased to pray.

There had been some fears, that on account of the heavy rains and the freshets the friends would not be able to come together with their tents. However, in the over-ruling providence of God, a cool wind soon began to sweep over the land, that scattered the clouds and dried somewhat the freshets, so that on the day of meeting the tents could be promptly pitched, and not a single sermon or prayer-meeting was hindered by rain. Immediately, however, after the close of the meeting there occurred such terrific torrents of rain that the inhabitants declared it unprecedented.

At a point called Long Grove, six miles west of Wheeling, our people had succeeded, by means of the truth, in gaining a solid foot-hold among the Germans. A few had already been converted. But the false teachers and their followers became excited and embittered, and gave vent to their anger and malice by scoffing, railing, blaspheming and lying against God's people and His work. They spared no pains to hinder the progress of the truth, even persecuting the dead. The Bishop says: "Certainly this is the place to look for religious zealots. The antiquated slanderous inventions that the sainted Jacob Albright had been a horse-thief and the like, have emigrated westward and have been industriously circulated here. But when one of their *orthodox* (?) preachers commits

17

adultery, or gets drunk, or cuts up other capers, he is quickly forgiven.   I rather suspect if these '*faithful watchmen*' (?) had lived thirty or forty years ago in Pennsylvania, no horse-thief would have been allowed freely to preach in churches, school-houses, government buildings and market-places, in cities and villages, and in the forests, to thronging thousands, until the holy fire of God had set half the United States in a blaze of religious fervor, — until the work of the hated Albright and his Church had gained such a foot-hold that the devil with all his brood of hell could never put it down again.   Yes, these brave watchmen (?) would have promptly imprisoned or murdered Albright and nipped the movement in the bud, had they actually believed their own statements concerning him.   O ye shameless, disgraceful falsehood peddlers *(Luegenkræmer)*, who show that you are children of the devil by the fact that ye love falsehood rather than truth, be ashamed of yourselves! And be converted from the old father of lies to the true and living God, before you receive your portion with all liars, hypocrites and unbelievers, where the smoke of their torment ascendeth forever and ever.

" Notwithstanding all their efforts to the contrary, these beautiful groves with their wealth of flowers, and their grassy slopes, shall no longer belong to the father of lies, but to the Lord Jesus, to whom belong the riches of the Gentiles.   Let these groves and prairies be consecrated unto Him, for the truth has already triumphed."

Thence he crossed the Mississippi into Iowa, and across the Wisconsin river, where many Indians were still living. The German settlers whom he found on the outskirts of civilization, "where twilight struggles with gloom", were morally in a deplorable condition. Many were skeptical and nearly all extremely wicked. This mission is a very difficult field of labor and involves a heavy outlay of money.

After spending seventeen days on this rough mission field, he went to the Milwaukee mission, going by way of Madison, Wisconsin. The trip was very hard, as the streams were much swollen, and the roads frightfully muddy. Five miles west of Milwaukee he dedicated our first sanctuary in the State of Wisconsin. The boundaries were at that time extending mightily in the North-west, and the prospects for conversions good. Bishop Seybert remained in this vicinity six days, and then traveled southward to Des Plaines circuit, where he organized an auxiliary missionary society, on which occasion the members, despite their poverty and privations in this yet untamed wilderness, subscribed over one hundred dollars for the holy missionary cause.

At Peoria he helped in a protracted meeting, which was "especially lovely, because our members and the German Methodists were united in love, labored and shouted and wept together, glorifying God by their unanimity."

On the way to Peoria, Seybert also found entrance in a society of the Amish communion, to whom he preached from Matt. 5: 1–12, with great liberty. He found them a very devout and attentive congregation. Evidently they were greatly delighted with this plain and simple messenger of grace, for they strongly urged him to tarry among them for a time, but ·he was obliged to hasten on.

He finally reached Naperville, Ill., again in September.   Here he was much refreshed in being permitted to spend a few days among brethren whom he had learned to know years ago at Warren, and in Schuylkill and Lancaster counties, Penn'a.

During this year an unwarranted attempt was made by Rev. L. S. Jacoby, a German Methodist preacher, to smirch the fair and honorable reputation of our honest and artless Bishop, by writing an article for the " *Christliche Apologete,*" the organ of the German Methodists, and edited by Dr. W. Nast, in which he charged Bishop Seybert with making an unfair attempt to rob the German Methodist preacher of the results of a revival near Peoria, Ill. Jacoby charged the bishop with having taken advantage of the Methodist pastor's absence, to raise his " Evangelical banner " and seeking to draw the people over into his own Church. To sum up the article briefly, Seybert was charged with proselyting in a surreptitious manner, and causing a sore division among the people there.

The publication of this paper caused some excitement and uneasiness among the membership of the Evangelical Association and others who knew Bishop Seybert. The universal belief was, that nothing could be farther from Seybert than such conduct. His ambition was to "break the ice" for his Church in new regions; like St. Paul he was loth to enter into other men's labors, or build on another man's foundation. Upon all sides, therefore, it was clamorously demanded that the Bishop should defend himself in the public prints against the accusations of Jacoby. This he finally did in a straight-forward account of the whole affair, through the columns of the *Christliche Botschafter.* Previously, however, a refutation appeared from the pen of Rev. L. Heis, who, it was alleged, had been sent as Seybert's tool to steal the M. E. Society, at Peoria, in which Jacoby's misrepresentations were indignantly exposed. Thereupon the society at Peoria itself published a communication, fully exonerating Bishop Seybert from the base charges made by Jacoby.

Finally the Bishop, who had intended to treat the attack with the contempt of silence, yielded to the demand, and wrote for the *Botchafter* a strong article, in which he plainly showed that Jacoby had entirely misrepresented the matter. The three independent statements corroborated each other, and Jacoby's attack was so completely refuted, that nothing was ever heard from him on that subject thereafter. Bishop Seybert was vindicated and his innocence established.

Seybert's elevation to the highest office in the Church did not put him above doing the hardest and humblest service. He was born to break the way. In his episcopal journeys he not only visited the churches and established societies, but went even beyond the circuits of the preachers, keenly watching for new openings, and planting the Gospel banner "in the regions beyond."   This was his occupation in the Spring of 1845, while Bishop Long was holding the Pennsylvania ·conferences.   For the first time in a quarter of a century he was absent from the session of the East Pennsylvania conference.

He also presided in 1845 at the first session of the Illinois conference.   This conference session in the "far West" (as it was then designated) was richly blessed.   It had seventeen itinerants and a number of local preachers.   The conference was held in Des Plaines, Cook Co.   At noon of the fourth day the business was all disposed of.   The examination of the preachers closed already before noon of the first day, for there were no charges against any; no preacher was expelled, nor deposed from office, nor put back on probation, nor otherwise punished. Neither did they hear any one say, "I want to stop itinerating," nor complain of his hard appointment, Though some of them had very difficult and severely laborious fields of labor, yet all seemed satisfied and determined to work together in love.

The Lord seemed to look with special favor upon our work in the great West, for the boundaries extended astonishingly and already covered Indiana, Illinois, Iowa and Wisconsin.   Often Bishop Seybert used to wish, that before he was called home he might see this "hind-most, untempered wall broken through".   He wanted to see our Church out-step the westward march of the formalist teachers, and his desire had now been fulfilled. He said, "we are now proclaiming the Gospel beyond the ramparts of our principal enemies, and our 'little banner' waves on the frontiers of civilization, amid the tents of the savages. It is not likely either, that the wolves in sheep's clothing will trouble us much here, for the pay is too small. These *diletante* do not care to expose themselves to the hardships and perils of this waste howling desert. Besides, the call for them is not so urgent as formerly. Since these people have become enlightened by the Gospel and see that the men, who like the apostles of Jesus, volunteer for no earthly reward to undergo the privations of life among frontier settlers, are best calculated to do them good. These settlers in their primitive huts could not accommodate the clerical aristocracy to satisfaction at any rate." At this conference session, J. J. Esher, he says, was received into the itinerancy.

After the session of the Illinois conference Seybert tarried several days longer in that State, and then started eastward.

June 26th he reached Indiana, and preached on the 29th at South Bend. Upon urgent request he spoke in the Methodist church to the German citizens. Here he also became acquainted with Captain Price, the celebrated temperance orator, who, by his great industry and extraordinary energy, had extended his influence over North America, England, Scotland and Ireland, and by his eloquence, under God's blessing, had persuaded more than ninety thousand people to sign the pledge and enlist in the temperance cause.

The pastor of the M. E. church at South Bend invited Captain Price and the Bishop to dine at his house, and the two temperance apostles had great pleasure in conversing upon the temperance cause and the work of the Lord generally.

Captain Price was greatly interested in Bishop Seybert, for he found in this plain and disingenuous German church dignitary a warm and zealous advocate of total abstinence. For the Bishop was indeed a noted apostle of temperance, and frequently delivered addresses of thrilling interest on the subject to his German fellow-countrymen.

Bishop Seybert next went to Ann Arbor mission, in Michigan, where more than fifteen hundred Germans, mostly foreign immigrants, lived closely huddled together. He spent nearly a week visiting the sick and the well, together a large number, and preaching daily. The people were hospitable and received the servant of the Lord gladly. Many attended the preaching services, among them a number of Catholics, upon which he said: "If therefore the *'Friend of Truth'* (a German Roman Catholic newspaper) should feel itself prompted again to ridicule 'Bro. Seybert's melting meetings in the West', he may also add in a vein of seriousness, that some of his Catholic brethren have actually attended some of those meetings, and have themselves been wonderfully *melted*, and it appears that some of them are not far from the Kingdom of heaven."

On July 31st he visited Bishop Long at his home near New Lisbon, Ohio. Next day, after they had arranged their affairs, they again parted with mutual good wishes, Long going to the West, and Seybert to the East.

August 19th he crossed the Niagara River at a point three miles below Buffalo, and landed in Upper Canada. In company with the Presiding Elder, he visited in twenty days nearly all our societies there and attended several "big meetings", which were blessed with awakenings and conversions. At Hamburg a sad state of affairs had prevailed a few years before this. The people were wicked beyond measure, and no wonder, for their pastors were drunkards! But since the truth is being preached in power, many vicious characters, and also formalists have been converted. Our society had erected an excellent brick church, which was to be dedicated soon.

The people were quite enthusiastic in their admiration of Bishop Seybert. They had never seen a bishop before, and had imagined such an official as being a very exalted and extraordinary personage, who would at least be very dignified and unapproachable. How agreeably they were surprised when their eyes fell upon the slight, nervous, simply clad form of Seybert, and they were told "This is the bishop!" And they were still more curious to know, how a man so tortured with rheumatism could endure such protracted journeys, and preach with such power.

In September he had a blessed meeting north of Toronto, in a Lutheran church. On Sunday they celebrated Holy Communion, and all were greatly blessed. In the morning he preached an ordination sermon, upon which Bro. W. Schmitt was ordained as a Deacon in our Church. On Saturday evening he was unable to be present, on account of severe rheumatic pains. During this visit he also preached for the Stony Creek society, who gave him quite a sum of money for Pittsburgh mission. The fact that this donation was unsolicited, and came from a strange country, and that from a people who have a debt on their own church, made it specially praiseworthy in his estimation.

In October he reached Albany, the capital of the State of New York. He spent three days with this people, and preached three times on Sunday. In the evening they labored with penitents, and the prayers of the saints at this place, in behalf of seekers, were, he says, "peculiarly touching and impressive". Above all, there were several Sunday-school scholars here, who prayed with wonderful pathos for the conversion of relatives and the extension of the Redeemer's Kingdom, which moved the bishop deeply.

Apropos to the surprise of the citizens of Hamburg, at the unpretentious appearance of Bishop Seybert, mentioned in this chapter, the following similar incident occurred in no less a place than Cleveland, Ohio:

Bishop Seybert having been announced to preach, an honest German informed his still unconverted wife, as he started to the church, that he intended to bring the bishop along home to dinner. The good housewife was quite amazed at the idea, but reluctantly consented. Accordingly she set her house in order, and exhausted her culinary art to prepare a dinner, which she thought would be fit for a bishop. She even called in a neighbor to assist her. Finally the dinner hour arrived, and with fluttering heart the poor soul awaited the arrival of her husband with their distinguished guest. After waiting for some time, she presently espied her husband coming up the street,—but no bishop! A poorly clad little man, with a heavy, broad brimmed hat, leather shoes, short, round, well worn coat, ornamented with a heavy row of large brass buttons, was walking beside him. On seeing this, the woman's countenance fell in disappointment. "Now I've gone to all this work and trouble for nothing," she said; "Instead of the bishop, he's got nobody but some common old man." Angrily she went back into the house, not knowing what to do. Soon the party arrived and went into the parlor. Then the husband went out to his wife, who greeted him with: "I thought you were going to bring Bishop Seybert; what did you bring *this* fellow for?" "Why it *is* the bishop, my dear," was the demure reply. "*This a bishop?* This is *no* bishop!" That was settled with her. But he insisted. She finally put the dinner on the table, but in no pleasant mood, and not until she was compelled to, did she believe that her guest was indeed none other than the famous and powerful preacher, whose name she had so often heard. If she had known his character, she would have prepared a plain, common dinner, without much ado.

Seybert's indifference in the matter of clothes was well known. With him clothes were for protection, not for display. It is probable, however, if he had not been a homeless bachelor who had no one to look after his wardrobe but himself, he would have been a little more prim. He thought nothing of a patch on the knees of his pantaloons, or on the elbows of his coat sleeve. Fortunately for him, too, he lived in an age in which this sort of thing did not give so much offense, especially as the Bishop was otherwise an affable and entertaining guest. He was much more concerned to have on his soul the beauty of holiness.

CHAPTER XII.

VARIED EXPERIENCES—CONTINUED.

In the Spring of 1846, Bishop Seybert presided at both the Pennsylvania conferences, was present at the session of the Ohio conference over which Bishop Long presided, and, on account of the sickness of Bishop Long, presided for him at the Illinois conference.

During his visit among the churches in Wayne county, in Ohio, Seybert was greatly annoyed by a traveling show of some twenty wagons. He expressed his disgust that the people of this country spend their time and their money to witness the barbarous performances of such outcasts as usually constitute a circus troupe or a theatrical company. "Such practices," he said, "must demoralize society and injure public morals. Government ought to prohibit these worthless and indecent exhibitions as inimical to the public good." — What would the good Bishop say in our day, when many church members and professors of religion, both old and young, patronize these circus shows? Surely there are better ways for a Christian to spend his time and money.

May 25th (1846) he reached Columbus, Ohio, just as the news of General Zacharia Taylor's dicisive victory at Buena Vista in the Mexican war had arrived. The city was already making preparations to celebrate the victory. All the bells of the city rang. This would have been all right in itself, the Bishop thought, but it was only the signal for a general and excessively dissipating uproar. As night came on, the carousal began. "There was shooting of fire-arms and sky-rockets; there was drumming and piping; there was shouting and cheering; there was drinking and drunkenness, which turned the festivities into a disgraceful fiasco. A great bonfire was kindled, which illuminated the city and burned all night, and around it the rabble behaved as if they were imitating the barbaric orgies of some pagan idol worship. Instead of giving God the glory due unto His name, for the good fortune which attended our arms in battle, they gave the honor to the devil in heathenish disorder."

Intending to return to Cincinnati, Ohio, per canal, on official business after the Illinois conference had been held, he started for Cambridge, but reached that place too late for the boat. He was therefore obliged to follow along the tow-path. The tow-path was rough, besides he had his saddle-bags to carry, so that he became foot-sore and weary, until at eleven o'clock in the night he finally overtook the boat. Rest was sweet that night. Next day his soul was vexed and grieved by the frivolous conduct of the crew and passengers.

At Cincinnati Bishop Seybert visited Dr. W. Nast, the editor of the *Apologete*, and enjoyed his visit greatly in the growing metropolis on the Ohio.

From Cincinnati he started back again to Mt. Carmel, Ill. On the way he was accompanied by Rev. J. Drometer of the Illinois conference, who was stationed at Mt. Carmel. From June 27th to 30th, three days, they were detained in the vicinity of Drometer's home, by incessant torrents of rain. Meanwhile Drometer became dangerously ill with a fever that threatened his life. This greatly increased the Bishop's concern. He also noticed that the family were very sad and depressed. On visiting him one day, the Bishop felt a mighty inward constraint to pray. Accordingly he fell upon his knees by the bed-side, and in earnestness and simplicity besought the Lord to restore the sick brother, if it were in accordance with His will. After prayer Seybert departed, leaving his benediction upon the family. Presently Drometer arose from his bed, and with Seybert resumed the journey to Mt. Carmel, riding thirty miles that same day. He was thoroughly restored, in an instant, in answer to prayer. For this bishop Seybert gave glory to God.

Arriving at Mt. Carmel, the Bishop and the missionary were received very joyfully. The bells were rung and the people invited to services. It was July 4th.

The popular manner of celebrating the birth-day of the Republic was anything but agreeable to Seybert. On this particular day he was specially annoyed at the demonstrations quite early in the day, and promptly determined for once to show the world how God's servants can put in a full day at their work on that day; he says:

"The ungodly celebrated that day with gluttony, drinking, swearing, shooting, and howling, besides other Satanic exercises, I, however, was on my feet betimes, hastily visited nine families in the morning, shaved, bathed, greased my shoes, and put on clean clothes and rode thirty miles the same day."

Traveling through Illinois in company with Bro. J. G. Miller, they came upon a number of our members, living in Macon Co., eight miles east of Decatur, who had come from York Co., Pa., and had neither seen nor heard an Evangelical preacher for seven years. Their joy at the appearance of these two preachers among them is more easily imagined than described. Miller remained with them to preach for them and their neighbors, and Seybert continued on his way to Peoria circuit.

On this tour he traveled quite extensively through Illinois, and had many interesting experiences. At one place he was obliged to stay all night in a very miserable hut, sleeping on a buffalo robe on the floor. But for such hardships he in common with the pioneer preachers of those days cared little, only so that they found the lost sheep of the house of Israel.

Near Decatur he found friends, formerly Pennsylvanians, who had not seen an Evangelical preacher since they settled there. Their joy knew no bounds, when Bishop Seybert unexpectedly came among them. He was received as an angel from heaven. He remained several days visiting and preaching. It is easy to imagine that he also must have enjoyed his labor among them. On departing he was loaded with provender for his horse and provision for himself, and one of the brethren rode quite a distance with him.

At Dr. Nothwagel's he preached to a congregation of six hearers, with much pleasure. Dr. Nothwagel was a converted drunkard, who had been delivered by Divine grace from the appetite for liquor.

September 5th he attended a two day's meeting with Bro. Blank on Racine mission. The people were very attentive to the Word, and a number came unsolicited and joined our Church. "At least these were certainly not *deceived* nor *seduced* by us," he adds.

The work in the West was prospering at this time. The boundaries of the Illinois conference had been greatly extended. It was impossible for the Presiding Elders to do their districts justice. After stubborn resistance a firm hold had been gained in northern Indiana, and the truth began to triumph in many parts of the great West. The seed that was sown in tears was now bringing glorious fruit. The missions had been so extended that there was a lack of preachers to supply the territory properly. The Evangelical Association had carried the banner of truth forward across the Wisconsin River, and planted it among the tents of the red man. The German settlements were open beyond Green Bay.

During his somewhat protracted stay in the West, Bishop Seybert was greatly troubled with ague. After the fever had somewhat subsided, he left Bloomington, Iowa, and started eastward in great

18

weakness. He traveled a distance of over 500 miles, through disagreeable weather and bad roads, crossing the State of Illinois, Indiana, Michigan and Ohio, reaching Greensburg, Ohio, near the end of September. Here he found a protracted meeting in progress, which was blessed with conversions and revival.

The Bishop stopped at Greensburg, simply because he could not proceed any further, and left again as soon as he could walk, notwithstanding the bad state of weather which prevailed at that season of the year. He traveled throughout the eastern portion of the Ohio conference, and despite his enfeebled health and the bad roads and stormy weather, he attended five special or protracted meetings. The Bishop was highly pleased with the missionary zeal manifested by the people at that time, and commended the liberality with which they supported this sacred cause.

On a cold Winter day, during one of his horse-back trips through Ohio, Seybert fell in with some one hauling a weaver's loom on a sled. Seybert was a man of sociable habits, and was always interested in artisans and the laboring classes in general, and at once began a conversation. A few direct questions revealed the fact that the man was a constable, who was about to sell the loom, which had been attached by law to pay a debt; and that the unfortunate weaver, to whom the loom belonged, was a poor man with a large family, who had no other means of support. On inquiry he also learned the amount of the debt. The fact that the loom was the man's only means of securing a livelihood, awakened Seybert's sympathy, and he exclaimed with earnestness, "This is hard!" The officer remarked, "Well, you see, as a constable I must do it, hard as it is, and I confess it is hard for me to perform my official duties in cases of this kind." After a brief pause the Bishop asked the officer, "Would you mind taking the loom back to its owner again, if I pay you the amount of the debt?" "I will gladly do it," replied the constable, "all I want is the money to pay the debt." Upon this Seybert reined up his horse and ordered a "halt". "Turn", said he, "go with me and we will bring the man his loom. I will pay the debt." The officer obeyed.

As they came up to the house, the man, his wife and the children all came out, curious to know what had happened that the constable brought the loom back again. Seybert spoke up at once, saying, "I told the constable it is too hard that a man with a family should lose the instrument by which he earned their support, and concluded I would pay the debt, and give you back your loom." While saying this he had alighted from his horse and thrown the rein loosely over a fence post. He immediately reached into his pocket and counted out the exact amount to the officer of the law. "You may write me a receipt," he said. This done the constable rode away. The Bishop stopped to speak a few words to the family, who were embarrassed with surprise and perplexity, and stared with open wonder at their strange and eccentric benefactor. They wanted to know who he was. "My name is John Seybert," he modestly replied. On their inquiry as to where he lived, he said, "My native place is Manheim, Pennsylvania, but I am a traveling preacher, who hardly knows that he has a home except the heavenly home, where all the saints shall rest forever."

He then gave them a little admonition, briefly telling them what to do to inherit eternal life, and then started for his horse. The family, however, objected to his going, put his horse into a dilapidated barn, gave it the best fodder they could find, and prepared a meal for their guest. The interval he employed in conversation on the subject of religion, and the weaver and his wife were both much affected. The weaver now wanted his benefactor to preach for them. Seybert hereupon left an appointment for the time when he expected to come by that way again.

At the appointed time he was on the spot and preached in the weaver's house, to a large number of people who were deeply moved by the Word. The result was, that the weaver and his family were soon converted to God, and henceforth received the preachers of the Evangelical Association with joy. A work of grace began in the community and a good class was organized of which the weaver became the class-leader, and a church was afterwards built. He had a good income, lived a pious life with his family, was useful in the church and was soon enabled to pay back the money again which Bro. Seybert had given him. Seybert finally accepted the principal, but declined the interest. This was characteristic. In whatever he did, he had in view the salvation of souls and the interests of his Church.   He knew how to turn circumstances into account for this purpose.

During the latter part of 1846, he labored under great bodily weakness.   He had not reached his aim at all, on account of physical infirmities, having traveled "only four thousand seven hundred and five miles and preached only one hundred and sixty-seven times".

During the Winter and Spring of 1847 he continued to endure great pain, and his debility was a great hindrance, so that he only preached nine times and traveled a hundred and fifty-eight miles in April. *"Lord,"* he exclaimed, *"do make me well again!* if it be Thy will; but if not, give me grace to be patient and to quietly resign myself to my lot, and to suffer according to Thy righteous will, for the sake of Jesus Christ, Thy dear Son.   Amen."

In this condition he held the Ohio conference, May 12th, and afterwards, in spite of his great weakness, started westward to attend the Illinois conference. He rode through Indiana and Michigan to Joliet, Ill., through terrible roads.   On the way he had repeated attacks of fever, and his rheumatic affection was also greatly aggravated.   Most men would have succumbed.   But Seybert fought his way through, and reached Naperville, the place of the Illinois conference session, one day before the conference began. This session, was a blessed one; especially were the communion and ordination services accompanied with visitations of Divine power.

On this great journey he was greatly troubled on

account of a lack of preachers, which he anticipated. But he was agreeably disappointed, as a number of applicants appeared, and the wants of the conference were amply supplied. This made him glad, and his anxiety was allayed. He says: "But a few years ago we had a single mission in the great West, and now we have a whole conference of three extensive Presiding Elder districts. The Lord hath done this. Praise Him!"

During the Summer of '47 he attended two camp-meetings in Illinois, one at Wheeling, the other at Naperville, where at times a score and more lay at the altar of prayer, who obtained pardon one after another. "Some of these had just arrived, fresh from Germany, and had been warned against us before coming, by their relatives, who called us deceivers and liars. Notwithstanding this, they came to the meetings to see for themselves, were convinced that it was the Lord's work, yielded, were converted, and became members of our Church."

At Naperville the flower-decked meadows surrounding the encampment, the dark green grove, hedged in as holy ground by a beautiful circle of large white tents, the spiritual singing, the touching pleadings of penitents, altogether stirred his soul to its depths as he arrived. The scene made a deep impression on his mind. There was beauty and grandeur of nature hallowed by the influences of heavenly grace.

After these meetings the bishop started for the East. The eastern people began to charge him with unfairness, and thought he paid more attention to the West than to the East. And so he did. But he justified himself with the assertion that it was more needed in the West. In the East the work went on in its usual manner, as there was no lack of experienced men, while in the West the battle was much more severe, and in his opinion it was his calling to stand *where the fight is hottest.* This could not be gainsaid. He had helped to storm the enemy's castles in Pennsylvania and planted the banner on the most perilous ramparts, and then concluded that they could help themselves without him, while he wanted to be among the pioneers in the West. As the line of battle and conquest moved westward, the old hero on his white horse rode bravely ahead, and kept pace with the westward sweep of the star of empire. In his hand he brandished no gold-hilted sword, but a tried Damascus blade, the two-edged sword of the Spirit, which in his hand was never allowed to rust or grow dull. Small of stature, and quick of movement, he rushed hither and thither, managing a longer line of battle from the Atlantic to the Mississippi than the greatest general ever did, his keen eye always detecting where the heaviest fighting was needed, his countenance beaming with enthusiasm and holy courage, and his voice of encouragement ringing out like a clarion, thrilling the wavering lines with the inspirations of hope and victory! The Church could not grow indolent while a man of such fiery enthusiasm and indomitable heroism stood at the head. Wherever he went, fresh courage filled the hearts. Like

Bonaparte, Seybert's presence was worth an army, and for many years his name was a terror to the black battalions of sin. This man never was fully appreciated. Had he lived under more popular surroundings, his fame would rank with the greatest of his generation.

Leaving Illinois he went through Indiana, Michigan, Ohio and Pennsylvania, visiting, preaching and doing an incredible amount of work in a very short time, and reached New Berlin, Pa., just a day before the General conference convened at that place, September 29th, 1847. This body elected Seybert to the episcopacy for the third term. He made the following entry in his journal: "To-day, October 22d, 1847, the conferences attended to the election of General Superintendents and again elected two for the four ensuing years, namely, Joseph Long and John Seybert. Thus this to me unspeakable important office has been imposed upon me again. O Lord, help! O Lord, give success! Amen."

CHAPTER XIII.

VICTORIES.

After the General conference in the Fall of 1847, Bishop Seybert traveled quite extensively through both the Pennsylvania conferences, and "had good times" among his eastern friends, witnessing much shouting and rejoicing. In the East Pennsylvania, there had been a great drought all Summer and Autumn, but in the Winter the Lord had mercy, and visited this part of our Evangelical Zion with a gracious rain, and times of refreshing came from the presence of the Lord. There were many conversions and many revivals among the members. Especially had the work increased in Lancaster, Lebanon and other counties, in the cities of Reading, Philadelphia, Orwigsburg, Lebanon and New York. The brethren had also pushed into new regions of darkness; the conference lengthened her cord, and strengthened her stakes, and widened the place of her tent. The conversions, he observed, were genuine, which "enraged the devil and his servants". This was the long looked-for result of twenty years of faithful and seemingly useless effort. Ever and again the Lord's captains were repulsed, but at last their preaching began to tell, and the Lord made a way for His truth.

In the Spring of 1848, Seybert held the two Pennsylvania conferences, and soon after started for the West. His health was good, and his soul was full of courage to "*drive* the work of the Lord." That was a suggestive phrase of his, thoroughly characteristic of the man. He anticipated much pleasure in soon again riding through the green groves and over the broad prairies of the West, decked with their unrivaled wealth and beauty of flowers, and there to sing of victory in the humble dwellings of the saints. It is not to be denied that Seybert was in love with the West. He was in spirit, enterprise and pluck a western man by nature.

On his way to the West he spent forty days in Ohio, and attended the session of the Ohio conference. May 29th he reached the State of Michigan and spent Ascension Day on Ann Arbor mission, preaching three times on that day. In the morning his theme was "The Incarnation of Christ in the Flesh"; in the afternoon "The Ascension", and in the evening "Christ's Future Coming to the General Judgment". He says it was a blessed day, and they realized the gentle breathings of the Holy Spirit. After spending seven days in Michigan, he reached Mishawaka, Indiana, where he preached the closing sermon of a protracted meeting, from Matt. 7:13, 14. This was undoubtedly a remarkable effort, for two souls were converted during the sermon, and the demonstrations of the congregation were so great that the Bishop was obliged to cut his sermon short and sit down, unable to proceed.

At Cold Water, Michigan, he chanced to be present at an M. E. conference session, where he heard Bishop Hamline preach. But Seybert remained incognito, not even revealing his official station to the preachers with whom he stayed at the hotel.

Pentecost found him in Cook Co., Ill., at a camp-meeting. The Bishop says it was a genuine Pentecost, as the Spirit of the Lord was poured out upon them. Two hundred and eighty-six communicants participated in the celebration of the Lord's Supper, and penitents crowded to the altar in throngs and sought and found pardon.

Soon afterwards, the conference met at the same place, and the session was a great blessing to the community. The reports showed that the work had increased on their hands during the year, and the membership had enlarged considerably. There was also a goodly number of young recruits to the itinerant ranks, which pleased the bishop. He said, if these men all seek the equipment from above, and continue in the work, they can be a great blessing to the West.

At this session of the Illinois conference, the first steps were taken towards sending a missionary to Europe, to labor among the Germans in the fatherland. Bishop Seybert was appointed as a steward to receive and manage the moneys that should be contributed for this purpose.

From here, after attending another camp-meeting, he went to Racine, Wisconsin, to dedicate a new church edifice. This was an occasion of joy to him, as the building was substantially built of brick, well arranged and commodious, situated in a large and growing city of the great Northwest, and the work gave promise of permanent growth and success.

October 13th found him in Indiana. Here somewhere the friends had erected a large log church, which pleased him. Presumably it was just such a plain, unpretentious structure as suited him. He says, the work began there three years before. Two years before conversions took place, but the devil rose up in wrath, and would not let the brethren into the school-house. However, a society of three classes was formed, and they built the log church, consequently they were no longer dependent upon others. Seybert preached to. them from Psalm 126, and the Lord blessed the friends so powerfully that some of them were, so to speak, "spiritually drunken". It has been noticed, that he often took that text' on such occasions, when he intended to pour out the "best of the wine". In connection with this text, it is said, he seldom used a hymn from the hymn-book of the Church, but recited from memory, and with the greatest accuracy, a poetical composition of Schiller.

In the Autumn of 1848 he attended a camp-meeting on Dubois circuit, of which he says: "Our people at this place have a well arranged camp-ground, with permanent log tents and preacher's stand, close by the church, which is a refuge in rainy weather. The whole institution stands on a forty acre strip of woodland, which is dedicated to Almighty God as Church property, and that by poor German people, who but recently came to this country. Where will you find a similar arrangement among our well-to-do American brethren?—*But these latter need more for their devotion to the fashions and the luxuries of the day.*"

About this time the first important revival took place in the city of Cleveland, Ohio, which has since become the official headquarters of the Church. We had the privilege a few years ago to hear, from the lips of the first member of the Evangelical Association in that city, the story of its small beginnings. This was old "Mother Schnuerer", who but recently entered into rest.

The Schnuerers had been converted in Buffalo, N. Y., and now lived by the lake in the small city of Cleveland. One day Mrs. Schnuerer saw a man riding along the street dressed unmistakably in the garb of an Evangelical itinerant. She could hardly believe for joy, for it had been years since they had seen any of the preachers of their Church. Mrs. Schnuerer hailed him, and asked him if he were not a preacher of the Evangelical Association. He affirmed that he was. The joy was mutual. Arrangements were promptly made to have preaching at Schnuerer's, and Cleveland became a regular appointment of one of the pioneer circuits of Ohio. This was in 1840, and the preacher was either A. Stroh or John Holl, who traveled on Lake circuit that year. For an account of this beginning, the reader is referred to Orwig's "History of the Evangelical Association", p. 310 et seq., English edition.

February 22d, 1849, Seybert says: "At last our desire concerning Cleveland is being realized. During a recent protracted meeting, both old and young were converted. Yesterday I preached twice there. It was a profitable day. A goodly number of promising people have been converted and added to our number, while many others are certainly under deep conviction. It has long been our wish to witness such a season on Cleveland mission, and the time has come. The Lord has heard our prayers and sent us help. Blessed be His holy Name!"

During this year Bishop Seybert again presided at the Ohio and Illinois conferences. From the session of the former conference, which was held in Emanuel church, Pickaway county, he proceeded northward. After spending Pentecost, and *having* a real Pentecost at Gideon Falk's in Hancock Co. (probably now Mt. Cory), he went by way of Perrysburg, Ohio, and Adrian, Michigan, to Ann Arbor, where he labored several days, preaching and visiting from house to house. The work there was prosperous, and a church edifice had been begun.

The Illinois conference met June 20th in Naperville, Illinois. The session lasted nine days. The religious services were richly blessed and largely attended.

At Freeport, Illinois, Seybert's horse ran away with the wagon, and finally leaped over a heap of lumber, breaking harness and conveyance, to the great annoyance of the Bishop. He naively asks: "Was this of the devil, or did it simply occur accidentally?"

Towards the end of July he hastened through Indiana, Ohio, Michigan, Upper Canada and New York, to Pennsylvania. He calls attention to the fact, that though he was nearly a broken down man he was yet able to travel through cities and communities, where the cholera and other epidemics were at that time raging with fatal fury, without being himself harmed, and could preach two and three times daily, as necessity might require.

On this trip he was forced at one place in Indiana, by a great rain and flood, to stop at a hotel. This was in a place popularly called Centre of Hell.

Its real name was Centreville, but on account of its wickedness was given this suggestive cognomen. It was Seybert's custom, if he caught a glimpse of the hostler, to ride directly to the barn, so as to give his personal care to his horse. He says: "When I reached the barn I found myself at once among the Belialites. They were on the hay-loft in large groups, playing cards and carousing at a terrible rate. Then I went to the house and found it worse yet. Here they were engaged in worse than bestial intoxication and debauchery. A few yards from the hotel was a saloon, in which a Democratic office seeker was haranguing the crowd. Here was

"Confusion worse confounded."

It was the Bishop's judgment that this ugly cognomen was as appropriate as could well be, "for here certainly is the *devil's nest*, an open gate of hell. The veritable devil lives here."

During the journey described above the Bishop

lodged with a family in the State of Michigan, with whom he had already been acquainted for nearly thirty years. The visit was the occasion of mutual pleasure. After supper and family worship had been concluded, Seybert united in matrimony an estimable pair of young people in the presence of the family. The evening was spent in earnest religious conversation. "This", says the Bishop, "was a genuine Christian wedding, free from drunkenness, gluttony and carousal, and without display, frivolity and extravagance of any kind."

After he had traveled through part of the New York conference, he crossed Niagara and invaded the Queen's dominions again. He spent some days at Stony Creek, preached at Puslinch and on Black Creek and Home circuits, and in the towns of Hamburg, Waterloo and Berlin. He was permitted to see the work of the Lord prospering in all these places, and witnessed conversions almost everywhere. In one of his meetings on Black Creek, the Bishop had among his auditors a Mennonite bishop and a woman ninety-five years old. At this place a glorious work of grace was in progress, which had begun in the Sunday-school. Afterwards at a meeting in Sodom Bush many Mennonites "broke through into spiritual life", and joined our people at the Lord's table. They had to suffer derision and persecution, however, from the unconverted. The Lord was with His own. The converted Mennonites now received the Evangelical preachers, and the prospects for still greater success were good. The Bishop spent three weeks in Canada. At his meetings in Waterloo, Berlin and Hamburg, the people came to the services in such throngs that it was impossible for the churches to hold them. The Bishop had great pleasure among the plain zealous friends there, and found them alive unto good works, upright in life and "hating the fashions". He gave this as a reason for expecting many conversions.

Then he returned to the State of New York, preaching at Buffalo, Lyons, Rochester and Syracuse. At Oswego, where we had no church, he intended to remain till next day. He quickly inquired after the Germans of the place, visited them, and preached to them that same evening. He had a good meeting. These Germans were without a preacher, and greatly desired our preachers to come among them. The Bishop spent sixty-three days in this conference, traveling sixteen hundred miles, and then crossed over into East Pennsylvania, the scene of his early labors, sufferings and successes. He was much pleased to find a spirit of enterprise here, which manifested itself in building church edifices and supporting the missionary cause. Learning that a project was on foot to build a Memorial church at the grave of the sainted Jacob Albright in Lebanon Co., Pa., Seybert expressed his unqualified approval. It had long been his fervent wish. He hoped the enterprise would be liberally supported by the friends near and far.

In that unusually benighted vicinity called "Devil's Hole" the work of the Lord was spreading. At this

19

place, which owed its ugly name to its ugly character, a church was built soon after the Bishop's visit, to which then eighbors, not belonging to the society, contributed from fifty to a hundred dollars a piece. As a great reformation took place, the name of the locality was then changed to the more euphonious Lewistown Valley.

At the close of the year of 1849 he recorded the fact, that his health had been preserved, while thousands, less exposed, died of cholera, fevers and other scourges. On the whole, he traveled five thousand six hundred and ninety miles, preached about three hundred times, besides visiting many hundreds of families, praying with the well and the sick. But to the Lord he gave all the praise.

The year 1850 was celebrated in the Evangelical Association as a year of jubilee, it being the completion of a half century since the first organization of the Church by Jacob Albright. Bishop Seybert wrote at the beginning of the year: "In all probability this will be a prosperous year in our Church. I am expecting a glorious year of jubilee, for all the indications are favorable. I hope it will bring abundant fruit to our little Zion."

Bishop Seybert celebrated this event in his own peculiar manner. He refused to receive any salary whatever, and absolutely insisted on paying all his expenses out of his own private purse. In fact, from that time he never accepted traveling expenses at all, and would not have accepted his salary, had he not been severely censured by the brethren for such a

course. They insisted he should receive his salary,
and then, if he desired, he might dispose of it for
benevolent purposes, according to his own judgment.
This advice he followed. Though he accepted his
salary, he never thereafter used any of it for private
purposes, but devoted it all to the funds and enterprises of the Church, paying his personal expenditures.
out of his own private purse. He thus not only
preached liberality, but practiced it on a truly magnificent scale.

CHAPTER XIV.

IN PERILS OFT.

In 1850 Seybert had to hold both the Pennsylvania conferences and the New York conference. On his trip to the New York conference session he had much pleasure in his intercourse with the friends, who received him everywhere as an angel of God, especially in Clinton, Centre and Lycoming circuits, Penn'a. On his way he made numerous calls and preached nearly every evening. About this time he began to ride in a conveyance, as he could not endure horseback riding any longer. His conveyance, however, was a very primitive affair, in which the Bishops of the High Church of England, or the lordly prelates of the Roman Church would hardly consent to ride. He was humble and economical in this respect also. His rig was in fact only an old-fashioned, rural one-horse "dandy wagon", without springs, having a broad and deep seat, upon which he laid a sheep skin, in lieu of a cushion. He always carried a chest of books with him, and the inevitable saddle-bag—a double leathern pouch, made to be strapped across the saddle when riding on horse-back. It took the place of the modern "grip sack" of the itinerant. With this out-fit the Bishop started northward into the State of New York, in the month of April. Near Williamsport, Pa., south of the Alleghanies, he came to Lycoming creek, above the city, a swift and powerful stream, large enough to be called a river. It flows down from the Alleghany mountains, and hence has a tremendous fall, besides being quite deep and wide. Just at this time the snows were melting on the mountains, causing an extensive freshet.

It was April 5th. He found the stream reaching far beyond its natural channel, and saw at once that great care would be necessary in crossing, as there was no bridge, but only a ford. He stopped, surveyed the wild and dangerous scene, and thought to himself, "I am familiar with this ford, and I have often crossed it at flood tide; my animal is a good swimmer; I have appointments on the other side and must hasten on; in the name of the Lord I will venture in." He accordingly drove in. He soon realized, however, that his famous swimmer would have all he could do to get its rider through. He headed up stream, and for a while made good headway. But when he got into the central current, the flood lifted his conveyance up, and forcing it down stream, upset it finally, and spilled out bishop, books and saddle-bags. This greatly hindered the horse in swimming, and also began to float down with the mad current. But for this, the faithful beast would have landed everything safely. As it was, horse, conveyance, Bishop, book-chest, saddle-bags and all, lay scattered about on the resistless tide of the river. The Bishop now let go the lines, so as to give the horse all the liberty possible, to land the wagon and itself. The horse succeeded after a brave struggle. Seybert himself fought the flood, swam and struggled as best he could, and succeeded in reaching the shore in safety. Horse and bishop reached the dry ground about the same time. Some men who were near, then came to his assistance, and recovered his saddle-bags and bookchest, which were floating rapidly down the tide. His loss he estimated at about fifteen dollars. The current volume of his journal also fell into the water, but he dried its soaked leaves again and used it for his daily entries for two years after that. Only the last few pages were too wrinkled to write upon. The book still shows the effect of this adventure in every page.

This perilous adventure and narrow escape had the effect to make him far less venturesome than formerly. Until that time he had scarcely known fear, and made many dangerous ventures in his extensive pioneer travels through the wild and unimproved regions of the new continent. But after this he frequently hired conductors and guides where there was no real danger.

April 11th he reached the New York conference district, and called a halt in the vicinity of Seneca Falls. He found it necessary to "rest a little", but as usual his resting was done by visiting numerous families through the day and preaching at night. This is what *he* called "resting", or "having a vacation", or "recuperating from the fatigue of a journey".

In spite of perils and hardships Bishop Seybert reached Syracuse, N. Y., April 15th, where the session of the conference began on the 17th. The business of the conference was transacted with unusual dispatch, and the preaching services were instructive and powerful. The ordination service was exceedingly impressive, and at the missionary meeting on Sunday afternoon the friends manifested special liberality in the good cause. In the British dominions — Upper Canada — the prospects were reported good, and the conference established another mission there. The missionary zeal was alive and the Bishop thought, "so long as we are active in this, there is hope that the Lord's work among us will flourish, as well in the established societies as in the mission fields. Should we lose the missionary spirit, however, there must necessarily be retrogression among us in efforts for the glory of God and the salvation of the world."

For a short time after this conference session, the Bishop had business to transact in New York in the interests of the "Benevolent Society of the Evangelical Association". Meanwhile he also preached here and there, especially on Lake circuit, where he says he had "good times". He also visited many sick, and learned that "our members were resigned to their lot, and satisfied, whether the Lord let them live or die".

After his special business affairs had been adjusted in the State of New York, he went to Canada, where he enjoyed himself hugely and felt at home. He always seemed pleased with the character of the work in the Dominion, and this time praised it in his journal as follows: "In this part of our large field of operations there exist several good and decidedly praiseworthy features, namely: First. A thorough and most healthful kind of conversions. Second. A lively worship in Spirit and in the truth. Third. A spirit of self-denial which abhors ungodly pride and the worldly fashions. ·

On his return from Canada Bro. Seybert crossed Niagara at Buffalo, from where, in company with a brother, he made a visit to a settlement or colony of Germans who were known as the *"Inspired"*, but who called their organization *"Ebenezer"*. This society owned eight thousand acres of land six miles south of Buffalo, and numbered about a thousand members. Within a space of three miles they laid out three villages, and made great progress during the six years of their settlement in the cultivation of the soil, and in the erection of mills and manufactories. They also built a large meeting-house, in which their teacher or prophet, Mr. Christian Metz, preached and enforced their doctrines. This man sometimes became '*inspired*'. On such occasions he employed certain scribes, who acted as his amanuenses and recorded his words. His utterances at such times, served as the rule of conduct for these people thereafter, as well as the Holy Scriptures. This 'prophet', however, seemed to Seybert to be a very estimable man.

These people led a temperate life in eating and drinking, and were very plain in their dress. The "devilish pride" and fashionable display did not exist among them, neither conformity to the world, therefore, the Bishop remarked, "they do not suffer from that loss of time and sinful extravagance in expenditures which are required by vanity. They also prefer the celibate state of life, and lay great·stress upon virtue and continence". The genial Bishop wished them God's blessing.

On his way west he preached extensively in Ohio. At the home of Bishop Long in Columbiana county he waited two days, which he considered a long time, for the return of Long, who was to meet him there by appointment. The two bishops appointed September 9th for the meeting of the Board of Missions at Pittsburgh, which was to select and send a missionary to Germany. This was in 1850, as per Seybert's journal.

At Ann Arbor, Michigan, he says:

"Recently a 'spiritual guide' (?) here re-christened a child which our missionary had already baptized. On this occasion he also let loose upon us as the 'deceivers' and 'false teachers'. But if this person wanted to re-baptize all the children that have been baptized by heretics and unconverted ministers — especially by such as teach baptismal regeneration, —he will have his hands full for a while. How can such men re-baptize children, who pledge themselves at their ordination into the sacred office, to follow and defend the Augsburg confession? And especially where children have been baptized by regularly ordained ministers? Does not the Augsburg confession in the original unchanged edition say, in the article on Baptism, that *all re-baptizers are accursed*?

According to that dictum this man is accursed. — Or is that article in the Augsburg confession a heresy? But they now want to justify this re-baptizer by reporting that our missionary baptized the child in question in his own name, instead of the name of God. Such liars and lie-peddlers ought to read the Bible diligently, so that they might learn into what an awful place all liars are consigned; perhaps they would then be persuaded to be converted to God and inherit eternal life — a consummation devoutly to be wished for."

Early on the morning of July 4th he "felt a most blessed influence from the world of light", and suddenly had a great enlightening on Rom. 13:12: "The night is far spent, the day is at hand, let us therefore cast off the works of darkness, and let us put on the armour of light!" He felt God's gracious presence early and had a blessed day. The heat was great, and he was now traveling in real pilgrim fashion, with the staff in his hand, as his horse was lame; but it made him tired.

Bishop Seybert was now in his sixtieth year. He says of himself: "I am well and hearty, and still able to endure hard journeys, and to preach daily. If necessary, I could preach three and even four times in one day, a thing I could do to-day. But I am admonished that the night cometh, when no man can work, and I am therefore determined to help all I can to gather sheaves into the Lord's garner before sunset." Leaving Michigan he turned his face westward, and went through Indiana to Illinois.

His journey through Indiana was very exhausting. In the northern part of the State his route lay through dense, dark and extensive forests, where the roads were bad, but the spiritual meetings encouraged him. These gatherings of the saints were to him like so many Elims in the desert. The months of September and October he spent on the grassy meads and in the groves of Illinois and Wisconsin. His programme was to spend the Autumn in the far West; Christmas he wanted to spend in Dayton, Ohio. From September 14th to 16th he was at a camp-meeting at Naperville, Ill. The meeting was blessed with great power and life, with convictions and conversions. The sons of Belial carried on a terrible, devilish uproar at night around the camp, but, says Seybert,— "There we have a solid foot-hold—let Satan rage!"

He found a state of universal prosperity on the mission fields of the West. On Sauk mission there were many penitents and conversions when he was there. On the day of the Jubilee celebration he attended two good meetings, and the benevolent contributions on that day were liberal. In Stephenson Co., Ill., he had much pleasure among old friends, who had removed thither from Pennsylvania. In the city of Freeport arrangements were being made to build a house of worship. The Bishop thought it was high time, as the many Germans there were much in need of a place in which to worship God in Spirit and in truth. In North Grove, Illinois, he helped at a meeting held in a hall which had formerly been a sanctuary of Bacchus. But when the owner and his wife were converted, they dedicated the room to the service of God. Thus this portal of hell was changed into a gate of Heaven.

Towards the end of November he began to turn his face eastward, so as to reach Dayton, Ohio, by Christmas. His purpose was accomplished. He spent the closing days of 1850 in that city. In his journal entry for the close of the year, which is dated Dayton, O., he says:

"In this year I have received much good from the hand of the Lord. The year is now almost gone, and I am thankful for its blessings. Under God's blessing my travels have been as follows: In Pennsylvania, one hundred and six days; in New York, fifty days; in Ohio, sixty days; in Michigan, eleven days; in Indiana, thirty-four days; in Illinois, eighty-one days; in Canada, only three days; in Wisconsin, fourteen days; in Maryland, six days; *total:* three hundred and sixty-five days. According to conference districts, the time was divided as follows: East Penn., forty-six days; West Penn., fifty-four days; New York, fifty-one days; Ohio, one hundred and one days; Illinois, one hundred and thirteen days. Total, three hundred and sixty-five days. My journey was five thousand one hundred and sixty-nine miles long."

Thus the restless preacher traveled through eight different States of the Union, besides Canada, — a territory extending from the Atlantic coast to the Mississippi river, in one year. When one remembers that he seldom, if ever, employed the swift iron horse, but only a private conveyance, and even part of the time went on foot, it will be seen what a herculean activity Bishop Seybert manifested in his sixtieth year. It appears also that there was not an idle day in the year. Few men observe such system, or are able to give such accurate account of themselves.

January 8th, 1851, Seybert came to Columbus, Ohio. As he wanted to stay all night, he inquired for a German hotel, where he could stay "all night in a decent manner". He was shown one, to which he went, supposing he had found a decent place. Hardly, however, had his horse been put away, before he discovered that he had made a mistake. One of the servants, intending to tell the stranger good news, said, "*This evening we have a ball here!*" "So!" said Seybert with a sigh, while his blue-gray eyes opened widely. He had a mind not to stay now, but his horse was already unhitched, and it was getting dark.

After supper he started off to take a stroll through the city. But at leaving, he was strongly urged to take part in the dance, which he abruptly refused, and went on. He soon learned that the German Methodists had a protracted meeting in progress in the city. He sought their place of assembling, and entered the church, softly and unnoticed, where the congregation was on its knees, engaged in earnest prayer, and in laboring with penitents. Here the unobserved and unrecognized Bishop felt at home. The cry of penitents, mingled with the hearty spiritual German singing, made a pleasing impression upon his weary mind. It was to him the house of God and the gate of heaven. But alas! all too soon for him did the young pastor close the services. It was the signal for the distressed Seybert to go back to his hotel, which was a perfect hell to him. Unknown he left the church and went to the hotel, where the children of the devil were assembled in large numbers in a capacious hall, in the rear of the building. *Their* meeting was not over yet, in fact it was just fairly beginning. They were just getting into the stream and excitement of the occasion. The Bishop declares that such fearful raging, howling, stamping and carousing he had never heard in all his life—and we know that he had seen and heard much in those barbarous days. The devilish carousal continued until daylight. In vain did the weary prophet try to sleep. He says; "Here I was in hell, in which we are told there is *no rest.* O that the spiritual advisers of these deluded people would take pains to put an end to such disorder!"—And this was a night in a *"decent"* German hotel in the city of Columbus, Ohio, in 1851.

Seybert spent the Winter and Spring of '51 in Ohio. From Columbus he went northward, in the midst of very severe weather, and reached Mohican district Feb. 1st. Near Big Prairie, Wayne Co., he preached at a place where the friends were building a new church. A revival broke out in a large settlement of European Germans, mostly drunkards and Sabbath-breakers. The work of the Evangelical preachers had resulted in changing this benighted people

into a company of true children of God. This was
what afterwards became the well-known Hope church,
in the vicinity of the Sprengs. The establishment of
that society was indeed a wonderful work of grace,
and resulted in sending out no less than four ministers
of the Gospel in later years. Bishop Seybert, when
he saw the grace of God here, was glad. He remained
several days.

The dedication of this church in March, 1851, as
Seybert records it in his journal, was a memorable
occasion. There was great rejoicing among the
people of God, and many sinners were converted.
The meeting was continued several days, and, as
was his custom, the Bishop organized at once an
auxiliary missionary society. These, in fact were
notable features of the dedicatory occasions of those
times.

After the session of the Ohio conference in May,
Seybert started for the Illinois conference, taking his
route through Michigan and Indiana, where, on
account of much rain, the streams were everywhere
swollen, bridges swept away and the roads almost
impassable. In Indiana, however, he was joined by
other brethren, who also were going to conference.
Their company greatly alleviated the toil of the
journey for the sociable and friendly Bishop. June
3d they reached Illinois, and enjoyed rich spiritual
feasts in the meetings they attended in Chicago,
Des Plaines, Dutchman's Point and other places.

Three days he spent in the vicinity of Wheeling.
He says: "In these three days I had great pleasure

among my spiritual sons and daughters. I visited above thirty families, and was permitted to rejoice in spirit at the Christian courage and pious zeal of these my spiritual children, whom I have begotten in the Gospel. God gave me these children as seals to my ministry during the last eighteen years. God hath done it, — and love receives the gift devoutly. To Him be all the praise."

On the ninth the company reached a camp-meeting at Naperville, which was blessed with notable displays of Divine saving power. Penitents great and small, young and old lay at the altar in great numbers, and their cries for mercy continued through the entire night.

On his way back to the approaching session of the General conference, Seybert had the pleasure of traveling three hundred and fifty miles in company with his colleague, Bishop Joseph Long. They enjoyed themselves greatly in the religious services they attended. As usual, however, Seybert took a long, round-about way to his destination. Though he started in Illinois, and the conference was in Ohio, he went all the way to the cities of New York, Philadelphia and Reading, and attended camp-meetings in Pennsylvania before returning.

Of the close of his third term of office he writes:

"I am happy, healthy and of good courage to prosecute the work of the Lord. Still, my old almost broken-down body sometimes becomes very faint through these long journeys in the great heat. I am also at the close of my term of service again. General conference is at the door, to which I must now hasten westward."

This General conference met in the old stone church at Flat Rock, Seneca Co., Ohio, where Seybert's body found its last resting place afterwards, and now awaits the glory of the resurrection morning.

He was here elected to his fourth term as bishop. This was but another occasion of humiliation before God, and he resolved to strive still to become more perfect in the love toward God and his fellow-men, and to dedicate the rest of his life *entirely* to the Lord.

At this session also it was resolved to remove the Publishing House of the Evangelical Association from New Berlin, Pa., to Cleveland, Ohio, where it now is, as soon as nine thousand dollars should be subscribed for such purpose.

John Nicolai, of the Ohio conference, was appointed as a missionary to Germany.

After the tenth session of the General conference was over, Seybert again started eastward.

October 18th and 19th he spent in Pittsburgh, and was greatly edified in the meetings there. He says that after great trials and severe conflicts, at last a better time had come there, and a friendly "star of hope" beamed upon our work in that important city.

During the Winter of 1851—1852 there were many conversions in the Pennsylvania conferences, and Bishop Seybert published the following manifesto in the "*Botschafter*":

"My retrospect of the work in the two Pennsyl-
20

vania conferences in the past Winter moves me to heart-felt thankfulness for the love and kindness which the dear friends have shown me. But I would specially remind the friends in the East, of what the Lord has done during the last conference year, in the moral elevation and spiritual reformation of some of the most benighted regions. Genuine conversions have taken place there in a manner that is not often witnessed. The newly converted, however, who, at these revivals, have found the priceless pearl of a change of heart, I would admonish, as an humble co-laborer in the vineyard of the Lord, to adopt the sentiment of the holy David: 'Bless the Lord, O my soul, and let all that is within me bless his holy name. Bless the Lord, O my soul, and forget not all his benefits. Who forgiveth all thine iniquities, who healeth all thy diseases', etc. I beg also, that you die unto self, unto the world and unto all wickedness, by exercising Christian self-denial, by daily taking up the Cross, and following the Lord Jesus in a holy life and walk. Yea, that you may wrestle with tears and prayers, with all the heart, until you are purified from all sin, delivered from all evil, fully healed, and transformed by divine truth; that like Enoch of old you may walk with God, that is, lead a godly, chaste, righteous and devoted life in this wicked world.

"But this is a strange and despised doctrine in our enlightened and very corrupt age, and among the thousands of *new-style* converts. To become free from all sin, to purify one's self, 'even as He is pure', and then to be enabled to live without sinning

(1 John 3:3, 9), is carrying the matter entirely too far for the majority of our modern Christians. They hope to get to heaven without this. This also is the cause that among many so-called converted people fruits unto holiness appear so sparsely, and that the church swarms with such miserable, worldly minded, backslidden professors of religion. These people are only a stumbling block to the world, and probably are the chief cause that Deism, Atheism, Universalism and other damnable isms are gaining such prevalence in many places.

"It is, therefore, in my opinion, highly necessary, that all faithful teachers and disciples of Jesus, who are aware of this destruction, should with redoubled earnestness emphasize the doctrines of growth in grace and Christian perfection.—But let them also exemplify and demonstrate these doctrines by their own life and conduct, then it will have weight when they speak."

After the session of the East Pennsylvania conference in 1852, in Pinegrove, Pa., the Bishop delivered a brilliant temperance address in the evening, and next day started on an extensive tour over bad roads. He first went to New Berlin, Pa., on business with the Publishing House, and then went four hundred miles northward to Berlin, Upper Canada. This was a laborious trip. The weather was cold, stormy and inclement. Great hail storms occurred, and immense quantities of snow and rain fell, together making the roads almost impassable. At Lyons, New York, he was joined by several ministerial brethren, whose company relieved greatly the fatigue of the journey. The New York conference session was held in Berlin, Canada, April 14th. The conference was a rich spiritual feast for preachers and people. The religious services and the preaching were accompanied with great power from on high.

April 21st he again crossed the Niagara by means of that marvel of human engineering skill and enterprise, the Suspension Bridge. His objective point was Bristol (now Marshallville), Wayne Co., O., where the Ohio conference met May 12th. Seybert reached Bristol on the 11th. Bishop Long was also present, and was to have presided, but was sick, and Seybert took his place. The conference closed, leaving the sick Bishop behind. Seybert expressed the confidence that the Lord would restore his colleague again, and spare him to long usefulness in the Church.

The next point was Naperville, Illinois, the place where the Illinois conference was to meet. The Bishop calls the distance five hundred miles, which was undoubtedly the case, the way he went. On the way he attended two glorious camp-meetings, the one at Elkhart, Ind., the other at Wheeling, Ill. Both were seasons of power. The trip was otherwise also pleasant on account of the fine Spring weather and good roads.

The session of the Illinois conference was an important one. There was much business, as the Indiana conference had to be formed. The business was also difficult on account of the extensive fields of labor that had to be supplied. The religious services were also richly blessed here. As the church proved too small for the congregation, the ordination sermon was preached on the adjacent camp-ground. An immense congregation assembled, and listened with devout attention to the sermon of the Bishop. As the brethren of the conference separated into two conferences, the formal parting of the brethren was signalized by the celebration of the Love Feast, at which they had a touching time and a precious waiting before the Lord.

July 7th, 1852. "To-day I am sixty-one years old. O Thou eternal and marvellously good God! How much goodness I have received in these sixty-one years of my life! Daily, hourly, yea momentarily have I been blessed temporally and spiritually. Where shall I get the feelings, and who will represent me with words fit to praise Thee, O God, as I ought for this! Eternity will be too short."

> "Come, O my soul, in sacred lays,
> And sing thy great Creator's praise:
> But oh! what tongue can speak His fame?
> What mortal verse can reach the theme?"

In July the Bishop crossed the Mississippi, and spent ten days in the State of Iowa, hunting up old friends from Pennsylvania, preaching in new communities and prospecting for the Church. He crossed the "Father of Waters" at Rock Island, and visited old members in Louisa Co., held a quarterly meeting west of Iowa city, and preached in a United Brethren church at Lisbon, Linn Co. Here, he says, the people were so happy that they sang aloud while on the way home. The work in those regions was at that time weak as yet, the appointments few and far between, and the hardships of travel greatly increased by the crossing of many unbridged streams. But the prospects for success among the Germans there he thought good, as immigration to this large, beautiful, healthy and wealthy State was setting in very strongly. He wished, however, for men working here who had the spirit of love for men in a sufficient degree to adopt the sentiment of Paul when he said, "I could wish that myself were accursed from Christ for my brethren, my kinsmen according to the flesh."

After ten days in Iowa he took a tour through southern Wisconsin. There the work had hard struggling against superstition and infidelity, and was also opposed by those who claim to be orthodox, but live in wickedness and are decidedly the enemies of Christ's disciples. And yet the work had made great progress, souls were saved and the Lord was glorified. The prospects were good and the opportunities great, but means and men were wanting. There also the harvest was great and the laborers were few.

July 30th (1852) he reached Sauk City, Wisconsin. Though he had traveled thirty-nine miles that day, he afterwards walked four miles to a prayer-meeting, talked on Luke 18:1–8, and walked three miles with a brother afterwards to stay all night. In the vicinity of Ragatz's a society had grown up very rapidly. Seybert himself preached there in 1844, before there had been any organization whatever. The Germans were without preaching, and the community was in great darkness. "But the Spirit of the Lord brooded with His light-creating influences over the moral darkness, the brethren labored on in faith, and the people became convinced of the necessity of conversion. In 1851 a fine church was dedicated there. In 1852 the society erected a parsonage, though many of the people were themselves living in poor huts. One brother deeded six acres of land for the purpose. The society was large enough to be divided into five classes."

There was a place, however, east of Wheeling, Illinois, where the Church had not been so prosperous and fortunate. True, the Lord had done great things there, but Satan sowed tares. The seed of dissension was planted through several hypocritical members. For several years the leaven of evil worked on, and finally resulted in a permanent schism. This gave another denomination opportunity to reap, and they sent a preacher into the place, who happened to be one who had formerly been among us, but had recently left us. This man sought to gain adherents among the disaffected, making matters still worse. The new branch attempted to build a church for themselves, but also got a quarreling.—Thus, the Bishop concluded, one might paraphrase the Scripture, "Behold, how terrible it is when brethren dwell together in wrath. It is not like the oil that ran down Aaron's beard. There hath the Lord not promised the blessing", etc.

November 23d, Bishop Seybert had a narrow escape from imminent peril. He was riding along, it seems, somewhere near Springfield, Ohio, in his "dandy wagon" and with his faithful horse; his broad rimmed hat was pulled down over his eyes, the reins were but loosely held, and he was quietly musing as the old gray jogged along. "As he came near Lake Gundy, a teamster's horses ran away with a wagon. They came down the road at a tearing rate, maddened by fright, and bore directly down upon Seybert. The wagon caught his conveyance and jerked it hither and thither, and his horse became frightened, broke loose from him and ran off. Seybert got out of the danger in a manner that remained a mystery to him. His hat, of course, received several holes, but, so far as he knew he escaped without the loss of a drop of blood. How it all happened he did not know. His conveyance was badly damaged, but that was soon repaired. Thus the Lord preserved him from misfortune in the *midst* of misfortune. Praise to His faithfulness!

From early in the Spring, all through the Summer and Autumn the Bishop had labored hard in the great North-west. He now felt the need of rest, and longed for the milder climate of southern Ohio. On his return tour through northern Illinois and Indiana, he found the membership generally, earnestly engaged in working out their salvation. At Evansville he was saddened, because the work had to be suspended on account of the missionary's sickness. "O", the Bishop prayed, "that the Lord would awaken faithful shepherds and teachers and send them to reinforce the young and weak Indiana conference." In Ohio he found conversion going on everywhere. But on account of a severe cough and pain in the chest, Seybert was scarcely able to preach at all. December 2d he reached the home of Rev. John Dreisbach in Pickaway county, about five miles southeast of Circleville, where he "felt at home and intended to recuperate a little."

One would think that the society and hospitality of his venerable host would certainly be charming enough to detain him several weeks at least. And what a privilege it would have been to hear John Dreisbach, the first Presiding Elder of the Church, and the first to receive a preacher's license, signed officially by Jacob Albright himself, to relate to his episcopal guest the story of his eventful and useful life. What memories these old veterans could recall, — what thrilling episodes, what pitched battles, what triumphs, what struggles between hope and fear! But how long did Seybert tarry and rest? *One whole night and part of two days!*—Then he went on again. On the first evening after his departure he was not even able to preach, but on the second evening he succeeded. Day and night he hurried on with a speed that would have done credit to Jehu. With him the "King's business required haste". He traveled northward via Wooster and Lisbon to Cleveland, and then via Erie to Pittsburgh, and so on. Before December was over he had distanced two hundred miles and preached twelve times.

This is the manner in which Bishop Seybert "rested". It would be no calamity if men of his stamp would in our time take the place of the *dili-tante* clergy who bask in the sunshine of public favor, whose inspiration is popular applause, and whose only concern is to get large salaries. And then if the congregation will once in a while donate several thousand dollars, and send the "overworked" manuscript reader abroad for the Summer months, to some fashionable resort, the heart of such pampered idlers has nothing more to desire. Their "cup runneth over."

CHAPTER XV.

GROWING OLD.

In the Spring of 1853 Bishop Seybert held the Pittsburgh and New York conferences. The latter met in Buffalo N. Y. At this session he mentions as something remarkable the brief period occupied by the examination of the members of the conference. He says it took exactly one hundred minutes—Seven minutes for Canaan district, six for Albany, and eighty-seven for Buffalo. Whether by reason of more scrupulous strictness in the enforcement of discipline, or more frequent aberrations of moral or official conduct, we cannot say—but investigations were more frequent then, it would appear, than now. Certain it is that in those days examinations were by no means a mere formality.

From this conference session the Bishop started to fill a series of appointments stretching over a thousand miles in length. These appointments were principally in New York and Canada. He began May 1st, and June 19th the work was done. After attending several protracted meetings in the cities of Rome, Albany and Rochester, N. Y., he crossed Suspension Bridge and invaded Canada June 8th. In forty days he filled as many appointments. This extended beyond the limits of the original series. June 20th he attended a camp-meeting near Hamburg, Canada, which was one of the best he ever saw. There were from twenty to forty penitents at the altar daily, and that without any urging. The communion service was a season of mighty commotion. Four hundred and seventy-nine participated in the celebration of the Lord's Supper. July 10th and 11th he dedicated the new church edifice at King's Bush. Already during the first prayer a marvellous Divine power came upon the congregation. Sinners were awakened and converted at this church dedication. On this occasion also a Sunday-school Union was organized. "Thus", says Bishop Seybert, "we had a right glorious dedicatory feast in our plain house of worship there — an edifice without a *tower*, without a *bell*, and without *debts*, erected by poor people. To God alone be all the glory!" — These items he mentioned in his journal in a similar tone wherever it occurred.

The last three months of the year he spent in the East, attending camp-meetings, church dedications, protracted meetings, overseeing the work, and helping where it was weak. In New York City, Philadelphia and Baltimore he found the society greatly improved. But it is suggestive that Bishop Seybert always reports *conversions*, while accessions or increase in popular influence is seldom mentioned. In his view the work prospered wherever there were conversions going on, otherwise not. The conversion of sinners was with him the Church's reward for her effort and outlay. And in the nature of the case, persons in those days seldom joined the Evangelical Association unless they were soundly converted.

In connection with his visit to the metropolis that year, the Bishop relates that a certain sister, whose husband drove her out of the house for Jesus' sake, took refuge with a neighbor's family who were members of our Church. At the same time an incendiary had set fire to a row of buildings on the same street. The fire approached the house where the persecuted sister was. Upon seeing the danger, she fell upon her knees and pleaded most earnestly that the house might be protected from the fury of the advancing flames. Instantly the wind veered to the north and drove the fire in another direction, and so the Lord protected his own. The house was saved.

At Baltimore he notes that "the membership was united in love, which is always the case where it goes well." At Baltimore station he preached a missionary sermon, and the contribution amounted to one hundred dollars. He says: "Several made an offering of their jewelry, such as finger-rings and other ornaments, for the good cause."

He notes the fact that during this year not so much was accomplished in the Eastern conferences as in many earlier years. What the reason is *He* knows best, who knows all things.

In the Spring of 1854 Bishop Seybert presided at the East Pennsylvania conference, and was also present at the session of the West Pennsylvania conference. Then he started for the West.

The session of the Ohio conference was held in Dayton, and was a tedious one, on account of much business. The Indiana conference session was pleasant, and the business was dispatched with unusual rapidity. But there was a lack of preachers. It was impossible to supply all the fields of labor. "The harvest truly is great, but the laborers are few." "True," says Seybert, "there are many belly servants and hirelings; but these, of course, gather no sheaves into the Lord's garner — nothing, only money into their own pockets.

The Illinois conference also had a blessed session. A goodly number of promising young men were received into the conference, besides several experienced men from the East Penna. conference. And yet here also there was a lack of preachers, so that the work could not be sufficiently manned.

On his tour through the mission-fields in Iowa he had enjoyable hours, especially at a quarterly meeting in Linn county. There the Lord manifested himself mightily, and many tears, both of joy and of penitence, flowed simultaneously, as seekers were converted happily into eternal life. He says: "In this new region our friends have no desire as yet to serve the god of this world and the god of luxurious fashions. Nor can they spare time and money for this extravagance. They are much more inclined to spare the little they have for the service of the God of Heaven. The Lord grant that it may always remain so! Here again the benefit of our missionary institutions is manifest."

July 28th he was present at a quarterly meeting in Freeport, Ill., at which he deplores that no conversions occurred. This city was being visited with the cholera, but "the inhabitants do not seem to be concerned about it. The spirit of speculation is too prevalent. In this place the speculators — among whom are many professors of religion — are content to let the children of God have Heaven and God, if they only succeed in gaining large fortunes. The lament of Jeremiah is confirmed upon them: 'Thou smitest them, but they feel it not; Thou tormentest them, but they will not repent. Their face is like a flint, and they will not be converted.' These fools will some day lament their folly with the rich voluptuary of the parable in Hell. It will some time be said to them, 'Thou fool! this night thy soul shall be required of thee, and whose will those things be which thou hast gathered?'"

In the vicinity of Freeport the Bishop owned a good farm, on which he that year built a house, which he "dedicated" in September, 1854, by preaching in it a dedicatory sermon from Gen. 28:17: "This is none other than the house of God, and the gate of heaven." What a suggestive incident! Here this restless, practically homeless itinerant preacher, dedicates the house he built as a private residence, to the Lord. It contained a "prophet's chamber", where every preacher was to be at home. The tenant was under contract to entertain God's servants, for which the Bishop allowed him a stipulated consideration. In this way Bishop Seybert exercised the virtue of hospitality.

During 1854 an accusation was circulated that the Bishop last Spring, in a private conversation in

Centre Co., Pa., had expressed himself in opposition to High schools and Colleges. Upon this he wrote an article in self-defense, which, however, was never published, undoubtedly because he never put it into the hands of the editor. It was not his custom to concern himself greatly about the stories that were forever following his heels. He suffered in this respect like all great men. There are everywhere little puppets, whose life consists in barking at the heels of greatness. It was only when the interests of God's cause required, that he ever said anything at all. The following was found among his documents, and was evidently intended for the public, though for some reason it never appeared:

"I have been requested by several ministerial brethren to defend myself against the accusation, that I had, in a private conversation, spoken unfavorably of High schools and culture, and that in a certain sermon I had not dealt fairly with the subject. I therefore take the pen in self-defense:

"Neither in private nor public have I ever expressed myself against higher institutions of learning. I am not opposed to good schools. Everybody must know that. In April I visited and preached among our friends in Centre Co., Pa., and some of our members there expressed their fears and anxieties on account of the fact that now also high schools are being established among us, especially referring to Union Seminary, New Berlin, Pa. They even thought the East Penn'a Conference had resolved to form a theological seminary, where consequently wicked **and** unconverted men would receive their equipment for the ministry among us also. I then explained, as best I could, to these honest souls, what the object and aim of the New Berlin institution was, and assured them that there was no occasion for alarm. I told them there was no danger that we would now start "preacher manufactories" after the manner of the carnally minded and ungodly churches and sects, where thieves and robbers without conversion and without grace can become ministers of the Gospel, if they only have money and talents. In spite of all, some declared they would give nothing towards the school; upon which I begged them, at least not to do anything against the cause.

"As to my sermon at Millheim, I admit that it thundered a little there. I went through swiftly and sharply. But the subject on that occasion was not exactly ungodly high schools or theological training institutions, but rather the ordination to the ministry. Some overwise, scornful school theologian had emboldened himself to speak disparagingly of the sainted Jacob Albright, and to scandalize the so-called 'Albrights', by ridiculing our ordination. This was too much for me, and it was my place to speak. I therefore went through the matter in an *orthodox* manner, which I suppose aggravated some who were present. But I could not help that. The truth may contend for her own rights. Among other things I said that if I found as much in the ceremony of ordination as these fellows, and my ordination had no better basis than theirs, I would have myself reordained, and would try to have holy hands laid upon me, that could be lifted up without wrath or doubting."

The Bishop praises the general condition of the work in the great West. He traveled two thousand miles there, and saw and heard much that was good. He says, however:

"In the State of Wisconsin we have it to do with a powerful host of darkness, which has a *centre* and two *wings*. The centre consists of Rationalists and Infidels; the one wing of popularity Christians, the other of superstitious bigots. As against the truth and the Lord's work, these all blow through one horn, and unitedly go into the field against the servants of God. However, in spite of all the opposition of the devil, we are constantly gaining ground, and have already brought many souls to Christ. In Milwaukee our church is attended by a multitude of respectable people, and the star of hope beams more brightly than ever there."

The first two months of 1855 Bishop Seybert spent in Ohio. First of March he visited Cleveland, and then started eastward to his old field of labor at Erie and Warren. This trip he made *per pedes*, with the "pilgrim's staff". The weather was unusually raw and cold, and old Boreas, swept down from Lake Erie upon the itinerant messenger of the Cross with savage fury. April 1st he reached Buffalo, where he preached and visited. In good time he arrived at the "Conrad Settlement" in Oneida Co., N. Y., at which place the New York conference assembled April 25th. His trip from the interior of Ohio to New York was hard on the old veteran. The weather was inclement and rough, and the roads were muddy.

The business of the New York conference, he says, was transacted with such dispatch, that everything was finished Saturday afternoon at three o'clock. He also mentions that the poor membership had supported their ministers so well, that, when the pro rata division was made, every man had his full disciplinary salary, and a balance of eighty-four dollars was left in the treasury. This the Bishop praised.

For the benefit of the uninitiated it should be explained, that formerly the Discipline fixed the amount of salary of the preachers, both married and single. The disciplinary amount was understood to be the *maximum* allowed, and not the *minimum* tolerated. Every preacher had to report all the money received as salary. This was then aggregated, and the whole amount divided by the number of preachers; the result was the average salary, and that was what each man received. It frequently occurred that they received much less than the disciplinary allowance. If, however, as in the case above, the average was above the disciplinary allowance, the amount remained in the treasury to cover future deficiencies. In this way the matter was equalized. The good preacher received no more than the poor one, the faithful had to suffer for the unfaithfulness and incompetence of others. This element of unfairness was undoubtedly one reason why the plan was abolished years ago. On the other hand, there was this element, also of fitness, that the wealthier charges helped the poorer ones. However, the whole arrangement is now a thing of the past.

May 20th he attended the Ohio conference, which met at Hope church, Wayne Co., Ohio. Bishop Long presided, and Bishop Seybert did not arrive until the fifth day of the session. May 30th he presided at the Indiana conference, and then attended also the session of the Illinois conference; at which, however, his colleague presided. Then he made a tour through northern Illinois. July 7th, his sixty-fourth birth-day, he walked quite a distance through heat and dust to Freeport, where he renewed his life-long resolution to serve the Lord with all his powers of soul and body.

Turning eastward again, as Autumn approached, he reached Economy, the residence of his aged mother, September 1st. But he only stayed two days with her, and then hastened on to the General conference which was to meet on the 12th at Lebanon, Pa. He reached this point a couple of days before the General conference began.

On this tour from the extreme West to the East, Seybert wrote as follows concerning a camp-meeting which he attended in Sandusky Co., Ohio: "The Lord wrought mightily, but the ungodly raged fearfully. They howled worse than wild animals. So it is. When the Lord works powerfully, the devil rages horribly. Where the devil and the world remain quiet, there the religion of Jesus is not genuine, nor the preaching of the Word in power. Where Jesus Christ, Peter and John are, there are also Herod,

Pilate, Caiaphas, the Pope, Ceasar and the devil, together with the whole serpent brood of unbelievers, thieves, liars, swearers and murderers, who make common cause in persecution."

About this time he wrote a letter to a young preacher of the East Pennsylvania conference, in which he says:

"I wish you the blessing from above, and the full equipment for your work, for it requires a great deal in order to perform the work of the ministry according to the will and order of God, and for the welfare of the Church and the world. Even among converted preachers there is in our day far too great a lack of Divine power. We are now much more learned and have a much larger vocabulary of words than our preachers in the days of Albright and Walter, but we are also far more conformed to this world in our preaching, worship and entire bearing. This is the reason that we have already everywhere so many members, who have only the name that they live, but before God are nothing but a carcass of stench. O Lord, look in mercy down upon our ministry, and forbid this evil. The Lord bless thee and me and all the brethren, that the Evangelical Association be not ruined through us! There is certainly danger threatening her from this direction; let no one doubt it."

He had now completed sixteen years of continuous service in the highest office the Church has to give. The reader of these pages will not doubt this service had been faithfully rendered, and that his great interest in "our little Zion", as he was wont to call the Evangelical Association, caused him to devote himself with remarkable self-denial to the service of the Church and of her Lord.

At the eleventh General conference, in Lebanon, Pa., Bishop Seybert was elected to his fifth term as a Bishop of the Evangelical Association, September 24th, 1855. Instead of this making him vain, it humbled him greatly. It is safe to say, he could have stepped "down and out" with consummate gracefulness, and without the least feeling of injury. *The Gospel ministry* itself was in his estimation the highest office in the Church and in the world, and, whether in the regular rank and file of the itinerancy, in the Presiding Eldership, or in the episcopacy, he was always first a preacher of the Gospel — the election to these positions he regarded only as adding certain administrative duties and responsibilities to the legitimate work of preaching, which he also faithfully and punctually performed as an obedient son of the Church.

Soon after General conference Bishop Seybert attended a church dedication, October 21st, at Brownstown, Pa. This house was dedicated in the *proper way*, for several sinners were converted before the services closed. At Reamstown, Pa., there was another church dedication November 4th. The meeting was protracted and in a few days there were also conversions in the new house of worship. At this place, he says, the "sons of Belial" behaved barbarously in the night time, and demolished the windows of the new church. "Here one can see", he remarks, "what the devil would do by means of his Cain's-trash, if he could break his chain, and if the Pope could introduce his power and authority into our blessed western land. As long as no conversions occurred, all was well, but as soon as the Word became effective, persecution began." November 24th and 25th he attended still another church-dedication at Eaton, Pa., where Rev. S. Neitz — that greatest of German pulpit orators in the State of Pennsylvania at that time — preached the dedicatory sermon. Here also the dedicatory feast was sealed by the conversion of a sinner in the Sunday evening service.

In Eastern Pennsylvania somewhere, an economical sister handed Seybert $20 for benevolent purposes; but she did not want her name published; the left hand shall not know what the right hand doth. Seybert remarks further: "This sister is a good housekeeper, and does not waste any money for vain display and luxury. If she were addicted to the fashions and to modern extravagance in dress, like many of our so called sisters in the Church are nowadays, (God save the mark!) she would have nothing left for benevolent purposes. Worldliness makes us poor in benevolence." — [It is impossible to give an adequate translation of the above. The zeal of our fathers against fashionable dress, and their constant reference to it produce a peculiar, idiomatic vocabulary on that subject. Bishop Seybert had a number of untranslatable words on this subject that

he used with a peculiarly unctuous emphasis, not
unmixed with a certain tinge of satire. Such words as
"modeputz" "Luxus" "modesucht" were the peculiar
possession of these plain men. Their zeal against
fashionable extavagance has gone quite out of fashion,
and, indeed, has not been followed up by their successors. Hence our poverty of words on the subject.]

In the Spring of 1856, Bishop Seybert held the
East and Central Pennsylvania conferences. At the
session of the former that famous, eccentric and
powerful preacher, Moses Dissinger, was one of a
class of eleven who were ordained deacons. From
there he went to the session of the West Pennsylvania conference. He was at both conferences
unusually brilliant and powerful in his ordination
sermons. The sermon before the East Pennsylvania
conference was on 2 Tim. 2:15, and will be found in
its proper place, or so much of it as has been preserved. The sermon before the Central Pennsylvania
can be reported only in a general way. His text on
this occasion was: "See, I have this day set thee
over the nations, and over the kingdoms, to root out,
and to pull down, and to destroy, and to throw down,
to build, and to plant."—Jeremiah 1:10. Old preachers, who heard this effort, declared it was one of the
very best sermons the Bishop ever preached.

The points of this celebrated sermon were briefly
stated of follows:

First, The calling. Second, The qualification.
Third, The duties. Fourth, The results of the
Gospel ministry. His treatment of these points was

clear and forcible throughout, especially the second and third. In speaking of the qualification to the holy ministry, he, of course, emphasized grace and unction as the principal thing. But never before was the Bishop heard to speak so strongly on the necessity of learning and intellectual training. But with the proviso that human learning be the hand maid and not the mistress in the house. In that case he declared that the study, investigation and scientific learning were not only useful, but desirable and necessary adjuncts of ministerial qualification. He referred to the false report that had been circulated as to his position on this matter, namely that he was opposed to learning, schools and useful books. He branded it as a vile slander, and resented it as an insult, with some impatience. He declared himself opposed only to the *abuse* of learning, and to ungodly and corrupt institutions of learning, where preachers are manufactured out of unconverted men by "machinery". Such schools he termed "nests of serpents and holes of basilicks".

In speaking of the duties of the ministerial office, he insisted upon frequent pastoral visitation as a principal means of leading souls to Christ. He also urged in the same line the searching out of new appointments, and extending the borders. Those who were careless in these matters the Bishop castigated with vehement severity. He declared them to be *lazy* and unworthy of their high office. And such as "located", without sufficient cause he also gave some hard blows. The only sufficient cause for leaving the field, in his opinion, is, when it is *utterly impossible to preach.* Said he, "I am determined to die on the field. When I can't preach every day any more, I'll preach four times a week; if that is too much, I will preach twice, and if that won't go, I will preach once yet,—*I am bound to die on the walls of Zion!*"

This sermon lasted an hour and a half, and riveted the attention and interest of the large audience to the last. With breathless interest they followed the burning utterances of the speaker, and the effect upon the entire audience was profound.

Bishop Seybert was now in his sixty-fifth year, and in the Spring of 1856 he made one of the most laborious, extensive and fatiguing journeys of his life. One stands amazed at the aged Bishop's courage, fortitude and indomitable enterprise. Though the weather that Winter was unusually cold, he traveled daily. It is hard to understand how it was possible for him to endure so much exposure, especially because, as we are told by those who know, he did not wear warm clothing. He never wore an overcoat in his life, but at this time wore a sort of a cape or mantle worn thin by time and use.

He presided in March at the East Pennsylvania conference, and though a deep snow fell, he crossed on his way westward three tall, high, cloud-mantled mountains with his conveyance. For lodging he stopped at a hotel in Bedford Co., where a crowd of drunken rowdies came in, drank liquor, smoked tobacco, and caroused in a fearful manner. Later at night three other rowdies came, who wanted lodgings, but had no money. The landlord refused to keep them. One of them, however, begged so hard, that he was finally permitted to stay. In the morning the wretch went out to the barn, sold his shirt to the colored hostler for ten cents, bought with it a dram of whiskay, which he gulped down, and then trudged off without breakfast.

On the 20th he was at the foot of the Alleghanies. Here he again lodged in a hotel, and next morning wanted to proceed. But it was impossible to go any further with the conveyance. A farmer then loaded his conveyance on a sled and took him up the mountain. He also made him a sled upon which to take his regular vehicle along. On the 23d he only made ten miles. By this time it was Easter, and the Bishop was obliged again to lodge in a tavern among a lot of ungodly rowdies. On Easter Monday the Lord sent him some good friends, old acquaintances, who brought him over Laurel Hill, as his temporary sled was already broken down. The arrival of these friends was providential, for he was at his wit's end at this point in his journey. The snow on the mountains was said to have an average depth of five feet, and in some places it lay fifteen feet deep; it was very cold, there was much ice, and the sky had that dull leaden hue, that casts a gloomy, sombre, cheerless forbidding shadow over the landscape and over the lonely traveler's mind. Withal a biting "nor'-wester" blew fiercely through the ravines, and chilled to the bone the weary old man. On the 26th he reached Pittsburgh, greatly fatigued, but preached in the evening from 1 Cor. 15:58, and the Word was with power.

March 27th he encountered a severe snow storm and intense cold, but he reached Economy, and spent the night with his mother, who was still living, though feeble, at the age of ninety years. Next day he crossed the line into Ohio, and on the 29th reached the residence of his colleague, Bishop Joseph Long, at Greensburgh, Summit Co., O. Here he was happy, but could not stop long. He had still to cross Ohio and Indiana, before reaching the Illinois conference session, which was his objective point. His route lay through Cleveland, Sandusky City, Bellevue and Perrysburg, O. April 16th he reached Freeport, Ill., where the conference met on the 17th.

Here the Wisconsin conference was organized. After spending forty days in the territory of the new conference, the Bishop said:

"There is nothing to fear for this new conference. I have examined closely into the circumstances, and have come to this conclusion: In the prosperous condition, and with the noble liberality of our membership there, and the courage and zeal of their preachers, this conference will, under the blessing of God, which has hitherto attended it, conquer gloriously. She has already sent a missionary into Minnesota, even before holding a session of her own. Blessed be the eternal God for this enterprise."

Quite a large number of young brethren,—promising men, entered the itinerancy. At their reception Bishop Seybert asked them in the presence of the conference and all in the church, whether they were free from the use of tobacco; which they all were enabled to answer affirmatively. The younger ministry in the West he found generally studious, diligently engaged in searching the Scriptures and other good books — a fact which greatly pleased him. "For," he remarks, "it is to be hoped that the vacancies which will occur by our death, will be filled by thorough and capable successors, who by God's grace will be able to carry forward the work which we have begun."

September 11th, 1856, a severe accident befell the Bishop at Lincoln, Stark Co., Ill. His horse became frightened, upset the conveyance, throwing him violently to the ground, and breaking its harness into fragments. The Bishop was very dangerously injured. He says: "Here my old, dilapidated, storm-beaten tabernacle of clay, in which I had, during the last thirty-five years, preached about *ten thousand sermons*, came very near being totally demolished; for my hardships on the long and perilous journeys of my itinerant life have at last made me weak. But the Lord again watched over me in this accident. Blessed be His Name!"

In his modesty he makes no mention of the many thousand private calls he had made, which added much to the fatigue of his ministry. He now had to spend two days in a hotel in Lincoln, Ill., among strangers and ungodly people. He could neither eat nor sleep, suffered great pain, and it was a matter of doubt whether he would recover at all. He was, however, resigned and patient, only complaining that he was far away from brethren and sisters, and was among a rough crowd of "Satan's people". After this he stayed for three days with a converted Lutheran, named Daniel Altendorfer. This brother took him into his house, and took good care of him, all gratis.

Several days after this, Rev. Dengel, one of our missionaries, came through Lincoln, and took the sick Bishop along to Pulaski, where he was hospitably entertained. In great weakness he left here and went a hundred and thirty-four miles to Marshall, Ill., where he was compelled to halt again for ten days. He was "almost finished" when he got there. And no wonder, for he traveled fifty miles in a day. On the eighth day after his arrival at Marshall, he tottered out with a walking stick and visited a penitent family. On the eleventh day he traveled fifty miles with his conveyance. He had to "hurry", lest he get "too far behind in his journey".

At the beginning of October he writes: "When I first attempted again to make a beginning in traveling, preaching and visiting, after the accident, it was in a very feeble manner, but soon I improved daily, so that, in the course of some ten weeks, I was quite restored from my injuries, and was enabled to continue my journey as usual through cold and heat, through snow-storms and other inclemencies."

When he was yet quite weak he arrived at Warrentown, Indiana, where he was to preach in a church called Tabor, built on Mount Tabor. Weary with a long day's journey, he arrived late. The congregation was already assembled and waiting. He says: "There was no time left to *eat* — only to *pray*. I accordingly went out upon the church yard in the darkness, fell upon my knees, pleaded fervently with God for His help and his blessing. He also heard my cry and blessed His Word powerfully. His blessings descended upon the assembly like showers of rain, and there was a degree of joy in the camp that is seldom seen." — No time to eat, only time to pray, is a rare sentiment in such an emergency. It was a scene for an artist. The travel stained, weather beaten, aged itinerant, upon his knees, amid the marble monuments of the dead, under the shadow of night pleading with God for his waiting congregation in the temple of Jehovah.

In December the Bishop dedicated a church edifice at New Portage, Summit county, Ohio. After several days of service there were still no conversions, and Bishop-Seybert gave as a reason, that "the old people are hard-hearted, and the young people are vain and wicked, have had poor training, and some of them behave worse than heathens."

CHAPTER XVI.

TIRELESS ZEAL.

January 9th, (1857) Seybert had come as far east as Economy, and found his aged mother so feeble that she had to be cared for like a child. She was in her ninety-first year. It afforded both the son and the mother mutual joy to meet once more on earth. On the 10th, as his horse was lame he walked to Freedom, and preached there. This was a cold day. The thermometer registered 14° below Zero. On the 13th he bade his feeble mother adieu, with the thought that he would never see her face again until they met in heaven.

The Bishop now retraced his steps; he could go no farther eastward, as he had to hold the Illinois conference, which would meet April 22d. He spent the Winter in Ohio, preaching and visiting. He arrived in Illinois April 14th, when he complains, it was very cold, and a terrible snow-storm hindered his journey. From this conference he went to Jefferson City, Wisconsin, to preside at the first session of the newly formed Wisconsin conference, May 6th, 1857. The business of the young conference was soon dispatched, and the report of the stationing committee was already read on the second day. No sour faces were to be seen among the preachers. They were all happy, whatever their appointment. The Bishop expressed himself confident of a glorious future for this conference, on account of the liberality of the membership and the fiery zeal of the preachers. Then he remarks: "One thing more deserves mention, which affords me much pleasure, and is an honor to the conference, and that is, that with but few exceptions, all the preachers, especially the younger ones, are entirely free from the use of tobacco in any of its forms; they neither chew, smoke nor snuff."

Alexander Stephens, I believe, once had the privilege of reading in the papers, a journalistic history of his life, and eulogies upon his character, the report having been falsely telegraphed that he had departed this life. Bishop John Seybert, came near having a similar experience in 1857. Several times the report became current that he was dead and buried, and it finally also reached his own ears. Upon this he wrote to the *"Christliche Botschafter"* to inform his friends that he was still among the living. The article ran somewhat as follows:

"Inasmuch as the report has become current in different States of the Union that I have departed this life and am already buried, I would inform our friends through this communication, that, during the past Winter, notwithstanding the great snow-storms, intense cold, and bad roads, I have enjoyed good health, and got along well, reaching the thirteenth session of the Illinois conference in good time. This was a good session. The bounds have been extended again, so that we were obliged to form a new district

22

west of the Mississippi.   The membership exercised great liberality in supporting the Gospel.   The preaching, during this session was powerful.   *Hallelujah!*

"So much for this time.   Remember me in your prayers, ye friends of Zion, so that I may be enabled to discharge the office of a teacher to the good of the Church and the salvation of the world, through grace. Amen."

This time he seems to have forgotten his birth-day. For the first time no mention of it is traceable in his journal.   In July he visited Kankakee, Illinois, a city of three thousand inhabitants, which three years before, was only a wilderness of thickets and underbrush.   Our Church had already established itself in the place, built a good church, and had a promising Sunday-school.

After this he spent sixty-three days in the bounds of the Indiana conference, presiding at the conference session in September.

He praised very greatly the arrangement he found at a camp-ground in Marshall Co., Ind.   This encampment was enclosed, and the twenty-four tents were of lumber with doors that could be locked, so that the ground could be locked in during the year.   It was so arranged that after service at night, everything could be locked out that was objectionable. This was a new arrangement at that time, which now is in more general vogue.   The Bishop saw at a glance the utility of the plan, and commended it highly.

October 9th, 1857, Bishop Seybert visited one of

the old itinerants of our church, Rev. John Erb, near Flat Rock, Seneca Co., O., who was near his end. This brother had to suffer severely, from a cancer in the face. "But", Seybert says, "he is comforted in his God, and seems to have a comfortable hope, and a strong inward desire to be present with the Lord. The prospect of a speedy departure fills him with peace."

For more than forty years Erb was a faithful, diligent, humble and spiritual preacher.

Soon afterward this aged sufferer was released, and died full of patience and hope. He was one of the old pioneers of our church in Pennsylvania and Ohio.

On the thirteenth of October, at Bro. Kerns, near Lindsey, Ohio, the Bishop again hitched to his conveyance, after having ridden 2,500 miles on horseback since March 26th.

On the 24th and 25th of that month he attended the dedication of the Peace Church near Blatchleysville, Wayne Co., Ohio, (Felgers). The services on Sunday evening were blessed with a number of conversions. Upon which he remarks: "So then this house was dedicated indeed."

Thence he went on east, and made his last tour in his native State and conference.

In the Moravian town of Bethlehem, Pa., a characteristic incident occurred. One afternoon in the beginning of Winter, he came into Bethlehem from the North, walking along by the side of, or rather ahead of his conveyance, occasionally casting a glanceat the houses on either side as he passed along, and then turning his eyes upward toward the sky, or backward towards his horse. A sister happened to espy him, and, supposing him to be searching for some one, she called out to him, "Why, Brother Seybert! is it possible that you are here? — Whom are you looking for, any way?" "I am not looking for anyone here, sister," was the reply, "but I'm going down here to Texas, — there's a revival of religion down there!" With this the Bishop trudged on, turning his blue gray eyes toward the westering sun, to see how much time he yet had to get through thirteen miles, to his destination.

How absorbed this man was in the business of soul saving! He had not been among his friends at Bethlehem for several years, but he will not even stop to exchange greetings, etc., or rest. He has heard that at Texas the Lord is saving sinners, and there he wanted to be. That was the absorbing thought of his soul. Nothing else was worth consideration. — "I'm going down here to Texas, — the Lord's saving sinners there!" That was enough! John Seybert wanted nothing better.

In 1858 Bishop Seybert presided at the New York, Pittsburgh, Central and East Pennsylvania conferences. The latter was his original conference; in it he was converted, and began to preach; in it he served the Church until his election to the episcopal office. He always felt at home there, and naturally felt a peculiar attachment toward its members, many of whom had shared with him the hardships, priva-

tions and difficulties of the days of small things. The
session of 1858 was the last of that conference he
ever attended. In less than two years he was called
home, his work being done.

The parting scene on this occasion was most affecting. The aged Bishop seemed to have a presenti-
ment that it was his last meeting with these brethren
on earth. And evidently many of the brethren had
similar feelings. When the business was finished,
and the time for the usual farewell ceremonies had
arrived, the Bishop seemed embarrassed and agitated.
He was loath to conduct the solemn ceremony himself, and sought to induce two other brethren to relieve him of this duty, but they refused. Seeing
that he could not escape, he cast a glance at his chair
in the altar, and crept with timid steps to his place.
With deep and labored breathing, as if very weary,
he addressed the conference, admonishing them to
faithfulness, steadfastness, love, humility and all
Christian virtues. Upon this he announced a hymn,
and offered a most touching prayer, during which
there was much weeping. Seybert then left the altar,
and, in a hesitating manner began to give each
brother personally the parting hand. A feeling of
indescribable sorrow filled all hearts, and the scene
impressed itself indelibly upon all who were present.
Some wept, some praised God, and others sang
solemnly a parting hymn. Meanwhile the patriarchal
Bishop had spoken to all, and had disappeared from
view. Upon looking for him he was seen hidden
behind the pulpit and lamp pillars, where he sat

weeping convulsively! Never had Seybert been seen so agitated. His forebodings were correct. His sun was sinking low in the horizon, and he never saw these men again, except as, one by one, he has greeted them in the city above. He had climbed

"Where Moses stood"
And viewed the landscape o'er.

Thence he went to the West Pennsylvania conference, and thence to the Pittsburgh conference, and thence to the New York conference. At the latter place, after mentioning the names of those whom the conference lost—some five or six in number, while only one was newly received, he exclaims: "Lord, help!"

While visiting one day in June, in Canada, he called among others upon an aged sister of the Mennonites, 86 years of age, who had recently been converted. During the fifteen years of her widowhood, she had read the Bible through several times, and the New Testament twenty-four times. The Bishop was astonished at her profound insight into God's Word, and expressed his opinion that she was "possessed of a deeper knowledge of the Scriptures than most of the preachers of that day."

July 7th, 1858, being his sixty-seventh birth-day, he wrote, "O God, how much goodness I have enjoyed during my past life! My sixty-eighth year shall also be consecrated to Thee. And grant Thou that my long life may have been useful to the Church and to the world, and contribute to Thy honor for the sake of Jesus and His sufferings. Amen."

Two days later the following:

"What a fortunate man I am in my sixty-eighth year! My health is at present good, and I am of good courage. Eighteen years I lived without God, and without religion; in my nineteenth I found the Lord. I have now served Him forty and eight years, thirty-seven of this time in the ministry. In this time I have preached more than nine thousand times, and traveled over a hundred and fifty thousand miles, mostly on horseback. My hearing is yet acute, I can read without spectacles, which I frequently do, and if it were necessary, I would undertake to preach three times a day. To God alone be all the praise."

The bishops, Seybert and Long, were neither of them of literary propensities, and seldom wrote for the public. They were often censured for this, and in 1858 public communications appeared in the *Christliche Botschafter*, complaining that the bishops were so seldom heard from. This induced Bishop Seybert to publicly explain himself. He wrote the following:

"As a brother, in *Botschafter* No. 17, accuses the over-seers of the Church of not having any desire to write, I would offer some excuses for myself in the spirit of love and meekness.

"First, I have a very large field of labor, upon which I have to make many extended journeys, being obliged to preach almost every evening, however weary I may be.

"Second, It is also a proper official duty to visit the members of the Church, the sick and the pentitent, to instruct them all in the Kingdom of God, and to pray with them.   This takes away much time,

" Third, Besides, I have many important matters to look after, incident to my office, which must be done, if I am to be found faithful.

" Fourth, I have very many letters to write, of which, for lack of time, I can not even write the half.

" Fifth, We have many industrious, able writers for our periodicals, by whom the doctrines of the Christian religion are clearly and emphatically discussed.

" Sixth, I have placed my large and valuable library, including more than twenty thousand pages of missionary intelligence at the disposal of the Publishing House, and of the editors, both during my life and after my death which will soon come.

" Seventh, I do not know that God has specially called or fitted me for literary work, as also the holy apostle Paul was not specially sent to baptize, but to preach the Gospel.

" Still, I am thankful to my critic for his remark, and will endeavor in the future to write more for the *Botschafter*.   John Seybert."

Near Hamburg, Canada, a camp-meeting was held, at which there were from twenty to forty seekers at the altar daily.   Among them was a man who came sixty miles for the purpose of seeking religion. Nearly five hundred guests appeared at the Lord's Table.   The Bishop spent twenty-eight days in Canada.   At Buffalo, N. Y., he mentions that a philanthropist presented our people with a large building lot, on condition that they build a church on it, which was done. He spent in all one hundred and five days in the New York conference, and then labored forty-nine days in the Ohio conference, after which he crossed over to Indiana. At Bainbridge in the latter State, he mentions another of those church dedications which were blessed with the conversion of sinners. Here the Bishop had the pleasure of baptizing a converted Jewess. This place was wonderfully revolutionized as a result of our work. Seybert specially rejoices over the remarkable progress which the conference had made, exclaiming, "Hitherto the Lord hath helped us!"

Early in November he reached Illinios, and spent the Winter in the northern part of that conference. On account of increasing infirmities and the bad western roads he did not venture farther west. At Naperville he mentions the dedication of the large brick church edifice which was followed by a gracious revival, lasting five or six weeks, during which many sinners were saved. Seybert says he was surprised that this protracted exercise had not exhausted the friends there.

During this tour he traveled more than a hundred miles over "majestic icefields", where he endured fearfully cold weather.

At Aurora he also had a blessed church dedication, remarking: "*Aurora* signifies '*the dawning light*', and now the morning light has also dawned here in the ecclesiastical heavens, — the light of the knowledge of God and of the truth."

Then his report proceeds: "In Hampshire, Kane county, on the urgent request of friends, I remained three days to rest, preaching one evening to a crowded house. Our friends here, though mostly living in poor huts, have builded a good, plain house of worship, without tower or bell, and without leaving any debts. At the dedication about *thirty souls* were converted, — promising people, too. He remarks: "Here it seems the poor can do more than in many places the rich. Does anyone ask how this can be? I answer, for three reasons. First, these people have a warm love for God and perishing humanity. Second, they are not stingy. Third, they are not captives to the fearful, world and church ruining fashion-god. That is why they can accomplish such things."

Among Bro. Seybert's documents was found an interesting history of the work of the Evangelical Association in Upper Canada, written about this time. The account really does not belong here, but to the History of the Evangelical Association. . We therefore only give such portions as seem pertinent to this biography. In the main it is historical rather than biographical.

The Bishop first describes the terrible condition of the Germans of Victoria's realm. They were most deplorably depraved and demoralized. Denominationally they were divided into Catholics. Lutherans, Reformed, Mennonites and Tunkers. The United Brethren had at one time made an effort to convert these Germans, but were unfortunate on account of the bad conduct of their missionary. He was deposed and expelled for immorality, and the Campbellites picked him up. Sad indeed is the Bishop's pen-picture of the churches there. A few examples will illustrate the condition of things. At Puslinch, on the occasion of a christening, the parson got so drunk that he fell from his chair. When some of those present picked him up, the lady of the house remarked in disgust, "Why don't you let him lie on the floor?"

Near Hamburg, a pastor had announced the celebration of the Lord's Supper, but on arriving in the town for this purpose at the appointed time, he was met by a procession of his parishioners, on their way to a dance. One was carrying a beer keg on his shoulder, and another had a fiddle under his arm. They requested the "*Pfarrer*" to postpone the Sacrament as they had appointed a dance, which he did! The dance went on.

This parson came near having a serious adventure that night. He stayed all night with a member of his church, named Smith. After retiring late at night, one of the aforesaid parishioners called, and declared he came to pommel the pastor, because he had never given his people anything in return for the money he received as salary. The host, Mr. Smith, was obliged to interfere, to prevent the parson from getting a severe castigation. This Mr. Smith, who was a rationalist, afterwards was converted and became a minister of the Gospel in the Evangelical Association, and served for years as a Presiding Elder in the New York conference.

A Catholic priest, near Puslinch, refused Catholic burial to a child whose father would not permit anointing it at death. But the burial took place at night on the Catholic cemetery. The enraged priest then had the body exhumed and sold it to a physician.

A Lutheran church dedication degenerated into a veritable drunken carnival.

This is enough to show the need of evangelization. Into such benighted regions the preachers of the Evangelical Association always delighted to go with the blessed tidings of salvation. The Evangelical Association has often gone where she was not wanted, but never where she was not needed. In going into Canada, however, she followed earnest and pressing invitations from the people there. The first efforts in Canada were simultaneous with the organization of the Missionary Society of our Church. In the Winter of 1837, the Rev's. Hammer, Harlacher and Dellinger made visits there. Michael Eis was the first to achieve success. At Waterloo, in 1839 an unparalleled undertaking was carried to a successful execution: A camp-meeting was held before there was a single member of our church there. The missionary invited Bishop Seybert to attend his meeting, which he did. The Bishop was persuaded to go by the fact that preachers were scarce there, and the work certainly needed help. He accordingly made a forced trip, per horse-back, of three hundred and eighty miles. At Buffalo he was taken sick, but still rode fifty miles that day. "There were fifteen tents on the ground, before we had a single member in all

Canada." The meeting was wonderful. Many people were converted. The result was the organization of the first class in Canada.

Several influential citizens of Waterloo now assisted the work. One of these was a Methodist preacher, who attended this camp-meeting, and said that it was "*old fashioned Methodism.*" This man supported the cause liberally and remembered it in his last will and testament. He also was instrumental in securing the recognition of our Church by the government.

In short, the work prospered so that in three years, Bishop Seybert declared we had a solid foot-hold in British territory. Near Niagara a revival broke out in a large Mennonite society, in which one of their Bishops was converted. He was, however, soon cast over-board by his unconverted brethren. "This" says Seybert, "caused an earthquake in their society, and a great schism."

CHAPTER XVII.

SUNSET.

After the Illinois and Wisconsin conference sessions in 1859, the Bishop, during the Spring, traveled over the Wisconsin conference district and attended several camp-meetings there. One of these was held at Honey Creek, Sauk Co. While the two hundred and ten guests knelt at the Lord's table, there was a complete triumph of grace. On that day also a missionary auxiliary was formed, at which two hundred and thirty-one dollars were subscribed. The Bishop expressed his astonishment at this, as the people were very poor. But, he explains, "these people were truly Evangelical, industrious, economical, liberal, and not stingy. They were Swiss emigrants, and were no slaves to the American fashion craze. If they were guilty of following the devilish vanity of the day, they could not have raised twenty dollars for the missionary cause."

Speaking of the young Wisconsin conference in general, the Bishop remarks: "This conference has made splendid progress. In the three years of its existence it has extended its borders three hundred miles beyond the Mississippi, away up into Minnesota, where already a Presiding Elder district has been formed. The delegates to the last General conference would hardly have believed this to be possible if it had been predicted, and to the brethren here themselves it would have seemed incredible. And yet it has been done. Behold, the Lord hath done this."

During the Summer — the last of his life, on his trip through Illinois — he unexpectedly found his colleague, Bishop Long, ensconced in the "prophets chamber" in his house near Freeport. This pleased him greatly. Unfortunately, however, the circumstances were such that the two bishops could only spend two hours together at that time. They accordingly dispatched their official business and then gave each other the parting hand again. This was an informal meeting of the episcopal board. Bishop Long was obliged to leave, and Seybert himself could not even tarry all night on his own premises. Long went westward to Iowa, Seybert eastward to Indiana and *ad in finitum.*

During a tour through Wisconsin, he on one occasion served as substitute for a Presiding Elder who could not be present. On Monday morning, learning that an encampment was to be selected, the aged but agile Bishop offered his services, which were gladly accepted. He cut himself a stick for a measuring rod, and in a very short time he had selected and staked off a first-class piece of ground in the most appropriate manner.

Apropos to this incident we relate here a suggestive anecdote.

At one of these camp-meetings in Wisconsin, while assisting in setting the encampment in order, he asked a boy who stood by, to go with him to bring up some poles from the woods. The boy willingly obeyed, and, in childish enthusiasm seized hold of the heavy end of the pole. But the Bishop interfered. " No, no," he said, "you take this end; *I will take the heavy end!*" How faithfully he *always* took "the heavy end", the reader of these pages, can very easily understand. That was characteristic of the man. That boy has since become a prominent minister in our Church, and already for sixteen years a General conference officer.

In one of his sermons at the above quarterly meeting he stated that his beloved mother had passed away, and was now with the blessed in Paradise, adding, "Methinks she expects soon to see her son John with her in heaven." His presentiments, which he casually expressed on several occasions during the last year of his life, did not at this time impress his auditors very seriously, as he seemed to be hale and hearty.

During his stay at the above place, a Sunday-school festival was held in the vicinity, at which about three hundred children were assembled, and the Order of Good Templars participated in the ceremonies and festivities of the day. Several temperance speeches were made, and of course, the Bishop being present, he could not escape. His remarkably quaint and severely plain appearance was in striking contrast to the gaily festooned platform, on which flags fluttered and banners waved, and uniforms glittered. It was the fifth of July. His was the closing speech. His text was: "Righteousness exalteth a nation, but sin is a reproach to any people." After expressing his delight in the institution of the Sunday-school, and the blessing the children assembled there enjoyed on its account, he went on to amplify and illustrate the assertion of his text. Among other things he also spoke of the virtue of economy and the vice of extravagance, eulogizing the former greatly in its bearing upon domestic happiness and social prosperity. This he declared belongs to *temperance*, and is a splendid piece of abstinence. The Bishop became quite earnest and let loose in a lively manner on the sin of extravagance and luxurious indulgence. At this point some fellow sang out from the audience, " Well, what are we to do with the money?" Undoubtedly this rude interruption would have exasperated the audience, carried away as they were by the magnetic eloquence of the speaker, had not the Bishop been ready. Scarcely had the rude question been heard, before the answer crashed through the ranks, "Why pay your debts with it!" This sensible, prompt reply was rewarded with a storm of applause, especially because the audience knew that the interlocutor needed that particular advice. This was very likely Seybert's last temperance speech.

About four miles from this place he passed his *last birth-day* anniversary on earth, which he spent in visiting from house to house, reading his Bible and in making a short journey, being specially charmed with the delightful scenery of the season. In the evening he wrote in his journal:

" Oh how thankful I feel toward God, when I look

23

back over the sixty and eight years of my life! My God, what shall I render unto Thee for the great goodness Thou hast shown towards me? I have nothing but myself, and willingly do I consecrate my all to Thee. Oh that my entire life may be wholly consecrated to God, through Jesus Christ my Lord and my Redeemer. Amen."

Whenever a proposition was brought before General conference to change or amend the Discipline, Bishop Seybert was concerned, lest the amendment prove to be in the wrong direction. He was particularly opposed to several measures which were proposed from time to time. Among these was one to increase the power of the Bishops, making the office more like that of the Methodists. Another was to abolish the office of Presiding Elder. Then there was also a proposition made, to regard the children of our own members, if they were baptized by us, as members of our Church, and inscribe their names on the Church Records. Upon this he wrote to a brother in the East, in 1859, pending the General conference:

"I rejoice that the preachers of the East Penn'a conference are not so easily persuaded to approve and support the many new propositions to improve and change our Book of Discipline, especially that your conference does not approve of the proposal to take children into the Church simply by virtue of their having been baptized. Such a step I say would be to lay the foundation for a heap of dead bones among us. But I am comforted with the confidence that there is too much *salt* among us to allow such a motion to prevail. But you must be wide awake in the East, or else it might succeed. I have talked with the author of the proposition; he defended himself earnestly, but I withstood him to the face, and think it will fortunately fail."

In another letter, written just before the General Conference convened, which should be his last, he said:

"There are forty recommendations to the General Conference,—what will become of them all? If these recommendations for improvements — rather changes — keep multiplying at this rate, we will soon have them by hundreds. But it is to be seriously questioned, whether our Discipline, which in my opinion is one of the best in the world, will be improved in this way. Time will tell. The power of the episcopacy is also to be discussed again; and another perverse proposition is on foot, touching the abolition of the Presiding Eldership. This would be a wild, inconsiderate leap. In all probability, this measure will burst like a soap-bubble, before it does us any harm. My advice is, let us stick fast to the good arrangements which we have, and I am of the opinion that it is much better to observe and obey the laws we have, than to be constantly changing them. But we will pray the Lord to give us wisdom not to do anything detrimental to His cause."

September 7th, 1859, the Indiana conference convened in Indianapolis, which was the last annual conference session over which Bishop Seybert presided.   During this session he was attacked by a fever.   Sunday, however, was a great and precious day.

Notwithstanding his fever, he hastened westward toward Naperville, Illinois, where the General Conference was to begin October 13th.   He arrived a day before it began weak, and weary.   This was the last General Conference he ever attended.   He had now served the Church in the highest office. for twenty years, and this General Conference elected him for the sixth time.   But, since he was really growing old, and was manifestly debilitated, three bishops were elected, with the purpose of lifting some of the burden from the shoulders of the old veteran, and to give him better opportunity to spare himself in his declining years.   John Seybert and Joseph Long were unanimously re-elected, and W. W. Orwig was newly elected to the episcopacy.

During this General Conference he was extremely feeble, and was sometimes hardly able to ascend the stairway to the auditorium of the church, where the conference assembled.   It was observed that he would go a few steps and then sit down to rest, and after getting to the top of the stairs, he would sit down in the back seat, before he felt strength enough to go forward to the chancel.   His demeanor was reserved and quiet, and he took but little part in the deliberations and debates, except that he seemed very attentive to what was said and done.   He seemed to be communing with his own thoughts, and had the air of one who was wrapped up in profound meditations. This was attributed, however, to his "severe cold" as he called his indisposition, and the hope was entertained that he would soon recover again. Still some of the delegates expressed grave apprehensions, lest some indiscretion should speedily lead to fatal results. But the intrepid veteran replied: "O brethren, you see I just had an attack of fever in Indiana, and then contracted a cold too which has aggravated the pain in my chest and my cough. I have been weak like this before; besides the weather is now unfavorable. I will soon be better again." He had not strength enough to make an exhortation at this time.

Bishop Seybert approached his end with an almost unequalled calmness and composure. He had resolved to "look death right in the eyes" as he expressed himself, believing that the pale king of terrors would quail, if met bravely.

On the last evening of General Conference, the Lord's Supper was celebrated by the delegates. During this solemn service, he was particularly observed. With folded hands he knelt at the table in the chancel, beside the other bishops, and received the elements with an innocence that seemed hardly of this world. One of the delegates present says: "I had quite forgotten myself, so intensly did I observe Bishop Seybert's manner and appearance. And I thought, 'Bro. Seybert, you are undoubtedly near the end of your earthly career, and are approaching the boundaries of the spirit world, for out of your countenance there shimmers already the innocence and purity of a glorified one through the pale integument, as you sit here under the dim glare of the lamps. I shall never forget that face until I see him in the transcendent lustre of the resurrection morning. His great spirit of self-denial, the marks of his sufferings, his sacrificing love, his sincerity, his simplicity and humility and his benevolence toward his fellowmen together with his great zeal against all wrong—all this seemed to me to be shining in his almost transfigured face, and made an impression upon my mind that I cannot now describe, though I fully realized it at the time. He seemed so near heaven, that the possibilty dawned upon me that, should his spirit at that moment depart and step over, his body might remain kneeling at the chancel just as he was, with folded hands, until some one should carry him away."

Irresistibly we are reminded of a paragraph by a brilliant lecturer: "It is recorded that in an eastern city a martyr was once tried, and as all they who sat in the council looked steadfastly on him they beheld his face, as it were the face of an angel. Is it possible that the light present in this case and in approximately similar cases in our day is the same thing in each? It is recorded also, as we remember, now that we allow our minds to sweep through the vistas of historical examples, that a law-giver who yet rules the centuries, once had, as he came down from a certain mount, a face that shone. . . . Is it possible that the look which comes into the countenance whenever the loftier zones of feeling are in full action is of the same sort with that which appeared in the face of

Dante's Beatrice delighted to do good; and in the face of him whose countenance was like that of an angel; and in the face of Moses; and in the unfathomed symbolisms of the transfiguration? Is it of the same sort with that light which fills the world of those who have no need of the sun, because the face of the Lamb doth lighten them, and the glory of God is the lamp of their tabernacle?"

It remains only to record such events concerning Bishop Seybert as occurred between the General Conference in October and his death in January following. He visited many of his old battle-grounds in Illinois such as Wheeling, Dutchman's Point, Dunkley's Grove and other places. Some of these places gave him special invitations, as the impression was current that the Bishop would never see the West again. At Esher's, near Wheeling, a solemn baptismal service was arranged for. The people came together in throngs to see and hear the old veteran once more. On seeing the multitude he resolved to try to preach, which he did, and in a most powerful manner. His theme was, " Dying and living with Christ ", and he laid great stress on the total extinction of "all evil members", and the rooting out of all sinful passions and desires, and urged the people to sink away utterly in the merit of the great Mediator, and to be entirely resigned to God's will.

After the sermon he baptized sixteen children in the most impressive manner. He was so strengthened during this inspiring service, that at its close he felt better than at its beginning.

November 7th he started eastward, visiting the churches on his way, and preaching occasionally. In Indiana he attended a quarterly meeting, where, he says, J. J. Esher, the P. E., preached with great power. As he was obliged to recuperate, he remained a few days, attending the services as often as his strength allowed.

On Sunday morning he undertook to preach, and to conduct the sacramental service. His text was Rom. 6:19–23, and the sermon was a great effort. He proclaimed with great force and plainness the doctrine of "entire freedom". He always defended the doctrine of holiness with great zeal, and insisted not only upon instantaneous conversion through faith in Jesus, but also upon instantaneous sanctification through faith in Jesus. He believed in the possibility of living without sin through grace and sanctification of the Spirit. He labored with special earnestness to advance true purity of heart and life in the Church.

Nor did he insist on either outward form or inward condition alone, but both together, and that consistently. True, Seybert thought much of external simplicity, and was a special enemy of extravagance and vain display, but he was far from seeking to force upon anyone a particular cut of the coat or anything of that sort. A stingy or dishonest professor got no credit from him, were he dressed never so plainly.

Bishop J. J. Esher, Bishop Seybert's spiritual son, says:

"It was my high privilege to spend six weeks of the last year of Bishop Seybert's life in his company.

He assisted me in holding a number of quarterly and protracted meetings on my extended district. (Bishop Esher was then a Presiding Elder.) Seybert was so afflicted most of the time, that I could not resist the conviction that he would not tarry with us long. I also expressed this conviction in his presence. Still he took an active part in the services, and not in vain. We had glorious revivals. His discourses were more than ordinarily unctuous, instructive and powerful. Some of them were decidedly master-pieces. Especially is this true of the sermon near Wheeling, on Isa. 55:6, 7. His remarks on the phrase, "And he will abundantly pardon", will never be forgotten by those who heard them. In all his discourses he urged the experience and practice of heart purity. When he spoke of conversion he emphasized the necessity of thoroughly breaking through from death into life, and then upon this well-laid ground to complete the edifice of holiness. It often struck me as remarkable with what ardor and solemn earnestness he taught this.

"Though he was often so feeble that he could scarcely get from his lodgings to the church, yet he took the most active part in laboring with seekers, and never wanted to see a service close, so long as a seeker was yet unblessed at the altar. When a soul was blessed, and sprang up like the lame man at the beautiful gate, thrilled with the power of a new life, the Bishop was ready to sing one of his animated choruses,—such as, "O happy life" ("*O seliges Leben*"), or, "O yonder is joy" ("*O droben ist Freude*").

"It is well known how he delighted to be present where there was loud shouting and animated praise, but it is a mistake to suppose that he ever accepted this commotion in lieu of the real substance of religion.

"Feeble as he was he did not cease to visit the people, and so to be useful in private as well as in public.

"Feeling that Bishop Seybert would not long be with us, I observed with keen scrutiny, his entire conduct, for I wanted to improve well my opportunity. I must say that the longer I was with him, the more deeply was I impressed that he lived alone for God, and cultivated a deeper and more intimate communion with the Redeemer, than even appeared from his public labors and success. If there were any difference between his teaching and his life, his life was superior to his teachings; he lived even better than he taught.

"At the time when he wanted to start eastward, a cold Autumn storm was raging and an icy rain was pouring down. I admonished him to spare himself, and to go per railroad to Greensburgh, Ohio, where he intended to spend the Winter, and offered to care for his horse until orders from him. His reply was, 'That would of course be much pleasanter to go by rail; but in that way I could not visit the friends on the way.'

"This explains why Bishop Seybert persisted in enduring the hardships of traveling with a horse long after the swift iron horse was in general use. — He could not look after the work in detail so well, nor get among the smaller rural societies by personal visitation.

" 'My time is short, and I want to improve it as well as possible, and I guess God will help me through.' Giving me his paternal blessing, and the parting hand, he went on. In a few weeks it was announced that Bishop Seybert had gone home."

December 4th he reached the State of Ohio, through Indiana and Michigan. December 16th he came to Bro. Loos, at Tiffin, Ohio, a local preacher, and tarried several days. The weather was cold. December 18th he preached his last sermon at Bro. Kern's, near Lindsey, Ohio, using one of his favorite texts: " Seek ye first the kingdom of God and His righteousness, and all these things shall be added unto you." Christmas he attended the dedication of a church at Kern's, near Lindsay, Ohio. But Bishop Long preached the dedicatory sermon.

December 29th, 1859, was the last day he spent on the road. He arrived on that day from Kern's at the residence of Bro. Isaac Parker, four miles west of Bellevue, Ohio, and nearly the same distance northwest of Flat Rock. Here for the last time he alighted from his conveyance. Throwing the reins of his horse over a fence-post, and taking his saddle bags on his arm, he entered the home of Bro. Parker greatly exhausted. He never went any further in his travels. His long pilgrimage should close under that roof; his extensive travels ceased; the door of heaven opened there; he was not, for God took him. On the day previous — the 28th — he had already written his last journal entry.*　His intention, however, was to rest here only a few days.

The day was now far spent. The burden of life was heavy. But he complained only of a severe cold. However, fears were entertained that it might prove fatal, and medical assistance was called, but in vain. It was observed that he was sublimely composed, and everything indicated that he was deeply conscious of his approaching end. It was only a few days thus. These days he spent in reading; occasionally he would converse in low tones,. of God and His work. He never missed reading his usual morning lesson in the Scripture, and his pocket Bible lay by his side on a chair after his death. It was the last book he read. Besides this his favorite authors were Hiller, Thomas a'Kempis, and Tauler.

The last night he slept tolerably well, rose in the morning, dressed without assistance, and joined the family at breakfast, eating quite heartily. At about eight o'clock he sat in the family circle, and related a remarkable dream he had during the night. He said he dreamed of being at a place where a large number of preachers were together, who appeared greatly delighted at his arrival. Upon this he undertook to shake hands with them all, but the number was so great that it seemed he could not get through with it.

After relating this dream he was assisted to the lounge upon which he loved to recline through the day. He was very feeble, but did not lie down. He

---

* This was, suggestively enough, the laconic phrase :—"*one soul saved.*"

sat, folding his hands with the innocent grace of a child. Mr. Parker, somewhat apprehensive, hastened out to call in neighbors, that the family might not be alone in the event of the Bishop's demise. Mr. Parker's son remained with the Bishop. Suddenly Seybert began to speak. Said he: "How terrible death must be to a wicked man!" After a pause he remarked, "death begins at the extremities" (pointing downward with his hands), "then it comes further up, and when it gets here" (laying his hand upon his heart), "then it is over. So I too will fall asleep." They were his last words. His voice choked. He sank over upon the lounge, and in a moment more the great spirit plumed its wings for everlasting flight. *Bishop John Seybert was dead.* It was January 4th, 1860. His dream had become reality. In an hour after relating it, he was on "mount Zion, and in the city of the living God, the heavenly Jerusalem, and in the innumerable company of angels," and had come "to the general assembly of the first-born, and to the spirits of just men made perfect." This occurred at nine o'clock A. M. He had lived sixty-eight years, five months and twenty-eight days. He had served well his day and generation, had brought in many sons unto glory, and was gathered into the eternal mansions in peace. The homeless wanderer had reached *home* at last.

> "How sweet the hour of closing day,
> When all is peaceful and serene,
> And when the sun, with cloudless ray,
> Sheds mellow lustre o'er the scene.

"Such is the Christian's parting hour;
So peacefully he sinks to rest;
When faith, endued from heaven with power,
Sustains and cheers his languid breast.

"Mark but the radiance of his eye,
That smile upon his wasted cheek;
They tell us of His glory nigh,
In language that no tongue can speak.

"A beam of heaven is sent to cheer
The pilgrim on his gloomy road;
And angels are attending near,
To bear him to their bright abode."

Bishop Seybert's remains were buried at Flat Rock cemetery, January 6th. The day was cold, and the long funeral cortege followed the hearse in sleighs to the old stone church at Flat Rock, Seneca Co., Ohio, where Bishop Joseph Long preached an eloquent funeral sermon in the presence of a vast assemblage of people from near and far. The text was Dan. 12: 3, "And they that be wise shall shine as the brightness of the firmament; and they that turn many to righteousness, as the stars forever and ever."

The Bishop was so affected that at first, in the struggle with his emotions, he could speak but very slowly. He spoke: First, of the work of the Christian teacher. (The German translation has "teacher" instead of the "wise".) Secondly, Of the Christian teachers' glory and reward. He said, such a teacher as Seybert shines as the brightness of the firmament already on earth, in the kingdom of grace. In his doctrine he thunders, in his life he shines. But in the world to come such an one will shine like the stars in heaven.

Rev. Charles Hammer and Rev. C. G. Koch participated in the services. A Lutheran minister offered the closing prayer. Owing to the secluded location and the shortness of the time, not as many ministers were present as would have seen fitting and desirable. After the services, an opportunity was given to look once more upon the face of the honored dead. There he lay as if asleep. The face that so often had shone with the lustre of holy joy, was pale in death; the eyes that had so often flashed with the fire of inspiration were closed; the lips that had been so eloquent, when the message of salvation burned upon them, were silent. The remains were laid away in the adjacent city of the dead, where he now awaits the trumpet call of the first resurrection, not far from where stands Ebenezer Orphan Institute. A simple, but appropriate monument marks the place of his rest, and is the chief adornment of that humble enclosure. To it pilgrimages have been made, and many an itinerant of a later generation has stood by that mound with uncovered head, and prayed that the mantle of this hero might fall upon him.

Slowly and sadly the mourners retired from the spot that henceforth would be hallowed ground, feeling that a mighty man of valor had fallen in Israel. The Church for a while felt orphaned.

There were no human relatives present to mourn over his departure, but thousands of spiritual-kindred brethren, sisters and sons and daughters, — wept for one who had been to them a minister of good. Over the length and breadth of the land, from the Atlantic ocean to the Mississippi river and beyond, in thousands of homes, the people mourned for this simple, unassuming minister of Jesus Christ. At Indianapolis, Naperville, and other places, impressive funeral services were held, churches were draped in mourning, and the people wept as for a father.

Three months after his obsequies, the Ohio conference assembled in the Flat Rock church, to hold its annual session. During the session, formal memorial services were held. The conference marched in procession to the grave, followed by a long procession of citizens and laymen. Forming a circle around the mound of the buried Bishop, the presiding Bishop, W. W. Orwig, conducted a funeral service and delivered a eulogy. The scene was affecting, and the conference was glad for the opportunity of giving this unique but fitting tribute of honor to one so worthy.

At a public sale of Bishop Seybert's personal effects, the members of the church and other citizens bought the different articles of his dress, etc., as mementoes of this remarkable man. Father Weiker of Bellevue bought his horse and buggy. Bro. John Orwig of Bellevue bought his peculiarly made coat, and this was cut up into shreds and given away to importunate friends. Another bought his broad-rimned hat, etc. This indicates the interest with which this great and good man was regarded.

Several years before his death, Bishop Seybert

made his last will and testament, in which he made the Evangelical Association and her Institutions his exclusive heir, save a few hundred dollars bequeathed to friends. Bishop Long was named as his executor. During his life he made large donations to the Church, and practiced a singular economy, solely for the financial benefit of the Church. Besides he lost more than four thousand dollars, because parties whom he trusted and befriended, proved unfaithful and defrauded him of his possessions. His philanthropy was often poorly rewarded, and perhaps sometimes bestowed upon unworthy objects. Yet he had, by his great simplicity and economy, accumulated quite a respectable estate, which fell to the benefit of the Church he loved. One of the stipulations of his testament was, that none of his money should be employed in vain display. He once remarked: "I have declared life-long war upon fashions and extravagance, and even after my death I want the war to continue." It must not be forgotten to mention either, that in his will he remembered his mother, who was then living as yet, who, however, died but a short time before him.

Bishop Seybert served the Church a period of forty years in the holy ministry. From the time of his entering upon this work in 1820, to the time of his death in 1860, he never turned aside from the ministry for a moment. He died in the harness, at his post. In these forty years he traveled, per horse, one hundred and seventy-five thousand miles, preached about nine thousand eight hundred and fifty times, made about forty-six thousand pastoral visits, held about eight thousand prayer and class meetings, besides visiting at least ten thousand sick and afflicted ones. This seems like an herculean accomplishment. But his was a busy life.

CHAPTER XVIII.

GENERAL REMARKS.

CHARACTER OF BISHOP JOHN SEYBERT.

" Who builds a church to God and not to fame,
Will never mark the marble with his name."—*Alexander Pope.*

John Seybert lived for the unseen world, and therefore this present world has largely forgotten him. Schiller's assertion that " History is Judgment ",* is not always true. If history be judgment, then judgment is sometimes unjust. The fact is, if a man's goodness outshine his greatness, the world is dazzled and blinded. Hence ordinary history leaves the best men to lie buried in obscurity. The judgment at the end of the world will reverse the verdict of history in more than one instance. History, cold and heartless as it is, may be man's best judgment, but it is not always God's judgment.

The man, a record of whose life is herein given to the English portion of our Church and of the world, is an illustration of this. No mere man ever lived a nobler life for God and for humanity than Bishop John Seybert, and yet, outside of the Evangelical Association, he is but little known or remembered. Even in his denomination, many of the present generation

---

* Die Weltgeschichte ist das Weltgericht.

know little or nothing of him. "'Tis true, 'tis pity, and pity 'tis, 'tis true."

John Seybert belongs to the heroic age of our Church. There were giants in those days, and he was one of them.

He was a typical Evangelical preacher, an embodiment of all that is distinctively characteristic of the spirit of our institutions and the general character of our ministry as conceived by the sainted founder of our Church, Jacob Albright. The spirit of aggression, the fire of missionary zeal, the desire to carry the Bible into benighted regions, and to bring the Gospel where no other church would condescend to go, this is characteristic of the ministry of the Evangelical Association, and distinguished in an extraodinary degree Bishop Seybert. We are no interlopers, nor proselyters, but pioneers by nature. We break our own stones from the quarry, and do not shun the toil of beginning the work in the crude. We have polished more stones for others, than others have for us. Seybert delighted in "breaking the ice", as he called it. Like the white plumed Prince of Navarre, he was always seen nearest the enemy's lines, where the hardest fighting was to be done, where danger and need were greatest.

He was no creature of circumstances. Circumstances were creatures in his hands. It may be truthfully said that he did more to mold his Church, than his Church did to mold him. He stamped his individuality upon the Evangelical Association and infused her with his spirit. His individuality was strong, unique and original. He won the admiration and confidence of the Church to such a degree that she involuntarily or unconsciously followed his example and copied his ideal.

He was one of those men who are not easily molded by their surroundings, their age, or their contemporaries. Seybert would have been much the same man, had he lived in any other age, provided he had become a subject of saving grace. Had he lived in the days of the apostles he would have been another Paul. Our bachelor-bishop indeed reminds one strikingly, in so many instances, of the great bachelor-apostle. He exhibited the same restless zeal and tireless activity; the same absolute devotion to the Lord and His cause; the same talent of adaptability; the same quickness of movement which made him almost ubiquitous; the same fearlessness in danger and intrepidity among enemies; the same holy ambition not to build on other men's foundations, but to preach the Gospel where others had not been; the same simplicity in preaching; the same abundance in labor; the same grand success.

In personal appearance, Bishop Seybert was not prepossessing, but singular. Of ordinary height, he possessed a robust frame, somewhat spare in flesh; his eyes were blue, his forehead was large, his chin prominent; an artless expression of deep earnestness, relieved by the light of benevolence and the lustre of Christian joy, played upon his features. His manner was frank as his face, his movements agile and nervous. The general effect of his physique was height-ened by his peculiarly plain and artless garb. He was thoroughly a homespun man. He wore a broad-rimmed, stiff felt hat after the manner of itinerants fifty years ago; his coat, closing up to the neck, was adorned with a thick row of large buttons; his trousers were of corduroy; his feet were covered with common leather shoes tied with strings. Altogether his appearance was unique, original, remarkable. But it was not affected; it was part of the man, and was thoroughly consistent with his radical sentiments on the subject of dress. He believed gaudy, costly, and fashionable dress to be inconsistent with a Christian profession, and incompatible with the Christian spirit, but he did not ask any one to imitate the cut of his coat, nor to comb his hair as he did, straight down.

Bishop Seybert's intellect was acute and practical, rather than massive and sentimental. Though deprived of a classical education in youth, his intellect was by no means without culture. He possessed the power of concentration in a remarkable degree, and his analytical abilities were of a high order. The ardor of his soul made his mind the stronger, and enabled him to penetrate to the very heart of Scritpure truth. His sucessful careeer, under the disadvantages of his time and circumstances, is the best evidence that his mind was one of extraordinary power. Besides, during his entire life he cultivated his intellectual faculties by reading the best German authors. When we take into account that he neces sarily spent most of his time on the back of his horse, it is a mystery how he managed to read so many books, and master such ponderous volumes of German lore. The result was, that he attained great thoroughness in the treatment of themes, and great versatility in Scripture exposition.

He was a man of strong, positive convictions. He lived for his convictions, and maintained them with a tenacity and enthusiasm which at times laid him open to the charge of stubbornness. But he was not stubborn. He had reached his conviction by prolonged study, keen observation, and extensive experience,— and convictions which a sincere mind attains in that way are not easy to give up. Besides, he founded his beliefs in the Scriptures and defended them by an appeal to the Book of books. He rested on the authority of God, and held to nothing that he did not believe to be Scriptural. He was a keen observer of little things, and to a modern mind appears tinged at least with something of superstition. This may be true, but let him who is actually innocent of the least superstition, even in our day, cast the first stone.

In conversation Seybert was affable and entertaining. He was never morose, always cheerful and active. But his conversation did not take a wide range of subjects, — unless it be conceded that the one subject of religion is large enough for a great man during his entire lifetime. God and His cause, was his theme in private conversation; and his aim was, in every case to advance the spiritual interests of those with whom he conversed. Thus his conversation was chiefly profitable, but by no means unentertaining. Sinners he exhorted to seek God, and saints he admonished to faithfulness. He was never frivolous nor worldly in his conversation. Withal, his deportment in the family was modest, cleanly, sociable and kindly. His influence in this regard was always the best.

In the pulpit Seybert was indeed a power. The reader of these pages can find ample evidence of that. His public ministrations were marvelous for spirituality. That was his chief characteristic; he had an unction of the Holy One; he was full of the Holy Ghost and mighty in the Scriptures. This was because his preparation was made chiefly by prayer, and the study of the Word of God.

His matter was choice, and largely original. That is to say, he drew it forth himself from the Fountain of the Word, rather than using the artificial helps of too many commentaries. Consequently he was always fresh and alive. He never grew "stale, flat and unprofitable". No man will, who goes to the Fountain for his supplies. He seldom dealt in speculative abstractions, but was a master in the art of making Scripture truth practical, and in bringing it down to the comprehension of the people. He gave the truth a handle.

His manner was always animated and nervous, and, when he was in the tide of impassioned speech, even imposing. He swept along with electrifying enthusiasm, carrying his auditors irresistibly with him. It was no uncommon thing for him to electrify his audience to such a degree that their demonstrations quite drowned out the speaker's voice. When he reproved sin, he did it with a keenness that is hardly attempted in our day; when he spoke of the Redeemer, he presented Him in inspiring glory and grace.

His language was terse, his sentences direct and incisive, his propositions comprehensive and compact. He was plain in his speech, as he was plain in dress. He cared nothing for ornamentation, or for the polish of rhetorical grace. He had a rhetoric of his own, and that, like everything else about him, was adapted to practical purposes.

The same was true of his homiletical arrangement. There was no far-fetched, fanciful division of points. He treated his text naturally, logically and practically. Judged from the effects of his preaching, he was indeed a great preacher. What pungent conviction was produced! what enthusiasm was inspired! what results were achieved! In this respect he has far outdone many more famous preachers.

This was largely due to the fact that he was always and only a soul-saver. Whatever he did, was done with this in view. He prayed, he studied, he rode, he talked, he preached for souls, and realized his desire.

Bishop Seybert's Christian character, it is almost needless to say, was irreproachable. He loved God with all his heart, and his neighbor as himself. His life proved this. His religion was no mere sentiment; it was the living, ruling principle of his soul. He was the most consistent of men. He lived not for himself, but for God and for humanity.   He was consecrated to that.   It was the only thing he did.

The Evangelical Association can be justly proud of Bishop Seybert.   He was a great man, who owed his greatness to his goodness.   His character was so genuine, his disposition so serene, his life so pure and consistent, his career so illustrious, and his success so magnificent, that his name will prove one of the brightest on our escutcheon, and, whatever the surprises and glory of the future, the lustre of Bishop Seybert's career will never be less.

> " He was a man, take him for all in all,
> We shall not look upon his like again."

In order that the reader may have some idea of the opinion which Bishop Seybert's contemporaries entertained concerning him, we subjoin a few extracts from various sources.

TRIBUTE TO THE MEMORY OF BISHOP SEYBERT.

The following appeared in the *Evangelical Messenger* of February 23d, 1860.   It was written by *T. M. Young:*

> Like a lone devotee at evening kneeling
> In the cold shadow of a temple dim,
> Sees not the sable night shades round him falling,
> Lulled by the music of the vesper hymn ;
> So in the twilight still I linger
> With aching heart that craves a healing balm,
> While memory, like a sweet-toned cherub, singing,
> Soothes my sad spirit with a plaintive psalm.

Our Father ! whom we mourn with vain affliction,
Thou art the theme of memory's tender strain,
The thought of thee is like a benediction
Invoking peace upon our selfish pain;
For like a dove with olive branch returning
From life's dark waters to the sheltering ark,
Thy soul with holy peace was fondly yearning,
To fold its pinions in death's peaceful barque.

Oh ! with what bitter grief they saw thee, languish,
Like the doomed victim of the venomed asp.
Schooling thyself to smile at thine own anguish
That loved ones might not mark its deadly grasp.
Self-sacrificing at affection's altar,
Thy spirit, like the faithful carrier dove,
Nerved its faint pinions ne'er to droop nor falter,
Upon its mission of untiring love.

Ah ! memory turning o'er her written pages,
Findeth few records of a life like thine.
Thy faith was placed upon the Rock of Ages,
Meek charity, and blessed hope divine.
And Oh ! rare mind, so free from falsehood's leaven
That from false seeming did thy soul rebel.
Not with thy prayers alone didst thou seek heaven,
But through a life of faith, and love, as well.

No ! thou wast not content with life's devotion,
Nor yet with one for this sad world too nice,
Like fancy frost-work, on life's turbid ocean,
A temple wondrous fair, but made of ice !
No ! thy soul, with sympathies divinely human,
Could feel for others' woe and help their need.
Thou wast a gentle, charitable Christian,
A Christian both in thought, and word, and deed.

Though thou hast left us for yon realms elysian,
Thy seeming presence doth my being thrill.

So deeply art thou mirrored in my vision,
Where'er I turn I seem to see thee still !
The night-wind's sigh seems like thy soft voice calling,
The moon-beams like the light of thy calm eyes,
And the twinkling stars are to my spirit singing :
"Thus, thus the righteous liveth : and thus the righteous
    dies ! "

The efforts vain, to calm the pain by steeping
In many tears the wound of such a grief ;
For e'en the solace of ungoverned weeping,
Hath not the power to yield my heart relief.
For memory's burning pen too deeply traces,
The bitter moments when all hope expires.   ,
Not e'en the lapsing waves of time effaces,
From the grieved heart those characters of fire.

The editor of the *Evangelical Messenger* paid this tribute to the Bishop's character.

Bishop Seybert was a man of toil. Trained to habits of industry from his youth, being naturally of an active nature, and reared, not in the lap of luxury, but amidst rigid economy, self-denial, and hardships, his early life qualified him in a very great measure to become, what he really was, one of the most indefatigable workers that the world ever saw. Few men, if any, either on this continent or Europe, in ancient or modern times, preached more sermons, visited more families, and traveled more miles, than did old father Seybert, and we doubt whether Paul himself would be an exception. And in speaking of his travels, it should here be remarked that he very seldom made use of public conveniences, but always traveled by his own private conveyance. As a pattern of industry he deserves to be held up to the imitation of all.

As a preacher he was practical. He cared but little for the purity of style, excellency and force of delivery, clearness of diction, impressive and correct language and gestures, or any of the peculiar characteristics of the orator. But what he neglected in this, was more than made up by his intense earnestness. Everybody saw that the plain, unassuming, active man before him, was altogether in earnest, and if he could not see it, he was sometimes made to feel; for a man had to know distinctly on whose side he was, if he would be sure to escape the arrows of truth that he flung by a muscular arm from his bow of steel. His lips spoke earnest words, his eyes flashed earnestness, his countenance, and that inimitable nod of his head, all declared him to be in earnest. Four years ago we heard him preach in Philadelphia; and in the course of his remarks he said: "I wish to have it said, when I am dead, that Seybert was a practical preacher." We say this of him now, not to gratify his wish, but, as every one that ever heard him knows, in order to adhere strictly to the truth.

But it was necessary that he should be doctrinal and argumentative in order to be truly practical; for it became his duty to combat error, as well as preach positive Gospel truth; and in listening to him, many a one of far greater pretensions to learning has been astonished to perceive the evidence of a rich fund of knowledge dart forth like flashes of light from his discourses.

Being very plain, and somewhat eccentric in his dress, he was the avowed and uncompromising enemy

of the gew-gaws and fooleries of fashion.   Many a
hard blow has he dealt, and many a conscience has
he made to smart, when he came to speak of this.   It
was a subject on which he always grew warm, and if
his rebukes were not very chaste in style, or his zeal
duly tempered with discretion, yet his worst enemy
(if he really had any, which is doubtful,) could not
deny that every word he spoke bore upon it the impress of an honest heart.

His ecclesiastical statesmanship was of a very
respectable character, and considering the intensity
of his nature, his views were often remarkably broad
and liberal.   But it was not in this that he particularly excelled.   He was no intriguer at all; slyness
or cunning could not have found a nook or corner in
his honest heart.   He was always a much better
worker than schemer, and in administering the Discipline, he coupled a remarkable degree of mildness
with his firmness.   As a presiding officer he knew
his place; never forgetting that he was to maintain
order amidst, and not participate in, the debates of a
conference until the time for him to speak came.   He
has always received the credit of conducting the
business of a conference with dispatch.

Like Paul the apostle, and the devoted Asbury, the
first bishop of the American Methodist E. Church,
Bishop Seybert was never married.   We are half inclined to believe he had no time to marry, or at least
preferred to spend all his time in the immediate service of his Master, rather than permit the cares and
responsibilities of married life, to distract his atten-

tion from the great and all absorbing work of saving souls. Hence he has no heirs, and the few thousand dollars that were left of a patrimony which was made to contribute freely to the cause of Christ during life, was bequeathed, in his last will, to the same purpose. Three thousand dollars he willed to the Missionary Society of the Evangelical Association, and two thousand to the "Charitable Society of the Evangelical Association" located at Orwigsburg, Schuylkill Co., Pa. This noble example is worthy of imitation! Minor bequests he made to other parties.

He may be said to have grown up with the Church over whose councils he presided for many years. He joined it when she had a membership of but 426, with three circuits, and but five effective intinerant preachers, and the entire territory covering but a few counties in eastern and central Pennsylvania. He leaves it now with a membership of 40,000; 320 itinerant preachers, many of them his sons in the Gospel, and her territories expanded over all the Middle and Western States, Canada, and a branch even in Germany. Well may his soul glow in raptures while he contemplates the goodness of God toward our little Zion, with whose spiritual and temporal interests he had been identified for a life-time.

Bishop W. W. Orwig, in his eulogy at the grave of Seybert, said: "Bishop Seybert was a *man*, a Christian and a *preacher* of the Gospel, who has had few equals in the Church, and who is unexcelled in the faithfulness, zeal and industry with which he performed the duties of his calling. He was a man, who, like Barnabas, was full of the Holy Ghost and of faith, and who, wherever he was known, was esteemed and loved, as has been abundantly shown since his demise by the tears of the people, both within and without the Church. May his example of piety, faithfulness and activity be an undying inspiration to the entire Evangelical Association and to her ministry, and always find enthusiastic imitation, and may all of us follow his faith!"

———

The editor the *Christliche Botschafter* gave the following estimate of the man:

"Thus lived and died a man whose memory will survive in thousands of grateful hearts, and will continue even to future generations. True, he did not take a place among the learned and great in the earth; no title, such as "D. D." ornamented his name. He passed through the world, quite plain and unpretentious, and yet we would ask, where are the men of his times who have done more good, who have led more souls to the Fountain of Life, and who have been a greater blessing than he? If other noble men have labored successfully in their sphere, he has certainly done so no less, in his sphere of operations, notwithstanding that his achievements have not been appreciatively judged by the learned world and by high churchly divines. But history names One who was served no better.

"Bishop Seybert was an itinerant preacher in the fullest sense of the term. Like Paul he chose the unmarried state, as presenting the fewest hindrances. in the service of the Gospel to which he was wholly devoted. We doubt whether any preacher in our Church has traveled more than he, or visited more families.

"To many he was a father in Israel. Eternity alone will reveal the number of souls which this man has. saved.

"True, he was human and had human infirmities, defects and peculiarities, but we may boldly assert that no *sinful* infirmities or habits were to be seen in his conduct. A principal feature of his character was his gentleness and toleration, notwithstanding the severity with which, in his sermons, he attacked men's sins and the vices of the times. He was a childlike, harmless servant of the Master, whose exalted pattern he sought to imitate. He was unselfish in his devotion to his calling. While the prelates of the Romish church, and of other ecclesiastical hierarchies lived in luxury and splendid ease, he traveled and exposed himself, and was satisfied with a salary of $100, and frequently paid his frugal bills from his own private purse.

"Though he was not celebrated as a pulpit orator; though he freely allowed his hearers to perceive that the Pennsylvania German dialect was his native tongue, yet no one could doubt that he spoke from the depth of profound conviction and intelligent faith.. His words came from the heart and reached the heart, and this especially when, as was so often the case, he spoke under the overwhelming power of the Holy

25

Ghost.   Whatever men may have thought of his oratory, all agreed that he was a good and pious man; even his strongest opposers granted this.—But what need of describing a man so generally known throughout the Evangelical Association, and whose loss almost every member personally feels?

"But no special institution in the kingdom of God was so precious to him, or so fully enlisted his sympathies as the holy missionary cause.   He was indeed a whole-souled missionary; he possessed a genuine missionary spirit, and lived in the cause of missions, for which reason also, by far the largest portion of his property was devoted to this noble institution."

————

A writer, whose name does not appear, in the *Christliche Botschafter* of March 17th, 1860, said:

"His simplicity and humility, his sincerity and conscientiousness, his gentleness toward his fellowmen, his intense opposition against unrighteousness, his great talents and extensive knowledge, above all his untiring and self-denying zeal for the honor of God and the welfare of mankind, all this and much more that is excellent, has made him loved and honored, as few mortals have been loved and honored.

"He was a master in Israel.   He possessed the qualifications of a theologian and of a successful preacher in a high degree.   His conception of truth was thorough and evangelical, and his charmed listeners found many a pearl of truth in his chaste and simple sermons.   It is true, his discourses were

plain, and it has been said that he was no pulpit orator in the usual acceptation of that term; but it is also
true, that he was one among a thousand in his mastery
of an audience, carrying them with him with irresistible power, and few retain their freshness and mental
vigor to the last, as did Bishop Seybert. Beyond all
this, the thousands of souls whom he was instrumental
in saving, who are partly on earth, and partly in
heaven, are the most precious proofs of his efficiency
and success. The children whom he has begotten in
the Gospel, are found in all parts of the Evangelical
Association, and in all the various positions in the
Church, from the presiding elder to the Sunday-
school scholar, and the fact that so large a portion
of his converts are found in our ministry, and that
perhaps each of our eight conferences numbers such
among its preachers, is a particular proof of his great
power.

"But he was especially also 'a man full of faith and
of the Holy Ghost'. He began his Christian life and
official career with a profound, thorough conversion,
and right here lies, at least in great part, the secret
of his remarkably fruitful ministry. In consequence
of his sound conversion and rich experience in the
grace of God, his life was eminently pious, his self-
denial positive, and his faith in God immovable. To
live for God and his cause was the high and single
purpose of his life, and few accomplished this as he
did.

"We are told, 'had he spared himself more, he might
still be living.' Granted. But he could not spare

himself; he was bound by solemn obligations to labor while it was day, and not to cease until the night should come, and he was conscientiously determined to keep his vows. He would fulfill his commission to the utmost, and feared to do less than he could.

"The Evangelical Association, which he so dearly loved, bears the impress of his influence on all sides, and that as deeply as she now mourns his departure. In every enterprise which had for its object the progress of the Lord's work and the increase of our Church, Bishop Seybert was the foremost in zeal and activity."

"In conclusion—though I am by no means through, —in him God gave to our Association in its infancy a man who will stand to future years as an example and pattern, especially for our dear brethren in the ministry. We have had him with us for a long time, and yet we lost him before we were ready to give him up. But we thank God, that He gave him to us, and pray that henceforth the spirit which was in Seybert may be diffused through our Association from the senior bishop to the youngest member; then we shall have a future for which the circle of the earth will not be too great, nor the heavens too high."

CHAPTER XIX.

BEING EXTRACTS FROM THE SERMONS, ETC., LECTURES, CONVERSATIONS AND LETTERS OF BISHOP JOHN SEYBERT, ON DIFFERENT SUBJECTS.

We have but very few of Bishop Seybert's sermons on record, and not one of those that we have is complete. It was a mistake on the part of his cotemporaries not to note down more of his sermons and lectures. Seybert himself left no manuscript copies of his sermons. He seldom, if ever, wrote sermons. This is to be regretted. His sermons and lectures would form a contribution to our denominational literature of inestimable value. Words of such power as his, should not have been permitted to die. As it is, they only live in their perpetual results. We give in this chapter so much as is accessible.

SERMON ON JOB.

My text is the book of Job, and from this I will preach without a sketch, praying that the eternal God may add His blessing, power and life!

Much has already been spoken and written about Job, but right here in the first chapter I find something about him that no one has yet clearly brought out — namely, that Job was, at the same time, both very rich and very pious! Is not that a rare case? (Pause.) I guess he was entirely sanctified. Wonder whether there is another Job to be found now-a-days in the Church? I doubt whether there is one in the Evangelical Association. We have people who are as pious as Job was, but they are not so rich. Great God, how important it is that our rich professors of religion should be entirely redeemed and purified from all vanity, pride, avarice, and worldly-mindedness! O that the generation of Jobs might increase!

Here I find something in the fifth verse that each father should take to heart. Job offered burnt-offerings *every day* for his children, for he thought they might have sinned. This wealthy and respectable man was very much concerned for the salvation of his children. He was not satisfied with their worldly prosperity — he had great anxiety for the salvation of their souls. Fathers and mothers, how is it with you? Do you also pray and bring daily offerings to God in behalf of your children, that they may not be overcome of the world and of Satan? Or are you satisfied if your son is a greedy speculator, and your unconverted daughter struts about in such display that one's horse gets frightened at her and attempts to run away, when passing her on the street? O, ye parents, learn from this pious man to observe your family worship daily, and let the offering of living, believing prayer, often ascend for your children. But you must also be right, and live right before them, or it will avail nothing. We next find that the children of God met together, either at Job's house, or in his neighborhood, verse 7. Some think these "sons of God" were the holy angels. I will allow them to have their opinion, but I shall take the Word just as it stands; I think it must have been a meeting of real *live* children of God — human beings who were soundly converted — for if there was a Job at that time, there were also, it is likely, other pious persons. These held a meeting, and behold, Satan came in also. And so he does to this day—but, hallelujah! the eternal God was there among His children, for they had come before God with prayer, hungering and thirsting after righteousness.   Satan was behind time. (Here the Bishop described the schemes and tricks of the devil in trying to hinder the Word and Work of God in congregations, and then continued:) But here I come to a point that could never yet be found out by the wisdom of the world, but only by the Spirit of God. It is too deep for me, it is such a depth that one staggers in trying to look into it, and that is the severe trials and great suffering of Job.

Satan being in the assembly, among the children of God, was asked of the Lord, "Whence comest thou?" What have you to do here? You are out of place here.   The Lord knew that Satan was envious of Job, because he was such a light in the Lord; and he had come as an accuser of the brethren, to bring something against this good man, who was as a thorn in his eye.   And being a "liar from the beginning," he would not speak the truth even to God, but said, "I have been passing to and fro in the country, after my business; and hearing that there was a meeting here, I thought I would come and see what is going on."

Although this was full of lies, there was some truth

woven into it. The devil does pass up and down in the land and has a great deal of business. He must frequently go to the taverns, groggeries, gambling pits, frolics, parties, dances, etc., and see to it that everything goes on right devilish. He must help the thieves, whoremongers, adulterers, fraudulent, and especially the vain fashion-fools to do everything according to his will. How the old fellow must chase about, and order the little sub-devils around right and left, and in every direction! He must help the ladies before the glass to make their fool-fashions set right, and must see to it that the men chase after the world with the necessary earnestness. In politics, in the Church, in the theatre, in the pulpit, in the closet, in the ball-room, wherever men do congregate, in whatever men engage, he is busy in efforts to hinder the good and advance the evil. Especially where there are spiritual meetings, where sinners are resurrected into the life eternal, and where the children of God leap for joy and praise their Redeemer, there he begins to rage like a steam boiler, and his anger is wreaked on some pious Job.

The Lord very well knew that Satan was at this meeting to bring a railing accusation against Job, and so He anticipated the cunning old serpent with the question: "Hast thou considered my servant Job, that there is none like him in the earth, a perfect and an upright man, one that feareth God and escheweth evil?" Then the devil's envy boiled over, and with a hot poisonous snort, he answered: "Doth Job fear God for naught? Hast Thou not made an hedge about him, and about his house, and about all that he hath on every side? Thou hast blessed the work of his hands, and his substance is increased in the land. But put forth Thy hand now, and touch all that he hath, and he will curse Thee to Thy face. — Job only serves Thee from self-interest, because it pays so well. If Thou wouldst give and preserve everything thus for me, I would also serve Thee." I suppose the devil had not learned then yet that the grace of God can so transform fallen men that they can serve God without any motive of self-interest, but only because it is the will of God; and perhaps the Lord thought it was about time the devil should learn this lesson, as well as mankind (herein is a very profound depth), and therefore the Lord said to Satan: "Behold, all that he hath is in thy power; only upon himself put not forth thine hand. So Satan went forth from the presence of the Lord."

He had to confess a great truth, namely, that God had "set an hedge about Job" and all his possessions, and was protecting him. Hallelujah! the devil himself was compelled to acknowledge that God is like a wall of fire around His people! Satan had often gone prowling around Job like a savage beast, but he always found him hedged securely in till now; when all at once the Lord opened a door of permission, and Satan enters promptly upon his work of destruction. "Here" thought he, "I will shew Job and all the world how little there is in the service of God." And he went to work quite shrewdly; Satan is no fool, depend upon that. In one day he seized Job's children, cattle, and all his possessions, and destroyed them; and to effect this, he, by Divine permission, made use of the Chaldeans, the storm, the lightnings, etc. But mark! Satan had so arranged it that one messenger after the other came to Job, bringing him one terrifying message after another. While one messenger was yet speaking, Satan had another on the run; he so hurried him that he was quite out of breath, when he came to Job, where the first one was still speaking, and could hardly deliver his message for panting. So it was with the third and fourth. How these poor fellows had to hurry their feet to carry the devil's messages! He still makes men who serve him chase about thus till they almost die. But — but there was a devilish object in all this. If Job had had but one minute he would have fallen upon his knees, and by prayer obtained strength immediately. This Satan knew very well, and was anxious to prevent it. It was his intention to suddenly overwhelm Job, and felt quite sure of victory too. But if ever in his life he was beaten, deceived, and put to shame, it was now. After Job had heard it all, he fell upon the earth, praying, and said, "The Lord gave and the Lord hath taken away; blessed be the name of the Lord!" His praise to God struck the devil like a thunderbolt of surprise. "Ho! what is all this? This is not as I expected!" he exclaimed. Full of anger, shame and madness, he fled, feeling as mean as only a defeated devil can feel! But he could not rest yet, thinking, "if Job is possessed of such deep piety, what harm will he not do my cause upon earth?

I must go at him again." So he went to the assembly of the sons of God again. Impudently he now tells the Lord, if he would lay his hand upon Job's body and life he would curse God; "for all that a man hath will he give for his life," said Satan. Then the Lord said: "Behold he is in thine hand; but save his life". . . . So went Satan forth from the presence of the Lord, and smote Job with boils from the sole of his foot unto his crown. Behold, as soon he had permission he chased and tumbled himself after the man of God, and abused him most miserably, causing him to break out all over with boils, so that he had to scrape the corruption off with a potsherd, and sit in ashes. Now he had robbed Job of his children, his cattle, his lands, his health, and almost his life, leaving him only a cross and ugly wife, who under the influence of the evil spirit came upon him and mocked him, saying: "Dost thou still retain thine integrity? Curse God and die." The old enemy knows well what a great influence the wife often has over the husband, and he thought, "Now I have surely conquered! Job surely can't stand that!" But hark! Job answered her decidedly and with resignation, being fully in the light: "Thou speakest as one of the foolish women speaketh. What! shall we receive good at the hand of God, and not evil?"

Defeated again, Satan now turns Job's former friends loose upon him, to plague him with accusations until it was almost intolerable. Just think how this holy, pious, consecrated man was brought into distress; his possessions, his children, almost his life taken away from him; persecuted by his own wife and former friends; his soul enveloped in darkness! Satan thought he could worry and discourage him till he had him conquered; hence he listened with malignant joy to the lamentations of Job. But suddenly he heard, to his terror, a confident exclamation come up from the depth of Job's soul: "I know that *my Redeemer liveth*, and that he shall stand at the latter day upon the earth: And though after my skin, worms destroy this body, yet in my flesh shall I see God!"

No doubt the enemy now lost all hope, for he saw that Job did not serve God for worldly prosperity, but that he was anchored deeply in his Redeemer. The end and object of this great trial had now been reached. God turned again the captivity of Job, removed his wretchedness, and blessed him more abundantly than ever before, and the devil learned a lesson that he will never forget.

The devil hates no one so much as those Christians who are so entirely swallowed up in God, and so dead to all the vanities of the flesh and of the world, that they love God with all the heart. But he can not injure them. Hallelujah!

This history gives us a clear view of the realm of spirits, and into that we must look if we would rightly understand it. It gives us a look behind the scenes, and lays bare the hidden forces that work in our lives.

Oh my brethren and sisters! whatever you do, press deeply into God. Watch and pray, submit yourselves wholly unto the Lord, and trust him in the greatest adversities.   For,

> "The clouds ye so much dread
> Are big with mercy, and will break
> In blessings on your head."

ARRAIGNMENT OF THE LIQUOR DEALERS.

Notwithstanding the misery and fearful destruction that is produced daily, by the comnon use of spirituous and intoxicating liquors, the murderous robber business of manufacturing and selling of it, both at wholesale and retail, still goes on uninterruptedly, as if it were a necessary and useful business, without which the world could not go on.   As soon as a man publicly opposes this business, the brewer, the distiller, the seller, the moderate drinker and the rowdy, become his enemies.   The *sellers* of strong drink are really the men who are responsible for the continuance of the vice of drunkenness.   They help the drunkard along in his pathway of ruin, encourage him in his vice, and furnish him with the implements of self-destruction.

Here are a few of the innumerable examples of the unspeakable miseries of drunkenness, which these rum-sellers produce;

Not long since a drunkard, whom I could mention by name, injured himself in one of his limbs, and the poison which brandy had carried into the red tide of life, produced inflammation in the wound, and it became incurable.   He died, frightfully cursing his poor soul, and went into the solemnity of eternity with horrid oaths and imprecations on his dying lips. Forever and forever he has to reap the fearful harvest which he sowed, and for which the rum-seller provided the seed. After death his poisoned mutilated carcass was terrible to behold.

Come, rum-seller, see this poor inebriate in his coffin! He came to his untimely end *by your hands.* Behold the work of your hands! Look into his face and you can read amid its lines and furrows your own awful doom. — And what have you gained? His money! For it you have brought him to an early grave.

During the last year a drunkard in S—— pursued his poor wife with an axe, while he was intoxicated. The creature fled from her *"protector"* to a neighboring house, but he followed her and cleft her skull in two, inflicting also several other ghastly wounds in her breast. Before help arrived she was a corpse, and her murderer, whom the rum-sellers had converted into an incarnate devil, was in the act of cutting his own throat with a knife. His father had been a liquor dealer and kept a saloon — a gateway to hell.

Another instance where the man was formerly one of my personal acquaintances. I know him to have been a well-meaning, kind-hearted man by nature, and he had an excellent, industrious wife, and good children. But through moderate drinking he became an arch-drunkard. The family became a ruin. The husband and father in his frenzies would pursue his

good wife and children, with the axe, the gun, the
butcher-knife, or anything he happened to get, so
that they frequently escaped death narrowly, and
finally they all had to leave him.

Do you see, ye rum and brandy makers and sellers,
what your devilish business accomplishes and produces? The above mentioned facts are only examples
out of millions, of how you utterly ruin your victims
in soul and body, for time and for eternity. Cast but
a glance at the innumerable victims of your butchery.
The land swarms with them. See how many beg-
gars and paupers you create annually, who go in rags
from house to house, begging for bread and clothes —
or perhaps for money to buy more rum and brandy
of you. For when, in robber fashion, you have stolen
all their possessions, you send them out into the
world and oblige them to *beg* more money before you
give them any more to drink. Yes, when these poor
wretches have squandered their last cent in your
establishment, and have pawned their last coat for
drink over your bar, you drive the naked victims
of your avarice from your door, and if it be the cold-
est Winter night. Even if they freeze, and rush into
the abyss of hell, you are not concerned, least of all
if you first got all their money. Money is your object,
ye accursed liquor dealers.

Lift up your eyes and see the thousands you drive
into infirmaries, insane asylums and prisons. On
your account they are suffering there. Cast a glance
also into the black abyss of hell, where the millions
of drunkards must endure the fearful tortures of the

worm that dieth not, and the fire that is not quenched. Through drinking, these have shortened their lives, and you are responsible for their lamentable fate. O, listen to the thunder of their cries of anguish, their moans of distress, and think of the imprecations they will heap upon you when you get there too! For you will get there just as sure as you do not change your course and stop your nefarious trade. Then those will curse you, who, deceived by you, had chosen the path of vice. Then those' souls whom you tormented, will accuse you. And every pang that you have caused, and every fortune you destroyed, will haunt you with its woe.

Better, a great deal, that you should nourish your children by begging, if such a thing were necessary in this country, than to be engaged in this destructive business. For, were this accursed traffic banished from our land and nation, we would have a gain, annually, of at least one hundred millions of dollars.

BISHOP SEYBERT ON TOBACCO.

[In many things Seybert was in advance of his age. This is especially noticeable in his views of the use of tobacco. In an age when most Christian professors and preachers used the narcotic, and few in any church thought of protesting against it, he was outspoken, radical, and earnest in his condemnation of the evil. Before any conference passed any resolutions on the subject, Bishop Seybert was wont to inquire of candidates for the ministry, for orders, or for the Presiding Elder's office, whether they were free from the use of tobacco.   Below follow some paragraphs giving his sentiments fully and clearly. S.]

In his journal he wrote of a certain locality: "Around here the people are deeply corrupted; there are many tipplers, and both among *converted* and *unconverted*, the pernicious use, or rather *abuse* of tobacco prevails.   However a glorious work of grace has begun, and it is to be hoped that the people will be saved from the *idols*, and will get rid of them."

In a sermon he delivered himself in this fashion:

"The misuse of tobacco occurs ordinarily in smoking, chewing and snuffing.   The daily use of it in this way can not fail to have a harmful effect upon particular portions of the body. Tobacco is fit for medicine, and that is the only use of the weed. But whoever chews, smokes or snuffs it daily, will at last suffer harm in his physical system.   Among the symptoms which it produces are the following: various classes of headache, numbness, dizziness, nausea, pain in the eyes, and watering of the same, dullness of the sense of smell, smarting and blistering of the tongue, unpleasant odor in the mouth, rawness in the throat and irritation to cough, constant hunger, accompanied with nausea and fainting, stomach cramps, weakness and trembling of the limbs, palpitation of the heart, distressing pressure on the chest, gradual consumption, etc. Every slave of tobacco, if he will be honest, must acknowledge that he is troubled with one or more of these evils, though he may not have connected his sufferings with tobacco unless his attention was called to it.

26

"If a medicine be used habitually for years to cure a certain disease, it will eventually produce a disease of its own, according to its properties and power, especially if it be a poison, which tobacco certainly is.

"Even the demands of our physical nature should prevent us from using the weed, for nature rises in rebellion against it in every person who begins its use, with the intention of habituating himself to its use. Every tobacco slave knows by experience, how unwilling his system was to receive the obnoxious poison, because nature felt its harmfulness and protested mightily against its use. We ought to be ashamed before the dumb brutes, though we are endowed with reason, we do far worse than they in this particular. Do not dumb creatures select the vegetation that is suitable for their nourishment, from among poisonous growths? As a rule, they touch a harmful weed but once. Ought not we to act as wisely as our cattle and sheep? They avoid harmful indulgences. We do not accomplish as much with our reasoning faculties as these dumb creatures do with their instinct! O, inconsistency, where is thy blush!

"Smoking and chewing positively impairs the digestion, because it vitiates the salivary secretion, and the gastric juice, which are necessary to the transformation of food into the blood and material for physical building and repair. Snuffing only spoils what it is intended to improve, besides being a repulsive habit, which eventually destroys the sense of smell, so that one feels as if he had neither head nor nose, or imagines he is all nose.

"In many instances it requires grace to get rid of the habitual use of the narcotic, just as stopping the use of intoxicants often also requires grace. But as a general thing, even good breeding and common civilization without religion will keep a man from using it, for this filthy habit is such a violation of good morals and æsthetical delicacy, that a well bred person will not be guilty of it. Good breeding abhors it. To stop the habit, in short, costs generally nothing more than that *one makes up his mind never to touch the weed again, and keeps the resolution. That does the business.*

"The tobacco habit is also an occasion of extravagance. If one observes the great waste of time and money which is connected with the misuse of tobacco, it is hard to avoid the conviction that it certainly is not a proper indulgence for those who claim to be followers of Christ. I have also observed that this narcotic leads to indolence, and laziness knows nothing except how to kill time. Presumably, tobacco dealers and users will regard me as fanatical and peculiar, but I can not reconcile such a filthy habit, that costs so much money and time, with the character of a Christian who is under obligations to consecrate his goods and time to God.

"In our little Evangelical Association (1841) at least $7,000 are this year devoted to tobacco — much more than the offerings for the holy missionary cause amount to. *O God, have mercy!* But if all the money that is paid out for tobacco in America alone for one year, would be devoted to benevolent purposes, how many naked and neglected children in the land could be clothed, sheltered and educated! how many forsaken widows and their orphans would be relieved from want, and made happy! how many missionaries could be equipped and sent out to save immortal souls! Yes, how many more preachers could our own Church support on the field of the Gospel, with the money that is consumed by its members in this unrighteous way! But alas! we too must sacrifice to the idols yet!

"But how is it with the servants of the Word, the itinerant preachers? Are these free from this uncleanness? It is for them to leave this path of sin first, for they are called of God to show the people the way to heaven, and to teach them to crucify the flesh with its sinful lusts, to put off the old man with his works, and to keep themselves unspotted from the world. But are *they* unspotted, if they are bedaubed with tobacco juice, and infected with tobacco stench, so that to a decent person they are positively repulsive? I think not.. They are slaves, and I advise them, yea beg of them to cleanse themselves of this filthiness, and to use their money to a better purpose, for the day of judgment comes on a pace, where also the preachers must give account of their stewardship.

"I appeal to the ministry to go to work to root up this evil. If you will interest yourselves in it as you should, the cause will make better progress. · Up then, ye heralds of the Cross! ye embassadors for Christ! Your Master smoked no tobacco. I will vouch for that!   Up, ye watchmen of Israel!   Break down and tear away these idols.   Lift up your voices, and protest by your *example* against this squandering of time and money.   The people watch their watchmen, and imitate the example of their leaders. Through you a reformation can easily be effected. And what a blessing this would be to our little Zion! The missionary contributions could be materially increased—yes, doubled.   Our pulpits would be clean, and our pews fit for decent and well-clad people.   The behavior of our preachers would be more in accord with their office, and their character as ministers would be in higher estimation, and they would employ many an hour in prayer and study, which they now lose by their sinful use of tobacco."

―――――――――

"LOVE IS STRONG AS DEATH."—A FRAGMENT.

Text:—Song of Sol. 8:5.   For love is strong as death.

This is an everlasting truth, which Christ demonstrated when he died for us while we were yet sinners.   Rom. 5:8–10.   This truth has also been demonstrated by thousands and millions of people, who have been constrained by love to endure tribulation, to bear shame, to suffer the loss of all things, and to submit even to the most painful death for the glory of God and for the sake of the truth.

It is evident that no person in his wicked state has or can have this love in him.   We must therefore inquire how we are to get possession of this quality of character.　I answer, *by regeneration.*　It is not to be attained in any other way, as is clear from 1. John 5:1:　"Whosoever believeth that Jesus is the Christ is born of God; and every one that loveth him that begat, loveth him also that is begotten of him." Here the holy apostle represents faith, regeneration and love as being together.　According to Rom. 5:5 love is shed abroad in our hearts by the Holy Ghost who is given unto us.　This is said of those who are born again.

According to the commandment of God, and also the example of ancient saints, we must grow and increase in love as well as in every other grace of Jesus Christ, if we are not to grow indifferent and cold, and at last lose our souls.　Whoever continues in love to the end of life, shall be saved, but he who has forsaken his first love, let him consider whence he is fallen, repent, do his first works and seek his first love again — seek her continually, until he is submerged in the ocean of everlasting love.

This love which is spoken of in the text must be genuine.　Let us be sincere in our love.　Love is not deceitful.　Brotherly love should be hearty, in honor preferring one another.　Our love is not to be "in word, neither in tongue, but in deed and in truth."　Then all will recognize us as belonging to Jesus Christ, and that we are His true disciples.

Whosoever has within him this love which comes from God, loves also his foes, prays for them and does them good, as the ancients said.　A heavenly spirit must possess those who follow Jesus, and those who have entered the kingdom of grace can not hate anyone.   Love goes out after all men.

Without the love of God in our hearts we are unfit for good works or the performance of Christian duty. Though we were ever so learned, and understood all tongues, and all mysteries; though we could speak with the tongues of angels, and though we could remove mountains by the might of our faith, yea though we give our all to the poor, and our body to be burned, yet all this without love would not save us.

Love adorns all our actions, and makes all our works acceptable to God.   Love enables us to do the whole will of God with great delight.   Love is an active principle in the regenerate soul, which constrains him to clothe the naked, feed the hungry, visit the sick and those that are in prison, and to entertain hospitably the stranger and pilgrim.   She also constrains God's people to open benevolent hands, to spread the Gospel by the help of their earthly means.   I know of a sister who purchased a number of pocket Bibles, and distributed them among the poor around her, so that these might have the precious Word of God.   That is practising love.

Love also persuades men sometimes to devote fields and forests to the service of the living God, and to dedicate houses, work-shops and business places, as homes of worship and prayer.   It constrains God's children to be prompt and regular in the public services of God's house, and to attend assiduously to family and secret devotions.   Carelessness in these particulars betrays coldness of love. Love produces life and activity in those in whom she dwells, so that they are at times enabled to pray with great emotion and many tears for their unconverted friends, that such may also be saved. Yea, love constrains men who have talent and are anointed from above for the purpose, to leave father and mother, wife and children, to despise a comfortable living and earthly possessions, and to carry "the grace of God that bringeth salvation" over mountain and valley, over land and rivers, through cold and heat, through sunshine and storm, regardles of the sacrifice they make or the hardships they encounter, until the ends of the earth are full of the honor and knowledge of God. Such men, however, are not easily frightened off by the devil, or made timid by difficulties. They do not easily leave the field. No! so long as love is master in the heart of the minister of Jesus, he sails boldly on.

Love also makes us patient in suffering, and enables us, for God's sake, to endure with fortitude all the trials, burdens, toils and cares of this life, waiting calmly until our change come.

Now, beloved friends, who hear this, how is it among you? How stands this matter with us all? How is it in the Evangelical Association? How is it with me and with you? Are you still rooted and grounded in that love that is strong as death? To the glory of God I can say that I feel love's fires burning in my inmost soul with as much intensity and fervor as ever before in my Christian experience.

And how is it in the ministry? Ye messengers of the Lord, have ye this love burnig yet, or are her fires gone down? Have you still the courage and faith to continue in the field until evening, when the Master will call the laborers home and give them their reward? O, brethren, be faithful! Our work in the Lord is not in vain. Possibly, in some the love has grown so cold, that you have determined to retire from the Gospel field at the next annual conference, and go back to gathering earthly treasures or to seek a more comfortable living, than the minister has who is the servant of everybody.

Where is that youth, strong as Samson who slew thousands of Philistines and set their corn fields on fire? Has he, like the son of Manoah, yielded to the charms of some Delilah who, as the wife of his bosom, has shorn him of his strength? Oh, he went out so grandly into the battle! But he has taken a wife and now his strength and courage are gone. Where now is his zeal for God's honor, and the love for immortal souls? It is to be feared it has been extinguished. In a few the impulse to preach has been lost and the love of money has captured their hearts, for, without good cause they have have left the work, gone home, and are now engaged in worldly business. Brethren, have a care! Your Lord cometh soon and inquireth for the talent He entrusted to your hands. And what will you say? Though the Lord has set you as watchmen, you seldom blow the trumpet. Is there no danger any more, or has the Lord taken the office from you and given it to others? You can not put the blame for your retirement on our friends; for they are seeking year by year to make more and more perfect arrangements, and yearly sacrifice their thousands that your wants might be provided for, while you are spreading the Gospel. Of course, if all our friends had this perfect love that is stronger than death, they would still do much more for the spread of Christ's kingdom than they do. They could support twice the number of traveling preachers, and three times the number of missionaries. What a blessing that would be for the German population of North America!

THE EPISCOPAL OFFICE.

The Great Head of the church has appointed various offices for the good of the church, and the salvation of the world. Already in the Apostolic church the Holy Spirit anointed and appointed prophets, evangelists, shepherds, teachers and apostles; there were also deacons, elders and bishops in the primitive Church, through whom the saints were edified, and the body of Christ strengthened. Therefore it is proper and beneficial to have these officers in the Church to-day.

The higher the office which the Church entrusts to a brother, the more humility is required, and also a correspondingly greater treasure of grace and unction in the heart, in order to perform the duties of the office well pleasing to God, and for the good of the Church. THE HIGHER THE OFFICE, THE NEARER TO GOD.

Jesus Christ holds the highest office in the Church universal, and He, the great "Shepherd and Bishop", is in the "bosom of the Father". John was the most far-seeing of the apostles, and was entrusted with the greatest mysteries of the Kingdom, and he lay on Jesus's breast. Paul, who took the first rank among the apostles, "was caught up into the third heaven, the Paradise of God", so that he constantly felt a deep inward desire to depart and be with Christ.

The exalted apostle Paul could not be separated from Christ, by height nor depth, nor any other creature. So should a bishop be. He must not be like a dried, dead reed, shaken by the wind, if he is to be fit for his high position. Even every Christian is to be green and flourish like a cedar of Lebanon, the older the stronger, how much more necessary is this for a bishop! A bishop should also be like a wall of masonry, like a granite rock, so that something can be laid upon him and be secure. What does a bishop amount to, if he is not a pillar in the house of God, nor a patriarch in the family of saints?

A bishop should be distinguished for his spirit of self-denial. He must not seek a life of ease, nor honor from men, nor shun the Cross, nor aim at a high salary, neither should he in his own person nor in his family be conformed to the fashionable ways and display of the world. He should have well-bred children who are true Christians, so that even they will demonstrate the man's fitness to preside over a household. A bishop in the Evangelical Association must not make a long face if he becomes all men's

scape-goat.   Long ago the sun has burnt me black.
"The world is crucified unto me, and I unto the
world."   Nor do I care to know anything, save Jesus
Christ, and Him crucified.   A bishop must not "lord
it over God's heritage", but be an "ensample to the
flock."   He must not be conspicuous for personal
pride and official *hauteur*, riding in cruel pomp over
the rights, the consciences and the happiness of the
people, like the gilded prelates of the Romish
hierarchy.

One of the strongest evidences that a man is not
fit for the episcopal dignity, is when he seeks the
office.   Such an one misapprehends the gravity and
importance of this position in the Church, or over-
estimates his own talent and fitness.   According to
Augustine the episcopal title is itself the name of a
work which he has to perform who receives the title,
and that work is to take care of the subordinates in
the Church, and to be concerned for their spiritual
welfare.   He who has a bishop's office has a *work* to
perform through the heat and burden of the day, and
must not desire to be a mere idle *gentleman*.   The
episcopal office is by no means a sinecure.   The
fathers of the primitive Church feared the office and
its responsibilities so greatly, that some of them had
to be literally forced into acceptance.   Among his
brethren in the ministry, the bishop should be the
least and humblest. as we are taught by the example
of Jesus in washing his disciple's feet.

THE SLANDERER.

The slanderer has three swords on his tongue, with which he kills three persons with one stroke, namely himself, the one whom he slanders, and the one who listens attentively to his words. Sometimes slanderers do not even let the dead alone. Lying and murder are inseparable, and Jesus says of the devil, that he is a liar and a murderer from the beginning. The slanderer is no better. For one thing he has the devil's nature and disposition, and then he is a tool of the devil. Nobody is safe from the devil, and much less from the slanderer's tongue. No one can tame the devil, neither can the backbiter's tongue be tamed, which is set on fire of hell. Consider this, you who speak bold lies against your neighbor. You are a devil. The devil concealed himself already in Eden in a serpent, and who does not know that a serpent carries its poison in its mouth? No sword cuts so keenly, no wound pains so severely, no arrow pierces so deeply, as a slanderers's tongue. A scourge makes furrows of blood, but a wicked tongue crushes the bones and kills the marrow. Many have fallen by the sword, but more by wicked tongues. Nor is any wound harder to heal than that which is made by the mouth of the slanderer, especially when the slanderer is influential. Herein is the greatest power of this evil, when it has the authority and influence of the great.

THE BLESSED AND HOLY LOT. — A SERMON.

[This sermon was preached by the Bishop in a private house in Bucks Co., Pa., and was greatly blessed to those who heard it. Some of his auditors regarded the hearing of the sermon as an event in their lives. About half an hour before the appointed time to preach, the Bishop took the chair behind the table upon which lay the Bible and hymn book. For some time he sat with folded arms in a meditative mood, occasionally casting a glance at the books before him. After singing and prayer, during which he seemed to enjoy no liberty whatever, he sat down again, manifestly nervous and embarrassed. Finally he rose and read his text, remarking, "I have read a big text, which ought to be treated with homiletic system, whoever can do it."]

Text: Blessed and holy is he that hath part in the first resurrection; on such the second death hath no power, but they shall be priests of God and of Christ, and shall reign with Him a thousand years. Rev. 20:6.

I have thought often and much about the millennium. · In studying the writings of pious and learned authors, it appears that they by no means agree. For myself I have come to this conclusion: I will see to it that I am a child of the King, so that I may have part in the first resurrection, and then in course of time I shall find out what the millennium is, and shall myself reign with Christ in the millennial kingdom. I will *first* show what the "first resurrection" is, and *second* contemplate the assertion, "Holy and blessed is he" etc.

1st. Concerning the *first resurrection* the learned are also disagreed. But there is a resurrection which at all events may be called the first, and which must take place first, if we are to have part in the holy and blessed lot, and that is *the resurrection from spiritual death, into the spiritual life with Christ in God.* This is the first. To be clear, however, it will be necessary to say something here of spiritual death. Spiritual death came into the world through the Fall, and has propagated itself in Adam's race until our time. It is because men are spiritually dead that they are naturally hard-hearted, impenitent, ungrateful, dead to everything that is good, alive only to sin. O how sad is the condition of humanity. To describe this universal spiritual death I have a good key in Ezek. 37. There the Lord took the prophet into a large valley, which was full of dead bones, very dry, and lying about in great confusion. The feet were where the head should be, and *vice versa;* one part lay here and the other there, as if a whirlwind had brought them there. Such is the condition of men in their natural state; evil desires and passions rule the soul, while the reason and the will, which ought to be on the throne, are under the yoke. Heads of families, who ought to be examples of self-control and piety, are intemperate and profane, in which case the head is where the feet should be. Clergymen, who assume the care of souls, frequently preach the devilish doctrine that men can not be made free from sin in this life, instead of the glorious Gospel truth, and then set their flocks a bad example in their lives. Does anyone want to be converted to God? These clericals say, "What! you want to be converted? You *are* good Christians. I have baptized and confirmed you, and you go to the Lord's Supper. Be satisfied, or you will get into fanaticism, and even may lose your reason yet! Go into jolly society, read the newspaper more and the Bible less, and you will feel easier!" Surely, in such a case everything is wrong end foremost and wrong side up, yea also everything spiritually dead and very dry, as was shown the prophet in the vision.

But the eternal God does not want the sinner to die forever, and has made provisions to bring him to life in Christ Jesus. He has also instituted the ministry. As of old He called Ezekiel, led him into the valley of dry bones and commanded him to prophesy; so it is to this day His plan and order to call His own preachers. Nor does He call them to spend first five or six years in high-schools, so as to get a diploma that they are educated preachers; but when God calls men, He calls them to *go* and *prophesy* unto the dry bones. At times the Lord's servants are severely tried, when they contemplate the hopeless condition of mankind and the Lord asks, "Son of man, can these bones live?" There is nothing left them but to answer, "Lord, thou knowest!" Often, too, they are led to feel their own weakness and unfitness.

This has often been my experience. Sometimes I am enabled to preach in perfect victory and grace, and then I think I will keep myself in this stream;

but soon there comes a season of poverty, fainting fits and emptiness, so that I learn anew that God alone is mighty, that all depends upon His blessing, and that He must be all in all, if the work is to increase. But under such circumstances His servants must work on, and not be easily discouraged. Even should they become sick, or other misfortunes befall them, they must not sit down in despair. Once I had a series of appointments a thousand miles in length, and when I began I was taken with a fever. Each forenoon I had to lie in bed, but in the afternoon I would bestride my horse, and until evening was at my next appointment, and held my meeting. At last, one day, I became so feeble that I scarcely reached my destination at all, and was obliged to go to bed immediately, for I was sick almost unto death. But when evening came, I heard the house filling up with many people. I was too sick to preach, but I thought it a pity that so many people should meet, to hear God's Word, in vain. Accordingly I arose, and staggered down stairs as best I could. There were many *strangers* present, and I thought, "Why, you ought to try to pray with these people anyhow." I made the attempt in great weakness. During prayer, a text came to my mind, and I determined to announce it, perhaps I could say a word to them at least. As soon as I began, the eternal power of God came down from heaven, and I felt suddenly perfectly well, and in the congregation there occurred a tremendous commotion. Sinners cried for mercy, and obtained peace and pardon, and blessed the Lord with a loud

27

voice, while God's children wept and shouted at the same time, because of the rushing among the dry bones that were coming to life. Next day I went on my way as free as a bird, and perfectly restored. We must not give up so soon. Only keep on prophesying, the mighty breath of the Spirit causes a rushing in the valley of dry bones, and the spiritually dead will be made alive; the life of God will enter into them, and they will stand upon their feet, when the servant of God prophesies. The noise and shaking will be heard.

II. Now the Spirit saith in the Revelation, "Blessed and holy is he", — the man who has been made alive spiritually, and is happily delivered from the guilt and curse of sin. As the Scripture saith, "Blessed is the man to whom the Lord imputeth not iniquity." Such an one has the forgiveness of sins, and peace with God through Jesus Christ. Therefore he is *"blessed"*. But the Holy Spirit has yet added something here, namely, the word *"holy"*. And these two words, "blessed" and "holy", have been bound together tremendously strong by the little conjunction "and", so that it hangs together like a chain which no man can break; for "what God hath joined together, let no man put asunder." Thus these two things, "blessed and holy", are inseparably united by divine authority. One who has been resurrected spiritually, has also received, in his regeneration, such a measure of the divine nature, that he is enabled to reign over all actual sin, and to live a *"holy"* life If he will watch and pray, he can also master his passions, crucify the "old man", and attain Christian perfection, in which state he entertains a holy hatred toward all evil, and even abhors his darling sins, for he possesses power to love God with all his heart. By love, all envy, pride, the adulterous vanity of fashion, all unbelief, avarice, backbiting and all evil will be burnt out of the soul, just as a fire will burn dry stubble. *That* Christian is perfect in love, who instantly repels every temptation, and who, when Satan tempts him to pride, replies, "I will go a step farther down"; if tempted to avarice, reaches into the pocket-book and brings an offering to God; when cursed, blesses the curser.

The devil, however, has a ministry in the world now-a-days, who can not abide this truth. It is indeed well understood, where the light is so clear, that a man must be converted, which is admitted by them. They will also allow one to feel something of the nearness of God, but there must be no stir and no noise connected with it. Then it is also taught that a person must always be a weak Christian, must sin every day and repent daily. We can not be saved from sin until we get into the grave. Sin will not end with us until our bodies are dust. Those who desire to become free from sin in this life are branded as proud pharisees and self-righteous people. In this way the devil's preachers seek to tear the "holy" and the "blessed" apart. But the Lord has put the *"and"* between them, which binds them together as with a vise, so that no devil nor man can separate them. *Hallelujah!*

However, the Lord has a ministry in the world which He himself has called and sanctified, and anointed with his Holy Spirit, who are enabled to preach the whole counsel of God *from experience.* These preach the Word of God as they have learned it in the school of Christ. They present holiness and happiness to the people in conjunction, and tell the people that "without holiness no man can see the Lord." In their preaching the Word of God cuts and pierces in every direction, for "the Word of God is sharper than a two-edged sword, piercing to the dividing asunder of soul and spirit, and of the joints and marrow, and is a discerner of the thoughts and intents of the heart." That is the way to preach, and so I am bound to preach until my eyelids close in death, for the truth must be enthroned and the right of the Lord must triumph!

These blessed and holy ones are also priests unto God and his Christ. Through their union with Christ, the everlasting High-priest, they have become a spiritual priesthood, to bring unto God a sacrifice of praise continually. They often praise God with a loud voice as they shout with the angels, *"Glory to God in the highest!"* or sing with David, "Bless the Lord, O my soul, and forget not all his benefits." As spiritual priests they intercede for a wicked world, the man, as head of a family offers daily morning sacrifice at family prayers. Such people are the heirs of God, and obtain the Millennial kingdom in, whatever it may prove to consist; yea, they inherit what is a thousand times better,—the kingdom of *eternal* glory. *Hallelujah!*

NEGLECTING APPOINTMENTS.
(Written for "*Der Christliche Botschafter*", 1852).

In the first number of the "*Botschafter*" for June, I noticed something that pleased me greatly, namely, that one of our itinerant preachers, who has traveled for many years, and on heavy circuits, says, that he has never missed an appointment yet. I am informed, however, that there is another, in the Indiana conference, who has traveled for seven years, of whom the same can be said. But where is the third, who is so fortunate as to be able to say this? Let us hear from him. There is hardly one in ten who is so prompt.

In all our conferences, and in nearly all our districts and circuits, I must constantly listen with grief to the complaint that the preacher carelessly neglects appointments to preach. By this destructive evil we have lost many communities, where there was good prospect of success. And the evil has increased terribly during the last few years. Preachers send one appointment to preach after another, only to neglect them, and so the appointments become *dis*-appointments, and the deceived people finally send for preachers who will serve them more faithfully, but often get such as only comfort them in their sins. In this way the hearts of the people are closed against us and against the truth which saves. I would urgently recommend to our young preachers who were received into our conference last Spring, to read, inwardly digest and observe the fourth and fifth paragraphs in the Rules for the reception of preachers, and the second paragraph in the General Rules for our preachers. The same advice I would also give to all who in the future may be received among us.

As regards those who have already contracted the pernicious habit of neglecting appointments, I would affectionately advise them to be converted without delay from it, and then prove the change by their conduct. In this way the trouble can be obviated.

FROM AN ORDINATION SERMON AT ALLENTOWN, PA.

Text: "Study to show thyself approved unto God, a workman that needeth not to be ashamed, rightly dividing the word of truth." 2. Tim. 2:15.

In the first place an "approved workman" must above all things be soundly converted *deep into eternal life.* Such conversion must not only appear from his outward manners and morals, but it must appear from a living inward testimony by the Holy Spirit, that he is a child of God. It is extremely censurable and a sacrilegious assumption of authority for men and youths to venture into the pulpit as shepherds of souls, who have never gone through a genuine evangelical repentance, and have never experienced a change of heart. Before my conversion the thought of preaching was far from my mind. I was converted while I was still a cooper. My penitential struggle was a hard one. I had less assistance too, than people have now-a-days. But after my conversion the Lord laid the ministry upon me.

I care not how beautiful, smooth and polished a "workman's" appearance in the pulpit may be; it matters not how systematic his discourse, nor how rhetorical his language; it is of little importance how great the burden of learning he may carry with him; if the man is not *converted*, — *soundly* converted, — converted from *pride*, his work will be nothing, *nothing, nothing!* It will be "faultily faultless, icily regular, splendidly null." That's the end of it. Perhaps there is such a theological scholastic under the sound of my voice to-day, who still maintains the ancient notion, that it makes no difference how the preacher's heart is, if he only preaches the Word aright; the people are to do according to his words. Perhaps he supposes that the doctrine of the positive necessity of conversion is only *our* peculiar doctrine. Hark! come here! I will promptly give thee a corrective from Matt. 7, that may possibly purge you of this error: "*Do men gather grapes of thorns, or figs of thistles?*" with an addition from Matt. 12th, "*Either make the tree good, and his fruit good; or else make the tree corrupt, and his fruit corrupt; for the tree is known by his fruit.*" Take this pill and digest it.

In the second place, an "approved workman" needs the *anointing of the Holy Spirit* for his office. All the polish of human learning avails nothing. The power of God, which alone can save sinners, must be in the Word. I know very well that there are those who trust in their acquired or stolen qualifications, and care nothing for the *one thing* that drives all the wheels of the evangelical ministry. Yea worse, they even speak deprecatingly of those who seek this one thing needful with sincerity.

But some one asks, What is this one little desideratum?   It is *fire!*

Listen, Brethren!   And ye people, listen also! Let me illustrate this truth, that all display, and expensive and polished machinery in church work is useless when the *little something* is lacking.   I take a locomotive, put it on the track, attach the passenger coaches, fill their cushioned pews with elegantly dressed people, put the conductor at his place, as also the engineer and the fireman.   The boiler has been filled with water, and the furnace with the best of fuel.   For aught I care, the passengers may also admire and be astonished at the mechanical skill displayed in the construction of the splendid locomotive. They may congratulate themselves on the auspicious prospects of a successful trip.   At last the signal bell in the depot strikes the time of departure; the conductor pulls the bell, signalling to the engineer to pull out.   The engineer pulls the lever — back — open again — but the machine will not move.   There the thing stands!   What's the matter?   Certainly it looks as if it ought to go.   No sir!   *Something* is lacking.   *There's no fire in the furnace*, therefore no steam in the boiler, no power in the wheels.   The mighty enginery will not draw as much as a cat.

Perhaps while the thing is standing there immovable, there comes a horridly sooty, smoked-up old engine, steaming, puffing, smoking, groaning, up a side track, drawing, with majestic strength, a hundred loaded cars of coal.   Why, what has this homely, black and sooty engine got within, that enables him to put to shame our attractive, handsome machine, possessing all latest improvements? It has *fire!* *Fire* is what it has! That engine with fire represents the soundly converted and divinely anointed workman, and the other represents the lifeless, spiritless man, who has every qualification, save that most necessary, which God's Spirit must supply. The most elegant workmen are seldom the best. But those who have the appearance of *workmen* set the corn-fields of the Philistines on fire.

THREE VICES AMONG CHRISTIAN PROFESSORS.

To all sincere persons who stand in the grace of God, I wish prosperity in the well begun work. But it is necessary to this purpose that all the heads of the Church should die unto the world and sin and all temporal things, and, as ensamples of the flock of Christ, live a holy life. Nor is it necessary to preach repentance and regeneration alone, but also growth in grace, until perfect holiness of heart be attained. When this is once accomplished, there will be few if any backsliders among professors of religion, and fewer lame and crippled would stop along the way of life and be lost.

But there are certain vices which greatly hinder progress in holiness, of which I will mention three of the worst. The first is *avarice* — the desire for money and worldly treasures. In our times this evil is so mighty, that many are in debt to such an extent that they are not only ruining themselves, but cause many of their fellow-men to lose all their possessions, and to be destroyed soul and body. Paul says: "They that will be rich fall into temptation and a snare, and into many foolish and hurtful lusts, which drown men in destruction and perdition. At no time has this saying been more strikingly demonstrated than now in the United States. How little many professors of religion, — some preachers not excepted, — regard the command of the Holy Spirit to "owe no man anything, but to love one another." Money making is the order of the day, but "the love of many has waxed cold."

Another vice, that grows worse and worse amid all our misery, is *vanity*, — the fashion-craze, and extravagance in general. This occasions a fearful expenditure of money, and many professors of religion exert themselves to the utmost, not to be behind the world in this regard. They even bring their infants in the cradle as offerings to this all-consuming, cruel Moloch. Therefore it is not hard at all for the devil to pull the rising generation down to destruction by this rope of iniquity. O what a curse this is for our nation. This evil, which is coupled with idleness and revelry, is the cause why hundreds of thousands in our day annually are suffering hunger, misery and want. *"But who hath believed our report?"*

One other vice that prevails in nearly all societies to a greater or less extent, is *hatred*, envy, want of brotherly love. Really there are few societies wholly free from this. It has even invaded the ministry, though John says, "He that hateth his brother is a murderer." Let him who reads this, examine himself, and see whether he is not infected with this evil, and therefore belongs to the generation of Cain, who was the first-born of the devil.

These three evils are only a few of the many that prevail among professors of religion, and which hinder the work of grace in the hearts of believers. If one should enlarge upon all the others, it would take more time and wisdom than I possess.

(USURY.—FROM A PRIVATE LETTER.)

Above all, however, I desire that our membership be saved from the ten and twenty per cent. interest system of the robber band of Freeport, Ill. and other western cities; also from the American fashion craze, and that they be cleansed from the uncleanness of tobacco. Then one would not have occasion so often to pray, " Help, Lord, for the godly man ceaseth; for the faithful fail from among the children of men."

SEYBERT ON SLAVERY.

Our Bishop was decidedly opposed to traffic in human souls and bodies, and an enemy of slavery, in accordance with the position of our Church, but he did not live to see its abolition. He left this world, just as the war cloud was gathering in the horizon of our country, under whose artillery blasts this great national evil was atoned for with the blood of patriots. He never enjoyed laboring in a slave State, and whenever he came back from an expedition below Mason's and Dixon's line, he expressed himself happy to have got away from *"the accursed ground"*. Several times he declared in profound earnest that he would not want to stay in a slave State even if he were dead, and he had carefully instructed his brethren, that if it should happen that he died in a slave State, they should inter his remains in a free State. He boldly lifted up his voice in the pulpit against this heaven-crying national sin, and declared his belief that no slave-holder, and much less a slave-trader, could inherit eternal life, unless he would desist from his evil practice in time.

In early years Seybert belonged to the old Democratic party, and still defended it in later years, on certain points. A western preacher took him to task on one occasion on this account, and expressed his surprise at the Bishop's affiliation with that party, when it upheld slavery, while he (the Bishop) was so radically opposed to slavery. After a pause, Seybert proceeded to show that the original principles of the ancient Democracy were right, but the devil, said he, had sown this weed. Slavery did not belong to Democracy. Then he went on, rising to his feet: "Slavery is of the devil, and if I were called to it, and the government would give me fifty thousand armed men, I would go into the South and root out this national evil tee-totally!" "Well! Well!" said his auditor. "Yes sir," said the Bishop. "A rod for the fool's back, hell for the devil's reward, and absolute destruction for slavery!"

If anyone should feel disposed to ridicule the Bishop's notion of destroying slavery with fifty thousand men, it may be enough to remind ourselves of the fact that when President Lincoln and his wise advisers issued the first call for men, they only wanted seventy-five thousand men, and grave West Pointers jocosely spoke of finishing the affair "before breakfast".

SEYBERT AS A TEMPERANCE APOSTLE.

The Bishop was extensively known as a distinguished German temperance apostle. He frequently delivered temperance lectures, and never failed to draw a crowd. The people streamed to his meetings from every direction to hear him, and all who ever heard him on the subject, agreed that he was a successful defender of the cause. His extensive travels and habits of observation gave him a rich fund of facts, figures and incidents. The use he made of these, made his efforts grand and irresistible. He would heap up one calamity upon another, one impoverishment upon another, one lost life upon another, one brutal act upon another, one crime upon another, one imprisonment upon another, and one hangman's execution upon another — all caused by drunkenness. It poured from his lips in a torrent of eloquence so majestic that it might be said of him as the old Romans were wont to say of Cicero, "Thunder and lightning are on his tongue." He presented calculations, showing how many drunkards there are in the United States, and how many moderate drinkers, whom he designated "the nursery garden of drunkenness", and from which whole fleets are driven into the glassy throat of this Maelstrom of destruction. He showed how many annually sink into a drunkard's grave, how many citizens are ruined by this vice and get into poor-houses, hospitals and prisons; then the amount of expenses the State incurs in litigations and prosecutions caused by the rum traffic, the amount of time and money that is squandered, the number of widows and neglected orphans that in this land of plenty are constantly crying and groaning in want, and how many souls are lost in hell annually. This was done with such emphasis and earnestness, and with such divine power, that the ordinary flippancy of temperance mass meetings disappeared, and his large audiences melted in tears. Of course, his quaintness and eccentricity which he manifested on the platform as well as elsewhere, frequently excited the risibles of his auditors, for his style of oratory was strikingly original and inimitable.

Rev. S. Neitz relates that he once heard him deliver a temperance address before astonished thousands in an important city of Eastern Pennsylvania. There were in the audience all classes of people, lawyers, magistrates, doctors, editors, theologians, professors, merchants, artisans, farmers, day-laborers and others. It was a popular audience in the broadest sense, brought out by public desire to hear the Bishop. Mr. Neitz observed a row of aristocrats, who beguiled the moments of waiting in making sport of the homespun little man who sat on the platform, at the same time somewhat piqued that such an enthusiastic audience should assemble to hear him.

However, he had not proceeded far in his address before they changed their manner, and began to be ashamed of their hasty judgment, and yet still somewhat of the opinion that nothing eloquent could come from such an ordinary source. Soon they were smiling audibly at his witticisms, and the next moment weeping at his touching allusions.

His text was Prov. 23:29, 30. "Who hath woe, who hath sorrow, who hath contention, who hath babblings, who hath wounds without cause, who hath redness of eyes? They that tarry long at the wine," etc. This was his great temperance text. His second great temperance text was, "Wine is a mocker, and strong drink is raging, and whosoever is deceived thereby is not wise." The Bishop described the "woe", the "sorrow", the "contentions", the "babblings", the "wounds", and the appearance and conduct of drunkards in an unequaled style. Among other subjects upon which he came to speak in this celebrated speech, he referred to the fact that the poison of alcohol becomes hereditary, and is transmitted from parent to child. "The inclination to drink intoxicants", he said, "is inherited by the child from the parent." Then he exclaimed with thrilling vehemence, "IT RUNS IN THE BLOOD! IT RUNS IN THE BLOOD, YE PEOPLE!! I can prove it. Up there in the Pennsylvania Iron Works there was a drunkard who had eleven sons, and of these *ten* became drunkards. *It runs in the blood*, my friends!"

Then he addressed himself to the brewers, distillers and dealers in liquor in a merciless manner. "You have no right to engage in a business that involves your neighbor in loss both in soul and in body, therefore you ought not to sell him liquid fire to drink. Alcohol may have a legitimate place in medical science, and I suppose it could be dispensed with in that too, if our physicians had more skill, but for this *one distillery would be enough for the whole United States.* What shall we do with the rest of them? What are they good for? They are manufactories where they prepare a death potion for our citizens in large vats. O God, root them all out of our land!

All who sell strong drink in a promiscuous way, are national poisoners and murder our citizens at wholesale. Their eyes know no pity nor sparing, but they drive our people in great fleets to destruction. And what is their profit? Why, the blood of these poor sots. No need of envying them their large possessions and palatial homes, for they are full of blood. The curse of God rests on their lands and in their palaces. The blood of their fellowmen is upon them. It cleaves to the stones in their walls, to the timber in their frames, to the costly furniture of their rooms. The curse of the Almighty is on their arbors of ease, follows them on their journeys and withers their forests. It is a fire that burns on down into the deepest hell. Wherever the dealers and the manufacturers dwell there is blood, blood is the foundation of the wall, blood is the capstone of the arch, blood is the covering of the roof. The floor, the walls, the ceiling are red with blood! Blood everywhere! O thou bloody man, canst thou hope that thy blood-money will reach the third or fourth generation of heirs? Your fields of blood will not reach the third! There lives in Heaven a righteous God, and as thou dost spoil thy neighbor's soul and body and family, so will God spoil thee and root out thy very name from beneath the sun."

In such strains the Bishop went on, and carried his audience with him on the resistless tide of his burning eloquence. He was full of enthusiasm, full of sincere earnestness, full of information and full of divine love, and these things together made him an orator whose power over his audiences was seldom excelled.

At one time, in his great interest in the cause, he ordered a lithograph of a great temperance painting, which portrayed in a striking manner the work of alcohol from the still to the gallows. It was known as "Bishop Seybert's Whisky Dragon".

One evening, on his way to an appointment, he passed a distillery, and a little further on a drunken wretch prostrate by the road-side in the gutter. He told his congregation that on the way he had "passed one of the devil's hog-pens, (meaning the distillery), and a little further on, one of the devil's hogs!"

FINIS.

GENERAL INDEX.